The
Beggar King

OLIVER PÖTZSCH

The
Beggar King

A Hangman's Daughter Tale

Translated by
LEE CHADEAYNE

MARINER BOOKS
HOUGHTON MIFFLIN HARCOURT
BOSTON   NEW YORK

First Mariner Books edition 2013
Text copyright © 2010 by Oliver Pötzsch
English translation copyright © 2013 by Lee Chadeayne

For information about permission to reproduce selections from this book,
write to Permissions, Houghton Mifflin Harcourt Publishing Company,
215 Park Avenue South, New York, New York 10003.

The Beggar King: A Hangman's Daughter Tale was first published in 2010 by
Ullstein Buchverlag GmbH as *Die Henkerstochter und der König der Bettler*.
Translated from German by Lee Chadeayne.
First published in English by AmazonCrossing in 2013.

www.hmhbooks.com

Library of Congress Cataloging-in-Publication Data
Pötzsch, Oliver.
[Henkerstochter und der König der Bettler. English]
The beggar king: a hangman's daughter tale / Oliver Pötzsch;
translated by Lee Chadeayne. — First Mariner Books edition.
pages cm
ISBN 978-0-547-99219-8
1. Fathers and daughters — Fiction. 2. Executions and executioners — Fiction.
3. Germany — History — 17th century — Fiction. 4. Murder — Investigation —
Fiction. I. Chadeayne, Lee, translator. II. Title.
PT2676.0895H4713 2013
833'.92 — dc23
2012038023

Printed in the United States of America
DOC 10 9 8 7 6 5 4 3 2 1

For Katrin, with love.

It takes a strong woman to put up with a Kuisl.

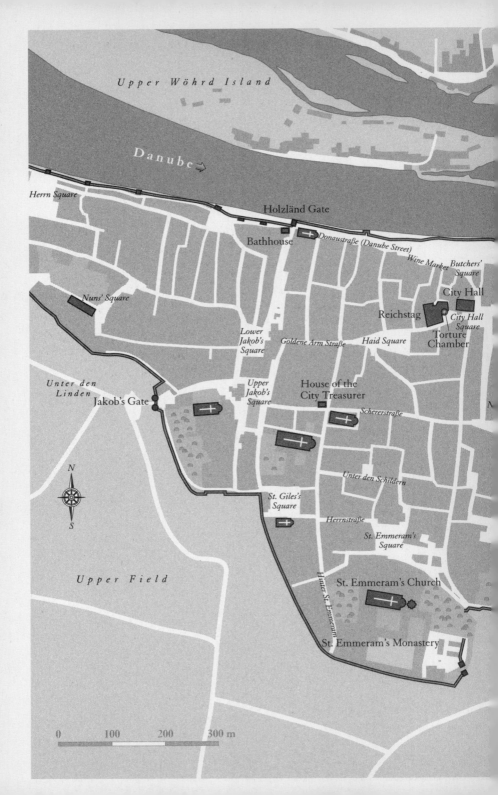

Upper Wöhrd Island

Danube →

Herrn Square

Holzländ Gate

Bathhouse

Donaustraße (Danube Street)

Wine Market

Butchers' Square

Nuns' Square

City Hall

Reichstag

City Hall Square

Lower Jakob's Square

Goldene Arm Straße

Haid Square

Torture Chamber

Unter den Linden

Jakob's Gate

Upper Jakob's Square

House of the City Treasurer

Schererstraße

N

S

Unter den Schildern

St. Giles's Square

Herrnstraße

St. Emmeram's Square

Upper Field

Hinter St. Emmeram

St. Emmeram's Church

St. Emmeram's Monastery

0   100   200   300 m

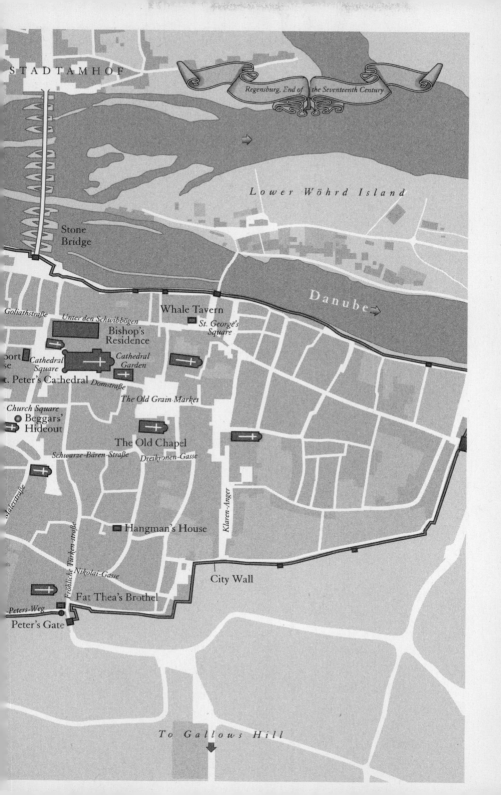

STADTAMHOF

Regensburg, End of the Seventeenth Century

Lower Wöhrd Island

Stone
Bridge

Danube

Goliathstraße

Whale Tavern

Unter den Schwibbögen

St. George's
Square

Bishop's
Residence

Cathedral
Square

Cathedral
Garden

St. Peter's Cathedral   Domstraße

The Old Grain Market

Church Square

Beggars'
Hideout

The Old Chapel

Schwarze-Bären-Straße   Dreikronen-Gasse

Klaren-Anger

Hangman's House

Fröhliche-Türken-straße

City Wall

Nikolai-Gasse

Fat Thea's Brothel

Peters-Weg

Peter's Gate

To Gallows Hill

DRAMATIS PERSONAE

PRINCIPAL CHARACTERS

JAKOB KUISL, hangman of Schongau
SIMON FRONWIESER, son of the town doctor
MAGDALENA KUISL, the hangman's daughter
ANNA-MARIA KUISL, the hangman's wife
GEORG AND BARBARA, the hangman's twin children

CITIZENS OF SCHONGAU

MARTHA STECHLIN, midwife
JOHANN LECHNER, court clerk
BONIFAZ FRONWIESER, Schongau town doctor
MICHAEL BERCHTHOLDT, master baker and alderman
MARIA BERCHTHOLDT, the master baker's wife
RESL KIRCHLECHNER, the master baker's maid

PEOPLE OF REGENSBURG

ELISABETH HOFMANN, the bathhouse owner's wife and Jakob
   Kuisl's sister
ANDREAS HOFMANN, Regensburg bathhouse owner
PHILIPP TEUBER, hangman of Regensburg
CAROLINE TEUBER, the Regensburg hangman's wife
SILVIO CONTARINI, Venetian ambassador
NATHAN THE WISE, king of the Regensburg beggars
PAULUS MÄMMINGER, Regensburg city treasurer
KARL GESSNER, Regensburg raftmaster
DOROTHEA BÄCHLEIN, brothel owner and prostitute
FATHER HUBERTUS, the bishop's brewmaster

HIERONYMUS RHEINER, president of the city council
JOACHIM KERSCHER, president of the Regensburg tax office
DOMINIK ELSPERGER, doctor

THE BEGGARS

HANS REISER
BROTHER PAULUS
CRAZY JOHANNES

Sobald ein Soldat wird geboren,
sind ihm drei Bauern auserkoren.
Der erste, der ihn ernährt, der andere,
der ihm ein schön Weib beschert,
Der dritte, der für ihn zur Hölle fährt.

Whenever a soldier is born,
three peasants are chosen for him:
One to provide his fare,
another to procure him a lusty wench,
and a third one to go to hell in his stead.

——A VERSE FROM THE THIRTY YEARS' WAR

PROLOGUE

The riders of the apocalypse wore blood-red leggings, tattered uniforms, and coats that fluttered in the wind like flags behind them. Their weapons were rusty and battered from killing, and their horses nothing but mangy old nags with dull, mud-encrusted coats. Silent, hidden behind a dense line of trees, the men stared at the sleepy village to which they would shortly bring death and destruction.

There were twelve of them, a haggard, hungry dozen. They had looted, murdered, and raped, again and again. Years ago they may have been men, but now they were just empty shells. A consuming madness flashed in their eyes. Their leader, a wiry young Frank in colorful mercenary garb, chewed on a frayed blade of grass and sucked in saliva through a space between his teeth. He saw smoke rising from the chimneys of the houses nestled along the forest edge and nodded with satisfaction.

"Looks like we may have found ourselves something here."

He tossed the blade of grass and reached for the blood- and rust-stained saber at his side. The sounds of women and children rose up from below. The man grinned. "Looks to be women, too."

A pimple-faced youth at his side giggled. He looked like a ferret, slightly stooped, clutching the reins of his scrawny nag with long, thin fingers. His eyes darted back and forth restlessly. He was not a day over sixteen, but the war had made an old man of him.

"You're a real bastard, Philipp," he rasped, running his tongue over his cracked lips. "You think of only one thing."

"Shut up, Karl!" said a stout, potbellied bearded man on the left. He had the same straggly black hair as the Frank and the youth next to him. They were all brothers, with the same empty stare, as bitter and cold as a violent hailstorm in midsummer. "Didn't Father raise you not to speak until spoken to?" the fat man growled. "So shut your mouth."

"To hell with Father," the youth replied. "And to hell with you, Friedrich."

The fat man was about to reply, but the group leader beat him to it, his hand shooting out, seizing Karl by the throat so hard that his beady little black eyes bulged out of his head like giant pinheads.

"Don't you ever bad-mouth our family again!" replied Philipp Lettner, the oldest brother. "Never again, do you hear? Or I'll tear your hide to shreds, until you cry out to our dead mother. Do you hear?"

Karl Lettner nodded as his face swelled up and turned bright red. The older brother let him go, and Karl fell to the ground like a sack, coughing.

Philipp's expression changed as he looked down, almost with pity, at his brother panting and gasping on the ground. "Karl, Karl," he said, sucking on another blade of grass. "What can I do with you? Discipline, do you hear? Discipline is everything in war. Discipline and respect!" He bent down to his little brother and stroked his pimply cheek. "I love you as if you were a part of me, but if you blacken our father's name once more, I'll have to hurt you — bad. Do you hear?"

Karl remained silent, chewing his dirty fingernails and looking down at the ground.

"I said, do you hear?" Philipp Lettner demanded one more
time.

"Yeah, I hear." His little brother lowered his head meekly,
though he clenched his fists in tight little balls.

Philipp grinned. "Good. Now we can finally get on with it
and have a little fun."

The other riders had watched the spectacle with interest.
They acknowledged Philipp Lettner as their undisputed leader.
Though not yet thirty years old, he was the most ruthless of the
three Lettner brothers and had enough shrewdness to keep his
place at the head of this gang. When, the year before, his men
had started going out on their own unofficial raids in the course
of the general campaign, Philipp Lettner had always managed to
keep their young sergeant from getting wind of it. Even now,
while the troops were supposed to be laid up in their winter
headquarters, they found a way to make little excursions into the
surrounding villages, though the sergeant had expressly forbidden it. They sold the booty to women who followed the army in
wagons peddling goods, so the gang members always had money
for food, drink, and whoring.

Today it looked as if they'd have an especially good haul.
The village in the clearing, hidden behind dense firs and beeches,
seemed almost untouched by the ravages of the Great War. In
the setting sun the mercenaries could make out newly built barns
and stables, and cows grazing in the lush meadows near the forest edge. The sound of a child's flute rose from down below.
Philipp Lettner spurred his horse, which whinnied, reared up,
and then galloped off through the copse of blood-red beeches.
The others followed their leader, and the killing began.

The first person to see them was a stooped, white-haired old
man crouched in the bushes relieving himself. Instead of fleeing
for cover in the forest, he stumbled back down the road toward

the village with his pants hanging down. Philipp Lettner caught up with him and, with a single blow of his sword, severed the man's right arm as he galloped by. Hooting and howling, the others ran over the old man, trampling his twitching body under their horses' hooves.

The villagers were going about their usual chores when they saw the mercenaries approach. With loud cries the women dropped their pitchers and bundles and ran away in every direction, into the fields and forest. Giggling, young Karl aimed his crossbow at a boy of about twelve trying to hide among the broken stalks of a freshly harvested wheat field. The bolt hit the boy in the shoulder, and he fell to the ground without a sound.

While the women ran off toward the forest, Friedrich Lettner and some of the other mercenaries fanned out to corral them like a herd of wild cows. The men laughed, picking up the women and setting them down on their horses or dragging them by the hair behind them. Philipp turned now to the anxious farmers who came running out of the houses to save their dear lives and the lives of their women and children. They carried flails and scythes, and some even sabers, but none was experienced in battle and all were weakened by illness, half starved from having nothing to eat but thin porridge. Perhaps they were strong enough to cut the heads off chickens, but against a mercenary on horseback they were no match.

In a few minutes the slaughter was over. The villagers lay in their own blood—in their houses amid smashed tables, beds, and stools or outside in the street, groaning, as Philipp Lettner went from one to another, slashing their throats. Two mercenaries threw a dead farmer into a well in the village square. The rotting flesh would poison the well and make the entire town uninhabitable for years to come. In the meantime the other mercenaries ransacked the houses, looking for something to eat or anything else of value. There wasn't much to be had—a few rusty coins, two silver spoons, a few cheap necklaces, and some rosaries. Young Karl Lettner tried on a white wedding gown he found in a trunk and danced around clumsily, singing a wedding tune in a shrill falsetto. The others laughed uproariously when he fell head over heels into a mud puddle. The blood- and mud-stained dress ripped and hung down on him in tatters.

Most valuable were the animals: eight cows, three pigs, a few goats, and a dozen chickens. They would fetch a fine price from the merchant women who followed the army.

And then there were, of course, the women.

Darkness was falling, and a cool dampness settled over the clearing. To keep warm, the mercenaries threw burning torches into the ruined houses. The dry reeds on the floors and the thatched roofs caught fire in seconds, and soon the flames were shooting out the windows and doors. The loud crackling fire served as a backdrop to the screams of the sobbing women.

The men corraled the women in the village square—about twenty of them. The monster Friedrich Lettner went from one to the other, pushing aside the old and ugly. When one old woman pounded him with her fists, he threw her into a burning house. Her screams didn't last long. In the silence following, all that could be heard from the farm women was an occasional whimper.

Finally the men picked out a good dozen women. The youngest was a girl about ten years old who stared off into space with an open mouth and bulging eyes. She seemed to have already lost her mind.

"All right," Philipp Lettner said, walking down the line of the trembling women. "This is how it goes. If you do what we say, you'll live to see the sun rise tomorrow. It isn't such a bad life being a soldier's wife. You'll get more to eat than what your old goats gave you here."

The other soldiers laughed. Young Karl giggled in a high, shrill voice—a falsetto in a chorus of madmen.

Philipp Lettner stopped abruptly in front of one of the girls.

Her disheveled black hair was probably tied up in a bun most days but now reached almost down to her waist. She was perhaps seventeen or eighteen years old. With bushy eyebrows and flashing eyes, she reminded Lettner of an angry little cat. She trembled, but she held her head high. Her coarse brown farm dress had been ripped, exposing one of her breasts. Lettner stared at the little nipple, which had hardened in the cold air. A faint smile passed over his face as he pointed at the girl.

"This one here is mine," he said. "For all I care you can bash your heads in fighting over the others."

He was about to reach for the young farm girl when his brother Friedrich, standing behind him, cleared his throat. "You can't get away with that, Philipp," he growled. "It was I who found her in the cornfield, and she's mine."

"Oh, indeed?" Philipp's voice was cold and sharp. "You found her, did you? That may be, but you apparently also let her get away."

He stepped closer to his brother until they were standing directly face-to-face. Friedrich was obviously the stronger of the two and as big around as a barrel of wine, but he stepped back a bit nonetheless. When Philipp got mad, strength no longer mattered — that's the way it had always been, since they were kids. Now, too, he seemed ready to explode. He looked at his brother without blinking, and his lips formed a narrow, bloodless line.

"I found that one hiding in a trunk over in the big old house," Philipp whispered. "She thought she could scurry away and hide like a little mouse. Well, we've had a little fun already. She's stubborn, and somebody will have to teach her some manners. I think *I'm* the best one to do that."

All at once, the harshness disappeared from Philipp's eyes. He smiled again and patted his brother on the shoulder.

"But you have a point. Why should the leader get the best woman, especially since I've already taken three cows and two pigs, right?" Philipp's gaze wandered down the line of his men, but nobody dared contradict him. "Do you know what, Friedrich?" he said finally. "We'll do just as we used to do back in Leutkirchen in Müller's Tavern. We'll let a throw of the dice decide."

"We'll cast dice for her?" Friedrich hesitated. "The two of us, now?"

Philipp shook his head and furrowed his brow as if he were thinking hard about something. "No, I don't think that would be right," he continued. "We'll *all* cast dice," he said, looking around. "What do you say? We all have a right to this juicy little tart!"

The others laughed and cheered. Philipp was a leader after their own hearts. In his eyes they were all equal — brothers as well as comrades-in-arms. *A young devil, with a heart as black as the devil's ass.* Young Karl hopped around in a circle like a whirling dervish, clapping his hands. "We'll gamble for it!" he shouted. "Just like old times."

Philipp nodded and settled down on the ground as he took out two worn dice he had carried around with him all through the war. He tossed them in the air and then caught them deftly in his hand as they fell.

"Well, who wants to play with me?" he called out. "Who? For the woman and the cow. Let's see what you're willing to gamble."

They drove the black-haired girl to the middle of the village square like a cow and sat down in a circle around her. With a desperate cry the young girl tried to flee, but Philipp slapped her twice in the face.

"Back off, whore! Or we'll all pile on you together and cut your tits off!"

The girl crouched down in a fetal position, her arms wrapped around her legs and her head bowed. Overwhelmed with grief and pain, she could hear the dice rattling in a cup, coins tinkling, and men laughing.

The mercenaries started singing a tune the girl knew well. When her mother was still alive, they sang it together as they worked in the fields. And later, on her deathbed, her mother hummed it one more time to herself just before she passed on and was gone forever. It had always been a sad song, but hearing it now suddenly seemed strange and gruesome. As the drunken mercenaries bellowed into the dark night sky, the sound wafted to her from across the field like a veil of fog. She could almost feel cold fingers wrap around her throat.

> *There is a reaper. Death's his name.*
> *From God his power came.*
> *His blade keen and steady*
> *To mow us is ready,*
> *And soon he will reap us*
> *In swaths for to heap us.*
> *O tender flow'r, beware!*

As the men laughed, Philipp Lettner swung the leather cup around in the air. Once . . . twice . . . three times.

With a soft click, the dice fell into the sand.

The
Beggar King

I

In the Danube Gorge near Weltenburg,
August 13, 1662 AD
Twenty-five years later

The wave caught Jakob Kuisl head-on and swept him off the bench like driftwood.

The hangman reached frantically for a handhold as he felt himself slip across the raft boards, feet first, toward the gurgling, swirling river. Slowly yet inexorably, the weight of his body dragged him into the cold water. His fingernails scraped along the planks as he slid, and he could hear frantic shouts nearby, though they were muffled as if by a thick wall. He managed at last to grab hold of a carpenter's nail jutting out of a plank and was hauling himself up just as someone came sliding past him toward the churning water. With his free hand, he lunged, seizing a boy by the collar. About ten years old, the boy thrashed about and gasped for air. The hangman pushed him back into the middle of the raft, where his relieved father grabbed the boy and hugged him.

Wheezing, Kuisl crept back to his seat in the bow. His linen shirt and leather cape clung to his body, and water streamed down his face, beard, and eyebrows. Looking downriver, he realized the worst was yet to come. The raft was drifting helplessly toward a towering rock wall over forty yards high. Here, in the Weltenburg Narrows, the Danube narrowed abruptly, transforming this part of the river into a roiling cauldron that had cost many a raftsman his life, especially in times of high water.

"My God, hold tight, hold on tight, for heaven's sake!" The forward helmsman leaned on his rudder as the raft plunged headlong into another whirlpool. The tendons in his arms stood out like knotted roots, but the long pole in his hands didn't budge. Heavy thunderstorms had caused the river to rise in the last few days so that the otherwise tranquil gravel banks along both shores had been swept away entirely. Branches and uprooted trees raced by in the white foam as the huge raft sped faster and faster toward the rock face. Next to him Kuisl heard the terrifying sound of the raft's timbers scraping the limestone cliff that now loomed directly above, casting its shadow over the small group of passengers like a stone colossus. Sharp rocks cut deep into the port side of the raft, slicing through the outermost logs lengthwise like they were butter.

"Holy Saint Nepomuk, patron protector from the flood, be with us! Hail Mary, full of grace, help us in our distress! Blessed Saint Nicolas, spare us . . ."

Kuisl looked sullenly to one side, where a nun sat, clutching an ivory rosary and wailing incessant prayers into the clear blue sky. So, too, the other passengers sat on the wooden benches, crossing themselves and mumbling petitions, their faces white as chalk. A portly estate farmer awaited his certain demise with eyes shut tight and drops of sweat on his brow. A Franciscan monk appealed in a cracked falsetto to the Fourteen Holy Helpers, orphan saints who couldn't have been much older than him when the Plague made martyrs of them. And the lad whom Kuisl had just saved from drowning now clung to his father and sobbed. It was only a matter of time before the rocks would rip these timbers apart and grind them to a pulp. Most of the passengers were unable to swim, but in such turbulent waters that wouldn't have saved them anyway.

"Accursed water! Blast it!" Kuisl spat into the river and heaved himself toward the bow, where the helmsman still struggled to redirect a rudder fastened to the raft by rope. With legs spread, the Schongau hangman braced himself beside the raftsman and leaned into the pole with his powerful torso. It felt as if the rudder had snagged on something far below in the ice-cold water. Running through Kuisl's head were the horror stories raftsmen told about malevolent, slimy monsters lurking at the bottom of the river. Just the day before, some fishermen had told him about a catfish five yards long that supposedly lived in a cave near the Danube Gorge. *What in heaven's name could be down there, holding fast to the rudder's pole?*

All of a sudden he could feel the rudder moving just the tiniest bit. He pushed harder, groaning, feeling that at any moment his bones might break. With a final grinding sound, the rudder came free. The raft spun out from the whirlpool and, with one last shudder, was catapulted away from the rock face.

Moments later they were shooting swift as an arrow toward two small rocky outcroppings on the right riverbank. Some of the travelers carried on screaming, but at this point the raftsman had gained control of his raft. They rushed past the foam-splashed rocks, plunging headfirst into the water until at last they'd made their way out of the dangerous gorge.

"Thank you very much!" The helmsman wiped the sweat and water from his eyes and reached out a callused hand to Kuisl. "The Long Wall might have had us for supper. Do you have any interest in rafting yourself?" He smirked at Kuisl, reaching out to feel the hangman's biceps. "You're as strong as two oxen, and you sure can curse like a natural-born. So, how about it?"

Kuisl shook his head. "Bless you for that, but you wouldn't enjoy having me. One more whirlpool like that and I'd throw up right there in the water. Solid ground under my feet is what I need."

The raftsman laughed, and Kuisl shook his wet, matted mop of hair so that droplets flew in all directions.

"How long before we get to Regensburg?" he asked the helmsman. "This river is driving me crazy. I've thought our time was up at least ten times now."

Kuisl looked back at the rock walls that overshadowed the river on both sides. Some reminded him of stone beasts, and some of the heads of giants who stared down at this swarming mass of tiny mortals far below. Just a moment ago they had passed by the Weltenburg Monastery, now little more than a ruin consumed by war and high water. Despite its sad condition, many travelers on the Danube still stopped there to offer silent prayers. After a heavy rain, the narrow gorge below was considered a challenge for even the most experienced raftsmen. It certainly couldn't do any harm to pause for a few Hail Marys beforehand.

"The Long Wall is, by God, the worst stretch along here," the helmsman said, making the sign of the cross. "Especially when the water is high. But from here on out it's a calm ride, I promise. We should get there in a few more hours."

"I hope you're right," the hangman grunted, "or I'll give *you* a good paddling with that damned rudder."

Kuisl turned away and padded cautiously along the slippery narrow aisle between the rows of benches, toward the back of the raft where the cargo was stored. He hated traveling by raft, even if it was the fastest and still the safest way to get from one town to the next. The hangman preferred to feel the solid forest floor beneath his feet. Tree trunks were good for building houses and tables and even gallows, if you like, but they surely weren't meant for this tumbling around, pitching, and tossing in raging river rapids. Kuisl would be happy when this was all over.

The travelers, who had meanwhile regained some color in their faces and were now praying or laughing loudly in relief, looked to Kuisl with gratitude. The father of the boy he'd saved tried to embrace him, but the hangman brushed him off and turned away grumpily, disappearing between the crates lashed down in the stern.

Here on the Danube, a four-day journey from Kuisl's home, neither the passengers nor the crew knew that Kuisl was the Schongau executioner. For the helmsman up front that was fortunate; if it had gotten around that a hangman had lent him a hand, he probably would have been expelled from his guild. In some regions, Kuisl had heard, just touching, or even being looked at by, an executioner could strip a man of his honor.

Kuisl climbed onto a barrel of pickled herring in the back of the cargo area and lit his pipe. Now, with the infamous Weltenburg Narrows behind them, the Danube widened again. The little town of Kelheim appeared on the left, and heavily loaded barges passed so close to the raft that Kuisl could almost reach out and touch their cargo. A fiddle could be heard on a vessel farther off, accompanied by the jangle of a tambourine. Behind that, a raft the size of a house plowed through the current at a leisurely pace. Loaded with lime, yew wood, and bricks, it lay so low in the water that small waves kept washing over the logs. In the middle of this slow-moving vessel, next to its tiny makeshift cabin, the captain rang a bell whenever smaller fishing boats drifted too close.

The hangman exhaled a few clouds of tobacco smoke into the almost cloudless summer sky, trying for a few minutes at least to forget the somber reason for his trip. Six days ago a letter from far-off Regensburg had arrived at his house in Schongau. Its contents troubled him more than he wanted his family to know. His younger sister, Lisbeth, who was married to the owner of a bathhouse and had been living in the distant Imperial City for years, had fallen seriously ill. It was a lump in her stomach, or so it was thought, accompanied by dreadful pain and a thick, black discharge. In the hastily scrawled lines of parchment his brother-in-law entreated him to come to Regensburg as soon as possible, since it was uncertain how long Lisbeth would survive. The Schongau hangman therefore emptied the medicine chest at home, packed his linen bag with opium gum, mountain arnica, and St. John's Wort, and was on the next raft heading down the Danube. As executioner, he wasn't allowed to leave town without prior approval of the city council, but Kuisl had simply ignored the prohibition. Just let Court Clerk Johann Lechner have him drawn and quartered when he got back! His sister's fate was far more important to Kuisl. He didn't trust the educated quacks, who would likely just bleed her until she was as white as a drowned corpse. If anyone could help his sister at all, it would have to be him and nobody else.

The Schongau executioner killed and healed. He was a master of both.

"Hey, big fellow! Would you like to join me for a drink?"

Jarred from his reveries, Kuisl looked ahead, where one of the raftsmen was raising his glass in a toast. The hangman shook his head and pulled his wide-brimmed hat down low over his forehead to protect himself from the blinding sun. His large hooked nose and, below that, the stem of his pipe were all that were visible under the brim. From beneath his hat he could observe both the travelers and the raftsmen among the crates in the middle of the raft, toasting their successful passage through the fearsome gorge with slugs of brandy. Like an annoying insect, a thought was troubling Kuisl. It would come and go, and the whirlpool at the Long Wall only briefly succeeded in displacing it.

Ever since his departure he had had the strange feeling he was being watched.

It wasn't tied to any one thing in particular, but a combination of instinct and his many years of experience as a mercenary in the Great War had taught him to heed the little twitch between his shoulder blades. He didn't know who was watching him or why, but the twitch persisted.

Kuisl looked around. Among the passengers he counted two Franciscan monks and a nun. In addition, there were traveling tradesmen, journeymen, and a handful of simple merchants — altogether around two dozen travelers, who along with the hangman had joined the convoy of five rafts. On the Danube it was possible to travel to Vienna in just one week, and within three weeks even as far as the Black Sea. In the evening, when the rafts moored together along the shore, everyone would meet around the fire, exchange a few words, and tell stories of previous travels and adventures — everyone but Kuisl. He didn't know a soul and usually sat alone, which was fine by him, as he considered most people nothing more than gossiping simpletons. From where he sat, off to one side, the hangman observed the men and women each evening as they sat around the fire, laughing, drinking cheap wine, and nibbling on legs of mutton. And again and again, he thought he felt someone's unwavering eyes upon him. Even now, under the bright noontime sun, he felt an itch or a tickle between his shoulder blades, as if a little bug were creeping across his back.

Kuisl, acting bored, dangled his feet from the wooden barrel. He filled his pipe again and looked out at the far shore, hoping to seem as if he were intently observing the horde of children standing there, waving at him.

Abruptly he wheeled around to face the stern of the vessel.

For a fraction of a second he did notice someone staring at him: the second helmsman, who operated the rudder in the stern. If Kuisl remembered correctly, the man had boarded in Schongau. The man was thickset and almost as tall as the hangman himself. From his blue Tyrolean jacket hung a hunting knife as long as a man's forearm. His shoulders were broad, a hefty paunch bulged over his copper belt, and he wore his knee breeches stuffed into tall, coarse leather boots and a Tyrolean hat commonly worn by raftsmen. The most striking thing about him, however, was his face. The entire right-hand side was furrowed with little pockmarks and scars, likely the result of severe burns. Over one eye the man wore a black patch. A shiny pink scar extended from his forehead to his chin as if embossed on his face, and it seemed to twitch like a thick, iridescent worm.

For a moment Kuisl felt as though he weren't looking at a face but an animated grotesque.

A hateful face.

When the moment passed, the helmsman bent down again over his oar. He sat with his back to the hangman as if their eyes had never met.

An image from Kuisl's past flashed through his mind, but he couldn't quite grasp it. The Danube flowed by lazily, taking the memory with it and leaving only a misty, vague presentiment.

Where in the world . . . ?

Kuisl knew this man. He couldn't say from where, but his instinct warned him. As a mercenary soldier in the Great War, the Schongau executioner had come to know all kinds of people — both cowards and heroes, some crooked and some upright, victims as well as murderers — and among them were many whom war had driven mad. One thing Kuisl could say with certainty: the man standing just a few steps from him, calmly guiding the tiller through the water — this man was dangerous. Dangerous and shrewd.

Deliberately, the hangman adjusted the larch-wood cudgel on his belt. All in all, there seemed no cause for concern. There were plenty of people who might say the same thing about him.

Kuisl got off the raft in the small town of Prüfening, still a few miles short of Regensburg.

He grinned, shouldering his medicine bag and waving to the raftsmen, merchants, and craftsmen. If this scar-faced stranger was in fact on his trail, that man had a problem now. As helmsman, he could hardly leave the raft before it arrived in Regensburg. And, sure enough, the raftsman stared at him with his one healthy eye, as if he was contemplating abandoning the raft and setting off after Kuisl. But then, evidently, he thought better of it. With one last hateful look, so brief it went unnoticed by everyone else, he turned back to his work, wrapping the slick rope, thick as a man's arm, around the posts in the jetty.

The raft remained moored there until a few more travelers boarded for the short trip to Regensburg. Then it cast off and began to glide slowly toward the Imperial City, whose tallest spires were now visible on the horizon.

Kuisl watched the raft drift away. Then, whistling a military march, he started down the narrow road leading north. Soon he'd left the little town behind and was surrounded on either side by fields of grain rippling in the wind. A stone marked the border where Kuisl left Bavarian territory and entered the lands belonging to the Free City of Regensburg. Until now he'd known the place only from stories. He knew that Regensburg was one of the greatest cities in the German Empire and was subject to no one but the kaiser himself. And he'd heard that the electoral princes, bishops, and dukes all convened there as a Reichstag to determine the empire's fate.

When Kuisl's gaze took in the towering spires and city walls in the distance, homesickness came over him. The Schongau hangman was not a man made for the wide world—the Sonnenbrau Tavern tucked behind the church, the green Lech River, and the deep Bavarian forests were good enough for him.

It was a hot August afternoon, and the fields shimmered gold in the sunlight. In the distance, black storm clouds were beginning to gather on the horizon. To his right, a gallows hill rose up from the fields; several corpses swayed gently in the breeze.

Now-derelict trenches served as reminders that the Great War was not so far in the past. By now the hangman wasn't alone on the road anymore; coaches and lone men on horseback rushed past him, as well as oxen slowly pulling farmers' overladen carts. A broad stream of noisily babbling people, all on their way to Regensburg, had apparently come to a stop near the entrance to the high gate in the city's western wall. Among the throng of poor farmers clad in wool and other coarse cloth, the pilgrims, the beggars, and the wagoners, Kuisl also caught sight of quite a few magnificently attired noblemen, mounted high on horseback, making their way through the crowd.

The Schongau hangman frowned as he watched this strange procession. Evidently one of the Reichstag meetings was close at hand. He took his place among the people in line before the gate. Judging from all the complaints and curses, this seemed to be taking longer than usual.

"Hey, big fellow! Which way is the wind blowing up there?"

Kuisl bent down to a farmer who was apparently addressing him. When the little man found himself eye to eye with the grim-faced hangman, he swallowed hard before continuing. "Can you see what the problem is up in front?" he asked with a modest smile. "Twice a week I bring my carrots to market, usually on Tuesday and Saturday, but I've never seen such a throng."

The hangman stood on his toes. Now he was almost two heads taller than the people standing around him. Kuisl could see a half-dozen armed watchmen standing guard at the gate, holding tin boxes in their hands, in which they collected a toll from each traveler. To the sound of furious protests from the farmers, soldiers plunged their swords into wagons filled with corn, hay, and cabbages as if they were looking for someone.

"They're inspecting every single wagon," the hangman groused, sneering down at the farmer. "Is the kaiser in town, or do you always make such a fuss?"

The man sighed. "Ah, it's probably because some important

ambassador has just arrived. But the Reichstag doesn't even meet till next year! If it continues like this, all the market stands will be taken before I make it to the Haid Square. Damn!" He cursed and took an angry bite out of a turnip he plucked from a basket in front of him. "Damned ambassadors! A plague—they're no better than the Moslems! They bring us nothing but trouble. They don't lift a finger and just hold up traffic."

"But why are they here?" Kuisl asked.

The farmer laughed. "Why? Why, to eat us out of house and home! They don't pay a cent in taxes, plus they bring their own servants along, taking the work from the rest of us! They claim they're here to figure out how to keep the goddamned Turks from invading the German Empire. But if you ask me, that's all hot air!" He sighed deeply. "Why can't the kaiser hold his Reichstag somewhere else for once? But no, every few years they come around again, and we have to put up with it. It seems like the envoys are always here."

Kuisl nodded, though he hadn't really paid much attention. What did he care about the Reichstag? All he wanted was to see his little Lisbeth. In the meantime the high and mighty could go right on planning the next war. They'd have no trouble finding people willing to follow them, to let themselves be slaughtered for the promise of wealth and glory. As for himself, he'd have nothing more to do with that old cut and thrust.

"And how about yourself? What are you doing here?" the farmer asked. "Have you found a place to stay yet?"

Kuisl closed his eyes. Apparently he'd stumbled across the chattiest farmer in all of Regensburg. "I'll be staying at my sister's," he mumbled, hoping that the little fellow might leave him in peace now.

All the while, the hangman and his companion had being moving along the line, and now only two wagonloads of hay separated them from what people were calling Jakob's Gate. The watchmen peered beneath the wagons, prodded the hay with their swords, then waved the wagons through and turned to the next traveler in line. The first rumble of thunder could be heard in the distance. A storm would not hold off for long.

Finally it was their turn. The farmer was allowed to pass without further ado, but Kuisl was waved aside.

"Hey, you . . . Yes, you!" A guard wearing a helmet and a breastplate pointed at the hangman and ordered him to step closer. "Where are you from?"

"Schongau, down by Augsburg," the hangman replied, looking at his interlocutor as he would a stone.

"Aha, from Augsburg . . ." replied the watchman, twirling his fancy mustache.

"No, not Augsburg, from Schongau," the hangman replied in a gruff voice. "I'm no dirty Swabian. I'm Bavarian."

"No matter," the watchman said, winking at his comrade behind him. He looked Kuisl up and down as if measuring him against some mental image. "And what brings you here, Bavarian?"

"My sister lives here," the hangman replied curtly, refusing to indulge the mocking undertone. "She's gravely ill, and I'm paying her a visit, with all due respect."

The watchman grinned smugly. "Your sister, indeed! Well, if she looks anything like you, you should find her in no time." He laughed and turned back to his comrade with a smirk. "Living and breathing lumps of rock with hooked noses are pretty uncommon 'round these parts, isn't that so?"

Laughter broke out all around. Kuisl remained silent as the watchman continued poking fun at him. "I hear they feed you Swabians on noodles and cheese until you got 'em coming out your ears. You're living proof that this stuff'll make you fat and dumb."

Without batting an eye, the hangman moved a step closer and seized the man by the collar. The watchman's eyes bulged like marbles from their sockets as Kuisl yanked him off the ground and looked him in the eye.

"Listen, young fellow," he snarled. "If there's something you need me to tell you, just ask straight out. Otherwise, hold your tongue and let me through."

Suddenly the hangman felt the point of a sword at his back. "Put him down," a voice behind him said. "Nice and easy, big fellow, or I'll ram this sword through your guts so it comes clean out the other side. You hear me?"

The hangman nodded slowly and set the frightened man back down. When he turned around, Kuisl saw a tall officer in a polished cuirass before him. Like his colleague, he wore a twirled walrus mustache and a helmet that gleamed in the bright sunlight and covered a mane of blond hair. He now had his sword positioned directly at the base of Kuisl's throat. A small crowd of onlookers gathered around them, eagerly waiting to see what would happen next.

"Fine," the captain said, his lips pressed in a thin, mirthless smile. "Now you will turn around and we'll go together to the room in the tower. We keep some cozy quarters there, where Bavarians such as yourself can take time to reflect."

The officer pressed the point of his sword a fraction of an inch into the hangman's neck to emphasize his point. For a moment Kuisl was tempted to seize the man's sword, pull him up close, and drive his larch-wood truncheon straight between his legs. But then he noticed the other watchmen standing around with lances and halberds raised, whispering among themselves. Why had he let himself get riled up? It almost seemed as if the watchman had deliberately gone out of his way just to provoke him. Was this how Regensburgers dealt with all strangers?

Kuisl spun around and marched off toward the tower. He could only hope they'd let him go before the good Lord called his sister home.

As the door closed behind the hangman, the first raindrops began to fall on the pavement outside, and within moments the rain was drumming down so hard that the people waiting at the gate had to pull their cloaks over their heads or seek shelter in nearby barns. Hail as big as pigeon eggs fell from the sky, causing many a farmer to curse himself for not having brought the harvest in earlier. It was already the third raging thunderstorm that week, and people were praying. Each family crowded together around an altar in their homes; not a few of the inhabitants of the surrounding villages took the deluge as an expression of God's righteous anger, and of his punishment for the debauched ways of the accursed city folk — the fancy clothes, their swindling ways, their shameless whoring, and all the arrogance of building ever taller, ever grander houses. Hadn't Sodom and Gomorrah perished in a similar way? With the Reichstag set to take place next January, all the pompous nobles would show up again; they would drink and whore and, instead of attending mass, would celebrate their own power — while, in fact, it was God alone who would decide the weal or woe of the German Empire!

With a deafening crack, a bolt of lightning struck the walkway atop the battlements, followed by such a loud clap of thunder that children as far away as Emmeram Square started wailing. In the brief flash of the next bolt of lightning, a figure could be seen struggling along the road from Jakob's Gate into town. He walked with a stoop, his face lashed by the hail and rain. No one else dared go out in such weather, but the man had an urgent message to deliver, and it wouldn't wait.

The scar on his face throbbed as it so often did when the weather was changing. The hangman had almost slipped away from him, but the man knew his enemy would have to pass through Jakob's Gate — there was no other way into town from the west. The man had run from the raft landing to the gate as fast as possible to warn the guards. A bit of money in the right hands had won them the time they needed to carry out their plan.

Revenge! How long they both had been waiting for that . . . !

The man grinned, and the scar on his face began to twitch nervously.

2

THE OPPRESSIVE SUMMER AIR LAY OVER SCHON-gau like a musty blanket.

Magdalena Kuisl ran down the narrow overgrown path from the Tanners' Quarter to the Lech, her skirt fluttering behind her. Her mother had given her the afternoon off and her strict father was far away, so she raced through the cool, shady land along the river, happy to escape the stuffiness and the stench in town.

Magdalena looked forward to a swim in the river, as the odor of manure, dirt, and mold clung to her matted black hair. She and her mother had been busy in town all morning collecting garbage and shoveling it into their cart. Even the nine-year-old twins, Georg and Barbara, had to help. The work seemed harder than usual because Magdalena's father had left for Regensburg a few days ago. As the family of the hangman, it was the Kuisls' job to clear the streets in Schongau of garbage and animal carcasses. Every week mountains of trash piled up at the corners and intersections in town, rotting in the hot sun. Rats with long, smooth tails scampered about on top of the piles, glaring at passersby with evil little eyes. At least Magdalena had the afternoon to herself.

After just a few minutes the hangman's daughter arrived at the riverbank. She turned to the left, away from the raft landing where there were already a half-dozen rafts tied up. She could hear the shouts and laughter of the raftsmen as they unloaded the barrels, crates, and bales and took them off to the newly re-built storage building, the Zimmerstadel, on the pier. She turned off the narrow towpath and made her way through the green un-derbrush, which now, in midsummer, was shoulder-high. The ground was swampy and slippery, and with each step her bare feet sank in with a slurping sound.

Finally Magdalena reached her favorite spot, a small, shal-low cove invisible behind the surrounding willow trees. She climbed down over a large dead root and removed her soiled clothes. Then she scrubbed the dress, apron, and bodice thor-oughly, rubbing them over the sharp, wet pebbles. She laid them out to dry on a rock in the warm afternoon sun.

As Magdalena stepped into the water, the current flowing past tugged gently at her ankles and she sank gradually into the mud. A few more steps and she slipped completely into the river. Here in the cove, hollowed out of the river ages ago, the current wasn't quite so strong. The hangman's daughter swam out, tak-ing care not to get too close to the whirlpool in the middle of the Lech. The water washed the dirt from her skin and hair, and after a few minutes she felt fresh and rested again. The foul-smelling city was far, far away.

As she swam back to the shore, she noticed her clothes had disappeared.

Magdalena looked around, unsure of what to do. She'd laid her wet clothing out on the rock right there, and now all that re-mained was a damp spot gradually vanishing in the hot sun.

Had someone followed her here?

She looked up and down the shoreline but couldn't see her clothes anywhere. She tried to calm down. No doubt some children were just playing a joke on her—nothing more. She sat down on a tree root to dry off in the sun. Lying back with her eyes closed, she waited for the pranksters to start giggling and give themselves away.

All at once she heard a rustling behind her in the bushes.

Before she could jump up, someone wrapped a hairy, sinewy arm around her neck and placed a hand over her mouth. She tried to scream, but not a sound came out.

"Not a word, or I'll kiss you until your neck is red all over and your father gives you a good spanking."

Magdalena couldn't help giggling as she sputtered through the hand held over her mouth.

"Simon! My God, you nearly scared me to death! I thought robbers or murderers . . ."

Simon kissed her gently on her neck. "Who knows, maybe I am one . . ." he said, giving her a conspiratorial wink.

"You're weird, a runt, and a quack, and nothing more. Before you even touch a hair on my head, I'll wring your neck. God knows why I love you so much."

She extricated herself from his grip and threw herself at him. In a tight embrace they rolled across the wet pebbles in the cove. Before long she had pinned Simon to the ground with her knees. The medicus was slender and wirier than he was muscular. At just five feet tall, he was one of the smallest men Magdalena had ever known. He had fine features with bright, alert eyes that always seemed to sparkle mischievously, and a well-trimmed black Vandyke beard. His dark hair was lightly oiled and shoulder-length in accord with the latest fashion. In other respects, as well, Simon was well groomed, though at the moment his appearance was somewhat in disarray.

"I—I give up," he groaned.

"Oh, no you don't! First you're going to swear to me there's no other woman in your life."

Simon shook his head. "No—nobody else."

Magdalena rapped him on the head and rolled down next to him. She'd never quite forgiven him for flirting with the red-headed merchant woman more than two years ago, even though Simon had sworn a dozen times there really hadn't been anything between them. But the day was just too beautiful to waste quarreling. Together they looked up into the branches of the willows swaying back and forth above their heads in the gentle breeze. For a long time they were silent, listening to the wind rustling in the trees.

After a while Magdalena spoke up. "My father will probably be away for a while."

The medicus nodded and gazed out at two ducks flapping their wings as they rose from the water. Magdalena had already told him about her father's trip to visit his ill sister. "What did Lechner have to say about that?" he finally asked. "As the court clerk, he could have simply ordered your father not to leave town—now of all times, in summer when the garbage stinks to high heaven."

Magdalena laughed. "What was he to do? Father just got up and left. Lechner cursed and swore he'd have him hanged when he came back. It was only then that it occurred to him that my father would have trouble hanging himself." She sighed. "There will probably be a big fine to pay, and until he comes back, Mother and I will just have to work twice as hard."

Her eyes took on a dreamy look. "How far away is Regensburg, anyway?" she asked.

"Very far." Simon grinned as he playfully drew his finger around her belly button. Magdalena was still naked, and droplets of water sparkled on her skin, tanned from her daily trips into the forest to collect herbs.

"Far enough at least that he can't torment us with his lectures," the medicus said finally, with a big yawn.

Magdalena flared up. "If there's a problem, it's your father who's always hounding us. Anyway, the purpose for my father's trip was serious—so stop your silly grinning."

The hangman's daughter thought now about the letter from Regensburg that had troubled her father so much. She knew her father had a younger sister in Regensburg, but she never realized how close the two of them had been. Magdalena was only two years old when her aunt fled to Regensburg with a bathhouse owner. They left because of the Great Plague but also because of the daily taunts and hostilities in town. Magdalena had always admired her for her courage.

Silently she threw some pebbles, which skipped a few times before finally being swallowed by the rippling water.

"It's a mystery to me who's going to clean up all the garbage in town for the next few weeks in all this hot weather," she said, more to herself than to Simon. "If the aldermen think I'm going to do it, they have another thing coming. I'd rather spend the rest of the summer in a hole in the ground."

Simon clapped his hands. "What a great idea! Or we can just stay here in this cove!" He started kissing her cheeks, and Magdalena resisted, though only halfheartedly.

"Stop, Simon! If anyone sees us . . ."

"Who's going to see us?" he replied, passing his hand through her wet black hair. "The willows certainly won't tell on us."

Magdalena laughed. These few hours spent down at the river or in nearby barns were all they had to show for their love. They'd always dreamed of getting married, but strict town statutes wouldn't permit that. They'd been courting for years, and their relationship was like a desperate game of hide-and-seek. As the daughter of the hangman, Magdalena wasn't allowed to associate with the higher classes. Executioners were dishonorable, just like gravediggers, bathhouse owners, barbers, and magicians. Accordingly, marriage to a physician was out of the question, but that didn't keep the couple from clandestine meetings in the fields and barns around town. In the springtime two years ago, they'd even made a pilgrimage together to Altötting, basically the only longer time they'd been together. In the meantime the affair between the medicus and the hangman's daughter had become a hot topic of conversation in the Schongau marketplace and taverns. Moreover, Simon's father, old Bonifaz Fronwieser, was urging his son with increasing insistence to finally settle down with a middle-class girl. That was actually essential in advancing Simon's career as a doctor, but he kept putting his father off—and meeting secretly with Magdalena.

"Maybe we should go to Regensburg, too," Simon whispered between kisses. "A serf gains his freedom after living a year and a day in the city. We could start a new life . . ."

"Oh, come now, Simon." Magdalena pushed him away. "How often you've promised me that! What will become of me, then? Don't forget I'm dishonorable. I'll just end up picking up the garbage again, no matter where I am."

"Nobody knows me there!"

Magdalena shrugged. "And what will I do for work? The cities are full of hungry day laborers and—"

Simon held his finger to her lips. "Just don't say anything now—let's forget it all for just a while." His eyes closed, he bent down and covered her body with kisses.

"Simon . . . no . . ." Magdalena whispered, but her resistance was already broken.

At that moment they heard a crackling sound in the willow tree above them.

Magdalena looked up. Something seemed to be moving there in the branches. All of a sudden she felt something warm and slimy hit her and run slowly down her forehead. She put up her hand to feel it and realized it was spit.

She heard giggling and then saw two boys, about twelve

years old, quickly climb down the tree. One of them was the youngest son of the alderman and master baker Michael Berchtholdt, with whom Magdalena had often exchanged strong words.

"The doctor is kissing the hangman's daughter!" the second boy shouted as he ran away. Disgusted, Magdalena wiped the rest of the spit from her forehead. Simon jumped up and shook his fist at the smirking boy.

"You impertinent little brats!" he shouted. "I'm going to break every bone in your bodies!"

"The hangman's daughter can do that better than you!" cackled the second boy, disappearing into the bush. "Do it on the rack, you scum!"

Then little Berchtholdt stopped short. He turned and looked at Simon defiantly, with clenched teeth, trembling slightly as the medicus charged after him like a madman, his shirt open and his jacket undone.

"It wasn't me," he squealed as Simon raised his hand to strike. "It was Benedikt! I swear! Actually, we were just looking for you because — uh — "

Simon had raised his hand to strike the boy when he noticed that young Berchtholdt was staring open-mouthed at the half-naked hangman's daughter, who was trying to hide as best she could behind a rock while she buttoned up her bodice. The physician gave the boy a gentle poke on the nose strong enough to send the boy reeling backward into the mud.

"Didn't the priest teach you any sense of decency?" Simon chided. "If you keep staring like that, God will strike you blind. So what are you up to here?"

"My father sent me," the boy mumbled. "He wants to see the Kuisl girl."

"Old Berchtholdt?" asked Magdalena, stepping out from behind the rock, now fully dressed. "What could he possibly want from me? Or is he sitting up there somewhere in the tree staring at me, too?"

The Schongau master baker was known around town as a lecherous old philanderer. He'd made a pass at Magdalena some years back and been rebuffed. Since then he'd been spreading gossip that the hangman's daughter was in league with the devil and had cast a spell on the young medicus. Three years ago the superstitious baker had almost succeeded in having the midwife, Martha Stechlin, burned at the stake for alleged witch-craft—something Magdalena's father had just barely been able to prevent. Since then Berchtholdt had harbored a deep hatred for the Kuisls and, whenever he could, tried to make life miserable for them.

"It's on account of his maid, Resl," the boy said as he continued to stare at Magdalena's low neckline. "She has a fat stomach and is screaming like crazy."

"Does she have a child on the way?" Magdalena asked.

Puzzled, the boy just stood there, picking his nose. "No idea. People think the devil has gotten into her. You should have a look, my father says."

"Aha, so now I'm good enough for him." She looked at the boy suspiciously. "Doesn't he want to go see Stechlin?"

"Berchtholdt would rather cut his own guts out than send for the midwife," interjected Simon, who'd dressed himself in the meantime. "You know, he still thinks Stechlin is a witch and would love to see her burn. Anyway, many people in town think you're just as good a midwife as she is, maybe even better."

"Enough of your nonsense!" Magdalena tied her wet hair up into a bun as she continued talking. "I only hope there's nothing seriously wrong with Berchtholdt's maid. Now come along, let's go!"

The hangman's daughter hurried down the narrow towpath to the Lech Gate, turning around to Simon once more as she ran.

"Perhaps we'll need a professional physician, even if it's just to go and fetch water."

As soon as they arrived at the narrow Zänkgasse, Magdalena was sure this was no ordinary birth. Through the small bolted windows of the baker's house the screams sounded more like a cow awaiting slaughter than a woman giving birth. Farmers and workers had come running to the door of the bakery and were whispering anxiously to one another. When Simon and Magdalena approached, the group stepped back reluctantly.

"Here comes the hangman's daughter to drive the devil out of the baker's maid," somebody said.

"I say they're both witches," an old woman whispered. "Just wait, and we'll see them fly out through the chimney."

Magdalena pushed her way past the gossiping women and tried not to take what they were saying too seriously. As the hangman's daughter, she was accustomed to people thinking of her as the spawn of Satan, and ever since she started working for the midwife, her reputation had grown even worse. Mostly it was the men who were convinced the hangman's daughter could prepare magic elixirs and love potions, and in fact, a few of the aldermen had already obtained such preparations from her father. Up to now, however, Magdalena had always refused to swindle people with such nonsense, primarily to avoid arousing even more suspicions about her being the devil's consort. But to no avail, she had to admit to herself with a sigh.

As the crowd continued whispering and gossiping, she entered the bakery with Simon, where they were received by Michael Berchtholdt, who looked as white as a sheet. As so often, the scrawny little man smelled of brandy, and his eyes were ringed in red circles as if he'd passed a sleepless night. He was rubbing a dry bouquet of mugwort between his fingers to ward off evil spirits. His wife, who was just as skinny, knelt before a crucifix in a corner of the room, murmuring prayers, which were, however, drowned out by the screams of the maid.

Resl Kirchlechner lay by the fire on a bench covered with dirty straw. She writhed in pain as if a fire burned inside her. Her face, hands, and legs were covered with red pustules, and the tips of her fingers had turned a shiny black. Her belly was distended into a little round ball and almost looked like a foreign object on her otherwise spindly body. Magdalena presumed that, until now, the maid had wrapped her dress tightly around herself to conceal the pregnancy.

At just that moment, the young woman sat up as if someone had rammed a broomstick up her back. Her eyes were vacant and her dry lips opened as she let out a long, drawn-out scream.

"He's in me!" she gasped. "My God, he's eating through my body and tearing out my soul!" A loud moan followed. "Oh . . . I can feel his teeth. I can hear his lips smacking as he gnaws through my belly! I want to spit him out like a rotten piece of fruit!" She made a retching sound as if preparing to regurgitate something large and undigested.

"My God, what is that?" Simon asked in horror from the doorway.

"Can't you see? The devil is in her!" Maria Berchtholdt moaned from the corner of the room, rocking back and forth on her knees and tearing at her hair. "He's eating her alive from the inside out. Holy Mary, Mother of God, pray for us sinners . . ."

Her prayers turned into a wailing monotone as Michael Berchtholdt stared silently at his maid thrashing around in spasms.

"It looks like Resl took something to abort the child," Magdalena whispered to Simon so the others couldn't hear. "Perhaps castoreum, or rue." All of a sudden she frowned. "Wait—she didn't . . ."

Magdalena cautiously approached Resl Kirchlechner and felt the pustules on her arm. When the maid started thrashing around again, the hangman's daughter jumped back. "I think I know what it is now," she whispered. "It must be Saint Anthony's Fire. Resl probably took ergot to abort the child."

Simon nodded. "I don't know much about it, but I think you're right. The pustules . . . the black fingertips . . . and then the feverish dreams. Everything points to that. My God, the poor girl . . ."

Magdalena squeezed his hand and then cursed under her breath. As a midwife, she knew about ergot, a fungus that grew on rye and other kinds of grain and was used now and then to abort a pregnancy. But ergot could be taken only in small doses or it would cause cramps and horrible visions of witches, devils, and demons. The victims' fingers and toes turned black and finally fell off, and because they felt like they were being burned by fire inside, the sickness was called Saint Anthony's Fire.

Simon turned to Michael Berchtholdt. "This girl isn't possessed by the devil," he replied, pointing to the girl's swollen belly. "Resl took ergot, and I wonder who might have given it to her."

"I — I have no idea what you're talking about," the master baker stuttered. "It may be that Resl has been fooling around with some young fellow and — "

"No, with Satan!" his wife interrupted. "She's been carrying on with Satan!"

"Nonsense!" Magdalena whispered softly enough so Berchtholdt couldn't hear it. She dabbed the face of the screaming maid with a damp cloth and tried to comfort her. But all of a sudden Magdalena couldn't stand it any longer. Her eyes flashed as she turned around and glared furiously at the baker.

"Nonsense! It's not Satan," she growled. "Everybody in town knows that you've been running after Resl! Everybody!"

"What are you trying to say?" Michael Berchtholdt asked softly. His facial features looked even sharper than usual. "Are you saying that maybe I — "

"You impregnated your own maid!" Magdalena blurted out. "And so that nobody would find out, you gave her the ergot. That's what happened, isn't it?"

Berchtholdt's face turned beet red. "How dare you talk about me like that, you fresh little hangman's girl!" he gasped finally. "You're forgetting that I sit on the city council and all I have to do is to give the word and you Kuisls can pack your things and leave. All it takes is one word from me!"

"Ha! And who will give your wife her little sleeping potion then?" Magdalena jumped up and pointed at the praying Maria Berchtholdt. "How often has she come to my father for a little potion to calm down her husband at home so he will nod off after drinking his wine?"

The baker glared in disbelief at his wife, who looked down at the ground, embarrassed, her hands folded. "Maria, is that right?"

"Quiet!" Simon said. "It's disgraceful to quarrel like this while the poor girl is probably dying. If we are to help, we at least have to know how much ergot she took and who gave it to her." He looked at Michael Berchtholdt in desperation. "For God's sake, say something! Did you give the medication to the girl?"

The master baker remained defiantly silent, but then his wife spoke up in a soft voice. "It's true," she whispered. "It would be a lie to say anything else. God help you, Michael! You, and all of us!"

The baker struggled for words but gave in at last. He slumped over, sighing, and ran his hand through his hair, which was thinning and matted with flour. "Well, yes, then, I — I gave it to her," he stammered. "I — I told her to take it all at once just to make sure it worked."

"All at once?" Magdalena looked at him in horror. "And how much was that?"

Berchtholdt shrugged. "A little bag, perhaps as large as my fist."

Simon gripped his forehead and groaned. "Then there's no way we can save her. All we can do is try to relieve her pain." With clenched fists he advanced toward Michael Berchtholdt. "Who in God's name gave you so much ergot?" he shouted. "Who, damn it! What quack?"

The baker retreated toward the doorway and finally mumbled something so softly that Simon couldn't understand him at first. "It was your father."

The young medicus stood there dumbfounded. "My father?"

Berchtholdt nodded. "The stuff cost me two guilders, but your father said it was the surest way."

Simon had trouble speaking. "Did my father at least tell you how much to give her?"

"Actually he didn't." The baker shrugged. "He just said it would be better to take too much than too little, just to make sure it worked. So I just gave her all of it."

Simon was tempted to seize the baker by the throat, but at that moment the maid began to scream again — this time longer and higher pitched than before. Resl reared up so far it seemed her spine would break. Her pale thighs were spread far apart, and the white sheets between them were stained with blood. The next moment the maid slumped down, and a bloody little body the size of a cat fell from the bench onto the floor.

A stillbirth.

Simon rushed over to the maid and felt her neck for a pulse. Her face was now relaxed and peaceful, and her dead eyes appeared to stare down at the bloody straw spread out on the floor. The medicus closed her eyes and laid her out gently on the bench.

"She's in a better place now," he mused, making the sign of the cross. "With no more pain, or demons, or people who would do her harm."

For a moment all was silent, except for the whimpering of the baker's wife. Finally Michael Berchtholdt came to his senses. He walked over to the fetus still lying on the floor next to the stove, picked it up gingerly, and walked out through the back door into the garden. When he returned a while later, he wiped his muddy hands on his trousers and attempted a slight smile that froze midway in a grimace.

"Resl is dead, and that's a shame," he said in a soft voice. "I'll see to it that she gets a decent burial in Saint Sebastian's Cemetery with a priest, funeral meal, and all the trappings. I'll also see that her parents are taken care of financially. As for everything else —" He gave an embarrassed smile. "— we don't want word to get around that the devil possessed our maid. That could end badly. And as the young physician here can certainly attest, Resl had a high fever — that can lead to bad dreams, can't it?" The baker looked at Simon expectantly.

"You don't seriously believe that —" the medicus began, but Berchtholdt raised his hand, interrupting him.

"I know your house calls are expensive. How much? Tell me — five guilders? Ten? How much do you ask?" He pulled a trunk out from behind the table and began to rummage through it.

"Just keep your money and choke on it!" Magdalena shouted, slamming the lid closed on Berchtholdt's fingers. He pulled them out, whining and clenching his teeth. His wife looked back and forth from one to the other as if they were ghosts. Simon assumed the shock was too much for her. Maria Berchtholdt had decided to withdraw into her own world.

"I'm going to tell everyone — everyone! — that you jumped on your maid like a randy old goat and let her die of ergot poisoning," the hangman's daughter whispered. "It's always we women who are expected to pay for men's lechery. Well, not this time!"

The baker's little weasel eyes took on a glassy sheen. "Aha, and who is going to believe you?" he asked. "A hangman's daughter and the horny son of an army doctor. What a pair! Go on, go and tell the people, and I promise I'll make your life hell!"

"My life is hell already." Magdalena turned to go and beckoned Simon to follow.

With a facetious bow the medicus took leave of the alderman and master baker Michael Berchtholdt. "If the hemorrhoids in your ass itch or your bowels get plugged up," Simon said in a cloying tone, "you know where you can find me."

They walked out together and were met by a group of curious onlookers. Behind them they could still hear Michael Berchtholdt's muffled cries and shrill curses. Magdalena stopped for a moment and looked into the faces of the bystanders, who were staring back at them with expressions of disapproval and disgust.

A hangman's daughter and the horny son of an army doctor. What a pair . . .

Magdalena was no longer certain anyone would believe them. The farmers and workers moved aside to make way for them, as if they had some infectious disease.

As Magdalena and Simon headed down toward the Lech Gate, they could feel the looks directed at their backs for a long time.

3

Late in the night Simon was awakened by noises outside the Fronwieser home. He reached for a stiletto he always kept in the trunk next to his bed. But judging from the pounding on the door and the crude cursing that followed, it could only be his father, who, no doubt, was staggering home from some tavern out behind the Ballenhaus.

Simon rubbed his eyes and stretched. Ever since that afternoon he had wanted to speak with his father about the ergot, but Bonifaz Fronwieser had disappeared without a trace. That was no cause for concern, as in recent months the old man had often vanished for days, boozing his way through the taverns of Schongau, Altenstadt, and Peiting. Once he finally ran out of money, he'd find a barn, sleep it off, and return home the next day, disheveled and hung-over. After a few weeks' respite, he would start up all over again. Simon guessed that at the local taverns his father had already freely distributed the two guilders he'd fetched for the ergot.

The young medicus sighed and reached for a cold cup of coffee on the trunk next to his bed. The bitter brew helped him to bear his father's increasingly erratic moods. In recent years their quarreling had escalated. Bonifaz Fronwieser had been an army surgeon before he found a position as doctor in Schongau. Simon's mother had died long ago, and his father wanted nothing more than to see his son better off in this life than he'd been. So, he'd sent Simon to the university in Ingolstadt, where the latter spent less energy on his studies than he did money on clothes, card games, and pretty women. Around the time Simon returned from Ingolstadt without a diploma, his father started drinking.

His father's loud singing interrupted Simon's thoughts. The young medicus listened as his father threw his boots in the corner, then promptly collapsed. With a loud crash, a few dishes fell to the floor and shattered. Blinking, Simon noticed the first light of day filtering through the shutters. He got up and started to dress. It was probably pointless to speak with his father now, but anger was rising in Simon, and he couldn't go back to sleep.

As he started down the steep staircase, he could see his father sitting on a bench downstairs. With a vacant look, old Fronwieser pushed a few rusty coins across the table, apparently all that remained from his drinking spree. Alongside him was a cup half full of brandy. Without saying a word, Simon picked it up and poured the contents onto the floor. It was only then that his father seemed to notice him.

"Stop that!" the father said angrily. "I'm still your father."

"You sold ergot to Berchtholdt," Simon said in a flat voice.

His father stared at him with small, tired eyes. For a moment it seemed he was going to deny it, but finally he shrugged. "And if I did . . . what business is it of yours?"

"The baker gave the ergot to his maid, Resl, and she died yesterday from taking it."

There was a long pause, and Bonifaz appeared unwilling to reply.

Finally, Simon continued, "She screamed so loud that all of Schongau could hear it—like a pig being slaughtered. But you were out carousing and didn't hear a thing, I'm sure."

Old Fronwieser folded his arms over his chest and threw his head back defiantly. "I gave the stuff to Berchtholdt because he positively begged for it. What he did with it is his business and doesn't concern me. If his maid —"

"You told him it would be better to take too much than too little!" Simon interrupted, his voice quivering. "You gave him the ergot as if it were herbal tea or arnica, but it's poison! Deadly poison! You're nothing but a charlatan, a quack!"

The last words, which slipped out by accident, sent his father over the edge.

"Quack?" he growled, digging his fingernails into the table-top. "You call me a goddamned quack? Let me tell you who's a quack in this town. It's your damned hangman! Folks are always begging him for their elixirs and their salves. Now that he's away, I finally have a chance to make a little money, and you make me out to be a murderer! My own son!" The old man stood up and pounded the table so hard the cups on the wall started rattling. "The damned hangman! That quack! That devil! I'll burn his house down."

Closing his eyes, Simon turned his face toward the ceiling. Bonifaz's jealousy had been a thorn in his side for years, a thorn tipped in poison. Many Schongauers preferred to take their sicknesses and little aches and pains secretly to the hangman rather than to the town doctor. This was, of course, far cheaper, and moreover executioners were considered better not only at treating the broken bones and external injuries they had often themselves inflicted but also at healing internal diseases. By virtue of their experience with torture and executions, they had a more thorough understanding of the human body than any doctor with a university diploma.

What angered old Fronwieser most, however, was that his son was a good friend of the executioner. The young medicus had learned more from Kuisl than from his own father and the entire faculty of Ingolstadt University put together. The hangman owned books on medicine that couldn't even be found in most libraries. He knew every poison and medicinal herb and had studied writings that traditional scholars considered the work of the devil. Simon idolized the hangman and was in love with his daughter—two things that got under Bonifaz's skin and made him seethe with rage.

As the old man continued his rant about the hangman and the hangman's family, Simon walked over to a pot of hot water that had been standing on the hearth all night. He knew he would need some coffee if he hoped to withstand the next few minutes.

"I'm not going to be scolded by the likes of someone who'd go to bed with the hangman's daughter." His father's tirade was approaching its climax. "It's a wonder, in any case, that you're at home and not out with that little harlot of yours."

Simon's hands curled around the hot rim of the pot. "Father . . . I beg you!"

"Ha! You're *begging* me!" his father said, mocking him. "How often have I begged you—how often?—to put an end to this shameful affair, to help me here in my work, and to marry Weinberger's daughter or even Hardenberg's niece, who at least does decent work at the hospital. But no, my son carries on with the hangman's daughter, and the whole town gossips!"

"Father, stop it! At once!"

But by now Bonifaz had worked himself into a frenzy. "If only your dear mother knew!" he scoffed. "It's just as well the reaper carried her off so long ago—it would have broken her heart. For years we tramped along behind the military, serving them as field surgeons, saving every last kreuzer I could so that our son might attend the university and have a better life some-day. And what did you do? You squandered the money in Ingol-stadt and wasted your time loafing around with riffraff."

Simon was still clutching the pot by its rim. Although it had become painfully hot from the fire, he seemed barely to notice the heat, and his knuckles turned white with the force of his grip.

"Magdalena is not riffraff," he said slowly. "Nor is her father."

"He's a damned quack and a murderer, and his daughter is a whore."

Without a second thought, Simon flung the pot against the wall. With a loud hiss, the near-boiling water splashed over the shelves, table, and chairs, filling the room with a cloud of steam. Dumbfounded, Bonifaz looked back at his son. The pot had just barely missed his face.

"How dare you . . ." he began.

But Simon was not listening anymore. He dashed out the door into the early-morning light with tears streaming down his face. What had gotten into him? He'd almost killed his own father!

Distraught, Simon tried to pull his thoughts together. He had to get out of here, away from this stifling town that was making a recreant of him, a town that forbade him to marry the woman he loved, a town that tried to prescribe everything he did or thought.

He stepped out into the narrow street where foul-smelling garbage was pushed into huge piles. All of Schongau smelled that way—like muck, feces, and urine. Simon staggered through the empty streets, past the closed shop doors and bolted shutters. Another sweltering day had dawned in town.

The mouse was close to Jakob Kuisl's ear. He could feel it brush past his hair, its tiny nose grazing his cheek. The hangman tried to breathe as softly as possible so as not to frighten the little creature. It sniffed his beard where tiny bits of yesterday's stew still clung.

In a single, rapid motion, the hangman reached up and

nabbed the rodent by the tail. The mouse dangled in front of his face, squeaking and flailing its legs in the air as Kuisl calmly examined it.

Trapped, just like me. Thrashing around and getting nowhere . . .

He'd spent the night locked in this hole in the Jakob's Gate Tower in Regensburg: a little room in the cellar that was apparently most often used for storage. Surrounded by rusty cannons and disassembled matchlock guns, the hangman awaited his fate.

Could he just be imagining it, or was somebody really out to get him? Some of the guards had whispered among themselves when they took him into custody, pointing at him as if they somehow already knew who he was. Kuisl thought about the leering grimace of the raftsman who'd watched him for days. And what about the farmer he'd met while waiting outside the city gate? Had he been trying to pump him for information, too? Was it possible they'd each played a part in some conspiracy against him?

Is it possible I'm just losing my mind?

Again he tried to remember where he had seen the raftsman before. It must have been long ago. In battle? A tavern brawl? Or could he be one of the many whom, in the course of his life, Kuisl had put in the stocks, beaten with whips, or tortured? Kuisl nodded. That seemed most likely. Some minor offender who had recognized the Schongau executioner. The guards had him arrested because he'd assaulted one of their colleagues. And the curious farmer—well, he'd been just a curious farmer.

So there was no conspiracy, just a series of coincidences.

Kuisl set the mouse down carefully on the ground and let go of its tail. The animal scampered off toward a hole in the wall and disappeared. And just a few moments after that, the hangman was startled by a noise. The door to his cell opened with a creak and a narrow gap appeared, letting in the dazzling morning light.

"You are free to go, Bavarian." It was the captain of the guards at Jakob's Gate, with his twirled mustache and gleaming cuirass. He held the door open wide, gesturing for the hangman to leave. "You've had enough lolling around on your ass at the city's expense."

"I'm free?" Kuisl asked with surprise, getting up from his bedraggled sheets.

The captain nodded impatiently, and in his eyes Kuisl noticed a peculiar nervous flicker that he couldn't quite put his finger on.

"I hope you've cooled down a bit. Let it be a lesson to you not to tangle with the Regensburg city guards."

With a face as impassive as a rock, Kuisl pushed past the captain, headed up the stairway, and stepped outside. It was early morning, but another long line of people had already formed in front of Jakob's Gate, and merchants and farmers were streaming into the city with their full packs and carts.

I wonder if the scar-faced raftsman is among them, the hangman thought, casually observing the faces. But he couldn't see anything that looked suspicious.

Stop thinking about it and concern yourself with your little sister!

Looking straight ahead, Kuisl left the dungeon and started out through the city. From the few letters he had had from her, he knew that Lisbeth, along with her husband, ran a bathing establishment near the Danube, right alongside the city wall. As the hangman plodded along the broad paved avenue that led away from the gate, he was now no longer certain his directions would suffice, and amid the bustling crowd he soon lost his way. Houses four stories high rose up along both sides of the road, casting their shadows on the narrow, winding streets that branched off the main road at regular intervals. Sometimes the buildings stood so close together there was barely a patch of sky visible between them. From far off Kuisl could hear bells tolling in innumerable church spires. It was only six o'clock in the morn-

ing, yet there were more people out and about on the main road
than on a Saturday afternoon in Schongau. Kuisl saw many
richly clothed citizens but also countless poor, among them beggars and wounded veterans of the war, holding out their hands
for alms at every other street corner. Barking dogs tore past his
legs and down the street, as did two little piglets, squealing
loudly. Towering up into the sky to his right was an enormous
church whose stone portal, adorned with columns, arches, and
statues, looked as if it were the entrance to a castle. Day laborers
and derelicts loitered or lay dozing on the broad stone steps.
Kuisl decided to ask one of them for directions.

"The Hofmann bathhouse, eh?" The young fellow grinned,
revealing two remaining teeth. When Kuisl addressed him in his
broad Schongau dialect, the young man sensed a chance to make
some easy money. "You're not from around here, are you? Don't
worry, I can take you there, but it will cost you a couple of kreuzers."

The hangman nodded and handed the derelict a few old
coins. Then he quickly seized the beggar's wrist and twisted it
until it cracked softly. "If you cheat me or run off," the Schongau
executioner whispered, "or mislead me or tip off your buddies
and try to ambush me, or if you even *think* about doing any of
that, I will find you and I will break your neck. Do you understand?"

The fellow nodded anxiously and swiftly decided against his
original plan.

Together they turned left, away from the stone portal and
onto the next major thoroughfare. Once more Kuisl was astonished at how many people were bustling about in Regensburg at
this hour of the day. They all seemed to be in a hurry, as if the day
itself were somehow shorter here than the days in Schongau.
The hangman had trouble keeping up with the beggar through
the labyrinth of the busy little streets. A few times he felt a hand

reaching for his purse, but a severe glance or a well-aimed shove sufficed to dissuade the would-be pickpocket each time.

Finally, they seemed to be nearing their destination. This lane was wider than the preceding ones, and a tiny brook polluted with excrement and dead rats flowed languidly down the middle of it. Kuisl sniffed the air — sharp and rotten, an odor that the hangman knew only too well. Strips of leather hung like flags from balconies and windows. It was clear he was in the Tanners' Quarter.

The beggar pointed to a large building at the end of a row of houses on the left, where an opening in a narrow gate led down to the Danube. The house looked neater than the others, freshly plastered, its trim painted bright red. The bathhouse coat of arms, a tin banner depicting a green parrot in a golden field, hung above the entryway, squeaking in the wind.

"Bathhouse Hofmann," the man said. "As promised, bone cruncher." He bowed and stuck his tongue out at the hangman before disappearing into a little side street.

As Kuisl approached the bathhouse, he again had the unmistakable feeling of being watched, perhaps from one of the windows across the way. But when he turned around, he couldn't see anything behind the leather hides covering each window.

Damned city crowds! They're driving me crazy!

He knocked on the solid wooden door in front of him, only to discover it was already open. With a loud creak, it swung slowly inward, opening on a dimly lit room.

"Lisl!" Kuisl called into the darkness. "It's me, Jakob, your brother! Are you home?"

A strange feeling of homesickness came over him, memories from his childhood when he'd looked after his little sister. Lisbeth had been so happy to escape Schongau, to get away from the place where she had always been — just like Kuisl's own daughter now — the free-spirited hangman's daughter. She really seemed to have made it in the city, but now she was deathly ill and far from home . . .

Kuisl stood in the doorway, his heart pounding.

Cautiously he entered the room. It took some time for his eyes to adjust to the dim light of the large, long room that extended the length of the house. Fragrant reeds had been spread over the smoothly planed wooden floors, and from somewhere in the house he heard the steady sound of water dripping — a gentle, steady tapping.

Tap . . . tap . . . tap.

Kuisl slowly stepped further into the house. Wooden partitions divided the room into private niches at regular intervals along either side. The hangman could see that each contained a bench and, next to it, a large wooden tub.

In the last tub on the left he found his little sister alongside her husband.

Elisabeth Hofmann and her husband, Andreas, lay with their heads tilted back and their eyes open wide, as if they were watching some invisible spectacle play out across the ceiling. For a brief moment the hangman thought the couple was taking their morning bath; only then did he notice that both were fully clothed. Lisbeth's right arm hung over the edge of the tub, and something dripped from the tip of her index finger to the floor like heavy melted wax.

Tap . . . tap . . . tap.

Kuisl bent over the tub and passed his hand through the lukewarm water.

It was deep red.

He jumped back, the hair on the back of his neck standing up straight. His little sister and her husband were bathing in their own blood! Now Kuisl saw the slit across Lisbeth's throat, grinning up at him like a second mouth. Her black hair floated like a matted net on the surface of the bloody water. The slit in

Andreas Hofmann's neck was so deep that his head was almost severed from his body.

"Oh, God, Lisl!" Kuisl cradled his little sister's head in his arms and passed his hand gently through her hair. "What happened? What's happened to you?" He clenched his jaw as his eyes filled with tears, the first tears he'd shed in years.

Why? Why didn't I get here sooner?

His sister's face was as white as chalk. He held her in his arms and rocked her back and forth, stroking the hair from her forehead as he'd always done when she was a child in bed, restless with fever. In a deep, faltering voice he began to sing an old nursery rhyme.

Maikäfer flieg, dein Vater ist im Krieg, deine Mutter ist im . . . May bug fly, your father's gone to die, your mother is in . . .

A sound made him pause.

He turned around to find a contingent of at least five guards quietly entering the room. Two had crossbows trained on him and stood poised to shoot as a third slowly approached him with his sword drawn.

It was the captain from that morning.

The man twirled his mustache and smiled at Kuisl as he pointed at the two corpses. "Looks as if you have a problem on your hands, country boy."

"But not all of the St. John's Wort! Good Lord, girl! Pay attention!"

Magdalena was startled by the voice of Martha Stechlin shouting right into her ear. The hangman's daughter, who had been busy spooning herbs into a pot, knew how important it was to use just the right quantities of ingredients. But her thoughts were far, far away. When the midwife shouted at her, Magdalena couldn't say for the life of her how much St. John's Wort she'd already put in the copper kettle over the fire. The strange aroma coming from the green liquid bubbling in the pot distracted her even further.

"How often must I tell you: follow the recipe!" Stechlin grabbed the spoon from her hand and began stirring the remaining ingredients into the kettle herself. "You might get away with that when you make green oil," she mumbled, "but if that were to happen with belladonna or lily of the valley, we'd be convicted for brewing poison and end up burned at the stake. So please, do pay attention!"

"I'm . . . I'm terribly sorry," Magdalena whispered. "I'm not quite myself today."

"I've noticed," the midwife replied. "But there's nothing you can do for Resl anymore. We can only hope people will come back to us midwives now when they need ergot. Those doctors with their university diplomas don't know a thing about it."

Sighing, the hangman's daughter put the crucibles and glasses back in the drawers. She had gone to Stechlin first thing in the morning to tell her about the baker's maid who had met such a horrible death the day before. In the last two years a genuine friendship had developed between Magdalena and the midwife, even though Stechlin was older by almost twenty years. Neither was thought of very highly in town, even if people kept calling on them secretly for their aid. The townfolk whispered behind their backs; the men especially gave them a very wide berth, convinced that the women meddled too much in what they believed should be the dear Lord's work.

Nevertheless, Magdalena took great pleasure in her vocation, probably because, as the daughter of a hangman, she'd been dealing with herbs almost all her life. Magdalena knew that hops dampened sexual desire in men and that lady's mantle helped during pregnancy. She knew the preparations that made a woman fertile — as well as those that would promptly abort an unwanted fetus. Since the moment she'd learned to walk, her father had been introducing her to medicinal and toxic plants alike, and as time went on, new ones were always being discovered. By now she was almost more of an expert in the subject than the hangman himself. More than once Magdalena had spared a young maid the disgrace of raising a fatherless child by selecting the appropriate herb. The hangman's daughter had likely saved some of those girls from murdering their own children, and from execution at the hands of Magdalena's own father.

She'd arrived too late to save Resl Kirchlechner, however.

"The flask, quick!"

Once again Martha's voice tore Magdalena from her gloomy thoughts. She hurried to the cabinet, found the tall flask, and set it down carefully on the table. The midwife took the pot from the hearth and poured a fine stream of the bubbling green liquid into the flask.

As the hangman's daughter held the flask upright and watched the green liquid slowly filter to the bottom of the container, she couldn't help thinking of the master baker's maid. What cruel injustice that Michael Berchtholdt was still walking around, a free man, while a woman had died by his hand! Women had to bear all the shame while high and mighty, privileged men could do as they pleased! Vividly, Magdalena imagined her father with a switch in his hand, driving Berchtholdt from town. But, of course, this wasn't realistic. Should she appeal to the town council? Tell court clerk Johann Lechner about it? No doubt she'd be laughed out of town herself. Besides, Michael Berchtholdt was dangerous, and his parting words no idle threat.

Go on, go and tell people, and I promise I'll make your life hell!

At that moment a fist-size rock, followed by a second and a third, flew in through an open window. The women heard a crash as the flask burst, and hot oil splashed Stechlin in the face. The midwife staggered backward, bumped into the table, and finally collapsed onto the ground, screaming and covering her eyes with her dirty apron. More stones came crashing in, shattering the pots and phials on the shelves where they landed.

Magdalena ran to the window and peered warily over the sill. Outside, in the middle of the lane, stood a group of smirking young men, apprentices and journeymen, none of them older than twenty. The hangman's daughter immediately recognized three of Michael Berchtholdt's sons among them.

"Brew your stinking potions down in the Tanners' Quarter, hangman hussy!" spluttered a lanky, pimply boy making an obscene gesture. Peter Berchtholdt was no more than sixteen years old. "Father says you're responsible for what happened to our maid! You gave her the draught that turned her into a witch. Now she's gone, and you're to blame, you pernicious, murdering witch!"

Magdalena seethed with rage as never before. She burst out the door into the street and, after running up to the group of boys, kicked young Berchtholdt in the groin. He folded up like a jackknife as he fell with a groan to the ground, his face flushed, unable to speak, much less defend himself. Everything happened so fast that none of the other boys had been able to intervene.

Arms akimbo, Magdalena looked down at the master baker's son. "I'll tell you who the murderer is," she shouted, turning her fury to the two other Berchtholdt boys standing uncertainly off to one side. "Your father gave Resl the poison himself because it was he who fathered the child, and now he wants to blame it on me. Believe it or not, your father is a dirty liar *and* a murderer! Now get out of here, all of you, or I'll scratch your eyes out before you can say *hallelujah.*"

She raised her right hand, showing off her long, dirty fingernails. Peter was still lying on the ground in front of her. The boy hesitated — for a brief moment Magdalena thought she recognized something like doubt in his eyes — but then he pulled himself together, struggled to his feet, and staggered back to his brothers.

"You'll be sorry for what you said about our father," shouted the eldest Berchtholdt. "I *will* tell him, and then he'll see to it that Kuisl has to chase his own daughter with a whip through town and throw her in the stocks." He spit on the ground and made the sign of the cross with his right hand.

As the boys turned to leave, Magdalena shouted after them. "Wipe your own ass first, mama's boys! You Berchtholdts are nothing but cowards and loafers!"

She looked up; several windows had opened now and a dozen pairs of eyes stared down at the ruckus.

"And all you up there are not one bit better! *Not one bit!* To hell with you all!"

Cursing loudly, she stomped back into the midwife's house, where Stechlin now sat at the large table holding a damp cloth to her scalded face. Magdalena was relieved to see that apart from a few red blotches on her skin, no real damage had been done. The midwife's eyes had thankfully escaped injury, but the broken glass and the green puddle on the floor showed the stones had shattered more than just a flask and a few phials. Magdalena felt as if a stone had struck her straight in the heart.

Only now did she break down, leaning on the midwife and sobbing, as wave after wave of grief and pain surged through her body. Stechlin whispered softly to her, stroking the young girl's hair as if she were a child. Finally the midwife whispered, "They will never accept us; it's like a law of nature, like budding, blooming, and dying. You must try to live with this.'

Magdalena rose. Her eyes were red and swollen from crying, but her gaze was firm and unyielding. "To hell with the laws," she whispered. "I'll never accept them—never. I'll do what suits me, now more than ever!"

Stechlin moved away a bit and cast a furtive glance at Magdalena. There was no doubt about it—the girl really was the Schongau hangman's daughter.

A few hours later Magdalena's anger had subsided a bit. She

and her mother were busy getting the twins ready for bed, a job that always occupied her so completely she had no time left for gloomy thoughts.

"Just one more story, Magda," little Barbara pleaded. "Just one more! Tell us the one about the queen and the house in the forest! You haven't told us that one for a long time!"

Magdalena laughed and carried her nine-year-old sister up the narrow stairs to the bedroom. Her back ached under the weight of the squirming child. The twins had grown an astonishing amount in the last year, and soon she wouldn't be able to lift Barbara anymore. Clearly they took after their father.

"Oh, no, it's time to go to bed," Magdalena said with feigned severity as she put her little sister in bed, covered her up, and blew out a smoking pine chip standing on a stool in the corner. "Look, your brother's eyes are already closed."

She pointed at Georg, Barbara's twin brother, who in fact seemed to be asleep in his narrow little bed.

"Then at least sing something for me," Barbara pleaded, trying hard not to yawn.

With a sigh, Magdalena began to sing a soft lullaby. Her little sister closed her eyes, and soon her breathing was regular and calm and she seemed to drift off to sleep.

The hangman's daughter looked down at Barbara, stroking her cheek tenderly. She loved her younger brother and sister, even if they sometimes got on her nerves. To Georg and Barbara their father was a growling bear who fought off bad men but was loving and tender with them, his own children. It almost made Magdalena a bit jealous that the hangman seemed to develop a kindlier attitude as he grew older. When she'd misbehaved as a little girl, she'd received a good spanking, but with the twins, her father usually just growled his displeasure — which didn't necessarily achieve the desired effect.

Magdalena was thinking about her father in faraway Regensburg when she heard footsteps behind her. Her mother smiled as she entered the room.

Anna-Maria Kuisl had the same long, black locks as her daughter, the same bushy eyebrows, and the same temper, as well. Jakob Kuisl had often complained he was married to two women, both of whom had a tendency to flare up. When they both were angry with him, he would often go and brood over the medical books that he kept in his pharmaceutical closet.

"Well?" Anna-Maria asked softly. "Are the children finally asleep?"

Magdalena nodded and stood up from the bed, exhausted. "A dozen stories and certainly a hundred rounds of bouncing up and down on my knees playing horsie! That should be enough."

"You spoil them too much." The hangman's wife shook her head. "Just like your father. He was like that with his little sister."

"Lisbeth?" Magdalena asked. "Did you know her well?"

Anna-Maria bit her lip, and Magdalena sensed that her mother really didn't want to talk about Magdalena's aunt, certainly not on such a beautiful summer evening. Just the same, she persisted with her question until her mother was finally persuaded to tell the story.

"After Lisbeth and Jakob's mother died, she lived here in the house with us," Anna-Maria said. "She was so young — almost a child — but then this owner of a bathhouse came along and took her back to Regensburg with him. Your father cursed and scolded, but what could he do? She didn't care a whit what her big brother thought — she was just as stubborn as he was. She just packed up her things and left. For Regensburg, of course . . ."

She stared blankly into space for a while, as if some macabre image had arisen from the past like a monster emerging from a dark abyss. She remained silent for a long while.

"Why?" Magdalena finally asked, breaking the silence.

Anna-Maria merely shrugged. "Love, perhaps? But to tell you the truth, I think she just couldn't stand it here anymore. The constant whispering, the evil glances, how people would make the sign of the cross whenever she passed by." She sighed. "You know yourself it takes a thick hide to be a hangman's daughter and stay in a place like this."

"Or maybe just stupidity," Magdalena said softly.

"What did you say?"

Magdalena shook her head. "Nothing, Mama." She sat down on a stool in the corner and looked at her mother in the moonlight that fell through the open shutters.

"You never told me how you met Papa for the first time," she said finally. "I know so little about you. Where did you grow up? Who are my grandparents? You must have had a life before Father came along."

In fact, her mother had always kept silent about her past. Father, too, never spoke about his time as a mercenary. Magdalena could vaguely remember Mother crying a lot, and in her mind's eye Magdalena could still see her father rocking her mother gently in his arms to console her. But this was a very distant memory, and in listening to her parents speak, it almost seemed as if their life hadn't begun until Magdalena was born. Everything before that was darkness.

Anna-Maria turned away and glanced out the window and across the river. Suddenly she looked very old.

"Much has happened since I was a child," she said. "Much that I don't want to be reminded of."

"But why?"

"Let's leave it at that, child. We'll save the rest for another day, perhaps when your father returns from Regensburg. I don't have a good feeling about this trip." She shook her head. "I dreamed of him just last night, and it wasn't a nice dream but a bloody one."

Anna-Maria stopped speaking and laughed. But it sounded like a tormented laugh.

"I'm already behaving like a silly old woman," she said finally. "It must have something to do with that accursed Regensburg. Believe me, a curse lies over this region, a bloody curse . . ."

"A curse?" Magdalena frowned. "What do you mean by that?"

Her mother sighed. "As a child I went to Regensburg often. I went to the market there with your grandmother, as we lived not far from the city. Whenever we passed by the city hall, Grandma said that the noblemen inside were plotting wars." She closed her eyes briefly, then continued in a soft voice. "It made no difference whether it was against the Turks or the Swedes; it was always the little people on the anvil who had to suffer the blows. Why did your father have to go to Regensburg, of all places?"

"But the war ended long ago," Magdalena interrupted with a laugh. "You're seeing ghosts!"

"The war may be over, but the scars remain."

Magdalena didn't get to ask her mother what she meant, because at that moment they heard footsteps and whispers in front of the house.

And in the next moment chaos broke out.

Simon washed the sweat from his face at a little washbasin in the consulting room, then buttoned his jacket and stepped warily out of the house.

All day the young medicus had been treating consumptive farmers, feverish children, and old women covered in boils. Since the hangman had been away, over a week now, more patients than ever had visited the Fronwieser house in the Hennengasse. Simon's father had retired upstairs to his room with a terrible hangover and needed treatment himself. Simon had his hands full. Only now, after sundown, did he find the time to visit Magdalena down in the Tanners' Quarter. He needed to speak with her, alone, to discuss Michael Berchtholdt's threats. Just the day before he'd agreed with Magdalena that she should enter an official complaint against the master baker, but in the course of the day he'd begun to wonder whether that really was such a sensible idea. Berchtholdt still held a seat in the city's Outer Council, and his voice carried weight — in stark contrast to Simon's, and especially Magdalena's as the eldest daughter of the dishonorable Schongau hangman.

In the meanwhile night had fallen. With lantern in hand, the medicus crept through the pitch-black streets of Schongau. At every corner he paused and listened for the footsteps of the night watchmen. Only when the streets were completely silent did he dare proceed, always on the lookout for curious neighbors who might happen to be watching from their windows. No one in Schongau was permitted out after nightfall, and anyone the constables caught would face a hefty fine. On account of an occasional late night of drinking and his frequent visits to Magdalena, Simon had already parted with a not insignificant amount of money. If he was caught just once more, he ran the risk of being put in the stocks or having to wear the scold's bridle. The medicus shuddered at the thought of being punished by none other than Magdalena's father — and of being the laughingstock of the entire town.

When Simon noticed light flickering down by the Lech Gate, he quickly covered his lantern with his jacket. Relieved, he then realized that the light was coming from the gatekeeper, Josef. The old constable had often let him pass through the narrow one-man door so he might visit the Kuisls. A modest bribe of brandy or watered-down theriaca was cheaper for Simon than the punishment for being caught leaving the city at night. As he drew closer, however, he noticed something odd. Josef's face was as white as chalk, and his lips were pinched tightly together.

"Where — where are you going at this late hour?" the old

man stammered, clutching his halberd tightly as if he might fall over without it.

"Oh, come now, Josef." He raised his hands in a conciliatory gesture. "You know I'm going to see Magdalena. How about a nightcap, as usual?" He pulled a little corked bottle out from under his jacket.

The constable shook his head nervously. "I don't think that's such a good idea tonight. It would be better for you to stay in town."

"Why . . ." Simon began. At that moment he heard sounds down below, a rattling and howling, all to the accompaniment of an out-of-tune fiddle. The medicus didn't bother finishing his sentence, pushed the watchman aside, and ran to the doorway.

"Fronwieser, no!" Josef shouted after him. "You're going to regret it!"

Simon wasn't listening anymore. He unhooked the rusty latch, ducked through the shoulder-high door, and ran down the street toward the raft landing. As he ran, he saw bright lights flickering in the Tanners' Quarter. The noise was coming from that direction, and the sound was getting louder, swelling to a thunderous beat that reminded him of the Swedes' drumming just before they set fire to the town long ago. One man appeared to be shouting, and a chorus of voices answered—then the drumming continued. Simon could at last identify the lights as hand-held torches and lanterns, little points of light all in a row, advancing like a glittering snake toward its goal.

The hangman's house.

Simon stumbled more than he ran—the cobblestones by the raft landing were still slick from the thunderstorm earlier that night—but finally he arrived at the Tanners' Quarter and ducked behind a cart laden with sweet-smelling hay to watch what was unfolding.

Two or three dozen young men had gathered there, journeymen from Schongau and a few farmhands from the surrounding villages. They had blackened their faces with soot, and some of them wore sacks over their heads, their eyes peering out through slits and flashing white in the light of the torches. Despite their disguises Simon recognized a number of them by their voices and their gaits. In their hands they held threshing flails, rattles, and scythes with little bells attached in places. One of the journeymen had donned a hairy devil mask and leaped about in a sort of wild, demonic dance.

In the middle of the mob stood a man with a blackened face, a black coat, and a hat adorned with two white rooster feathers. It took the medicus a moment to realize that this was in fact Michael Berchtholdt. With his long, flowing robe and painted face, the lean master baker appeared bigger and more menacing. The others fell silent as Berchtholdt began to speak in a steady, strident singsong.

"The hangman girl, this Kuisl whore, she practices on you, and more. The belly swells, all plump and round, but her physician makes her sound. 'Tis true, my friends?"

The chorus of masked faces roared its reply in one voice: "'Tis true!"

"Then now you know just what to do!"

The rattling and stomping resumed once more, swelling now to an infernal racket. Meanwhile, in the nearby houses shutters had opened, but the faces that peered out seemed more amused than frightened by the clamorous, bloodthirsty mob below. How often, after all, did they get to see such a spectacle in sleepy little Schongau?

Simon crouched even lower behind the cart, trying desperately to figure out what to do. He'd heard of Vehmic tribunals and their secret vigilante proceedings, though never in Schongau. Their victims were often loose women or other members of society who had in some way offended the moral order: village drunks, lecherous priests, greedy estate farmers, or millers who

had defrauded their customers. The medicus had heard that the
accused were sometimes whipped and chased through the fields,
but in most cases they suffered only the humiliation of public
ridicule delivered in lines of satirical verse. Just last year in Kin-
sau, a few towns away, the young men of the village had smeared
human waste all over the walls of the building belonging to the
bathhouse owner and hoisted a manure cart up onto his roof.
The victim had watched the spectacle in silence, knowing there
wasn't much he could do against the majority of villagers.

This last thought worried Simon. He couldn't imagine Magdalena would ever tolerate such abuse without fighting back.
Would she physically assault her accusers? Claw at their sooty
faces with her nails? How would the men react? The physician
looked uncertainly at the shuttered windows of the hangman's
house, just as Michael Berchtholdt started to declaim another satirical verse.

"She gives the maids her witches' brew and turns them into
demons, too. And takes them off to live in hell. 'Tis true, my
friends? Do tell, do tell!"

"'Tis true!"

"Then now you know just what to do!"

Simon's anger was rising, and his ears started to hum. Michael Berchtholdt was trying to turn the tables on her, to make it
look as if Magdalena was responsible for what happened to
Resl—and the others actually seemed to believe him! Simon
knew he didn't stand a chance, but someone had to try to stop
this.

Prepared for a fight, he pulled out his knife and was about to
jump out from behind the cart when the shutters on the second
floor of the hangman's house flew open with a bang. There stood
Magdalena in a white linen nightdress, her hair disheveled, her
teeth clenched, her eyes ablaze. Simon shuddered. For a moment
he believed the vision standing before him was not his beloved
Magdalena but an avenging angel straight out of the Old Testa-

ment. The boisterous men below were also apparently so astonished by her appearance that absolute silence prevailed for a moment.

"Lies!" she shouted out into the night. "Filthy, cowardly lies! You all know what happened! Each and every one of you! And still you stand there like asses playing along with Berchtholdt and his ridiculous masquerade!"

She pointed at the master baker, who raised his right hand in a sign meant to ward off the devil. "*You,* Berchtholdt, got your maid pregnant and administered the poison yourself, not I! I'm going to Secretary Lechner, and I'll tell him everything. When my father, the hangman, is through with you, you'll want to hide your face behind that mask. He'll cut your nose off and throw it to the dogs!"

"Hold your tongue, hangman's girl!" Michael Berchtholdt's voice trembled with hatred and anger. "It's about time someone muzzled that impertinent mouth of yours. You've been whoring around this town far too long. And as for your father . . ." He looked around, waiting for signs of approval. "Court Clerk Lechner will see to it that Kuisl is forced to chase his own daughter through the streets with a whip. Lewd woman! Isn't it so, my friends?"

"'Tis true!" The voices were not as loud as the last time, but the young fellows seemed to have regained their confidence.

Simon, still standing behind the cart, noticed Anna-Maria now, standing a ways back from the window alongside the frightened twins, who had apparently been awakened by the noise. The mother turned to her daughter, trying to coax her away from the window, but Magdalena remained adamant.

"Lewd woman?" she shouted over the din of the mob and pointed at their leader. "Who is lewd here, Berchtholdt? Didn't my father brew you a potion just last year to keep your rod nice and stiff? You dirty, lying sack of shit! And haven't you all come

by at least once seeking ivy and stoneseed for your barnyard liai-
sons with your sweethearts? I could sing a verse about every last
one of you. Listen up, Berchtholdt . . ." She paused for a moment
to concentrate before hurling her curse at the mob's leader.

"The wife of Berchtholdt has gone dry. The baker's got a
wandering eye . . . He mounts his maid, the lewd old steed, and
poisons her to hide the deed!"

"Lies, lies! I'll put a gag in your damned mouth, Kuisl girl!"
Michael Berchtholdt ran to the door of the hangman's house and,
finding it locked, kicked at it like a madman. When the heavy
oak boards wouldn't budge, he swung his lantern in a wide arc
up onto the roof.

"Burn down the hangman's house!" he screamed. "Go to it,
friends! We won't take that kind of talk from a whore!"

Hesitantly at first, but then faster and faster, the young men
rushed forward to toss their torches against the walls and onto
the roof. Soon some of the shingles caught fire, and a thin column of smoke began to rise up into the sky like a slight, black
finger. The roof smoked and the shingles crackled as the first
flames licked at the timbers, rising ever higher until finally en-
gulfing the entire roof.

"Get out of here, fast!" Anna-Maria shouted, pulling the
tearful children away from the window, "before we're burned
alive!"

She ran down the stairway with the children and out the
door, where a hail of stones, rotten vegetables, and stinking dung
awaited them. Magdalena followed close behind. Defiantly, she
stood in the doorway a moment and allowed herself to be pummeled with filth and malice.

A stone struck her forehead, and she staggered backward as
a thin trickle of blood ran down her right temple, dripping onto
her bodice. For a moment it seemed she was preparing to fight
off the entire mob of farm boys and journeymen by herself. She

clutched the door frame with both hands, cursing softly. But reason soon prevailed, and she ran off after her mother and the
twins, who had sought refuge behind a woodpile.

The flames rose toward the ridge of the roof, and at first
Simon just stood there in his hiding place behind the cart, immo-
bilized with terror, but as the fire started to consume the house,
he couldn't stand by any longer. Without a further thought, he
ran out from behind the cart directly into the mob.

"You dogs!" he roared. "Setting fire to a house with a mother
and her children inside! Is that all you know how to do?" The
young men turned around, astonished. When they saw Simon,
hatred flared in their eyes. At once three rushed the medicus,
who tried to hold them off with his knife. The razor-sharp blade
whistled through the air in a semicircle as the men stepped back.

"Not one step closer," Simon snarled. "This stiletto's done
the work of an army surgeon; it's amputated fingers and arms. A
few more won't make any difference!"

He heard the sound of feet running behind him, but before
he could turn around, a heavy, powerful body struck him and
pinned him to the ground. At once all the other men were on top
of him. One of the Berchtholdt boys drew back his arm and laid
into Simon's face with his fist, over and over, as if he were nothing more than a bag of flour. The medicus could taste his own
blood, and after the fourth blow the world went black. The
shouts and noise of the brawl sounded strangely distant, and
acrid black smoke wafted across his face.

*They're beating me to death. Like a rabid dog, they're beating me
to death! If this is the end . . .*

As if in a dream, he heard a sudden clap of thunder, then felt
something cold drip onto his upturned face. It took him a few
moments to realize they were raindrops—thick, heavy drops
falling harder and harder. Then a proper downpour was pelting
him and his enemies, turning the ground beneath them into a
muddy morass.

"Stop! In the name of His Majesty the Prince, I order you to stop at once!"

The voice boomed so loud that even in the torrential rain the command was clear. Turning his battered head from where he lay on the ground, Simon could make out in a haze a figure astride a horse. The medicus blinked several times before realizing through a veil of blood that it was the secretary, Johann Lechner. The rain streamed down his black coat, his hair clung to his forehead, and yet despite the storm the Elector's representative looked like an enraged and awesome deity. As the supreme authority in Schongau, he commanded a dozen city watchmen, who stood beside him now, their loaded muskets pointed at the mob. Their expressions made plain their displeasure at being awakened in the middle of the night only to stand here in the rain. And the secretary, too, was clearly annoyed he'd been called from his ducal residence, where he represented the electoral prince in matters of government.

"I shall give you exactly one minute to clear out of here," Lechner said in a soft voice. "After that I will give the order to shoot. Is that clear?"

Simon could hear whispering and the patter of running feet as cloaked figures fled into the darkness. In a matter of moments the area in front of the hangman's house was empty, except for a handful of cast-off flour sacks and extinguished torches that bore witness to the nightmare — these and a devil's mask that leered up at Simon maliciously from a puddle of mud and horse piss. A few flames still spluttered on the roof, but otherwise the heavy downpour had quenched the fire.

"For God's sake, see to it at once that the fire doesn't flare up again!" the secretary shouted to the city guards. "Accursed vigilantes! A plague on all those farmers!"

The guards filled buckets with water at a nearby well and ran up into the attic to put out what remained of the fire. Some of the men helped Anna-Maria to let the cows out of the barn, where they'd been lowing anxiously and beating their hooves against the boards of their stalls. Meanwhile, Magdalena contemplated the smoking roof from a safe distance. Speaking softly, she tried to soothe the children, who were weeping and burying their heads in her lap. The face of the hangman's daughter was vacant.

"They'll pay for this!" Magdalena seethed at last, rubbing the blood from her forehead. "Father will string them up for this, I swear!"

By now Simon had struggled to his feet and hobbled over to Magdalena. Bending down over the twins, he gave them a quick once-over, especially little Georg, who was having a coughing fit, apparently suffering from a mild case of smoke inhalation.

A few last drops fell from the sky before the rain ceased altogether. The thunder sounded far off now, like the drums of a slowly retreating army.

"Fronwieser, Fronwieser . . ." With a mixture of amusement and sympathy, Johann Lechner looked down on Simon from atop his horse. "You bring me nothing but grief. And now I'm awakened in the middle of the night to save your miserable life." He pointed to the smoking roof. "If it hadn't been for the rain, all of Schongau could have gone up in flames. And all because of a stubborn woman."

"Your Excellency—" the medicus began, but Lechner waved him off.

"I know what happened, and I know who's behind it, too." He leaned down in the saddle and regarded Simon as he might a disobedient child. "But believe me, something like this was bound to happen sooner or later. Haven't I told you several times you ought to put an end to your little affair with Kuisl's daughter? If you don't, people will never quit hounding you." Lechner sighed. "This time I came to your aid, Fronwieser, because the city's welfare was also at stake. But next time you're on your own. May God have mercy on you then."

Simon was too weak to reply. Blood had congealed in his mouth, his left eye was already swollen shut, and the right half of his face would probably be shining all shades of the rainbow in the next half-hour. His whole body felt as if it had passed through a grain mill. Shock and fear for Magdalena's safety had made him forget his pain at first, but now it rolled over him like a surging storm. He searched in vain for a suitable response.

"Is that all?" It was the voice of Magdalena, who had planted herself in front of the secretary's horse in the meantime. Her face was crimson with anger. "This rabble almost burns our house down, they beat Simon half to death, Berchtholdt poisons his maid, and *you* are scolding *us*?"

Lechner shrugged. "What should I do, lock them all up? Harvest is approaching, and I can't let the crops wither in the fields with no one to work them. Perhaps I should put Berchtholdt in the stocks . . . perhaps, yes." He shook his head, thinking. "But to do that I'll first have to present some evidence. He was disguised just like the others, and none of those farmers will snitch on the master baker. After all, he's the man who buys their grain year after year. Believe me, that would be an endless trial that wouldn't help anyone at all. Besides, the people are right." He turned his horse around and started back toward town, throwing one last glance behind him and shaking his head almost regretfully. "A medicus and a hangman's daughter . . . That won't do. We have to have rules, after all. Believe me, Magdalena, your father would see things in exactly the same light."

The secretary disappeared into the night with his guards, leaving the small, sodden group alone in the dark. A breeze blew across the courtyard and carried the last of the smoke away. Now that the fire was out, it felt as quiet as a cemetery. Anna-Maria rocked the children silently in her lap.

"Looks as if we'll have to spend the night in the barn," she said. "We can start cleaning up tomorrow. The whole attic is black with soot."

Magdalena stared at her in disbelief. "Pardon me? They set your house on fire and all you think of is cleaning up?"

Her mother sighed. "What else is there to do? You heard what Lechner said. None of those men will be held accountable." Angrily she tapped her daughter on the chest. "And don't think for another moment that you can keep playing the hero. That's over and done with! This time we were lucky, but the next time it could be the children burned to death in their beds. Is that what you want?" She looked intently at her daughter, who pursed her lips. "I'll ask you again: Is that what you want?"

"Your mother is right," Simon said. "If we go after Berchtholdt, then next time they just may burn your house to the ground. The man is an alderman, after all, and has the people on his side."

Looking up into the overcast night sky, Magdalena took a deep breath of the fresh air the rain had brought. For a while no one spoke a word. "You don't really think they'll leave us be, do you?" she whispered at last. "For them I'm fair game, now more than ever."

Her mother looked at her crossly. "Because you take it too far! Lechner is right. A hangman's girl and a medicus—it isn't proper. You've got to quit carrying on, or else it'll come to an even worse end. You can't marry; that's against the law. And after what happened tonight, you know they won't leave you in peace until you start keeping your hands off each other." Anna-Maria stood up, brushing the soot from her dress. "For far too long your father has just stood by and watched, Magdalena. But this is the end. As soon as he returns, we'll send a letter to the executioner in Marktoberndorf. I heard his wife died in childbirth, and he would be a good match for you, with a big house and—"

Magdalena leaped up in a rage. "So you want to hide me away, so I don't give you any more trouble. Is that right?"

"Suppose it is?" her mother answered. "It's only to protect

you and everyone else. You're obviously incapable of doing that yourself."

Without another word, Anna-Maria took the twins by the hand and went to the barn, where she made up straw beds for them. For a moment it appeared that Magdalena was about to call after her, but then Simon put his arm around her shoulder from behind. Her whole body started to tremble as she began to cry silently.

"She surely doesn't mean it that way," Simon whispered. "Let's go to sleep now. Tomorrow when the sun comes up—"

Suddenly Magdalena wrapped her arms around Simon as if she would never let him go. She clung so fiercely to him that he could feel the firmness of her body through their wet garments, and she kissed him long and passionately on his bloodied lips.

"This very night," she whispered finally.

Simon looked at her quizzically. "What do you mean?"

Magdalena put her finger to his lips. "Mother is right. As long as we're here, they'll hound us. Too much has happened already, and the next time it might not just be us who get hurt; something could happen to the children. We can't allow that." She looked deep into Simon's eyes. "Let's get away from here, this very night. I mean it."

Before Simon could reply, she went on hastily: "Berchtholdt will never leave us in peace. If the matter with Resl gets out, he'll be thrown off the council. He won't risk that, so he'll do anything in his power to see that I keep my mouth shut. One way or another."

"You mean, we should leave Schongau . . . for good?" Simon held her tightly. "Do you know what that means? We'll have nothing, nobody will know us, we'll—"

Magdalena stopped him with another kiss. "Stop your blathering," she whispered. "Don't think I don't know myself that it will be hard. But it's obvious we can't stay here any longer. You

heard what Lechner said. A medicus and a hangman's daughter
. . . 'that will never do' . . ."

"And where shall we go?"

Magdalena hesitated only briefly before answering. "Regensburg. Anything is possible there."

A roll of thunder signaled another rain shower passing over
the town. Simon pulled Magdalena close and kissed her until,
locked in a tight embrace, they sank to the ground in a puddle of
blood, mud, and horse piss.

A small bundle of humanity in the midst of the thundering
downpour.

4

THE HANGMAN KICKED THE IRON-PLATED DOOR
so hard that the cell walls shook. Like a caged animal, he'd been
pacing for hours, stooped over in the tiny chamber. His thoughts
circled with him as he paced.

They'd been holding him in this dungeon for five days now.
The room was made entirely of wood, an almost perfect cube
built so low that Kuisl couldn't stand upright inside it. Aside
from a tiny hatch that opened once a day so that a foul-smelling
soup and some bread could be passed to the prisoner, the room
had no windows, and the darkness was so complete that even
after hours in it, all he could make out were vague outlines. Fastened around Kuisl's right ankle, a chain clanked as he trudged
from one corner of the cell to the other.

The only piece of furniture was a hollowed-out wooden
block that served as a toilet. A while ago, in a fit of rage, he'd
picked it up and heaved it against the wall, a deed he now regretted, as the stinking contents had splashed all over the cell and
had even managed to soil Kuisl's cape. Never in his entire life
had the Schongau hangman felt so powerless. He was convinced
by now that someone had set a trap for him, a trap he'd stumbled

into like a clumsy oaf. Whoever had so gruesomely murdered his sister and her husband was now attempting to frame him.

It made no difference that he declared his innocence when the guards entered the bathhouse, that he swore on his soul he'd only just discovered the two bodies moments before. The verdict had been decided at the outset, a fact that became amply clear when he saw the captain's smirk. Now everything came into focus—his hasty arrest at the gate, his feeling of being watched, the unlocked door to the bathhouse. They had laid the bait and he'd taken it.

But why?

Ever since the Regensburg city guards had locked him in this cell, he'd been racking his brain to understand just who might be behind this conspiracy. He didn't know a soul in the city, and presumably people here didn't even know that Lisbeth Hofmann came from a hangman's family in Schongau. Or could this be some kind of payback for his impudence toward the constables at Jakob's Gate? Was it merely an accident that he crossed paths with the malevolent, scar-faced raftsman?

He was roused from his thoughts by loud footsteps echoing down the corridor outside his cell door. In the little window next to the door appeared the face of the captain with the shiny cuirass. "Well, country boy," he said, twirling his mustache and smiling. "Have we softened you up a bit? A few days in this cell always does that to a person. And if not, the hangman has his own special ways of loosening your tongue . . . so to speak."

When Kuisl didn't answer, the captain continued. "In the meantime we've questioned the witnesses and inspected your pack." He shook his head with feigned severity. "I don't know much about herbs, but what you have in there is a bit more than a man might need for a cough, don't you think? Opium, nightshade, hellebore . . . What were you planning to do with all that? Poison the whole city?"

Kuisl had been crouching in a corner so that the captain couldn't see his face in the dark. "Those are medicinal herbs," he said. "My sister was sick, as I've told you a hundred times. Her husband wrote me a letter, and I came here from Schongau to help her."

The soldier furrowed his brow. "You don't actually look like a physician, not even like a bathhouse owner. So, what are you?"

"I'm the Schongau hangman."

There was a short pause; then the captain spluttered. He laughed so hard, in fact, that it sounded as if he might choke. "The Schongau hangman?" he gasped. "Ha, that's a good one! Really good. We've never hanged a hangman here!" It took him a while to calm himself down again.

"Be that as it may . . ." he said, wiping a few tears from his eyes. In a flash his voice was cold and biting again. "You must know what's in store for you, hangman, if you don't confess soon. Believe me, the Regensburg hangman is a tough one and has brought many others much tougher than you to their knees."

Kuisl folded his arms and leaned back. "Even if you break every last bone in my body, I'll still be innocent."

"Well, then, what do we have here?" The captain held a sheet of parchment up to the little hatch. "We found this letter upstairs in the bathhouse attic. Hofmann's last will and testament. He had no children or surviving relatives, and upon his death a certain Jakob Kuisl from Schongau was to inherit everything. Your name is Kuisl, isn't it?"

Blinking after being in the dark so long, the hangman stepped into the dim light to get a better look at the sheet. The parchment was embossed with a red seal, the bathhouse coat of arms. The handwriting was erratic, as if it had been written in a great hurry.

"You can't possibly believe this rubbish, can you?" Kuisl said. "I've never even met this Hofmann fellow, and the last time I saw my sister was years ago. So why should I inherit anything? This scribbling is something you put together yourself. Give it to me!"

He thrust his hand through the hatch, but the captain pulled the parchment away just in time.

"You would like that, wouldn't you?" he snarled. "To destroy the evidence! Now let *me* tell you a story. You knew your brother-in-law ran a successful bathhouse, and you knew about the will. You were having money problems, so you came to Regensburg. Maybe you pressed your sister for money, but she wouldn't give you any, so you helped yourself. As a hangman you know only too well how to stick a pig."

"Rubbish," the hangman whispered. "Lisl is my sister. I would never so much as touch a hair—"

But the captain wouldn't be interrupted. "You killed her, then began plotting your getaway," he continued, "perhaps back to Schongau. There you could have safely waited until the postal coach arrived bearing the news of your sister's tragic death. A savage robbery-murder—how very tragic indeed—but no one would have suspected you. Who would ever have known you'd just been to Regensburg? But you hadn't reckoned you'd be controlled as you came through the city gate, and I saw right away that there was something fishy about you, country boy—"

"Dirty lies!" The hangman pounded his fists against the reinforced wooden door. "You're nothing but dirty gallows birds, all of you! Tell me, how much did they pay you for locking me in the tower overnight? Who ordered you to take me prisoner in the bathhouse? Who? Say something!"

The alarmed captain's face disappeared from the window for a moment. When he reappeared, he was smiling again.

"I really don't know what you're talking about," he finally said. "Whatever the case, the investigation has concluded now, and the paperwork is complete. The city council will probably meet tomorrow morning to determine your fate. In Regensburg we make short shrift of scoundrels like you." The watchman's eyes wandered over the excrement-splattered cell walls. "I hope your stay in our lovely city dungeon has given you time to reflect. The hangman is already polishing his pincers. But why am I telling you this? You know all about these things, after all. Have a nice day in Regensburg."

He winked at Kuisl, then walked away with a merry whistle.

Despairing, the Schongau hangman leaned back against the wall, then fell into a dejected heap in the corner. Things were not looking good for him. From experience he knew it was only a matter of days before torture would begin. According to age-old law, a suspect could be sentenced only once he'd made his confession, so the Regensburg hangman would use every means at his disposal to compel a confession from Kuisl. First, he would show him the instruments of torture. If this didn't induce a confession, he would apply the thumb screws and remove Kuisl's fingernails one by one. Finally, he would tie hundred-pound stones to his feet and hoist him up, arms bound behind his back, until his bones sprang from their sockets and cracked. The Schongau hangman knew the routine well; he'd performed it a dozen times himself. But he also knew that if the suspect wouldn't confess in spite of all this, they'd let him go.

At least what was left of him.

Kuisl lay down on the dirty wooden floor, closed his eyes, and prepared himself for his long journey through the world of pain. He was sure that if he confessed, he would be broken on the wheel, at the very least. Probably they would hang him first, slit his belly open, and pull the guts from his body.

His gaze wandered over the dark cell walls, where innumerable prisoners had carved not only their names but their pleas, prayers, and curses into the wood. The captain had failed to fully close the little hatch in the door, so a small sliver of light fell across the words. Every inscription told a story, a fate, or gave testimony to a life that had no doubt ended much too soon and too painfully. His gaze stopped at a message just one line in length, a message carved deeply, apparently with a knife.

There is a reaper, Death's his name . . .

Kuisl frowned. It was strange to see the words here, of all places. It was just the first line of a silly old mercenary's song, but to the hangman the line said volumes. A muffled roar sounded in his ears. Long ago the words had been banished to the furthest reaches of his mind — almost forgotten entirely — but now, as he read the inscription, it all came rushing back.

There is a reaper, Death's his name . . .

Images, sounds, even scents overwhelmed him — the smell of gun smoke, booze, and decay, a droning chorus of men's voices, the rhythmic marching of feet.

There is a reaper, Death's his name
From God above his power came.

The memory struck him like the blow of a hammer.

. . . The foot soldiers' ballad resounds through the city, though individual words are impossible to discern — a low thrum, like the sound of a thousand insects. The nearer Jakob comes to the market square, the louder it grows. He can feel his heart pounding as he sets eyes on the crowd before him — day laborers, tailors, cobblers, greedy adventurers, and penniless wretches. They're standing in a long line that snakes around the entire square, ending at a large, battered wooden table. Behind the table sits an officer with a big book, noting the names of new recruits. Drummers and fifers stand in tight formation behind the table, while brandy flows freely and anyone who is still able to sing is singing.

There is a reaper, Death's his name
FROM GOD ABOVE HIS POWER CAME.
HIS BLADE KEEN AND STEADY
To mow us is ready . . .

Slowly, very slowly, the book swallows the line until finally Jakob stands before the officer, who considers him with a smirk, chewing a wad of tobacco and spitting brown liquid onto the pavement.

"What's your name, boy?"

"Jakob Kuisl."

"And how old are you?"

"I'll be fifteen this summer."

The officer rubs his nose. "You look older. And damned strong, too. Ever been to war?"

Jakob shakes his head, silent.

"War's a bloody affair. A lot of honor, a lot of death. A lot like a slaughterhouse. Can you stand the sight of death, hmm? Bodies hacked to pieces, severed heads . . . Well?"

Jakob remains silent.

"Very well," the officer says with a sigh. "We could use a boy to carry supplies, or perhaps you could play the drums. Or——"

"I'm here to join the infantry, sir."

"I beg your pardon?"

"I want to fight——with a longsword."

The officer hesitates, then breaks into a broad grin. His grin turns into a soft chuckle, then to an outright laugh, louder and louder until he turns around at last to his comrades. "Did you hear that?" he cries. "The young sprout wants a two-hander. Hasn't even run a pike up a farmer's ass in his life, and he wants a two-hander!"

The crowd roars. Some of the fifers stop playing to point at the big, pimply, clumsy boy whose shirt and trousers are much too small for his shapeless frame. Jakob is growing too fast; his mother says he'll soon be able to spit on the heads of everyone in Schongau. But Schongau is far away.

Now the young man picks up a dirty bundle of linen covering a long and narrow object, which he handles as if it contains the kaiser's own scepter. He lays it out on the table carefully and removes the wrapping.

Inside is a sword so long it reaches to the boy's chest. With a short cross-guard and no point, its blade glints in the sun.

The crowd's jeers die down to a murmur as all eyes turn to the weapon. The officer bends down over the longsword and runs a finger along the blood groove.

"By God, a genuine executioner's sword," he whispers. "Where did you get this? Did you steal it?"

The boy shakes his head. "It belonged to my father, and to my grandfather and great-grandfather before him."

Jakob carefully wraps the weapon back up in the dirty, blood-stained linen. His words sound reverent and unusual from the mouth of a snot-nosed fifteen-year-old village boy who wants to enlist.

"My father is dead. Now the sword belongs to me."

Then the hangman's son walks down the silent ranks of infantry-men until he reaches the yoke, a horizontal pike supported by two halberds set in the ground.

An old ritual of mercenary foot soldiers: whoever passes through commits himself to war.

Jakob Kuisl was still lying on the floor of his cell at the Regens-burg city hall, staring at the inscription on the wall.

There is a reaper, Death's his name . . .

He got up at last, reached for a pebble on the floor, and began to scratch away the inscription.

Letter by letter.

At that moment Magdalena was farther from home than she'd ever been in her life.

Blissful, she stretched out on the hard planks of the river raft and looked up at clouds passing over her like white dragons. For the first time in a long while she was happy. The waves slapped rhythmically against the heavy boards, the raftsmen's shouts sounded far-off, and only Simon, humming softly beside her, seemed real. The medicus was leaning on a wine barrel, staring dreamily across the water at the passing riverbank. His face was still black and blue from the Berchtholdts' beating, but at least he could open his eyes again. From time to time he spat cherry pits in a wide arc into the water. When one struck the helmsman by mistake, he turned around and shook his finger playfully at Simon.

"If you keep that up, I'm going to have to dump you both into the Danube. Then you can swim all the way to Regensburg for all I care." He shook his head. "The river is no place for children and lovers—this is a place for work." He was grinning again, likely thinking back on how he'd met his own wife.

Magdalena picked up a cherry and let the soft, juicy flesh dissolve in her mouth. Schongau was so far away! Less than a week ago they'd fled to the ferry landing in the middle of the night, carrying no more than a sack and a bag. Heaviest were Simon's medical instruments and a few books he couldn't bear to part with. Other than that, they brought only a few changes of clothes, a little food, and two blankets. Everything else they left behind: their past, the satirical verses, the paternalism, their secret rendezvous, and the constant fear they might be discovered.

They'd traveled down the Lech past Augsburg in the direction of Donauwörth, then along the Danube on a raft transporting cloth and salt to the Black Sea. Along the way they'd passed the university city of Ingolstadt, where Simon had once studied; the little city of Vohburg; and finally the infamous Weltenburg Narrows, where the raft was whisked through whirlpools like a mere leaf blowing along the surface of the water. The steady movement and changing landscape gave Magdalena a feeling of greater freedom than she'd ever known before.

Away from home at last . . .

But a shadow passed over her face when she thought of her mother and the twins. She'd kissed the sleeping children farewell before closing the door to the house behind her for the last time. The letter she left for her mother was brief and tearstained, but never in her life had Magdalena felt so clearly that she was doing the right thing. Had she stayed, there surely would have been no end to the hectoring—the townspeople's prejudices were just too deep—and eventually one or another zealot would actually set fire to the house. Master Baker Berchtholdt would see to it that she never had a moment's peace.

Magdalena could only hope that her mother saw things the same way.

Ultimately, it wasn't a question of whether they would leave, but of where their journey might take them. In the end it was Magdalena's aunt who helped them make up their minds. Magdalena admired Aunt Lisbeth Kuisl for her courage in leaving everything behind. Magdalena could be just as strong herself! If her aunt was still alive, she would certainly understand. Magdalena would simply wait until her hardheaded father had left; then she'd knock on Lisbeth's door, her aunt would open the door and embrace her, and Simon would be given a position as Andreas Hofmann's assistant at the bathhouse. He could bleed the guests and treat their minor ailments. That would be a start, and who knows? With time Simon might even go on to become the Regensburg city surgeon. A new life would open up for them, a life in which no one would know she was a hangman's daughter.

But suppose her aunt had died in the meantime, of some kind of growth that even Magdalena's father couldn't cure?

She shook her head, trying to drive away these sinister thoughts. She wanted to enjoy the moment. Only the dear Lord knew what the future held.

"We're here! Magdalena, we're here!"

Simon's cries roused her from her musings. She sat up to see Regensburg emerge behind the next bend in the river—a silhouette of buildings, bridges, and churches gleaming in the afternoon sun. An imposing defensive city wall began at river's edge and extended, with its redoubts and outbuildings, far inland to the south. Beyond the wall towered the cathedral, the city's landmark. Bells chimed across the water as if in greeting.

With loud cries the raftsmen prepared for landing, tossing ropes and issuing commands. To the right, beneath the city wall, was a harbor vaster than anything Magdalena could imagine, almost half a mile of jetties and piers where boats and rafts were moored, bobbing up and down. Men hurried about, lugging barrels and cases, disappearing into the storage sheds that lined the city wall. Downriver an imposing stone bridge spanned the Danube, connecting the Free Imperial City with the Electorate of Bavaria. On the Bavarian side Magdalena could make out charred ruins from the Great War; even the suburbs to the south of Regensburg had apparently burned.

With a heavy thud, the raft docked at one of the many wooden piers. Simon and Magdalena shouldered their bags, waved farewell to the raftsmen, and took their places in a long line of laborers and travelers winding their way toward the city gate at the end of the Stone Bridge. The air was laden with scents—spices, brackish river water, fish, and fat sizzling over an open fire. Magdalena was hungry. The two had eaten nothing but cherries since that morning. She pulled Simon over to a little food cart set up with tables and benches behind the bridge. For a few kreuzers they bought some smoky sausages dripping with fat and a small loaf of bread. Sitting on a pier, they let their legs dangle over the side.

"And now?" Simon asked, wiping the fat from his lips. "What's your plan?"

"What's *our* plan, you mean," Magdalena corrected him with a laugh. "You forget we're in this together." She shrugged and took another bite of her greasy sausage. "I suggest we set out for my aunt's house right away and see if my father is still there," she said with a full mouth. "After that, we'll just have to see what happens. Come on, let's go!" She wiped her hands on her skirt and reached for her sack.

But it was gone.

A few steps away Magdalena noticed a gaunt figure about to disappear in the crowd with her sack under his arm. She jumped up and took after him.

"You blasted thief!"

Simon joined the chase, and together they ran through the crowd, bumping into travelers disembarking from their rafts, arms loaded with crates and sacks. Magdalena heard shouts and splashing behind her but had no time to turn around. The thief was already almost out of sight. Her dress fluttered behind her like a flag in the wind as she desperately tried to catch up with him. That bag contained everything connecting her to her home in Schongau, including a little faded portrait a peddler had once made of her mother. She mustn't lose it!

The thief was running along the edge of the landing now where, away from the crowds, he could run faster. Simon had chosen the same path and was right on the man's heels, followed close behind by an angry, cursing Magdalena. As they approached a line of storage sheds, the thief made a sharp turn toward a stack of logs and crates. On the other side a narrow lane crowded with carts, carriages, and people led into the city. If the thief got that far, they would certainly lose him!

At just that moment Simon stumbled over a rope on the ground and fell to his knees as Magdalena rushed past him.

"Stop, thief!" she shouted. "Stop him!" But the few raftsmen and dock workers standing among the stacks only glanced at her indifferently.

The haggard thief swung the sack over his head triumphantly as he clattered onto a pile of logs. Just as he reached the top, a figure appeared from the right. He had jet-black hair tied into a ponytail, and the muscles on his tanned upper arms rippled like little balls under his skin. He grabbed the bottom-most log with both hands and pulled it out from under the stack with one powerful tug. The logs on top came loose and started to roll, crashing down in all directions.

The thief teetered briefly like an acrobat on a rope, then fell with a cry and lay pinned between the logs, moaning.

The black-haired man reappeared from behind the piles where he'd taken refuge from the avalanche. Magdalena at first guessed he was in his early thirties, but as he drew closer, she could see he was considerably older. Folds had formed around the corners of his mouth and piercing blue eyes, lending him a mature and stately appearance. He wore a simple leather waistcoat over his bare upper body; his only adornment was a red cloth knotted around his neck. In his enormous hands Magdalena's sack dangled like a little toy.

"I believe you've lost something," he said, tossing the bag to Magdalena. "And as far as this fellow is concerned . . ." Grabbing the nearly unconscious thief, he dragged him to the edge of the landing. "A cold bath sometimes works wonders." With a wide swing, he threw the howling man into the Danube. When the man resurfaced, he floundered until the current carried him away at last.

"Don't worry," the man said. "He can swim. This isn't the first time I've had to cool off this hothead. He's just a little miscreant with whom even the hangman doesn't want to dirty his hands. But I won't tolerate thieves on my wharf. It's bad for business."

With a smile he approached Magdalena and held out his hand. A few tattoos adorned his muscular upper arm, among them some kind of sea monster emerging from a wave.

"My name is Karl Gessner," the man said with a broad grin that revealed nearly perfect white teeth. "I'm the city raftmaster. Sorry that your stay in Regensburg has gotten off to such a bad start, but at least you have your bag back." He pointed to Simon, who had finally gotten up and came hobbling over. "I hope your friend didn't get those bruises on his face around here. You're probably new in town and looking for work. Is that right?"

"It's possible," Simon said abruptly.

The raftmaster grinned. "I can sense that from three miles away, against the wind. If you wish, you can earn a few kreuzers from me today. Here on the docks there's always something to do. Lugging crates, caulking boats, tying logs together for the rafts . . ." Gessner whistled through his fingers, and several laborers came running over at once to help him restack the fallen logs.

"Thanks, but—" Magdalena began, but Simon interrupted.

"Believe me, that wouldn't be a profitable deal for you," the medicus replied, wiping the dirt from his trousers. "My hands are more suited to holding a pencil or a pair of tweezers than heavy barrels. But if one of your workers happens to have an infection in his leg or stomach pains, we'd be happy to show our appreciation for your kindness."

Gessner clicked his tongue. "A traveling barber, then! Well, I'd advise you to watch that the guards don't catch up with you. They don't much care for quack doctors."

"Simon is no quack doctor," Magdalena said firmly. "He studied in Ingolstadt."

"All right, fine, I didn't mean to offend your friend," the raftmaster said, trying to calm things down. "A physician with medical training is always welcome here. Perhaps I even have something for you . . ." He shook his head from side to side, thinking. "There's a tavern not far from here. It's called the Whale, and it's just the right place to go if you're new in the city. That's where everyone in Regensburg goes who's looking for work. I've even seen traveling bathhouse journeymen there. Just say that Raftmaster Gessner sent you and you have my recommendation." He winked. "I can trust you, can't I?"

Simon raised his hand solemnly to give his word. "I swear we're not quacks—you have our word on that." He smiled and bowed slightly. "Our deepest thanks. It's always a blessing when a person has someone he can trust in a strange city."

"Maybe we'll meet again sometime at this—uh—Whale," said Magdalena, tossing her sack over her shoulder after checking to see that nothing was missing. "But first we're going to visit my aunt. She's the wife of the bathhouse owner Andreas Hofmann. You don't happen to know her? I hear she's seriously ill."

The blood drained instantly from Gessner's face, and his whole body seemed to turn to stone. For a moment he was speechless.

"You—you—are . . . ?" he stammered.

Magdalena looked at him anxiously. "Is there something wrong?"

It took a moment for the raftmaster to get a hold of himself again. When he pulled himself together at last, he laid his hand on Magdalena's shoulder. "You've chosen an unfortunate time to come to Regensburg." The words came out slowly and ominously. "It's said that your aunt . . ." He faltered.

"What's wrong with my aunt?" said Magdalena, pulling away from the raftmaster. "Out with it!"

Gessner shook his head sadly. "I don't know all the details—perhaps it's best you have a look for yourself. Josef!" he waved one of the laborers over. "Take these people to the Weißgerbergraben. Right now!"

The man nodded and turned to leave. Again Magdalena tried to get the raftmaster to talk, but he turned aside, busily hammering heavy nails into a barrel.

"Come on," said Simon, nudging her gently. "We're not going to learn anything more here."

Magdalena turned away, her mouth set, and followed Simon and the workman as they disappeared down a narrow lane. As they left the dock area, though, they heard the raftmaster's voice behind them.

"God be with you!" Gessner called after them. "And remember the Whale! Perhaps you'll find someone there who can help you."

A few blocks away the harsh reality awaited them.

As the two breathlessly approached the bathhouse, they could see right away that something wasn't right. The entrance was blocked with a heavy chain and guarded by a grim-faced watchman, halberd in hand. Curious onlookers were milling about in the street, whispering to one another, while their close-lipped guide cleared out without another word to Simon or Magdalena about Lisbeth Hofmann.

The hangman's daughter tapped one of the bystanders on the shoulder and pointed at the building. "What happened in there? Why is everyone standing around gaping?" she asked as casually as possible, though she couldn't keep her voice from trembling. A white-haired old man in front of her had a sparkle in his eyes that betrayed something had happened here and, thank God, it hadn't happened to him.

"The bathmaster and his wife," he whispered. "Found in a pool of their own blood. It happened almost a week ago, but the house is still under guard. There's something strange going on here."

Magdalena's face went ashen. "Are the bathhouse people dead, then?" she asked hoarsely, as if she didn't already know the answer.

The man giggled like a child. "Dead like two old nags at the slaughterhouse. They say the blood ran ankle-deep in there. Must have been an awful mess."

Magdalena struggled to compose her thoughts. "Well . . ." she stammered, "do they know who's responsible?"

The old man nodded enthusiastically. "They caught the fellow!" he squeaked. "Hofmann's brother-in-law, a bear of a man, a real monster. They say he came from somewhere near Augsburg . . . Never heard of the place before, myself."

"Was it perhaps . . . Schongau?" Simon asked in an undertone.

The old man furrowed his brow. "Schongau . . . yes! Do you know the murderer?"

Magdalena shook her head quickly. "No, no, that's just what somebody told us. Where have they taken this . . . monster to now?"

The old man stared at them with increasing suspicion. "Well, of course, to one of the dungeons by city hall. You're not from around here, are you?"

Without answering, Magdalena pulled Simon by the sleeve into a small side street away from the bathhouse, where the old man was already starting to spread rumors among the onlookers about the strangers who apparently knew the monster.

"I'm afraid your father's in real trouble," Simon whispered, looking warily in all directions. "Do you really think that—"

"That's rubbish!" Magdalena said angrily. "Why would my father ever do anything like that? His own sister! It's absurd!"

"So now what do we do?"

"You heard it yourself. He's somewhere in city hall," Magdalena replied curtly. "So we'll go there; we have to help him."

"Help? But how do you imagine . . ." Simon started to say, but the hangman's daughter had already set off down the fetid, narrow lane, tears of rage and grief running down her cheeks.

Her dream of a new life had been cruelly shattered before it had even begun.

A dark figure broke away from the crowd in front of the bathhouse and silently followed the two newcomers. No onlooker would later recall someone crouched in the shadow of a nearby house, only steps away from Simon and Magdalena, someone as unremarkable as a wall or a parked cart—motionless, ever present, and unnoticed by all.

The man had long ago perfected this ability, lurking in the alcoves and doorways of burned-out cities, biding his time. He had feigned death on the battlefield only to slit the throats of foolish profiteers who tried to loot corpses of their weapons, clothing, and coins. He was a master of deception and, even more than that, of metamorphosis. He'd been living as someone else for so many years now that he was in danger of losing himself completely in this other identity—the identity of someone who had long been dead.

But then the past had come knocking at his door, reminding him who he really was. The burning desire for revenge returned and filled him with new life.

The hangman had returned . . .

It wasn't part of the plan that the hangman's daughter would also stay in Regensburg, but it wasn't without a certain irony. The man closed his eyes briefly and chuckled softly to himself. Had he believed in God, he would have uttered a prayer of thanks and donated a twelve-pound candle to the church.

Instead, he simply spat on the pavement and picked up the trail again.

The square in front of city hall was full of idlers this Sunday afternoon, as well as the pious who were streaming from the cathedral as mass came to an end. And then there was the usual crowd of beggars. It hadn't been hard for Simon and Magdalena to find this spot. Basically they let themselves be carried along by the current of the crowd that streamed down the wide paved road from the Weißgerbergraben and deposited them directly in front of the new city hall.

The three-story building had been partially finished just the year before, and the plaster gleamed white in the hot midday sun. To its left towered an even higher building with painted glass windows and richly decorated oriels. Through the wide portal came group after group of mostly older men, garbed in costly and, in some cases, rather exotic robes and deeply engaged in conversation. Snippets of sentences reached Simon and Magdalena in strange dialects they could only partially comprehend. So this, then, was the famous Reichssaal—the Imperial Hall, where the rich and mighty met with the kaiser to determine the destiny of the German Reich and to confer on how best to manage the ever-present and ever-increasing danger posed by the Turks. The raftsmen mentioned that the meeting would take place a few months from now, and apparently preparations were already under way.

Magdalena nudged Simon and pointed to a narrow doorway between the Reichssaal and the new city hall, where two watchmen stood guard with halberds. The gate behind them stood open, but the two bailiffs shared an expression as watchful as it was surly. And behind the gate was a dark archway.

"Look!" the hangman's daughter whispered. "The dungeon next to the city hall. That must be what the old man meant!"

Simon shrugged. "And what now? Push our way past the guards, knock down the doors to the dungeon, and smuggle the hangman out in your little travel bag?"

"You idiot!" Magdalena replied. "I just want to talk to him and find out what happened. Perhaps then we can figure out how to help him."

"And just how do you propose to do that? They won't let anyone in there."

Magdalena, who seemed to have calmed down somewhat, flashed him a devious grin. "We need someone to distract them while I have a look around in there. Can you do that?"

Simon looked at her in disbelief. "You're asking me to . . ."

She grinned again and kissed him on the cheek. "You're always quick on your feet; just think of something."

Then she headed briskly for the door, where the guards were already eyeing her expectantly.

"Have you got the monster locked up good and tight?" she asked them blithely. "Down in the Weißgerbergraben, the most blood-curdling stories are going around. They say the man is as big as a tree and tore the heads off the bathhouse owner and his wife like they were nothing more than chickens. What's going to happen if he gets out, eh?"

The guards' expressions went from attentive to boastful. "Let that be our concern, woman," one of them replied gruffly. "We've put all kinds of rascals in here under lock and key."

"Really?" Magdalena pursed her lips and batted her eyelashes. "Uh, like who?"

One of the guards puffed out his chest. "Well, you've probably heard of Hans Reichart, the swine who robbed and murdered five townfolk — stabbed them in the back, no less. We chased that shameless bastard all over city, but in the end the hangman got him on the wheel and impaled that broken bag of bones on a stake. As a reward, we each got to keep one of Reichart's fingers." The watchman held up his left hand and crossed himself superstitiously. "No one's so much as stolen a kreuzer from me since."

Magdalena swallowed hard. It was clear her father risked a similar fate.

"I wish I'd been there for the chase," she said finally. "You're both such big, strapping fellows." She winked and ran a finger down the breastplate of one of the guards, with a quick but suggestive glance downward. "Up top, I mean, of course."

The soldier grinned back. "You're welcome to have a look down below, you know."

At that moment laughter and noise erupted nearby, and with

a sigh, the guards broke off their brief flirtation and turned their heads to watch as a young man climbed onto a cart and began loudly extolling the virtues of some elixir.

"Dear citizens of Regensburg, step up and taste my newest miracle cure! This theriaca is brewed from dried snake meat and a secret mixture of exquisite herbs I myself gathered in cemeteries by the light of the full moon. It works wonders for cases of infertility, toothache, and stomach pain. On my honor, I swear it will give sight to the lame and make the blind walk again."

"Stay here, girl," one watchman growled, beckoning to his comrade to follow. "Let's see what all this racket is about before I get to tell you about how I worked over Schaidinger not long ago, a dirty dog who robbed the offertory box."

"Oh, um . . . wonderful," replied Magdalena, smiling grimly as the determined watchmen headed toward the cart.

Beads of sweat on his brow, Simon waved about a little bottle he'd hastily removed from his satchel: a harmless cough syrup containing ivy, sage, and honey, which was all he'd been able to find on short order. When he noticed how Magdalena had engaged the two watchmen in conversation, he couldn't think of any other way to create a diversion than to climb up on a cart and start making ludicrous proclamations. Simon had seen the itinerant quacks and mountebanks in Schongau, and during his student days in Ingolstadt. These self-anointed miracle doctors crammed their carts full of bizarre ingredients like scorpion oil, elephant fat, and pulverized stardust. In spite of, or perhaps because of, their exotic antics, these men were the highlight of every local carnival.

And indeed, it didn't take long for a group of curious onlookers to gather around Simon in the city hall square, all of them laughing and shouting.

A rotten head of cabbage just missed him as it flew past his head. "Hey, quack," one called, "how about you give some of your miracle drug to the bathhouse owner whose gut was slit wide open? Perhaps he'll come back to life!"

With a stiff grin, Simon shook his head, keeping an eye on the two officious watchmen who approached as Magdalena slipped through the narrow doorway.

"I would never dare interfere in God's mysterious ways," he cried out, his voice cracking. "When the Lord calls us, we are obliged to follow. It's not up to us to bring back the dead, were it even in my power to do so!"

Good God, what is this nonsense I'm spouting! Simon thought. *I can only hope that Magdalena is in and out in a hurry.*

"Hey, you!" The two bailiffs had finally reached the cart. "Get down this instant! Who the hell do you think you are, hawking your magic brew on a Sunday in front of city hall? Don't you know that around these parts quackery is against the law?"

"Quackery?" shouted Simon, tearing at his hair in feigned outrage. "I am a medicus with university training who has come upon hard times. Permit me at least to demonstrate my art."

"Nothing doing," one of the guards replied. "You'll come down right now, and into the stocks you'll go until morning. That'll purge this nonsense from your head!" He pointed at a stone column smeared with rotten fruit and excrement off to the side of the square adjacent to the market tower.

Simon's face turned a shade whiter. *Magdalena, I'll never forgive you for this . . .*

"Just give him a chance!" a bystander chimed in. "Maybe he really is a medicus, and if he isn't — well, you can still give him a good thrashing."

After a moment's consideration the soldier nodded. "All right, then, it's Sunday and the people want some entertainment; so come on, doc — show us what you can do."

The other bailiff appeared to have been struck by an idea

and, with a broad grin, waved for someone in the crowd to approach. "What good fortune! We've got a patient for you right here."

Ducking, Magdalena hastened through the gate, which was slightly ajar, and entered an expansive vault whose low ceiling was so covered with soot and dirt it was pitch black. A few cannons stood rusting in the corner. On her left she spied the wooden gate of a cell that turned out to be empty. Farther back, in a room next to a pile of cannonballs, a few soldiers were sitting around playing dice.

When Magdalena attempted to breeze by, one glanced up and glared. "Hey, girl," he cried. "What are you doing here?"

Magdalena curtsied and looked demurely at the ground. "The two gentlemen at the gate said I could have a look at the bathhouse monster." Feigning embarrassment, she fumbled with her bodice. "Is it true that at the full moon he changes into a werewolf, with fur and teeth and all that?"

"Who told you that?"

"The—the two gentlemen, upstairs, just a minute ago." Like a stupid farm girl, Magdalena drew little circles in the dirt with her right toe and pouted. "And they said I should come back at night sometime so I could see it—I mean, see how he changes."

The man laughed and winked at his comrades. "Sure, girl, go ahead and have yourself a look! And when the big bad wolf growls at you, we'll come and save you." He pointed toward a corridor on the left where a door stood open, then picked up the dice again. "You'll find the monster back there—just be careful he doesn't bite you."

She curtsied again as the other guards laughed, then entered the dark corridor. Looking around frantically, she saw a few sturdy doors with iron fittings. *Which one is it?* She didn't have much time. The guards would no doubt come after her soon enough, most likely with an invitation to join them in one of the cells for a little fooling around. She didn't even want to think about what might happen after that.

"Father!" Magdalena whispered, knocking against the wooden walls. "Can you hear me? It's me, your daughter!"

There was a clatter behind the middle door, and finally Jakob Kuisl replied.

"Magdalena! Good Lord, what are you doing here in Regensburg?"

The hangman's daughter pressed her forehead against a small hole beside the door no bigger than the palm of her hand. In the dim light she could see her father's head, his shaggy, matted beard, and the whites of his eyes gleaming out of a dark face. The stench of rot and excrement nearly took her breath away.

"I'll tell you about that some other time," she whispered. "Simon's with me. Now tell me what's happened to you and how I can help. The guards will come back at any moment!"

"Good Lord, who gave you two permission to just get up and leave Schongau!" Kuisl cursed. "Your mother's probably worried to death, and surely Lechner's hopping mad with nobody home shoveling the shit! When I get out of here, I'm going to give your ass such a whipping that—"

"Papa," Magdalena whispered, "you really have more important things to worry about. So tell me what happened!"

"It was a trap," Kuisl whispered once he'd calmed down. "Someone killed Lisl and her husband and wants to pin the murder on me now." Quickly he reported what had happened since he'd arrived. "I don't know what dirty bastard did this to me," he finally muttered, "but by God, when I find him, I'll break every last bone in his body."

"But you've got to get out of here first," Magdalena replied.

She looked around frantically for a key, but in vain. Finally she began to rattle the door handle.

"Quit that," her father said. "I can't get out of here, unless you can prove before the awful inquisition begins that someone else bloodied his hands with this dirty deed; then perhaps they'll put off the torture."

Magdalena frowned. "But how do we do that?"

Her father's mouth was now very close to her ear—she could smell his familiar scent, sweat and tobacco.

"Go to my brother-in-law's house and try to find some kind of clue," he whispered. "Anything. I'll bet the culprits didn't try very hard to cover their tracks. Why should they? They've already got their suspect in custody."

Magdalena nodded. "And if we don't find anything?"

"Then your father will meet his Maker. The Regensburg hangman, so I hear, is savage."

There was a lengthy pause; then voices sounded from just outside the dungeon gate.

"I think someone's coming," Magdalena whispered.

Kuisl pushed his fingers through the little hole and pressed his daughter's hand so hard she almost cried out.

"Quick now," the hangman said, "Get out!"

The hangman's daughter took one last look into her father's eyes before she turned and hurried down the corridor. Just as she was about to set foot in the vaulted anteroom, the watchman she'd been speaking with stepped in front of her.

"Well? Is the werewolf sprouting fur?" He ran his hands over her bodice and pushed her back down the long hallway. "Do you want to have a look at *my* fur?"

Magdalena pointed back down the hallway. "But—but the monster isn't there anymore. The door to the cell was just standing wide open."

"What the devil?"

Pushing her aside, the watchman ran toward the cells. In a flash Magdalena was in the sooty vestibule again. From there she could see sunlight streaming in through the open gate. Without slowing down, she fled past the astonished guards still playing dice and hurried toward the exit, then out the front gate.

When she finally reached the city hall square again, she could see that Simon had gotten himself into a mess of trouble.

Inch by inch, the point of a needle closed in on a wide-open eye. The beggar's head quivered, but the strong hands of the guard held him, vise-like, while two other guards pinned his arms to his sides. The old man had stopped whimpering and just stared in pure horror at the needle about to pierce his eye. There was no escaping now.

"Good God, keep still, man," Simon whispered, trying to focus fully on his quivering target. "I can help you, but only if you don't move."

Sweat streamed down the medicus's face as the merciless August sun burned down on the marketplace. The onlookers' boisterous cries had quieted now to a tense murmur. What they were witnessing here was better than the usual cheap theater traveling hucksters had to offer, especially since no one knew how this drama might end.

The watchman had spotted old Hans Reiser in the crowd and selected him as the ideal candidate for the self-proclaimed medicus to demonstrate whether he really was a master of his art or just some pathetic quack, as most onlookers suspected. For years old Reiser had been shuffling around the square with milky eyes. He was once a well-respected glassblower, but his trade had almost completely destroyed his eyesight. Now he was nothing more than a grumbling old man, without money or family—a blind old dotard whose presence at city hall increasingly irritated the watchmen.

The old beggar suffered from the gray stare—a disease of the eye in which the afflicted has the sensation of seeing the world as if through a waterfall, thus giving the condition its Greek name: cataracts. The pupils, gray in color, looked like two marbles. The operation could only benefit the watchmen: either Reiser would be cured and wouldn't annoy them anymore, or he would die. That would bring them relief as well — and as for the medicus they could prosecute him for quackery and hang him and be done with it.

All in all, a perfect solution.

Simon knew he'd never live to see next week if he didn't heal the beggar right here and now in the middle of the city square. Whether Magdalena managed to find her father was of secondary importance at the moment. He tried to put everything else out of his mind and concentrate only on the incision he was about to make. The needle was now just a few tenths of an inch from the pupil, and the beggar's eye stared up at him like the moon, round and full. The medicus knew that removing a cataract was one of the most difficult of all medical procedures, and it was for this reason — as long as anyone could remember — that it was performed mostly by traveling barber surgeons, who could be far, far away by the time complications developed. Simon himself had performed the operation only twice in his life. It involved inserting the needle sideways into the white of the eye and pressing the clouded lens to the bottom of the eye. Just one slight tremble, the tiniest false move, and the patient could go blind, and even die as the result of subsequent infection.

When the needle pierced the eye, the beggar jerked and screamed. A second incision followed in the other eye. This time Reiser whimpered but held still, his defiance broken. Simon held the needle against the eye for a while to keep the lens in place, then, as he withdrew it, staggered backward. The back of his shirt was soaked, and sweat was streaming down his face. Only now did he notice that a hush had fallen over the crowd.

"I'll put a dressing on it now," Simon said, his voice weak. "You'll have to wear it a few days, and then we'll see whether—"

"Good Lord!" Reiser interrupted Simon as he held his hands up to his face and shouted with joy. "I can see again! By God, I can see again!"

The raggedy beggar stumbled across the square, grasping wildly at passersby. It did in fact appear he'd been cured of his blindness, even though his plodding movements suggested he'd not yet regained his sight completely. Elated, Reiser ran his hands over every face within reach, grasping at coattails and the brims of hats. Many backed away in disgust—some even pushed the beggar away—but Reiser didn't lose heart. The old man staggered over to his savior, missing him twice in his attempt to embrace him. He finally managed on the third pass, pulling Simon firmly to his breast.

"You—you are a sorcerer!" he cried out. "Look, everyone, see for yourself—this man can work magic!"

"I . . . don't think that's the right word," Simon whispered, but Reiser dashed across the square again, embracing complete strangers as he continued pointing at Simon. "This man is a sorcerer, a real sorcerer! Believe me!"

The medicus cast a cautious glance at the watchmen, to whom this word alone gave the sudden opportunity—in spite of his successful operation—to seize him and send him to the gallows. Might this be enough to have him burned at the stake?

At this very moment Simon caught sight of Magdalena as she sneaked out through the main gate and waved at him furtively. He feigned a move in one direction, then dashed off in the other, disappearing into the crowd.

"Stop the sorcerer!" the guards shouted behind him. "In the name of the kaiser, stop him!"

Simon knocked over a vegetable stand, sending cabbages

rolling across the pavement and tripping up one of the guards. Another guard crashed into a maidservant and became entangled in a brawl with some indignant bystanders. Simon darted into a narrow alley leading away from city hall and toward the cathedral. Panting, he leaned against the side of a house to catch his breath. When he turned to pick up his things, he noticed he'd lost one of his two bags, the one containing most of his clothing, including his new petticoat breeches and his French-tailored jacket! At least he'd managed to hold on to his books and medical instruments.

Just as he was about to slip into the shadows of the narrow alleyway, he felt a hand on his shoulder. He started, then turned around to face a grinning Magdalena.

"Didn't I say you can't be left alone for a minute?"

The hangman's daughter gave him a kiss on the cheek and nudged him gently in the direction of the cathedral. They could still hear angry shouts and curses from the city hall square.

"It would be best if we don't show our faces here again for a while," she whispered, now in a serious tone. "We already have enough problems as it is!"

Simon nodded, still panting. "I say we take the suggestion of the raftmaster and go looking for that peculiar inn. It looks like we're going to need a cheap place to stay for a while."

"The *Whale!*" Magdalena rolled her eyes. "What sort of cheap tavern do you think it'll turn out to be?" She turned to leave. "I only hope it doesn't stink of fish."

As they rounded the next corner, a shadow followed. Dirty boots slid almost soundlessly through the dung- and trash-filled lane, almost as if they floated on air.

Hunched over, Jakob Kuisl moved from one end of the cell to the other. It was just four paces wide, but he had to keep moving if he wanted to keep his thoughts running.

Outside he could hear excited voices, shrill shouts and cries. Something seemed to be going on out in the market square, and Kuisl could only hope the tumult had nothing to do with Magdalena and Simon. Why — damn it — were the two of them in Regensburg at all? Had they set out after him because something had happened in Schongau? The hangman shook his head. His daughter would certainly have told him if that had been the case. Most likely his impudent girl had gotten it into her head to pay her sick old aunt a visit and take in a bit of the city life in Regensburg. The Schongau clerk, Lechner, would certainly be looking for Magdalena! It was her job, after all, in her father's absence, to cart manure from the city streets, and she would be lucky if they didn't throw her in the dungeon when she returned home for shirking her duty. And that cock of the walk Simon along with her! But Kuisl himself would most certainly be the first to give his daughter a good whipping.

The hangman paused at the thought that he might never again be in a position to reprimand his daughter, because it was here in Regensburg that he would die. Really, it was an act of providence that Magdalena and Simon had followed him — they were his only hope now of escaping death on the gallows. Besides, his anger at his reckless daughter was at least a welcome distraction from his memories. Though he'd scraped the writing off the wall, the old mercenary song took him back to a time he would rather have forgotten. But the seed of remembrance had been sown, and in the darkness and idleness of this cell his thoughts kept returning to the past.

Each time he reached the far end of his cell, his gaze fell on the blank space where the line from the song had been etched, and memories flashed through his mind like lightning — the murder, the violence, the brutality all came back to him now.

Instinctively, Jakob Kuisl began to hum the beginning of the song:

There is a reaper, Death's his name . . .
HIS BLADE KEEN AND STEADY
To mow us is ready . . .

The hangman listened to himself hum it, but the tune sounded as if it were coming from the mouth of another man. He bit down hard on his lip until he tasted blood.

5

THE EYE STARED IN COLD AS MARBLE — UNBLINK-
ing, motionless, and dry — without betraying the slightest flicker
of emotion. At times Katharina believed no being existed behind
this eye; that instead an evil, monstrous doll was observing her
like a caged bird or a beetle scampering back and forth inside
a jar.

Katharina couldn't recall how long she'd been imprisoned in
this room. Five days? Six? Or more? There was no window for
light to enter, only a small hatch in the door through which a
gloved hand supplied her with food, drink, and white candles in
exchange for her chamber pot. Her only contact with the outside
world was through a small fingernail-size hole above this hatch,
and though Katharina had tried and tried, all she could see
through it was a dark, torch-lit corridor. Now and then she could
make out the sound of soft music in the distance, though it wasn't
the kind of music she knew from fairs and church festivals, but
solemn and ceremonial, composed of trumpets, harps, and reeds.

It sounded to Katharina a little like the music of angels.

She'd discovered the eye would visit her at regular intervals.

Sometimes the visit was announced by shuffling and scraping at the door, and very rarely she would hear the sound of feet dragging or a soft, melodic whistle. But more often than not, only a prickling sensation between her shoulder blades alerted her that, when she turned around, the eye would be there again, staring at her, cool and curious.

Long ago she'd given up calling for help. At first she'd cried, cursed, and screamed until all that remained of her voice was a reedy squawk, but when she realized that this did no good and just made her hoarse, she curled up into herself like a sick cat and retreated far inside her head, where recently everything seemed jumbled together — horrible visions, visions of people impaled on stakes and tortured, of decapitated bodies and the corpses of infants with contorted limbs, of green long-necked monsters throwing helpless souls into vats of boiling oil. But there were also wanton images: naked young boys and tender young girls who caressed her in her dreams, fairy-like creatures who held her high in their arms and carried her to the mountain peak of Brocken, where she joined both men and women in wild orgies.

Sometimes Katharina would cry and laugh at the same time.

Whenever her thoughts came briefly into focus, she tried to remember what had in fact brought her here. She'd been hanging around behind the old grain market, heavily made-up the way men liked it, with brightly colored hair and a full flowing skirt that she had only to lift to service her clients. Katharina knew her work wasn't without risks. In contrast to many other prostitutes, she worked without a madam. Her friends bought protection from Fat Thea or someone else and paid a pretty penny for it, but Katharina worked alone. If the guards caught her, she would be thrown into the stocks in the city hall square, then whipped and chased out of town the very next day. It had happened to her twice already, first when she was only fifteen years old. Now in her early thirties, Katharina was an experienced prostitute and knew how to avoid the bailiffs. And if she got caught—well, she could always bribe them with her body.

But now misfortune had visited her at last, a nameless misfortune, a misfortune that she could never have imagined in even her worst nightmares.

The man had worn a black coat and a hat drawn over his face. His voice was refined and pleasant, not like one of those crude raftsmen whose breath stank of booze as he nailed her like a board to the wall. She knew this man had money to spend. He led her to a hidden doorway and pulled out a little silver bottle. The warm liquid inside tasted sweet like wine and went down as smooth as honey. The next thing she could remember was falling onto a bed in a strange room where the man covered her body with a thousand kisses. It hadn't been unpleasant. On the contrary, for the first time in a long while she'd felt desire welling up inside her again. When she finally came to much later, she was still lying in the same room, but with a pounding headache now. Her gums felt as if they were on fire.

There was no doubt the stranger had provided generously for her. In one corner of the room stood a bed made up with white linens, and in the other corner, a chamber pot. A table had been prepared with cheese and white bread on silver platters and wine in a fragile glass goblet. Never before in her life had she tasted white bread—it was heavenly, without husks, grit, or hard kernels. In the following days she was fed more white bread and other delicacies—sausages, sliced ham, creamy butter . . . As time passed, Katharina began to suspect she was being fattened up like a goose, but she kept right on eating, as it was her only diversion amid the endless, monotonous hours, the only way she could drive away the tormenting thoughts.

Where am I? What does he intend to do with me?

Once again Katharina felt a tingle creep across her back. She turned around and looked directly into the eye.

It was studying her. Something scraped along the outside of the door.

It was time for the next course.

Avoiding the main streets, Magdalena and Simon made their way through a labyrinth of narrow lanes and shadowy back courtyards piled high with rubbish and excrement. The squalid children and hapless, wounded veterans of the Great War who occupied these places stared out at them as they passed. Old soldiers leaning on crutches, some with horrible scars and burns on their faces, held out their hands as the two strangers hurried by in silence. Everywhere, mangy, scraggy dogs roamed the streets, snarling at them in packs. This was the other face of Regensburg, the dirty underside that had nothing whatsoever in common with the clean paved streets, the stately parliament building, the cathedral, and the towering houses where the patricians lived. This was a place of poverty and disease, where the daily battle for survival was waged.

More than once Simon thought he saw a figure peering at them from around a corner, someone pursuing them, lying in wait for just the right moment to plunge a dagger into their ribs or snatch their few belongings. But oddly enough the beggars and the wounded left them alone. Simon was sure this had less to do with him than it did with Magdalena, whose steady gait and fierce gaze showed possible thieves and muggers she wasn't an easy target. They could sense that the hangman's daughter was one of their own.

"If this tavern doesn't materialize soon, I'm going to die of thirst right here in the middle of the street," Simon lamented, wiping the sweat from his brow. Again he cursed himself for having eaten that salty, greasy sausage down by the river.

The heat continued to build palpably in the narrow lanes. Several times already they'd asked halfway reputable-looking passersby for directions to the Whale. Each time they'd been sent off in a different direction, and now they found themselves somewhere behind the cathedral, supposedly just a stone's throw from the elusive tavern.

"Surely it can't be much farther," Magdalena said, pointing ahead to a broad boulevard spanned by tall stone arches. "Those must be the arches they told us about. We just need to turn right here, and we'll be there."

As they walked, the hangman's daughter briefly recounted what had happened to her father. A few words were enough to give the medicus cause to worry. Was it really possible someone had framed the hangman? And if so, why? Simon wasn't especially enthused about Kuisl's idea to go looking for clues at Hofmann's house. He dreaded the thought of breaking into the bathhouse that night. What if someone caught them? No doubt they would be deemed the hangman's accomplices, thrown into the very next cell, then led to the gallows alongside him. But the medicus knew he wouldn't be able talk Magdalena out of it. Once the hangman's daughter had set her mind to something, there was no turning back.

At last they emerged from the labyrinth of narrow lanes and turned right, into a wide paved boulevard with huge stone arches overhead. Nestled discreetly between two warehouses stood a lopsided, two-story gabled house that looked as though it had been standing there since time immemorial. Above the entrance dangled a rusty metal sign depicting a whale and a man leaping from its mouth.

"Jonah and the whale," Simon said, nodding. "This must be it."

Magdalena tried to get a look inside, through a sooty bull's-eye windowpane, but even though it was the middle of the day, it was as dark as the grave inside. "It doesn't exactly look inviting," she ventured.

"It doesn't matter," replied Simon, reaching for a small

bronze fish that served as a door knocker. "The raftmaster seems to know his way about town, and his word clearly carries some weight. I think we ought to try it. We do need a cheap place to stay, since my savings can't last us much longer than a few more days." He pounded vigorously on the door.

For a long time they heard nothing. Just as Simon was about to suggest they look for somewhere else to stay, the door opened a crack and a long pointed nose appeared, attached to a haggard old woman with stringy hair and remarkably bad breath.

"What? What do you want?"

"We're . . . looking for lodging for the next few weeks," Simon replied hesitantly. "Karl Gessner sent us, the Regensburg raftmaster."

"If Gessner sent you, you must be all right," the old woman mumbled as she shuffled back inside, leaving the door wide open behind her.

Simon cast a cautious glance inside the taproom. Hanging from the wood-paneled ceiling was a giant stuffed catfish that stared back at him with mean eyes. Despite the summer heat, a tile stove with a bench built around it rumbled away in a far corner. The chairs and tables in the room were old and scuffed, and except for Simon and Magdalena, not another living soul seemed to be staying there. What fascinated Simon most, however, was the shelf that lined the opposite wall, holding objects he never would have expected to find in such a place: books.

Not two, or three, but dozens of them, all bound in leather and apparently in mint condition.

He entered the tavern alongside Magdalena and walked directly to the books. He knew at once he'd feel at home here.

"Where — where did you get all these?" he asked the old woman, who had disappeared behind the bar again and was polishing glasses with a dirty rag.

"My dead husband. Before he married into my family, dear old Jonas worked as a scribe down at the ferry landing, drafting

documents for the rivermen. He could never get enough books."
She looked at Simon suspiciously. "I'll bet you're a bookworm,
too. I could use someone like you at the present."

"I — don't understand," Simon stuttered.

The tavern keeper's widow gave a condescending nod toward the bench by the stove. Only now did Simon and Magdalena notice someone lying there, snoring loudly. The stranger
wore wide baggy trousers, a frilled white shirt whose lace collar
was spattered with red wine, and a tightly fitted purple jacket
whose silver buttons gleamed brightly in the dark room. The
man's legs, stretched out on the table, were shod in freshly polished leather boots whose bucket tops reached almost down to
the sole.

Damn! That outfit must have cost a fortune, Simon thought. *I
always wanted boots like that!*

"Ask the Venetian," the landlady replied. "He comes here
for the books — and for the wine and women, of course."

Simon took a closer look at the man passed out on the bench.
He didn't look like a penniless drunk. On the contrary, the unconscious man looked well-to-do, right down to his cleanly
clipped goatee. His black hair fell in curls across his shoulders,
his fingernails were manicured, and his cheeks had a soft pink
hue. Just as Simon was about to turn away, the Venetian opened
his eyes. They were dark, almost sad, as if they'd read more than
their fair share of tragedies.

"*Ah, ma che bella signorina! Sono lietissimo! Che piacere!*" he
said, still a bit woozy, then sat up, smoothing the wrinkles out of
his jacket. Simon was just about to bow when he realized that the
man was addressing not him but Magdalena. He stood up from
his seat by the stove, took Magdalena's hand, and brushed it with
his lips. Magdalena couldn't suppress a giggle. She never would
have thought it possible, but the Venetian man was even shorter
than Simon. Just the same, all of the Venetian's nearly five feet
positively pulsed with pride and nobility.

"May I introduce myself?" he asked in almost perfect, unaccented German. "Silvio Contarini from the beautiful city of Venice. I must have dozed off." He bowed slightly, and Magdalena noticed with astonishment that his hair slipped forward as he did so. Evidently he was wearing a wig.

"Gambling and whoring till the wee hours of the morning," the tavern keeper complained from behind the bar. "You and your cronies guzzled two gallons of my best muscatel last night."

"*Perdonate.* Is this enough?" The Venetian slid a few shiny coins across the bar, which the old woman quickly pocketed. Magdalena was aghast. The man had just paid as much for wine as her family spent in a whole week.

"Do you like books?" he asked Magdalena, pointing at the shelves behind him. "Do you perhaps know Shakespeare?"

"Actually," Simon now chimed in, "we're more interested in medical texts."

Silvio turned around in surprise, only just now noticing there was another person in the room. "I beg your pardon?"

"You know, Scultetus, Paré, Paracelsus, and so forth. You've probably never heard of them." Simon reached for his bag and turned to the innkeeper. "May we see the room now?"

Without waiting for Magdalena, he stomped up the narrow stairway. Silvio looked at the hangman's daughter in astonishment. "Is your friend always so . . . surly? These bruises all over his face! He must get into a lot of scrapes, yes?"

The hangman's daughter laughed. "Actually no. He loves books, just as you do. He's had a bit of a rough day is all. We've had a long journey, you should know."

The Venetian smiled. "Yet not so long as mine! *Ma che ci vuoi fare!* What brings you to Regensburg?"

"My . . . father." Magdalena hesitated. "We come from Schongau. My aunt lives here, or rather, she lived here . . . and we wanted to pay her a visit, but . . ." She waved her hand. "It's too complicated to explain in a few words."

Silvio nodded. "Then perhaps another time, over a glass of wine." Reaching abruptly into his jacket pocket, he pulled out a little book, which he handed to Magdalena.

"If you like, read this, poems by a certain William Shakespeare. I translated them into German myself. Tell me frankly what you think of them."

Magdalena graciously accepted the little leather-bound book. "But how can you be so sure we'll meet again?"

Silvio smiled. "I'm sure we shall. I come here often. *Arrivederci.*" He bowed politely and pranced out of the room.

Puzzled, Magdalena gazed after him for a while before climbing the narrow stairway up to the room where Simon was already lying on one of the flea-infested beds, staring up at the ceiling.

The hangman's daughter grinned. "Is it possible you're the tiniest bit jealous?"

Simon snorted. "Jealous? Of the dwarf?"

"Right. He's the same height as you, you know."

"Very funny," Simon snapped. "In case you didn't notice, the man was made-up like a woman. And he was wearing a *wig.*"

Magdalena shrugged. "Perhaps. I've heard that in France, at court, all the men wear wigs now. Doesn't look half bad."

Sitting up, the medicus looked at Magdalena as if she were a naughty child. "Magdalena, believe me, I know people like him. It's all a façade—fine clothes, witty repartee, but nothing at all behind it!"

With a sigh, she lay down next to Simon and pulled him to her with both arms.

"Strange. That sounds somehow rather familiar."

Late in the evening the gatekeeper Johannes Büchner strolled through the narrow city streets enjoying the mild summer air. Periodically he tossed a leather purse full of guilders in the air so the coins jingled like castanets. The lieutenant had been saving up for the coming Sunday, when he and a few friends had a game of dice planned for the back room of the Black Elephant. High stakes, big payoff—that was the way Büchner liked it.

Even as darkness fell, he had no fear for his safety. He was, after all, the head watchman at Jakob's Gate, and the riffraff knew him well. Beggars, thieves, and whores knew better than to trifle with him. Unlike many of the other guards for whom duty at the gate was just another annoying civic responsibility to be performed as a matter of course, Büchner was a trained soldier paid by the city. Besides, anyone who dared assault a city guard risked meeting his end on gallows hill with his guts spilling out. But not before Büchner's colleagues worked him over; by the time they were through with him, the poor bastard would wish he were dead already.

The lieutenant's route took him from the city hall square all the way to the wine market near the Danube. Büchner mulled over the exciting events of the past week. The trap set for that Bavarian had worked perfectly! When the man first approached him at Jakob's Gate, Büchner knew at once that this would be a profitable venture, even though he was surprised that such an influential person would want anything to do with someone as vile as an executioner. But that wasn't really Büchner's concern; the payoff was decent enough, and the man had made clear he wouldn't tolerate any questions.

Even though the man hadn't given his name, it was of course clear to Büchner who stood before him. As a longtime commander of the city guards, he knew who wielded power in this city. The man had promised him a whole purse of guilders just for seizing the Schongau hangman at Jakob's Gate and releasing him at the agreed-upon time the following day. An armed contingent was to follow the stranger in secret, and a surprise would be waiting for them all at the bathhouse. When the guard finally saw what the surprise was, he had to hand it to his client. You really had to be careful not to make an enemy of a man like him.

Büchner whistled as he turned into the narrow Wiedfang-gässchen Street, driving off a handful of whimpering strays with a few well-aimed kicks. A prostitute, cheaply made-up and haggard, winked at him from a street corner. For a moment the lieutenant considered spending the money he'd come by so easily not on wine but on women — then he thought better of it. In the last few weeks prostitutes had been disappearing left and right in Regensburg; the only ones who still dared to venture out into the streets were almost all old shrews.

"Get out of here before I put your bony frame in the pillory," Büchner said in a threatening voice, spitting at her.

With a suppressed giggle, the prostitute sauntered off, but not without first offering him a view of her bare, boil-scarred backside. Soon enough Büchner was alone again in the narrow street, and though he'd served as night watchman in this city for thousands of hours, the sudden silence gave him an eerie feeling.

You're getting old, Büchner, he thought. *Letting yourself get spooked by a whore? It's time for a mug of wine, or—*

Thinking he caught sight of something moving out of the corner of his eye, he made an abrupt about-face, prepared to show a purse snatcher just what he was up against. No doubt the robber would turn on the spot and flee.

"Who dares approach the city guard—"

The knife plunged into the small gap between his cuirass and armpit and cut straight through to his heart. As blood spurted from his mouth, he stared back at his attacker in disbelief.

"But . . . why . . . ?"

His knees buckled and he sank to the ground like a marionette whose strings had been cut. One final twitch, and he was still. The coin purse slipped from his limp fingers.

The murderer bent down to feel for the gatekeeper's pulse, then for good measure slit his throat. At the latest, his colleagues would discover their commander's stiff corpse the next morning, another tragic victim in a growing wave of crime in Regensburg. His attacker wiped the hunting knife on Büchner's cloak and, contented, sauntered off with the purse of guilders, humming softly to himself. It was simply not worth the risk of having some garrulous bailiff foil his plan, especially now that this girl had appeared on the scene. No one suspected she'd show up in Regensburg looking for her father. Now what was he going to do about her?

The man decided the matter could wait a while. The hangman's daughter wasn't going anywhere, and the more pressing matter now was to dispose of some of the evidence. All would be taken care of, all in good time . . .

Smiling, he fingered a matchbox in his coat pocket. Soon enough all his worries would vanish like a puff of smoke.

Simon and Magdalena waited until the night was as black as the bottom of the Danube before heading downstairs to the tavern of the Whale. With considerable reluctance, the medicus had finally agreed to Magdalena's plan to search the bathhouse for some clue that might exonerate Jakob Kuisl.

As he descended the creaking stairs, Simon noticed with astonishment that the tavern, empty just a few hours before, was now at full capacity. Every table was occupied with weatherworn raftsmen and craftsmen smoking their pipes, but more well-to-do citizens were there, too, with their lace collars and sparkling buttons. Laughing loudly and gossiping, they rolled dice as wine flowed so freely that the scrawny server could barely keep their steins full. A dark cloud of tobacco smoke enveloped the men, many of whom held women in their laps: garishly made-up and giggling, groping their patrons' crotches as they licked their dark, wine-stained lips.

At his usual spot in back by the stove, the Venetian reclined, staring dreamily at the chaotic scene around him and sipping his wine now and then. He was the only one in the room with a lead-crystal glass in front of him.

"Ah, *la bella signorina* and her brave protector!" he exclaimed in greeting as Magdalena and Simon entered. "Have you abandoned your love nest in order to devote yourselves to the joys of the night? Sit with me, *signorina,* and tell me whether you've read my little book yet! I'm — *come si dice* — dying to know what you think of it."

Simon shook his head coldly. "Sorry, we have other plans for tonight."

Silvio Contarini winked at them. "For that you could have just stayed upstairs, no?"

Magdalena smiled and pulled away. "Didn't your mother teach you not to stick your nose into other people's business? Enjoy your wine, and we'll see you later."

"But what about my book?" he called after them. "The poems? *Via piacciono questi versi?*"

"I'll wipe my backside with your book tonight," Simon replied softly, closing the door behind them.

They were immediately engulfed in silence; only the muffled sound of laughter could be heard through the thick windowpanes. A warm breeze was blowing a moldy odor off the Danube.

"Simon, Simon." Magdalena shook her head with mock severity. "Can you please be a little more polite? Or I might be tempted to believe you're jealous!"

"Oh, come now!" Simon stomped ahead. "I just can't stand it when someone uses such cheap tricks to seduce a woman!"

"Cheap?" Magdalena grinned, catching up to him. "*You've* never written me any poetry. But no need to worry; the Venetian is much too short for me anyway."

They avoided the large square in front of the cathedral and hurried westward through the stinking, narrow back streets. At this hour it was so dark in Regensburg that they could barely see their hands in front of their faces. Simon had brought along a little lantern from the Whale that he held under his jacket; this at least threw faint light a few yards ahead. They didn't dare risk any more light, as it was long past curfew, and if the watchmen caught them, they would no doubt both wind up locked in a cell and spend the next day in the stocks in the city hall square. More-over, the light attracted thieves and murderers, who even now were no doubt lurking in doorways and around dark corners, looking out for drunks on their way home from the taverns and hoping to relieve these poor, besotted souls of their purses, their sterling silver buttons, and their finely polished boots.

Just as he had earlier that day, Simon imagined a robber skulking around every corner: once when he heard the sound of pebbles crunching just a few yards behind them, and later when he heard the faint sound of footsteps. In a narrow passage where the houses were built so close they almost touched, a legless beg-gar reached for Magdalena's skirt; she rid herself of that nuisance with a single well-placed kick. But otherwise, except for a hand-ful of drunks they encountered, all was quiet.

After a good quarter-hour that seemed infinitely longer to the medicus, they finally reached the Weißgerbergraben. Along the road a canal flowed gently and emptied into the Danube, and before them the bathhouse loomed up out of the darkness. A tired watchman clutched his halberd in the entryway, looking as if he might just collapse at any moment.

"Now what?" Simon whispered. "Shall we ask the guard if we can have a look around?"

"Idiot!" Magdalena scolded. "But it is strange, isn't it, that they're still guarding the house? After all, the murder took place a while ago." She stopped to think for a moment. "Let's see if we can enter from the courtyard in back — nobody will see us that way."

Simon grabbed her sleeve. "Magdalena, think about it: if

they catch us inside, they'll draw and quarter us along with your father! Is that what you want?"

"Then you can stay outside."

Magdalena broke away and slipped through a little alleyway barely wider than her hips that separated the bathhouse from the neighboring building. With a sigh, Simon followed.

They climbed over slimy heaps of garbage and a foul-smelling mass of something that on closer inspection turned out to be a pig carcass. Dozens of rats scurried about. A few yards in, a hole appeared in the wall and, behind it, what seemed to be a back courtyard.

Simon's gaze wandered over a mildewed wooden tub, some nondescript piles of junk, and a newly built well. Behind this was a small garden with pots of soil neatly arranged in rows. A small door gave entry to an outbuilding.

Magdalena hurried over to it and shook the handle gently. It was locked.

"Now what?" Simon whispered.

The hangman's daughter pointed to a window that appeared to open into the bathhouse. The shutters were open a crack.

"Looks like my uncle wasn't especially cautious," she said in a soft voice. "Or somebody's been here before us."

The shutters creaked as she pushed them aside, then she boosted herself up and into the building. "Come on," she whispered to Simon before disappearing into the darkness inside.

Having crawled in behind her, Simon held up the lantern to illuminate the cavernous room in which they found themselves. It seemed to extend all the way to the front of the building and was divided into niches, each containing a wooden tub. Fresh towels were stacked on shelves all along the walls, and next to them stood rows of vials filled with fragrant oils.

Magdalena stopped short. The tub directly next to her was still filled with water, and dark spots spattered the ground in front of it. She bent down to run her finger along the floor, and in the light cast by the lantern she could see her fingertip was red.

"So this is where my aunt and uncle were murdered." She wiped the sticky substance on her skirt. "Right in the bathtub, just as my father said. Look, you can still see the drops there."

Slowly she approached a far window that overlooked the back courtyard and motioned to Simon. By the light of his lantern he could see a bloody handprint on the windowsill.

It was the handprint of a man of about medium build, certainly not of Jakob Kuisl, who had what were probably the biggest hands Simon had ever seen in his life.

The medicus shrugged. "The print could be from one of the guards who removed the corpses."

"What, out the back window?" snapped Magdalena. "Nonsense! The murderer entered the house back here, killed the two of them, and escaped again the same way. The size of the handprint proves it wasn't my father!"

"Nobody will believe that in court," Simon said, resuming his inspection of the room. By now his curiosity had gotten the better of his fear. He pointed to a door hidden at first glance behind one of the niches. "This seems to lead somewhere."

He pressed the door handle and found himself standing in a room with a brick oven. Stained copper kettles as big as slaughterhouse vats were arranged on the oven, and alongside it wood was piled high enough to burn a witch. A narrow stairway led to the second floor through a ceiling black with soot.

"The heating chamber," Magdalena said with an appreciative nod. "Aunt Lisbeth didn't exaggerate when she wrote my father that their bathhouse was one of the largest in the city. With all this hot water, the entire Regensburg city council could probably splash around in the tubs all day long, all of them at once. Look." She pointed to a circle of stones in the floor that surrounded a hole. A chain passed through the hole, allowing a

damp wooden bucket to draw water from a well below. "Their
very own well!" The hangman's daughter sighed. "What I
wouldn't give to have something like that at home in Schongau.
We'd never have to haul buckets up from the river again!"

She took a yard-long stick from the woodpile, wrapped it
with brushwood, and fashioned a torch to illuminate the dark
space below. Meanwhile, Simon ventured up to the second story,
where he found two additional rooms. In one, apparently the
Hofmanns' bedroom, stood a large bed and an open chest. Peering inside, Simon realized someone had already rifled through it.
An empty folder lay on top of tattered linens along with a crumpled set of Hofmann's Sunday best. The medicus assumed the
folder had once contained the bathhouse owner's official papers,
which the guards had seized as evidence.

Now Simon turned to the other room, and what he saw from
the doorway stopped him in his tracks. It looked as if some evil
spirit had wreaked havoc there. Over the fragrant reed-covered
floor bouquets of dried herbs had been scattered and trampled.
Shards of glass littered the floor, too, apparently broken cupping
glasses. To his left, one shelf had been overturned and another
held only a single bronze mortar; everything else had been hastily knocked to the floor. By the dim light of his lantern Simon
saw a hopeless mess of torn parchments, tattered book bindings,
leather purses ripped at the seams, and heaps of pills crushed to
powder — all strewn across an enormous oak table that spanned
the width of the room.

The medicus picked up a pill and sniffed the powder. It
smelled strongly of alum and resin. Clearly this was Andreas
Hofmann's treatment room. As bathhouse operator, he also
tended to his patrons' little aches and pains.

Simon frowned. Why in God's name would the guards have
made this mess? Had they been looking for something?

Or had someone else come back here after they'd left?

He picked up a tattered book from the floor and leafed

through it, a conventional herbarium depicting various kinds of grain. The pages with illustrations of rye, wheat, and oats were dog-eared and marked with red ink.

"Simon, come quick! I've found something!"

Magdalena's stifled cry roused Simon from his thoughts. He put the book aside and hurried downstairs, where the hangman's daughter was standing hip-deep in the well, pointing down excitedly.

"See for yourself! There are iron rungs built into the wall leading down! And I hardly believe my uncle was climbing down the well to fetch water. There must be something else down here." She continued climbing downward until she disappeared into the darkness.

"Upstairs I found——" Simon began, but Magdalena interrupted him with an astonished cry.

"I was right! There's an entrance here just a few rungs farther down. Hurry and come down!"

Queasy, Simon climbed down after her, arriving in just a few feet at a hole in the wall the size of a wagon wheel. He stumbled through, into a low chamber roughcast in white limestone. Inside, barrels, crates, and moldy sacks stood along the walls. Magdalena was already at work ripping open a number of them by the dim light of the lantern. She wore a disappointed look as she held up a few dried apples for him to see.

"Damn! The cellar is nothing more than a storage room!" she said with disappointment.

Simon thrust his stiletto into one of the barrels and stuck his finger inside. He tasted sweet, heavy red wine.

"Malvasia," he said, smacking his lips. "And not bad. At home only the fine burgomasters get stuff like this. Perhaps we should take a little keg for ourselves . . ."

"Idiot!" Magdalena cursed. "We're here to help my father, not to get drunk!"

"That's a pity," Simon replied, shining his lantern around the room. In one corner he saw that rats had helped themselves to a bag of flour, as a faint white trail led along the wall to where other bags of ground meal were stacked — basic gray linen sacks cinched with black cord. Stooping down, the medicus ran his finger through the dust. He stopped short. The powder was light blue in color and had a sickly sweet odor. He suspected the meal had already begun to mold in the dampness down here.

Simon followed the trail of dust until he came to a place along the wall where a sack had been torn open lengthwise. A half-dozen dead rats were lying on a mountain of flour, their bellies distended. Evidently the rodents had gorged themselves to death. As Simon nudged one of the cadavers with his shoe, he noticed footprints in the flour.

The footprints came to an abrupt halt in front of the wall. One of them —

All of a sudden he was startled by a rumbling from the room directly above them. The medicus ran to the hole where they'd entered the room and looked up. The darkness at the mouth of the well looked blacker to him now than before. He heard a splash, as if someone was filling one of the large kettles with water.

"What's going on up there?" Magdalena whispered, letting the apples fall to the ground.

"We'll find out soon enough," Simon replied, scrambling up the rungs of the ladder.

When his head struck something hard above him, his worst suspicions were confirmed. Someone had covered the mouth of the well with one of the large kettles from the boiler chamber and was now filling it with water.

Desperately Simon pushed against the copper base, but the kettle was already so full that it wouldn't budge, and they could hear the sound of ever more water pouring into the massive container. The sound of water pouring finally stopped, only to be followed by a crackling and wisps of smoke that penetrated the gaps between the kettle and the walls of the well.

"Fire!" Simon cried. "Someone pushed the boiler over the hole and lit the wood! Help! Somebody help us!" He pounded desperately against the bottom of the kettle, though he knew no one could hear them up above.

No one but whoever's setting the fire, he thought.

In the meantime the first tendril of smoke had grown to a dense and acrid cloud that was filling the entire shaft of the well. Coughing, Simon applied his shoulder to the kettle with all his might, but in vain. He couldn't get a good foothold on the slippery rungs. He nearly plunged headlong down the well and threatened to take Magdalena with him, who by this time had clambered up the rungs behind him.

"Damn it!" she shouted. "This is pointless! We can't both push against the kettle at the same time. Let's go back down and see if there's a way to escape through the water. Perhaps it connects with the well in the yard!"

"And if it doesn't?" Simon wheezed. He was hardly visible through the thick smoke above her. "Then we'll both drown like rats in the canal! No, there has to be another way!"

He pushed once more against the base of the copper kettle, but it was like trying to move the wall of a house. If only the kettle hadn't been filled with all that water!

The water?

Then an idea came to him. He drew his stiletto and jammed it repeatedly, in short, sharps jabs, at the bottom of the kettle. The metal was very hard, but after a while he managed to poke a tiny hole in it so a thin stream of water trickled down. Simon kept jabbing at it, and the stream became broader until a flood of warm water soon poured down over him and Magdalena. Once more he pressed his shoulder against the kettle, and now, finally, it budged! He continued pressing until the veins on his temples stood out and the smoke made him gag. With a crash, the heavy vessel finally tipped, and heavy smoke poured into the well.

"Let's get out of here!" Simon shouted as he climbed up the last few rungs. Coughing and struggling for breath, Magdalena followed. The boiler room was already filled with thick, caustic smoke, and Simon kept bumping into walls like a blind man until he finally stumbled on the door to the bath chamber. The medicus screamed as he touched the glowing-hot door handle; tiny shreds of his flesh stuck to the metal, hissing. In desperation Simon kicked down the door and stumbled into the large room where the bathtubs and wooden partitions were already ablaze. Someone had knocked over the oil containers, and waist-high flames rose from glistening puddles around the room. Simon was about to run toward the main entrance, but Magdalena grabbed his shoulder and held him back.

"That door is most certainly locked," she gasped. "And anyway, the guard is probably still there. We have to get out through the back again!"

With burning eyes and lungs practically bursting with pain, they staggered toward the rear window, which fortunately was still open. Simon pushed his way through the opening and landed hard on a pile of rubbish. Pain shot through his right ankle. Beside him he could hear Magdalena groaning loudly. She struggled to her feet and ran through the inner courtyard and down the narrow lane. All she wanted was to get away from this inferno. Simon could hardly stand now—on top of everything else, he'd sprained his ankle. When he turned around again, he could see the fire had already spread to the attic, and the roof timbers had started crashing down behind him. The flames licked at the neighboring houses like the tongues of malevolent spirits.

Somewhere nearby an alarm started to ring.

• • •

The old night watchman Sebastian Demmler smelled the fire before he saw it—a faint odor in his nose at first, then stronger, more biting, coating his palate with an acrid taste and awakening his worst fears. Demmler had lived through the great fire during the war and remembered the conflagration quite vividly from his childhood. Two entire city neighborhoods had been reduced to ashes back then, and the cathedral had just barely been spared. He would never forget how the townsfolk screamed as they leaped from their burning homes.

Demmler had been a night watchman for decades, and when he smelled this fire, his infallible instinct told him that such a time had come again. He took one step around the next corner to see the home of the murdered bathhouse owner blazing now like a gigantic torch. Three other buildings had already caught fire. This close, everything was lit up as brightly as on Easter night when they set bonfires to drive away the evil winter spirits. Demmler could feel the heat singeing the hair on his bare arms. Stepping back a few paces, he sounded the alarm with his little bell.

"Fire!" he shouted. "Fire in Weißgerbergraben! Help! Help!"

By now alarm bells in the nearby Scottish church were also ringing, and screams came from all sides. Demmler watched people run out of their front doors toward the burning bathhouse with buckets, tubs, and even entire barrels of water. In front of the house lay a watchman's lifeless body, buried slowly in the burning timbers crashing down. Residents of the neighboring buildings sought to save their homes from the fire by splashing buckets of water at the walls, but in vain, as the liquid vaporized on contact.

Demmler continued to sound his alarm, holding the stained sleeve of his coarsely woven coat over his mouth so as not to breathe in too much smoke. Where were the guards from the Westner Quarter? It was high time for them to show up in their new fire wagon with its hoses. For at least five of the buildings, however, it was already too late. This far into the summer, a single bolt of lightning could set an entire village on fire, and when a thatched roof started to burn, the fire could eat its way to the ground floor in no time at all. The old night watchman had seen too many buildings go up in flames like funeral pyres.

Only now did it occur to Demmler that there hadn't been any thunderstorms in the last few hours. He was by nature a bit slow-witted, but he nevertheless mulled this over as he continued ringing his bell and watching the other citizens attempt to extinguish the fire. Had someone once again failed to properly bank their fire for the night? But it was past midnight now, and who would be cooking at this hour? What else might have caused the fire?

As he pondered that question, Demmler noticed a figure dashing out of the little alley alongside the bathhouse. The figure was dressed in black, so all Demmler could make out was a dark shadow disappearing around the corner. Two other figures—a man and a woman—came staggering out of the same alley a short time later, and this time Demmler got a better look. The man was short, with delicate features, and wearing broad trousers and a tailored jacket like the ones young dandies wore. In the light of the flames Demmler could see a black Vandyke beard and a black head of hair to match. When he caught sight of the woman, he nearly gasped—she was clearly a beautiful woman, but in her simple gray dress, her bodice stained, and her face blackened with soot, she truly looked like the bride of Satan.

The bride of Satan?

Demmler wasn't an especially superstitious man, but the raging fire, the flickering shadows, and this soot-covered witch awakened terrible fantasies in him. Besides, wasn't Satan said to be petite and vain, with a weakness for the fair sex? Trembling, Demmler leaned back against the wall as the two figures turned into a side street just a few steps from where he stood. He tried to get a better look at their faces, but the only th.ng he was able to remark before they disappeared in the darkness was that the young man was limping.

The mark of Satan—the devil's cloven foot! Holy Mary, Mother of God, help me!

The night watchman crossed himself and swore he would say a hundred rosaries if Satan didn't drag him away first. He heard a final rasp and cough; then they were gone. His heart pounding, Demmler resolved to report everyth_ng to the head of the guards the next day. He would tell him exactly what the devil and his woman looked like, even if Demmler doubted such a description would be useful.

Presumably, by then, the Prince of Darkness would have assumed a different form.

Coughing and gasping, Simon and Magdalena pushed open the door to the Whale and came face-to-face with about three dozen astonished guests. A moment before, a boisterous mood had prevailed in the room—laughter, singing, and the clinking of mugs as toasts were made—but now the room fell as silent as a cemetery.

Nervously the medicus checked Magdalena and himself for any outward symptoms of a contagious disease. And only then did he notice with horror that they were both completely covered in soot. The white linen shirt Simon had put on that morning had taken on the color of burned wood and was now dotted with so many burn holes that the fabric was almost fall_ng apart. Ashes clung to Magdalena's matted, charred hair, and only her eyes shone brightly from her sooty face. Bewildered, the guests could only stare at them.

"There's . . . a fire down in the Weißgerberg-aben," the medicus blurted out breathlessly. "We tried to help but the fire was just too great. We . . ."

His last words trailed off and were drowned out in the immediate uproar. Guests who were stone drunk just a moment ago now jumped up, shouting all at once; some attempted to crowd through the door where Simon and Magdalena still stood, forcing the pair back through the doorway, where they stared out at the bright glow of fire in the western sky over the city. Bells were ringing everywhere now, and when Simon heard what sounded like the angry buzz of a swarm of bees, it took him a few moments to realize it was, in fact, the collective sound of a thousand screaming voices.

Oh, God, is that really the fire that started in the bathhouse? he thought. *How many houses are on fire now?*

He tugged at Magdalena's sleeve. "Let's go and get some water. Looking the way we do, we might be suspected of having something to do with the fire."

Magdalena nodded. She cast one last horrified glance back at the city skyline, silhouetted now against the bright orange blaze, then returned with Simon to the tavern. It had almost entirely emptied out, except for the Venetian, who was still sprawled out near the stove, just as they had left him hours ago. Silvio Contarini, whose curly black wig had slipped and was hanging crookedly across his forehead, looked besotted now. Alongside him three men were dozing, their heads resting on playing cards that floated in a puddle of wine in the middle of the table.

"*Ah, la bella signorina* and her valiant companion!" he purred. "What happened? You look as if you've only narrowly escaped your own funeral pyre."

"We — we've had an accident," Simon said crossly, nudging Magdalena forward. "If you don't mind, we'd like to go and clean up a bit."

"You must cleanse yourself *internally.*" Grinning, the Venetian pushed a jug of wine across the table. "Chilled Malvasia. That will rinse the ashes from your mouth."

"Some other time. The lady is tired." Tapping Magdalena on

the behind, Simon was about to head upstairs when he met the
lady's furious stare and realized he'd gone too far.

"The *lady* can still decide for herself," Magdalena snapped.
"Perhaps the *gentleman* declines the offer of a glass of wine, but
the *lady* would be pleased to relax and have a drink."

Pulling away from Simon, she smiled at the Venetian. "A sip
of wine would be just the right thing, thank you."

"*Certo!*" Solicitously, Silvio nudged one of the drunken card
players onto the floor so gently he didn't even wake up. "You'll
find no better medicine in all of Regensburg," the Venetian continued. "And no better place to forget your troubles." He pointed
to the empty seat.

Magdalena dropped down on the bench and helped herself
to a tumbler of wine. The moment the first drops ran down her
throat, she felt the alcohol's exhilarating but calming effect. After
the fire and the attempted murder, and after inhaling all that
smoke, she badly needed a glass of wine.

"But . . ." Simon tried one last time, before Magdalena's eyes
flashed, silencing him. With a shrug, he hobbled up the stairs.

"Is your *piccolo amico* angry at me now?" Silvio asked after
the sound of the footsteps had died away. He refilled Magdalena's glass. "I'm sorry if I've offended him."

Magdalena shook her head. "Oh, don't worry . . . he'll calm
down again." Then she picked up a cup of dice and shook it.
"The loser gets the next round. Agreed?"

The Venetian smiled. "*D'accordo.*"

Dawn was breaking already, and Jakob Kuisl's thoughts still tormented him. Memories plagued him, billowed through his mind
like poisonous plumes, and try as he might, he couldn't dispel
them. He shut his eyes, and his thoughts drifted back to the past
. . . *the scent of gunpowder, the screams of the wounded, the blank
eyes of the dead he tramples as he marches across the battlefield with*

*his two-handed sword. For ten days they have laid siege to Magde-
burg, and now Tilly orders the attack. Heavy artillery roars from bar-
riers the sappers have erected, and massive cannonballs crash into and
breach the city walls. Jakob and the other mercenaries run screaming
through the streets, slaughtering anyone who crosses their paths. Men,
women, children . . .*

*Little Jakob came of age in the war. He became a double merce-
nary—receiving twice the usual pay of ten guilders a month standing in the front line for Tilly. His colonel awarded him a master's
diploma for his use of the longsword, but mostly Jakob fights with a
katzbalger, a shortsword designed to be thrust into the opponent's gut,
then twisted to slice open the intestines. Jakob still carries his two-
handed sword on his back to terrify the enemy and win the respect of
his own people.*

*Meanwhile word has gotten around that Jakob is the son of a
hangman. That lends him a certain magical aura, even among his
comrades. A hangman is a shaman, a traveler between two worlds.
When Jakob needs money, he sells pieces of gallows rope, forges bullets that never miss, and sells amulets that make their wearers invincible. At eighteen years of age he is a bear of a man. The colonel has
already promoted him to the rank of sergeant, since he kills better
than most. Silent, quick, impassive, just as he learned from his father.
His own men fear him; they follow his commands and lower their
heads when he passes by, and they admire him when he stands at the
front, shoulder to shoulder with them, and engages the enemy.*

*And yet, when the battle is over, he stays on the smoking field
among the twisted, bloody bodies and he cries.*

There is a reaper, Death's his name . . .

*Jakob left Schongau to escape the bloody work of an executioner.
To refuse his inheritance, to escape his father's fate.*

But God put Jakob back in his place.

A sound outside his cell roused the hangman from his reveries.
He'd lost all sense of time, but the chirping birds told him it was

morning now. The cell door had fallen slightly ajar, and the outline of a man appeared there. In the light of a flickering torch on the wall behind him, the figure's shadow grew to superhuman size until it seemed to fill the entire room.

Kuisl knew who was standing before him before the man had uttered even a single word.

6

THE PROSTITUTE KATHARINA LAY ON THE FLOOR
of her dark chamber, trying to deflect the hairy hand that crawled
over her face like a spider. She felt it clearly, but each time she
opened her eyes, she could see nothing but her own hand, which
she then held up close to her face, wiggling her fingers until they
turned, before her eyes, into black insect legs covered with fine
hairs. Katharina screamed and pounded her forehead with her
fist again and again.

"Go away; why won't you just leave me alone?"

But the spidery legs crept down her neck and over her
breasts, where they lingered.

The creak of hinges stirred her from her hallucination. The
hatch in the door slid open, and a tray of bread, dried pears,
honey, and eggs was pushed through it. Katharina took the tray
and flung it against the wall so hard the eggs broke and viscous,
yellow yolk oozed down the whitewashed walls.

"Eat this stuff yourself!" she screamed. "I want out of here!
Out, do you hear me? Out!"

The eye stared down at her coldly.

"Let me out!"

Silence. The eye unblinking.

"You goddamned devil!"

Katharina ran to the door and jammed her finger through the hole, but the eye had disappeared. She kicked the heavy wooden door and hammered it with her hands, screaming louder than she ever had before.

"Bastard! Devil! Satan!"

She had the sudden premonition that someone was standing right behind her. She spun around. Had she seen a shadow dart across the floor? A hunchbacked man, with a tail and two horns on his head. Katharina put her fist in her mouth and bit so hard that a tiny trickle of blood ran across her pale, translucent skin.

I'm going mad . . .

Her screams fading to a whimper finally, she slid down against the wall and onto the floor next to the overturned tray. She could still smell the enticing aroma of fresh bread, and now, reluctantly, she was hungry again.

She reached for the bread and clawed hastily at the white interior, stuffing the still-steaming pieces into her mouth. Perhaps the shadows and visions would vanish with her hunger.

In her ravenous fit she didn't notice the eye once again staring down at her as she ate. Cool and pitiless.

"I've been expecting you," Kuisl said as he rose from the floor of the cell and extended his hand to his visitor. The ceiling was so low that for the hundredth time he knocked his head against it. Early-morning light streamed through the open cell door. "It's only too bad it's under circumstances such as these."

The Regensburg executioner's grip was viselike, and his rough, callused hand felt like the bark of an old oak. And though Kuisl's knuckles cracked, he barely registered the pressure.

"The ways of the Lord are inscrutable, dear cousin," his visitor replied. As was the custom among hangmen, he addressed Kuisl as he would a member of his own family. Most executioners were distantly related in one way or another.

The Regensburg hangman stepped aside and motioned for Kuisl to follow him out into the dimly lit corridor of the cell block, at least as far as his chains would allow.

Philipp Teuber was a good bit shorter than the Schongau hangman, though considerably broader. His body was like a wine barrel with a disproportionately small head screwed on top. He was all sinew and muscle; the Heavenly Father seemed to have forgotten a neck when he created Teuber, leaving the excess material for his arms and legs. In the middle of his round, full face stood two astonishingly cheerful, sparkling eyes surrounded by countless freckles. All of this was framed by a full reddish-blond beard and an untamed head of hair. The Regensburg hangman was about forty years old, but his whole appearance gave the impression that he was considerably older.

"Next time let me know when you're planning a visit to Regensburg," Teuber said. "Then I'll be sure to make a place ready for you in my house and have Caroline cook up some salted smoked meat."

Kuisl grinned. "It certainly would be better than the slop they serve here."

"You don't know my Caroline." Teuber flashed a row of dark yellow teeth as his face contorted into an expression the Schongau hangman could interpret only as a smile.

For a while they were silent. Then Teuber found his voice again, massaging his knuckles as he spoke. "It's looking grim for you, cousin. The inquiry is over, and the city council wants to start your trial today. If you don't confess, they'll send you down to me in the torture chamber, and you know what happens from there . . ."

They both fell silent again; only the buzzing flies circling over the chamber pot could be heard.

"Why did you come?" Kuisl finally asked.

"I guess I just wanted to have a look at you," the Regensburg executioner said, "before I put the thumb screws to you, that is. It's not every day that I'm asked to break one of our own on the rack, let alone draw and quarter him." He looked deep into Kuisl's eyes. "The president of the council says you're responsible for killing your sister and brother-in-law. Is that true?"

Kuisl cleared his throat loudly and spat on the ground. "What do you believe?"

Teuber's eyes probed Kuisl's body as if searching for witch's markings or suspicious liver spots under his clothing.

"How many people have you executed, Kuisl?" he finally asked.

The Schongau hangman shrugged. "No idea. Maybe a hundred? Two hundred? I've never tallied them up."

Teuber nodded approvingly. "Then you know at least what I'm talking about. Look here." He pointed at his round, bearded face. "With these two ears of mine, I've heard more people whining that they were innocent than you have dumb farmers in Schongau. And these two eyes have seen more gallows birds hanged than there are fat priests in Rome. Regensburg's a big city, and almost every month I have to hurt someone. And with time, Kuisl—" He sighed, looking at the inscriptions on the cell walls. "—with time, one learns to tell who's innocent and who's not," he continued. "Believe me, most are guilty."

"Don't preach to me," Kuisl growled. "I don't give a damn what you believe or think. There's nothing you can do once the higher-ups have made up their minds."

Teuber nodded. "Right you are. Though it's not nice when you have to lay the noose around someone's neck while the real murderer's still running free."

"So, you do believe I'm innocent?"

The Regensburg hangman looked deep into his colleague's eyes once more. "The city out there's like a ravenous beast," he said finally. "Every day she devours a few more, and it isn't always the villains."

Kuisl sensed his interlocutor was keeping something from him.

Teuber hesitated before attempting a smile again. "I'll make you a proposal, Kuisl. Confess the double murder at the trial and you'll at least spare yourself the torture. If they decide to break you on the wheel, I'll crack your neck first with an iron rod so you won't feel the rest. And if they decide to draw and quarter you instead, I have a nice little potion that will carry you off gently before your limbs are ripped from their sockets. How does that sound?"

Kuisl spat on the ground again. "It wasn't me, and I'm not going to confess. Now get out of here, and do what you have to do. No doubt you have a few pincers to polish."

Teuber took a deep breath. "You're too damn proud, Kuisl. Believe me, you'll end up screaming, and then all the pride in the world won't do you a damn bit of good. I've seen it all too often."

"By God, I tell you, it wasn't me!" Kuisl exploded. "Even if you break every bone in my body. If you believe I'm innocent, then help me or keep your damned mouth shut."

Teuber shook his head. "I won't do anything that will bring ruin upon my family."

"Rubbish!" Kuisl snapped. "Bring me some paper and something to write with—that's all I ask. And when I'm done, take the letter to my daughter. That shameless woman is gadding about somewhere in Regensburg."

"A farewell letter—I understand." Teuber nodded. "I'll have to ask the aldermen for permission, but that shouldn't be a problem. Where do I find your daughter?"

Kuisl laughed. "Who are you? The Regensburg hangman or his apprentice? Ask around, keep your eyes peeled, but do it in secret so that you don't drag my Magdalena along to the gallows, too."

Teuber stroked his beard. "Fine, Kuisl," he said finally. "I'll help you because you're one of us and because I don't think you're stupid enough to get yourself caught standing between two corpses with your dagger drawn. But as of tomorrow morning, I'll have to hurt you all the same."

"Let that be my concern." Kuisl had already returned to his cell and settled down on the floor. "Now leave me in peace, Teuber. I need to think."

The Regensburg executioner grinned as he slowly pulled the dungeon door closed. "Kuisl, Kuisl," he said, wagging his finger impishly. "I've seen many a sinner before I tortured them — anxious, raving, screaming, praying — but you are by far the boldest. I can't believe that will last long."

With a crash, the door slammed closed and darkness descended over Jakob Kuisl.

A huge beech tree waved in the breeze above Simon. Its green leaves were rustling, birds were chirping, and the hum of insects filled the air. The medicus took a deep breath and felt at one with the world. All at once, however, a raucous noise clashed with the pleasant sounds of nature. A huge saw seemed to be cutting through the ancient beech trunk. The tree began to sway, its enormous bulk threatening to topple at any moment and bury the medicus beneath it. Then, with an earsplitting crash, the beech fell to the ground. Simon awoke with a shout, opened his eyes, and realized he'd just been dreaming. No blue summer sky spread out over him, only the sooty ceiling of the Whale. Yet the noise persisted.

Chrrrrrrrr . . . Chrrrrrrrr . . .

Simon turned on his side to see Magdalena lying on her back next to him, snoring like a drunken sailor. He wrinkled his nose. The hangman's daughter not only snored like a drunken sailor, she smelled like one, too. Her mouth gaped open, and a thin string of saliva had formed in one corner. The medicus couldn't help but grin. If the little Venetian could see his *bella signorina* now, he'd most certainly put an end to his inappropriate advances.

The little Venetian?

Simon sat bolt upright and looked over at the other side of the bed. With relief, he found he was alone with Magdalena. Nevertheless, the very idea that Silvio might have taken Magdalena off to bed while Simon slept like an infant beside them made his blood boil. Who could say what had already happened between them? Simon knew from personal experience what men were capable of when alcohol turned girls silly and weak. He closed his eyes and suppressed his worst imaginings.

When he climbed out of bed, he felt a sharp, throbbing pain in his right ankle. In a flash he remembered how they'd broken into the bathhouse the night before and just barely made it out of the cellar. Cursing softly, he rubbed some arnica ointment on his swollen foot and wrapped it gently in a piece of linen. Then he dressed carefully. Fortunately, in the bag he managed to hang on to after being chased through the market square he discovered a fresh shirt and an only slightly soiled jacket among his medical instruments. He'd already given his trousers a quick, makeshift cleaning the night before with a cake of bone soap; he'd have to wear this outfit around Regensburg for the coming weeks—a prospect especially distasteful to him when he thought about how smartly dressed the little Venetian had been last night. Simon could only hope the bruises on his face had faded some in the meanwhile. In his present condition he no doubt resembled a small but dangerous barroom brawler.

Without waking the snoring Magdalena, he hobbled out of the bedchamber and down to the empty taproom, where he poured himself a mug of watery beer and found a bowl with stale pieces of leftover bread. Two drunks were dozing on the bench by the stove, and in front of a steaming pot sat someone Simon didn't recognize at first: the Regensburg raftmaster they'd met the day before at the docks.

Karl Gessner smiled and motioned for Simon to come closer. "Ah, the little quack from the raft landing! I knew we'd meet again soon." His smile immediately vanished. "Excuse me, I'm tactless. Right now you surely have enough worries." He pushed the pot of lentil soup to the middle of the table so the medicus could help himself.

"This double murder . . . was a heavy blow for the both of us," Simon said hesitantly, dunking his bread crust into the soup. "We thought perhaps Hofmann would give me a job. We—we wanted to make a new beginning here. And then this!" He shook his head. "Now they've taken Magdalena's father into custody because they think he's the one who did it. Ludicrous!"

"And? What do you intend to do now?"

Simon dunked another crust of bread into the soup and swallowed before answering. "For the time being we'll probably stay here at the Whale. There must be some way to prove that Magdalena's father is innocent. The murder in the bathhouse . . ." He paused because he wasn't certain how much he could trust the raftmaster. After a while he continued in a soft voice. "You seem to know your way around Regensburg. Do you have any idea who might be behind this murder? Something about it just isn't right. Yesterday the house was still under guard, as if it concealed some dark secret. Do you have any advice?"

Gessner shrugged. "You both certainly know by now that the house burned to the ground last night. If there was anything of interest inside it, nothing is left of it now."

"But did you happen to hear anything before that?" Simon was grasping at straws. "Something, anything, that might exonerate Magdalena's father?"

Gessner looked at him sympathetically. "I'm sorry. As raftmaster, I sit on the Outer Council, but with regard to the bathhouse murders I'm more or less powerless. That's someone else's responsibility. I know only that Kuisl will be put on trial soon." Falling silent, he poked around in his soup, but Simon could sense that Gessner had something more to say.

"The world is unjust—that's just the way it is," the raftmaster finally added. "And often it's the wrong man who suffers. But it's not for you to decide what's good and what's right."

Simon looked at Gessner and frowned. "What are you trying to say?"

Gessner sopped up the last bit of soup with the bread and stood up. "Be sensible and don't get mixed up in things that are much bigger than you may be prepared to handle. There's still time for you to return home. A good day to you, and greetings to your girl." He placed a copper coin on the table, bowed slightly, and disappeared out the door without another word.

Simon sat for a while thinking about Gessner's final words. What did the raftmaster mean when he said they oughtn't to get mixed up in things? What was going on behind the scenes?

Finally the medicus gave up. If there was anything to be learned, he certainly wasn't going to learn it sitting here all by himself in some cheap tavern. With a sigh, he headed out the door and into the blinding morning sun. He needed fresh air to get his mind off all this, even if his foot was still throbbing. The events of the previous day kept running through his mind. Obviously someone had set a trap for the Schongau hangman—but who, and why? Their visit to the bathhouse yesterday made it clear that someone had already been there looking for something. And that someone had followed them, locked them in the basement, and tried to burn them alive.

Because they had discovered something?

But what? Why had this arsonist tried to kill them, and what did any of it have to do with the plot against Magdalena's father?

Simon was so lost in thought that he didn't notice he was approaching the cathedral square. Only after a few people had

bumped into him did he think to look up, startled. A few peddlers had already set up their stalls, and people were streaming
out of the main church portal after early mass. Many, wearing
serious expressions, were deeply engaged in discussions about
the fire the night before, which had destroyed so many homes
and possessions. Each one seemed eager to outdo the others with
gruesome, detailed stories. Simon couldn't help but think of an
old saying:

Blessed Saint Florian, spare our house, and let the others burn . . .

A sudden rolling drumbeat sounded across the plaza, and
two guards approached from the right. One beat an old military
drum while the other held a parchment in his hand. As a crowd
began to gather, one guard broke the seal and began to read in a
booming voice.

"Citizens of Regensburg, lend an ear! A fire broke out in our
beautiful city yester eve, destroying three dozen homes. Lives,
too, were lost. Some say the devil himself is among us, along with
his playmate." Whispers went up among the crowd as it eagerly
awaited the grisly details. After a dramatic pause the crier continued:

"The city council is pleased to inform all citizens that it was
not the devil who set the fire, but it was a foul deed by the hand
of man. Two persons who were seen in the Weißgerbergraben
area last night are under strong suspicion of having committed
this dastardly crime. Persons in question are a little man with a
limp and a black-haired girl in a coarse linen skirt . . ."

What followed was a detailed description of the two sus-
pects. The blood drained from Simon's face as he listened. The
watchmen were looking for him and Magdalena! Perhaps someone in the cathedral square had recognized him already! In fact,
a murmur was passing softly through the crowd, and someone
rose and approached the guard, pointing toward the river in the
approximate direction of the Whale. Simon backed up against
the wall of a nearby building and peered into a small lane behind

it that branched into a labyrinth of ever-narrower alleys. A curious older couple stared down at him from a second-story window, so in spite of his swollen ankle, Simon hurried away, limping. He had to warn Magdalena as fast as possible! He only hoped it wasn't already too late.

Just as he was about to turn the corner, he heard a voice call to him from a dark entryway: "If it's through these alleyways you want to escape, let me guide you, or someone will surely cut your throat even before the watchmen can arrest you for arson."

An old man clad in rags emerged from a stone portal. In the dim light it took Simon a few seconds to recognize him as Hans Reiser, the blind beggar he'd healed the day before in the market square. Reiser's stubbled, pockmarked face beamed at Simon with joy. He wore a patch over his right eye, but he gave Simon a cheerful wink with his left as he ran up to the medicus with arms wide open.

"I prayed to God to send you back to me again so I could repay you!" he cried out. "Thanks be to God. He heard my prayers!"

"Very well," Simon said in a low voice. "Perhaps some other time. At the moment — well, I'm in a bit of a hurry, so please — "

Reiser put his finger to his lips and grinned. "You needn't tell me a thing. I know the authorities are looking for you and the girl because of the fire last night."

"But how do you — ?" Simon began.

"We beggars know many things," the old man interrupted in a whisper. "The citizens think of us as lice-infested, starving sacks of shit who hold out our hands for every last little coin, but in reality we're even more powerful than many of the guilds." He winked. "We even have our own guild house, though it's not as fine as those of the merchants, bakers, or goldsmiths. Believe me, nothing remains a secret from us for long."

"You promise you won't betray me?" Simon whispered.

Horrified, Reiser shook his head. "Betray my savior? Am I Judas? I wish to help you!"

"But what do you intend to do?"

"For starters, we'll make you and your girl disappear," the beggar replied. "I've already sent a messenger to the Whale who will bring the girl back here to us. I also know you're trying to find out more about the bathhouse murders. Let's see if we can't find some clues for you."

"But that's impossible!" Simon cried. "We haven't told anyone about the murders!"

"Aha, and your conversation in front of the bathhouse just yesterday morning?" Reiser grinned. "In Regensburg the walls have ears, and most of those ears belong to us beggars. Now quit standing there gaping like a fool and come along!"

Tentatively Simon followed. "Where are we going?"

Reiser looked over his shoulder to glance at the medicus with his good eye. "To the king of the beggars. I've already spoken with him, and he will grant you an audience."

"Who?"

Reiser giggled. "The head of our guild, you idiot! Consider yourself lucky; it's a great honor to be invited to see him. And now hurry along before the guards catch up!"

Shaking his head, Simon followed the old man through the labyrinth of narrow lanes and trash-filled courtyards. Darting shadows reminded them that they weren't alone.

Magdalena awoke to a knocking sound that grew louder and louder. She was about to get up and give the troublemaker pounding at the door a slap when she realized the noise wasn't coming from outside but from her own head. She slowly opened her crusted eyes but closed them again as a flash of light seared her pupils. Next she attempted a cautious squint as she groped for a pitcher of water she vaguely remembered had been standing beside the bed when she collapsed the night before. She grabbed it and poured its cold contents all over her face. Spluttering, she shook the water from her hair. The pounding had stopped, but a sharp ache still coursed through her head in waves.

The thought of waves immediately made her nauseous.

Suppressing the need to throw up, she tried to remember the night before. The fire in the bathhouse, their narrow escape, their arrival at the Whale . . . After Simon went up to bed, she'd loitered down in the tavern, showing the men there that holding one's liquor wasn't just a matter of body weight or years of training. The Kuisls were widely known for their cast-iron stomachs. The night before any execution, Magdalena's father would get so drunk that Anna-Maria Kuisl had to lug him cursing and hollering into their bed in the wee hours of the morning. Yet odd as it was, without fail the hangman would be on the scaffold stone-cold sober just a few hours later, even if he did look rather grim — an appropriate appearance for a hangman on execution day. Magdalena had apparently inherited this particular brand of stamina from her father. Throughout the night she had also chewed on some of the bitter black coffee beans Simon so adored, and that had no doubt helped her stay at least partly sober.

Simon?

"Simon? Are you there?" she croaked, feeling the empty bed beside her. She sat up with a moan. The medicus must have gone downstairs already. She wondered whether he was still angry at her for having stayed down in the tavern the night before, drinking with the little Venetian. She opened the door and staggered down the stairway, her head pounding. The scent of frying bacon permeated the air, causing her stomach to rumble loudly. In the main room she saw the tavern keeper behind the bar, helping herself that very moment to a slug of brandy.

When she noticed Magdalena, she pointed back to the

kitchen. "If you're looking for your drinking friend, he's in there," she mumbled, taking another swig. Magdalena nodded and went back to the smoke-filled kitchen where wood logs glowed inside an enormous hearth.

"Simon?" she asked, but the only person in the room was Silvio Contarini, who stood by the hearth, whistling as he stirred the contents of a clay bowl with a spoon. Next to him bacon was sizzling in a pan, permeating the room with a delicious aroma.

"Ah, you slept in?" The Venetian winked at Magdalena and pointed toward the pan. "I'm preparing an old Italian home recipe, *uova strapazzate allo zafferano,* scrambled eggs with saffron and bacon. Would you like some?"

Although Magdalena had intended only to inquire about Simon, now that she saw the golden egg hissing in the pan, she couldn't resist.

She nodded, and her mouth began to water. "A little . . . yes."

With the elegance of a royal cupbearer, Silvio set a plate, knife, and spoon down in front of her on the table and poured diluted wine from a carafe.

"The perfect cure for a hangover," he said with a grin, serving her a hearty portion of eggs and bacon. "Guaranteed to bring the color back to *una ragazza*'s cheeks. I hope it doesn't bother you if I call you *una ragazza,* a girl. You look so — well, so young."

"I just turned twenty-four this summer, if you want to know exactly. You needn't bow when you talk to me." Magdalena smiled to herself as she stared at the plate in front of her. She had never before seen a scrambled egg so yellow — it gleamed like liquid gold. "It looks wonderful," she said.

"The saffron does that," Silvio explained as he noticed Magdalena's astonishment. "I like my eggs to shimmer like the sun."

"But isn't saffron very expensive?" she asked, perplexed. The hangman's daughter knew that saffron was weighed against gold and therefore merchants often mixed powdered marigolds in with it, despite the high fines for being caught doing so.

The Venetian shrugged. "Food, drink, love . . . There are some things one doesn't scrimp on."

Magdalena nodded, her mouth full. "Stlishish!"

"Perdonate?"

She wiped the grease from her lips. "I said it's delicious. Have you ever heard of a drink called coffee?"

Silvio nodded. *"Caffè!* Ah, a wonderful brew! If I'd known you'd drink it, I would have gone to the market — "

"That's not necessary," she interrupted. "Simon always has a few beans with him. I was only thinking it would go well with the egg." Suddenly she remembered why she'd come to the kitchen in the first place. She took one more bite before she stood up. "Have you by chance seen Simon?"

"Your grim little *amico?"* Silvio rolled his eyes theatrically. *"No.* Can't you forget about him for once and, *come si dice,* chat with me for a bit?"

Magdalena smiled. "Didn't we do enough of that yesterday?" She turned to leave. "But as far as the coffee and the saffron egg are concerned . . . we'll do that again some other time. Thank you very much."

The little Venetian raised his hands to heaven. "You're ungrateful! At least allow me to accompany you. I know my way around this city almost as well as I do Venice. Surely I can help you find your friend."

Magdalena sighed. "All right, then; you don't give up, do you?"

Together they walked out into the dazzling daylight. The sun was so blinding that Magdalena didn't notice a figure crouched in an alley across the street, studying her every move.

Simon had to be careful not to lose sight of Hans Reiser. His guide kept turning ahead of him into little alleys, each one narrower than the one before, often groping his way along the walls with his hands; evidently Reiser still hadn't completely regained his sight. The medicus begged him again and again to keep the patch on if he didn't want to risk losing his sight again, but each time the beggar waved him off.

"Who will lead you to the beggar king, then, huh?" he replied as he continued to stumble through the dark alleys.

They clambered over piles of excrement, rotten vegetables, and animal carcasses piled up in the narrow streets. The sun almost never shone in these close, suffocating back alleys, and the stench was so bad that Simon had to hold his jacket sleeve over his mouth and nose to keep from vomiting.

"Aren't we almost there?" the medicus asked repeatedly, but the old man replied only with an impatient shake of his head.

"I want to make sure no one is following us," Reiser whispered. "It's better if we go around in circles a few times. If the guards learn where our guild house is, the beggar king will have my hide, personally."

"But how can you have a secret guild house that nobody knows about in a city as crowded as this?" Simon asked. "It's not like there are just a few of you, and the guards must certainly have noticed already."

"You might be surprised."

Reiser giggled and continued groping his way along the walls of the houses. Cursing, Simon followed, wading as best he could with his sprained foot through the muck, which was nearly ankle-deep in places.

The beggar came to a halt in the middle of a deserted, shadowy back courtyard, put his finger in his mouth, and whistled. Another whistle answered from somewhere nearby. Reiser pushed aside a rotting two-wheeled wooden cart to reveal a crumbling stone staircase underneath. Simon guessed that at one time a house had stood on the spot where the courtyard was now, and all that remained were these steep, deeply worn steps into the cellar. Grinning, Reiser made an imperceptible bow.

"The beggars' guild house! Please, after you, Your Honor."

Simon headed down reluctantly. After they'd gone just a few yards, he was surprised to see a line of torches along the walls, lighting the way. The walls themselves appeared to consist of weathered stone blocks painted with strange runes. It took a while for the medicus to recognize the markings as Hebrew, which he was unable to decipher.

After another dozen or so steps the stairway ended in a wide, sloping corridor that led further down into darkness. As they walked, they passed a number of forks and intersections, where they encountered ragged, stooped forms. Reiser seemed to know most of them and greeted them warmly. As the people shuffled past, it occurred to Simon that many of them walked with a limp, and some wore bandages over their eyes or hobbled along on just one leg with the help of crutches. All their faces were gaunt, and all were dressed in rags. Simon sensed he was walking step by step down into an abyss, past a virtually endless procession of the miserable and the sick.

Just like in Dante's underworld, he thought. *Good heavens, just what have I gotten myself into?*

The crowd of the downtrodden grew denser, whispering and pointing to the young medicus as he passed by, until at last Simon and his escort came to a low, vaulted torch-lit room. The flickering flames cast a mournful light on a ragged group gathered around an enormous oak table rotting in the middle of the cellar. The room was a good fifteen paces long and just as wide. On the ground and in the corners more people were dozing, gnawing on chicken bones, and quarreling loudly over jugs of wine. There was a strong stench of old men, urine, straw, and smoke, which emanated from wood fires in the room's corners and alcoves. The conversation that filled the room died quickly as Reiser entered with the medicus. Simon could feel dozens of eyes on him. He took a deep breath and returned the stares.

What is this place? A robbers' den? Or a vestibule to hell?

A figure emerged from the group of men sitting around the

table. In contrast with the others' ragged garb, he was clad in a threadbare jacket inlaid with golden threads and knickers that, though frequently patched, still looked magnificent. He wore a wide-brimmed hat over long gray hair, and an equally gray full beard framed his wrinkled face. As he began to speak, light flashed in Simon's eyes, and he realized that the man's upper incisors were made of pure gold! Thin wires seemed to attach these treasures to his brown gums and adjacent teeth.

"Is this the itinerant doctor who cured you?" the beggar asked, pointing to Simon with his scarred right hand.

Reiser nodded. "It is he! He's the one who stuck the needle in my eyes as carefully as if they were his own. This man is divinely gifted—"

"Or a devil and an arsonist!" interrupted the other with a grin. "At least if we were to take the word of those fools in the city guards." He turned to Simon, scrutinizing his now almost faded black eye, the last sign of the brawl in Schongau. "So," he asked, "are you the devil? From the looks of it I think you're probably just a little devil that Beelzebub roughed up."

The men sitting around the table roared, but Simon kept silent. Once more he cursed himself for having come here at all. How could these crazy, tattered creatures help him discover anything about the bathhouse murders? He was already cautiously backing away from the scene when the leader raised a finger, and immediately the laughter ceased. With a grin, he extended his hand to Simon in greeting.

"How rude of me," he said almost obsequiously. "I haven't even introduced myself. People call me Nathan the Wise. I am the king of the Regensburg beggars, the lord of the realm of night and of this wonderful guild house."

He made a theatrical gesture, causing some of the bystanders to break out in laughter. The beggar allowed Simon some time to look around before continuing.

"What you see here is only a small part of our own little city.

Above us the Jewish ghetto used to stand, but my brothers in the faith were driven out of Regensburg many, many years ago. Their buildings were razed, their homes robbed, and all that remains are these marvelous underground passages, which serve today as our guild halls."

He indicated the dirty men dozing along the walls in back, his gold teeth sparkling in the torchlight. "Every beggar in Regensburg belongs to our guild," Nathan continued. "Every day he pays his dues and in return is granted protection, a roof over his head, and care when he is sick. We are our own masters, just as in any guild."

The beggar king led Simon over to the large oak table where an extremely odd group of people was assembled. The circle of scruffy-looking men, with their wine jugs and moldy scraps of bread, looked like a surreal distortion of a respectable dinner party. "Perhaps you've made the acquaintance of one or another of my city councilors in the course of the last day or so." Nathan pointed at a man beside him who wore a monk's tonsure and a pale gray habit. "This, for example, is Brother Paulus. He collects alms for our church, even though he's never taken a vow and knows more about boozing and whoring. And this one here," Nathan said, pointing to a stooped, toothless little man with a thin line of drool hanging from his contorted mouth, "this is Crazy Johannes, who will do a Saint Vitus' dance for you on request. For an additional charge, of course . . ." With easy grace, the humped little man transformed himself into an upright, rather normal-looking person, bowing slightly as he extended his hand to the stranger.

"As for yours truly," Nathan said, "as a Jew, I did my time on the traveling stage many times over in my youth. I've since retired from the exciting life of a vagabond." He sighed. "I have so much paperwork now that barely a moment remains to go begging. Ah, well . . . You helped one of us out," he said, presenting

Simon with a glass of red wine, "so we'll help you in return. What can we do for you?"

Simon took a sip of the wine, which tasted remarkably good.

"The murder of the bathhouse owner and his wife that took place a week or so ago," he said finally. "Do you know who's behind it?"

Nathan's expression turned to disgust, and his golden incisors glinted. "A nasty, far too bloody matter, as I've heard tell. They locked up a hangman from out of town right off, but you already know that. Whether he's the one responsible or not I couldn't say." He leaned toward Simon and said in a conspiratorial tone, "I know only that the bathhouse owner was involved in some truly risky business."

The medicus frowned. "What do you mean?"

"Well, Hofmann had dealings with a handful of men who have quite powerful enemies in the city. Quite powerful, indeed, including members of the Inner Council."

"I don't understand what you're insinuating. What could a bathhouse operator—"

The beggar king interrupted him with a sigh, rubbing his hands together. "I see we'll have to fill you in a bit. But my advice comes at a price."

"I have no money."

Nathan gestured dismissively. "Money! Always money! As if there were nothing more valuable in this life!"

"What do you mean, then?" Simon asked cautiously.

Nathan turned serious, folding his hands as if in prayer and peering intently at the medicus. "Oh, come now, doctor, I'm sure you don't think I invited you into our hideout without thinking twice if I didn't have something specific in mind for you." He gestured at the crumpled figures lying in the corners of the great hall. "Reiser says you're a talented doctor. As you can see, we're surrounded by suffering here—folks with infected legs, flies all over them laying eggs in their flesh. Some are so tormented by open sores, festering boils, and wracking, incessant coughs that they're practically going mad. I want you to examine each and every one of them. At no cost, of course. Clearly, none of them can afford a doctor."

"And if I refuse?" Simon asked quietly.

The beggar king cleared his throat. "Not a good idea. Tomorrow morning when the hangman comes around to collect animal carcasses and garbage, he just might find a human cadaver, too. I've heard wonderful medications can be made from human fat and skin. The apothecary shops pay a fine penny for them."

"It doesn't really appear I have a choice, does it?" the medicus replied, his face ashen.

Nathan smiled. "Doesn't really look that way. From what I've heard, you're looking for a job now anyway. We can offer you room and board, as well as some information you just might put to use. That's a good deal, as far as I can see!"

"But who will guarantee that you won't do away with me anyhow, in the end? After all, I know where your hideout is."

Nathan clutched his chest in horror. "*Mon dieu!* You're speaking to the beggar king! Who can you trust in this snake pit Regensburg, if not me?" His voice took on a sly tone. "Naturally, the offer stands only if I can trust you to keep your mouth closed."

Simon sighed. "All right, then, I'll do it. What other choice do I have? Now tell me what you know."

The beggar king shooed the others away from the table and leaned so close to Simon that the medicus almost choked on his foul, garlicky breath.

"Hofmann was one of the *freemen,*" Nathan whispered, then paused dramatically before continuing. "A secret society of tradesmen and simple citizens who are revolting against the Regensburg patricians. The freemen seek to reassert the rights of the guilds, but the moneybags are fighting them tooth and nail. A few years back a couple of their leaders were hanged for inciting a revolution, and since then the freemen have operated underground, where they're making plans to break the power of the patricians, by force if necessary, and even, it's rumored, with the support of the Elector and the bishop."

"The bishop?" Simon asked, astonished. "But the church —"

Nathan rolled his eyes. "God help us! What kind of one-horse town do you come from? This is Regensburg!" He shrugged. "I can see I'll have to elaborate a bit. This is a Free City, ruled by the patricians, who are answerable to no one but the kaiser. *Capito?* But Regensburg is also a diocesan town — the seat of a bishop — and an important city in the Electorate of Bavaria. Thus, both the Elector's and the bishop's seats are here, and the bishop even has the power to write and enforce his own laws. For us beggars this complicates things, since we have no idea who will cut off our hands or drive us out of the city. Isn't that so, my friends?"

He winked at the other beggars, eliciting laughs of approval.

"Both the Bavarian Elector and the Regensburg bishop want to increase their influence in the Free Imperial City," he continued. "Any means is admissible in their attempts to undermine the kaiser's and the patricians' authority. It's quite possible, therefore, that the nobles are working in consort with the freemen. Is that clear?"

"Of course," Simon replied after a while, though he really hadn't understood much of it. "But what does that have to do with Hofmann?"

"Didn't I just tell you? Hofmann was a freeman," the beggar king said. "Perhaps he knew something that would be damaging to the patricians, just as the Reichstag was about to meet. So they . . ." He swiped his fingers across the front of his neck. "And they did the same to his wife. And so as not to arouse suspicion, they arrested this hangman — as a scapegoat."

"That . . . seems possible," Simon replied. "Or perhaps not. One would have to speak with these freemen first."

Nathan laughed. "Speak with the freemen? Who do you think they are? Washerwomen? They'll be strung up on the gallows should anyone discover who they are. Nobody can find them."

"Not even you?"

The beggar king thought for a moment. "Perhaps. But what will that accomplish? Perhaps they'll decide *you* are the real murderer. Believe me, the order to kill Hofmann came from high up in the city council. It's better for you and your girl to go back to your little Schongau. You are too young to die."

Of course. And I leave my future father-in-law to rot and die in Regensburg, Simon thought. *Magdalena would never forgive me for that.*

"I want to speak with one of these freemen," he said finally. "Make that happen, and I'll get to work right away on my patients."

The beggar king nodded. "As you like. I'll see what I can do. By tonight we'll know more." He snapped his fingers, and Reiser approached with two other beggars. "I'll have your things and your girl brought here, too. It's best if you stay with us for a while, not just because of the matter of the fire, but whores have been disappearing from the streets without a trace as of late." His golden incisors gleamed again as he began to laugh. "Consider yourselves my guests of honor for the time being."

Simon got up and went over to a corner of the hall for a better look at his patients. Fat blowflies swarmed around him as if to welcome their new guest.

What Jakob Kuisl missed most was not the sunlight and fresh air but his beloved tobacco. The guards had confiscated his pack, which held his tin of the sweet-smelling weed.

The hangman sighed and wet his parched lips with his

tongue. He'd paid a sinful price for the tobacco he ordered specially from Augsburg, and he needed it the way others needed
drink — especially when he had to think. He missed his beloved
pipe now more than ever, as he lay on the cold floor of his cell,
hands tucked behind his head, staring out into the darkness and
thinking back on the trial that morning, which had made him
realize just how hopeless his situation really was.

They had hauled him up to the office, where they read the
short indictment to him. The president of the council and the
three lay assessors were convinced of his guilt from the outset: his
presence at the crime scene and the will spoke volumes. Only
Kuisl's confession was needed to settle the matter. But the Schongau hangman insisted on his innocence and, in the end, even
grew combative. Finally it took four bailiffs to bind his hands
and feet and drag him back to his cell.

Ever since, Kuisl could do nothing but wait to be tortured.

He was certain they'd begin soon. The matter demanded immediate attention — the accusations were too grave. Once the
torture began, it all depended on him to determine how long it
was before the sentence was pronounced and the execution carried out. The longer he held out, the more time Magdalena and
Simon would have to find the real killer.

There is a reaper, Death's his name . . .

The hangman slapped his forehead but couldn't get the accursed song out of his mind. He felt as if he were imprisoned
twice over — once in this cell and again in his head. The memories were the prelude to his impending torture.

For the hundredth time his gaze wandered over the cell wall,
stopping at a bright, smooth spot in the wood. At Kuisl's request
the Regensburg executioner had left the small hatch in the door
open so that the scribbling on the walls was legible in the faint
light. Kuisl recognized some old sayings and names, among
them a handful of initials. Only a few prisoners were able to
write out their whole names, and some signed their confessions

with simple crosses or initials. Often their last messages to the world were therefore just a few lines or circles carved laboriously into the wood.

Kuisl read the letters and dates: D. L., January 1617; J. R., May 1653; F. M., March 1650; P.F.K. Weidenfeld, anno domini 1637 . . .

P.F.K. Weidenfeld, anno domini 1637?

Kuisl stopped short. Something clicked in his head, but it remained vague and diaphanous. Was it possible?

P.F.K. Weidenfeld, anno domini 1637 . . .

Kuisl was trying to concentrate when he heard footsteps coming down the corridor. The bolt was pushed aside, and a guard entered.

"Your grub, you dog." The soldier shoved a wooden dish toward him in which unidentifiable lumps were floating around in a grayish sludge. The man stood, waiting. When Kuisl didn't react, the bailiff cleared his throat, then dug around in his nostril with his finger, as if a fat worm hid up there.

"The hangman told me I had to bring the bowl back right away," he said finally. "And the paperwork, too."

Kuisl nodded. The Regensburg executioner had sent him some paper, ink, and a quill, as promised. Until that moment Kuisl didn't know what he wanted to say to his daughter. He hoped to give Magdalena some ideas about where to look for clues in the city, but the damned memories of the war kept distracting him. Now, all of a sudden, he had a vague thought, possibly just a whim, but Kuisl felt it worth looking into, since time was so short.

"You'll have to wait a while," the hangman said. He took out the pen and ink and hastily scribbled some lines on the paper while the guard drummed his fingers impatiently against the door. Finally Kuisl folded the paper and handed it to the bailiff. "Here. And you can take back the soup, as well, and feed it to the pigs."

The hangman kicked the steaming bowl, sending it flying into the corridor where it landed with a clatter.

"Later, I promise you, you'll beg for a bowl of soup half as delicious as that one," the surprised guard replied. "You'll whimper and pray when Teuber has at you with the red-hot pincers. You'll die like a dog, you goddamned Bavarian, and I'll be standing there, front and center, when he breaks you on the wheel."

"Yes, yes, very well. Now get moving," Kuisl snarled.

The guard swallowed his rage and turned to leave. Just as he was about to bolt the door, Kuisl looked up at him.

"Ah, and if you intend not to deliver that letter," the Schongau hangman said casually, "I'll see that Teuber breaks your bones, slowly, one after the other. He doesn't like it, you know, when people try to put one over on him, you understand?"

The door slammed shut and the bailiff withdrew. Once again Kuisl's thoughts turned back to the war, the murder, the pain. He stared at the initials on the wall and tried to remember.

P.F.K. Weidenfeld, anno domini 1637 . . .

The letters gnawed at his subconscious — eliciting just an inkling, an image from long ago, from another life.

Men's laughter, the crackling of burning rooftops, a long, excruciating wail, then silence . . . Jakob Kuisl is holding the sword in his hand like a scythe.

Kuisl knew that if he had just an ounce of tobacco, the pipe would bring the image into focus.

In the corridor the guard squeezed the folded letter in his hands and cursed softly. Who the hell did this damn hangman think he was? The king of France? Never before had a prisoner spoken to him like that. Particularly not one about to face the gallows. Just what was this Bavarian thinking?

The bailiff thought back on Kuisl's threat. The Regensburg executioner had indeed sent him to the cell to pick up that damned letter. No doubt Philipp Teuber was to pass the paper along to some relative—a last farewell from a condemned man seeking consolation and perhaps even a few sweets to uplift him at the end. That wasn't uncommon.

But what the executioner didn't know was that someone else had promised the bailiff a tidy sum for the privilege of having a look at the letter before handing it over to Teuber.

Grimacing, the guard secured the paper in his jacket pocket and strode out into the city hall square, whistling. As arranged, the stranger was waiting for him in Waaggässchen Lane in front of the constabulary. The man was stooped and, despite the summer heat, had turned up his coat collar to obscure his face. No one would be able to say later who he was; even the guard who delivered the letter in exchange for a bag of coins would be unable to describe him afterward. The man's movements were too fluid; his appearance, nondescript. Everything about the man was calm and collected, except for his eyes.

As he hastily unfolded the letter, they seemed to glow with hatred.

At once a cold smile spread across his face. He took out another piece of paper and wrote a few lines on it, then tucked the real letter inside his coat.

"I'll pose a riddle for the girl and this quack," he whispered, more to himself than to the guard. "Sometimes you have to throw the dog a bone so it has something to chew on. Or else they'll draw some very stupid conclusions. Here, give this to Teuber." With these words, he handed the guard the paper.

As the bailiff entered the bustling city hall square, he felt such relief that he dropped his first few coins right away on a strong glass of wine. Nevertheless, cold shivers ran up and down his spine.

There were people you wouldn't wish on your worst enemy, and then there were people you wouldn't wish even on an alleged murderer.

7

Do you have any idea what might be detaining your *amico*?"

Silvio Contarini gallantly offered Magdalena his arm. She hesitated briefly, then permitted the Venetian to guide her through the narrow Regensburg streets, while she towered over him by at least a full head.

"To be honest, no," she said uncertainly. "Perhaps he just stepped out for a breath of fresh air. I only hope nothing has happened to him."

"Didn't you say he likes coffee?"

Magdalena nodded. "Coffee and books, yes, he's addicted to both."

"Then I know a place where Simon could be."

Silvio guided her along a wide paved avenue with oxcarts and coaches rumbling by. He took care to walk on the outside to shield her from the occasional splashes of mud from passing vehicles. The hangman's daughter couldn't help but smile. This man was a real cavalier! She decided to allow herself to feel like a lady, at least for a short time—to give herself over to the care of her diminutive companion.

The two soon reached the city hall square. Across from the magnificent building was a neat, freshly whitewashed gabled tavern, complete with glass windows, bright stucco work, and a newly thatched roof. Patricians in wide trousers and tight-fitting jackets paraded in and out alongside brightly made-up women with broad-brimmed hats and elaborate pinned-up hair. Silvio tugged at Magdalena's sleeve impatiently, pulling her toward the entry.

"You don't believe they'll let me in, looking the way I do!" she whispered, horrified. "I look like a despicable chamber-maid!"

The little Venetian examined her uncertainly. "That may in fact be a problem. Take this," he said, handing Magdalena his cloak. Only then did she notice that a small dagger was tied to the inside of the Venetian's belt, its handle inlaid with rubies.

"Later we'll find you some clothes more befitting your beauty," Silvio said resolutely. "We can't allow a *bella signorina* such as yourself to go running around looking like a washer-woman."

Magdalena pulled the wide, much too warm woolen cloak over her shoulders until only her face and her shaggy black hair were visible. She could only hope that no one noticed her shoes. She also realized that after the previous night's events, she no doubt had a strong odor.

"Oh, God, I can't do it . . ."

"Come now!" Silvio nudged her into a lavishly furnished taproom filled mostly with elderly gentlemen and flashy young ladies at their sides. The Venetian found two free seats and snapped his fingers. Shortly thereafter a smartly dressed maid appeared, curtsied several times, and set out a steaming pot of coffee and two cups.

"As far as I know, this is the first coffeehouse in the whole German Empire," the Venetian said, filling Magdalena's cup to the brim. "At least I haven't heard of any other. And believe me,

I would hear of it." He slurped his coffee with great relish. "If your friend likes coffee as much as I do, it's quite possible we'll find him here."

Magdalena gazed around at the guests, though she knew in advance it was wasted effort. "Nonsense!" she whispered. "How would Simon know about a place like this?"

The Venetian shrugged. "So be it. At least the two of us will have the chance to get to know each other better now."

Chuckling, Magdalena took a sip of the hot, stimulating drink. "Admit it, you set this up. You wanted only to be alone with me."

"Would that be a crime?"

The hangman's daughter sighed. "You are incorrigible! Very well, then," she said, leaning toward the Venetian, "tell me about yourself. Who are you?"

"Let's just say I'm a frequent and welcome visitor in this establishment who is always scrupulous in paying his rather exorbitant bills," Silvio said with a grin.

Then all at once he turned serious. "This city is very important for *la vecchia Venezia,* you know," he continued. "Especially now, when representatives from all over the world are here to discuss how to proceed against the Turks." He raised his cup solemnly. "The Moslems gave us this marvelous drink, but unfortunately they now wish to do us the dubious honor of exporting their religious beliefs as well. Thus, my *doge,* in his infinite wisdom, decided I should take up residence as his permanent ambassador in the mightiest city of the German Empire."

"*You* are the representative of Venice in Regensburg?" Magdalena gasped. "But why then are you living at the Whale? I mean—"

Silvio waved her off. "No, no, I don't live there, but—*come si dice*—the boredom!" He rolled his eyes theatrically. "All these smartly dressed ambassadors, always the same old conversations . . . politics, ugh! This evening, again, I have to host another mindless ball." He folded his hands as if in prayer. *"D'una grazia vi supplico, signorina!* Lend me the honor of your company at the ball. It will be my only light in these dreary hours! You'll be my salvation!"

Magdalena's laugh stuck in her throat.

Seated at a neighboring table, a man in a dark cloak had pulled his hood far down over his face, but the hangman's daughter was nevertheless certain he was watching them. In contrast to the other guests, the stranger was neither smoking a pipe nor drinking coffee. He sat hunched over as if he had become part of his chair.

"The man opposite us," she whispered, assuming an icy, forced smile to avoid attracting suspicion. "Don't look now, but I believe he's watching us."

Silvio raised his eyebrows. "Are you sure?"

"Believe me, I've had some experience with this sort of thing as of late. This stranger isn't the first one in my life I've caught spying on me."

"If that's the case . . ." The Venetian ambassador placed a few silver coins on the table and slowly stood up. "We'll leave by the back door. If he follows us, we'll know you're right."

Nodding and greeting people amiably as they passed, the pair crossed the crowded room to an inconspicuous door. They hurried up a staircase to the floor above, ran along a dark corridor, and finally arrived at an opening so tiny it seemed more like a window than a door. Silvio pressed the door handle and nudged Magdalena onto a ramshackle balcony. A ladder led down into a back courtyard stacked with old boxes and barrels. The Venetian put his finger to his lips and pointed down. Magdalena sensed Silvio was well acquainted with this escape route. Her heart pounding, she began to descend the rungs behind him.

Just as they reached the courtyard below, the man in the black cloak appeared on the balcony above them.

Their pursuer's hood was still pulled over his face as he

leaned over the railing and stared down at them like a hawk eyeing its prey. Magdalena had no time to get a closer look, though,
for in the next instant he was clattering down the ladder. The last
several yards he took in a single leap, spreading his cloak around
him like wings. When he landed, he turned and started toward
them quick as a shadow in the dark, a long, narrow rapier glint-
ing in his hand.

Screaming, the hangman's daughter jumped behind a stack
of crates. From her hiding spot she watched in horror as Silvio
drew his dagger and attacked the man. The stranger was poised
for attack, his rapier in front of him, ready to lunge at any moment. Without the slightest sound, Silvio rushed forward, his
dagger circling in the air, but the man skillfully sidestepped him,
then thrust upward with his rapier, slicing the silk sleeve of Silvio's coat clean off.

Magdalena was shocked to see blood dripping from the tear
in Silvio's jacket and noticed he was limping slightly. It couldn't
be long before the stranger attacked straight on and plunged his
rapier into Silvio's chest.

And I'll be next . . .

Frantically, Magdalena looked all around until her gaze fell
on a huge wine barrel, almost as big as a man. She ran toward it
and shoved as hard as she could. It seemed empty. Groaning, she
pushed against its damp staves with all her strength until it teetered a moment, then tipped over with an earsplitting crash. It
rolled toward the stranger, gaining momentum, as he cursed and
struggled to jump aside. But it was too late — the barrel bowled
him over and burst against the opposite wall, sending splinters
flying through the air.

The stranger remained motionless on the ground for a moment, then struggled to get up, groping for his rapier, which had
landed nearby. Before he could pull himself together, however,
Silvio had seized Magdalena by the arm, drawn her to the door
of an adjacent house, pushed her inside, and slammed the bolt

closed. When the stranger arrived at the door, he started banging furiously on the other side.

"Grazie!" the Venetian panted. "That was close. You were right; we really were being followed."

They ran through the house and out the front door into the street, where the usual traffic—wagons, coaches, and pedestrians, all chattering and complaining—streamed by slowly. It was as if the pair had entered a wholly different world oblivious to the danger lurking just a few steps away. Most people didn't even turn to glance at them.

At the next street corner Silvio stopped, leaning against the wall of a house to examine the rip in his jacket and the blood on his finger, which he eventually licked off.

"Santa Madonna!" he panted. "What in the world have you gotten yourselves into?"

The hangman's daughter shrugged. "Unfortunately I don't know that myself. I don't know who this man is or why he's following us. He may be the very same man who last night . . ." She hesitated.

"What do you mean, last night?"

Magdalena shook her head. She decided for the time being not to tell the Venetian anything about their break-in at the bathhouse. "Nothing. I'm probably just seeing ghosts."

Silvio touched the bloody tear in his jacket again.

"Well, it certainly looks like I need a new jacket." He grinned and pointed at Magdalena. "And so do you."

The hangman's daughter looked down at herself. She'd lost Silvio's cloak in the scuffle. The coarse linen dress she wore underneath was tattered, and her bodice was splattered with red wine. She looked as if she'd just barely escaped a barroom brawl with a gang of prostitutes.

"You're right," she replied, embarrassed. "But I have no money to—"

"Money? What would you need money for?" Silvio interrupted. "We'll find something nice for you at my house. After all, you can't possibly come to my ball this evening dressed like that."

Magdalena hesitated. "You . . . you really meant what you said before? You want me to come to this ball with you?"

"*Mama mia!* Why should I be joking? A beautiful woman such as yourself is an honor to any house!"

The hangman's daughter had to laugh. Almost all the parties she'd ever been to were held in the market square or empty barns. There were sausages, sauerkraut, and beer, and maybe a few musicians to strike up a dance tune with a fiddle and castanets. The prospect of attending a *ball* was about as foreign to her as an invitation to paradise.

"I'm—I'm afraid I'll make a terrible fool of myself," she stammered. "I wouldn't have the first clue what to say—or do . . ."

"Your smile says more than a thousand words. Now, say you'll come!"

The chivalrous Venetian took Magdalena by the arm and led her through the streets of Regensburg as if she were the elegant wife of some wealthy patrician.

A few moments later the hangman's daughter stood with Silvio before a massive building on the bustling cathedral square. Above an entrance as wide as a barn door two stories rose up, each with a row of shimmering glass windows. The bays, pointed arches, and dormer windows gave the building the appearance of a noble country estate, while its size almost reminded Magdalena of the Regensburg city hall.

"This mansion belongs to *you?*" Her jaw dropped.

"No, no!" Silvio demurred. "I only rent quarters here. A patrician was kind enough to make some rooms available to me. Come along. I'll give you a tour. There's a room in here I know is certain to be to your liking."

The Venetian led Magdalena through the entryway into a shadowy courtyard. Fragrant flowers and plants sprouted from marble tubs and buckets along the gravel walkway, and wild ivy grew along the stone walls. Gaily colored birds chirped from a silver cage hanging from one of the rafters. Magdalena felt as if she had entered the Garden of Eden. She timidly fingered some kind of bright yellow fruit that dangled from the sun-dappled branches of a tiny tree in a corner.

"Those are lemons," Silvio explained. "In my homeland they grow in every garden. I'm trying to grow them here, but the German winter will kill most of them." He sighed. "When it's cold, I grow especially homesick for my beloved Venice."

"Do all the houses in Venice look like this?" Magdalena asked cautiously.

Silvio smiled. "I have friends there who decorate their villas in gold and travel in silver gondolas. I myself consider that pretentious, but if you live in the richest city in the world, it's tempting to begin to think you're better than others. Follow me, please."

They ascended a broad staircase flanked by banisters and marble statues. In contrast with the stench of the city, the air here was redolent of fruit and mint and filled with the soothing sounds of a harp nearby. Curious, Magdalena stopped in front of a small sculpture of a handsome young man smiling down at a girl holding an apple out to him. Inside his marble back, rats, snakes, and toads scurried about.

"What *is* that?" she asked the Venetian.

Silvio shrugged. "A gruesome statue. I should have it removed—it doesn't fit in very well among the beautiful figures here. But come now. I'll take you to my dressing room. It would be preposterous if we couldn't find something suitable there for *la bella signorina.*"

At that moment a maid approached them with a neat bundle of fresh laundry. She curtsied and lowered her gaze, and though Silvio seemed not to have even seen her, Magdalena could feel the maid assessing her out of the corner of her eye. Her mouth pinched, she turned up her nose in disgust. Apparently she considered Magdalena just another of the loose women whom the master of the house liked to bring up to his room — nothing more than a cheap streetwalker.

I can't really blame her, Magdalena thought, hurrying past the girl as quickly as possible.

They passed through an ivy-covered gallery, coming at last to a chamber with high, almost church-like windows. At first Magdalena was blinded by the light streaming through them, but once her eyes adjusted to the brightness, a small miracle appeared before her eyes.

Am I dreaming? How is this possible?

It seemed there were at least a dozen other women standing beside her, all around the room, all with the same dirty linen dress and the same disheveled black hair. Dumbstruck, Magdalena realized she was in fact staring at herself. The walls were covered by six-foot mirrors, which reflected her image over and over. Between the mirrors enormous, ceiling-high wardrobes were flung open, full of frilled garments, velvet gowns, and other splendid clothing. Some clothes had been carelessly tossed off and draped across a round table in the center of the room and over the chairs and gleaming inlaid wooden floor. Each piece must have been worth more than Magdalena's father earned in an entire year.

"I beg your pardon," Silvio said. "I wasn't sure yesterday what they — that is, what I should wear, so I made a bit of a mess. My servants were supposed to have cleaned this up."

Magdalena didn't even seem to hear him. She stepped into the middle of the room and began to spin around, faster and faster. Around her, dozens of Magdalenas danced, an entire dancehall full of her, which seemed to go on and on, a dancehall where she alone was the centerpiece.

The only mirror the hangman's daughter had ever seen was the small, cloudy pocket mirror her father had given her mother when they were first married. The old thing was cracked, and it distorted Magdalena's face so much that she'd put it aside in disgust more than once. Until today all she'd ever seen of her own face and body was what she'd been able to make out in her quivering image in the waters of the Lech. Now she could see for the first time what others saw when they looked at her. Awestruck, she passed her fingers through her black hair, tracing the lines of her eyebrows, nose, and lips.

Am I beautiful?

The hall of mirrors in the Venetian's house was the most impressive thing she'd ever seen.

"I ordered these mirrors specially from Venice," Silvio explained, dreamily passing his hand over a smooth silvery surface near the door. "Nowhere else on earth can you find such quality. I'm happy you like it," he exclaimed, clapping his hands together. "But now we must find something for *la bella donna* to wear."

The Venetian strode confidently toward one of the wardrobes. As he opened it, Magdalena, who was having difficulty tearing her eyes away from her reflection, saw countless women's dresses hanging in neat rows, as if they'd never been worn before—broadly tailored skirts, narrow bodices with puffy sleeves, dainty pointed bonnets, cloaks lined in ermine, and velvet jackets with fur collars.

"I have lady visitors on occasion," Silvio admitted. "And I've ordered some clothing so that the *signorine* can feel at home here with me. Take your time to look around, and perhaps you'll find something that suits you."

It was clear to Magdalena who the *ladies* were who visited this house, and she was tempted to turn back right then and there and return to the Whale. Simon would certainly be waiting for her, and this farce would finally come to an end.

On the other hand . . .

Magdalena's gaze wandered back to the mirrors and to the

magnificent colorful clothing. Never in her life had she seen such skirts, much less worn anything so splendid. Perhaps she and Silvio could just send a message to Simon, telling him that all was in order and she would be back at the Whale that evening — or first thing in the morning at the latest. Why shouldn't she browse around here a while and enjoy herself?

But then her conscience intruded on the fantasy. What about her father then? He was languishing in his prison cell while, like a cheap streetwalker, she let herself be tempted by the prospect of a night of dancing in the arms of Regensburg's rich and powerful men. How could she possibly . . . ?

Powerful men?

Magdalena turned to the Venetian ambassador.

"Tell me, Silvio. At the ball tonight," she asked casually, "just who will be in attendance?"

The Venetian grimaced. "Ah, the usual. Some ambassadors; some merchants with their overweight, garishly made-up wives; some important patricians from the city council. If the city treasurer shows up, I'll probably have to waste some time discussing Regensburg's ridiculous mountain of debt. *Madonna,* it's going to be an awful bore!" He fell dramatically to his knees in front of Magdalena. "Please! Grant me the favor of your company, I beg you!"

Magdalena tilted back her head in cool deliberation. "Who knows? That may not be such a bad idea after all," she said. "Surely these gentlemen have some interesting things to say."

With only the briefest hesitation, the hangman's daughter reached for a small red velvet jacket with lace sleeves trimmed in fur, and a wide hoop skirt. Why not marry pleasure and practicality? If anyone could help her father, it would be the men attending the ball tonight. She might even discover a few things that would otherwise remain strictly the province of the innermost circles of power.

Magdalena's gaze wandered back to the mirrors. Before her stood a proud woman, a woman determined to fight.

Tooth and nail, if that's what it came to.

Shortly after nightfall Nathan finally had news from the freemen.

All day Simon had been cooped up in the catacombs, caring for his destitute wards. He'd scraped scabies from the heads of three children, splinted a trembling old man's broken leg, treated countless festering wounds with arnica, prepared packets of dried blueberries for patients with dysentery, and pulled five rotten teeth. After all that work he was more than a little happy when the beggar king finally informed him the freemen were willing to meet him down at the raft landing that evening. Nathan agreed to act as his guide, with the qualification, however, that Simon would continue treating Nathan's crew of beggars, at least for the next few days.

The two set out, passing again through winding subterranean corridors before finally emerging into the cellar of a tavern. The tavern keeper didn't seem surprised in the least when Nathan and his companion appeared out of thin air from behind a stack of firewood. Simon had to assume the man was aware of the beggars' secret passageways, but when he asked Nathan about it, the beggar king replied in a disparaging tone.

"When there isn't enough room in the hospitals or among us down below, some of my brothers have to stay in lousy inns like this one," he said as they stepped out the back door. "That bastard demands two hellers a night, and if they don't pay, he reports them to the city." Then he winked. "But if the bailiffs throw us out at Jakob's Gate, we come right back in by Peter's Gate. Just like fleas—there's no getting rid of us."

From this point on, the moon illuminated their way through back alleys. No shadows leaped at them from dark corners, nor were any suspicious sounds to be heard behind them. The medicus felt certain that with Nathan by his side he was as safe as if he were home in bed in Schongau. Only a lunatic would dream of attacking the beggar king.

As they walked along, Simon thought constantly of Magdalena. When the beggars brought his medical instruments to him that morning from the Whale, they also brought news that Magdalena had disappeared. Simon was still not seriously concerned, though; it was quite possible she'd just gone out for a stroll around town or was making inquiries into the murders. Just to be sure, a beggar was waiting to intercept her at the Whale and bring her to the catacombs. But what if the guards had already seized her for arson? And then, of course, there was another possibility that tormented Simon . . .

Perhaps she was simply out enjoying herself with that puny Venetian!

This wasn't the right moment to indulge in jealous fantasies. Before them the wharves of the raft landing appeared. He was surprised to note that the place was deserted at this hour except for some rats scurrying across wet planks. From the Danube the stench of fish, algae, and decay rose up, and alongside the wharves, rafts bobbed lazily up and down in the water, their boards creaking as the languid current knocked them against the posts. Music and laughter echoed from nearby taverns—evidently the sounds of raftsmen tying one last one on before early-morning departures.

Just then they heard footsteps behind them, and Nathan pulled Simon out of sight behind some wine vats stored on the dock waiting to be loaded onto another vessel. A few moments later two guards came into sight, halberds slung over their shoulders, unshaven faces exhausted and red from alcohol. They looked bored as they sauntered from one end of the landing to the other.

"Damn it! What are they doing here?" the beggar king cursed. "I don't pay the outlandish bribes so these village idiots can come around here looking for a lady friend for the night!"

Simon looked at him with consternation. "You paid a bribe —"

"Why else do you think it's so quiet around here?" Nathan interrupted. "Two silver pennies for the pier warden to put his men down for a nap. But just for half an hour, so please be quick!"

No sooner had the two guards rounded the next corner than Nathan took hold of the astonished medicus and, crouching, ran with him toward another group of barrels next to the warehouse. The containers were positioned so that a small passage ran between them, one not directly visible from the raft landing. At the end of the passage they came upon a crate as tall as a man, old and smeared with tar; a tangle of nets spilled out of it. It smelled so strongly of rotten fish that Simon instinctively put his hand over his nose and started to gag. Paying the stench no heed, Nathan raised the lid with a creak.

"Follow me, keep a low profile, and pull the lid shut after you."

Horrified, Simon watched the beggar king pull himself up to the edge of the crate and climb inside. There was a clattering sound, and then only silence. Simon peered inside in disbelief to discover that Nathan was nowhere to be seen.

What the devil . . . ?

"Damn it all to hell, where are you?" The voice of the beggar king echoed strangely from very far away, farther in any case than the crate was deep.

Simon heaved himself over the edge, climbed inside, and closed the lid as instructed. Everything went pitch black at once; the foul odor of fish and guts rose around him as if he'd landed inside the belly of a whale. The medicus felt some matted nets under his feet and, as he groped around, discovered that one hung down farther than the rest. Carefully he crawled forward on his knees, patting the ground beneath him as he went, until he came upon a hole no wider than a man's hips through which the end of the long net dropped. The net served as a sort of rope ladder leading down into bottomless darkness.

Hand over hand, Simon made his way down the slimy rope ladder until he felt solid ground beneath his feet.

In front of him Nathan held a burning lantern in his hand and grinned. "I almost thought you'd gotten yourself tangled in the net like a fat carp," he whispered. "Now come along."

They hurried down a narrow corridor hollowed out of the damp earth that was so low in places Simon had to duck to avoid hitting his head. Here, too, the stench of fish and algae reigned, but a fresh breeze blew in from somewhere in front of them, and water dripped from the ceiling onto Simon's collar.

"An old escape tunnel crossing under the Danube," Nathan explained. "It runs all the way over to the Upper Wöhrd, the island in the middle of the river, and then past that to the north riverbank, where the Electorate of Bavaria begins." He giggled. "The bailiffs are flabbergasted about how we manage to smuggle so many goods across the river when customs are so strict on the bridges. If we wanted, we could clean out the whole city."

The beggar stopped so abruptly that Simon almost ran into him. His eyes glinted coldly, out of place on his otherwise friendly face, and his golden teeth flashed in the lantern light as he whispered.

"If you should ever betray our tunnel, you'd best know that we'll find you. Wherever you are. We treat traitors to our cause to slow deaths. Think of human leather . . ."

"I — wouldn't even dream . . ." Simon stuttered.

"So much the better," Nathan said, and continued walking. "I don't distrust you, but I have to make sure you understand."

Again he giggled, and the medicus followed him with a sigh. Simon couldn't quite figure Nathan out: one minute he treated him like a friend, and in the next his manner was cold and calculating.

Who's to say he's not just leading me into some trap? Simon thought.

When they arrived at the end of the corridor, another rope ladder led up through a narrow shaft. Again Nathan went first and, after arriving at the top, pushed a large black object to the side. Surfacing behind him, Simon recognized it as a rotting wooden fishing boat that lay hidden in underbrush not far from the shore.

The medicus took a deep breath of the fresh night air and looked around. By the light of the full moon he spotted a low-lying grassy island that stretched up and down the Danube. To one side he could make out the Stone Bridge in the moonlight where it connected to the island by a dam. Nearby were several large warehouses and other buildings attached to crumbling jetties that led down to the dark, rushing current. Mill wheels revolved, clattering and squeaking, causing something to pound inside the various buildings like the snore of a mighty giant.

"The mills on the Wöhrd," the beggar king whispered reverentially. "Do you hear that? The sound of the future! It will never cease to astonish me what man is capable of." He pointed at the rattling and whirring wheels that, like enormous machines, cut furrows through the river along the shore. "Sawmills, paper mills, textile mills, and naturally the large grain mill. Do you see the house over there with the gabled roof? The largest mill in all of Regensburg! The freemen are expecting you there. I'll stay here and wait for you."

Simon hesitated. "Why don't you come along?"

Nathan made an apologetic gesture. "They told me in no uncertain terms to stay outside. They're a bit fussy about their anonymity. To be honest, I don't really want to know who they are. It would only bring me grief. Now go before they grind you to bone meal in their millstones." He gave Simon a last wink before he disappeared into a nearby bush.

Once the medicus had looked all around and noticed nothing out of the ordinary, he started walking past piles of logs and wooden shacks toward the towering mill. An enormous water wheel was attached to the front, extending into the Danube and turning with an earsplitting clatter. From inside the building the pounding and rattling mill mechanisms were so loud they drowned out nearly every other sound.

At the back of the building Simon finally discovered a door left slightly ajar. Inside, soft moonlight filtered through tall windows, illuminating sacks of grain, worm-eaten wooden tubs, and old millstones stacked high on either side of the entryway. Narrow paths wound between the sacks and into the dark interior, while farther back a millstone as big as a wagon turned with that dreadful grinding sound. Simon could feel a fine, soft dust beneath his feet as he groped his way along the widest path through the building.

"Hey, is anyone here?" he called out, feeling instantly foolish. Who would ever hear him over all this racket?

Or maybe nobody is supposed *to hear me,* Simon thought with growing fear.

The deafening noise suddenly ceased, and silence reigned in the cavernous room—a silence almost more troubling than the grinding and pounding of the machines. The only thing audible now was the soft sound of grain trickling to the ground.

Simon stopped to reach for the stiletto hanging on his belt. "Whoever you are, come out now! I don't much care for this game of hide-and-seek." He tried to speak firmly, but his voice cracked at the end.

A small light flared up in the corridor on his right and started moving toward him. On his left, too—in front of and behind him—more and more lights materialized. Simon blinked as at least a dozen men with lanterns approached, all of them wearing brown cowls and hoods with only narrow slits at the eyes. Unhurried, they approached the medicus until they'd cornered him between two sacks of grain.

Simon looked around frantically like a trapped animal. There was no escape!

Slowly, ever so slowly, one of the men approached and, once he stood directly in front of the medicus, removed his hood.

Instinctively Simon raised his stiletto. Only at the last moment did he realize that the man before him was no stranger at all.

Chandeliers sparkled, bathing the ballroom in a flickering light. A small band of flutes, fiddles, trumpets, and a harp played a French dance while the ball guests moved in unison. Laughter and chatter filled the room, while a diminutive turbaned Moor passed around jellied hors d'oeuvres and kept the guests' glasses brimming with cold white wine from the Palatinate.

Magdalena leaned against the wall between two tall porcelain vases, observing the festivities in a tight-fitting bodice with a plunging neckline, a red velvet fur-trimmed jacket across her shoulders, and a hoop skirt to match. Her black hair, ordinarily so unruly, was pinned up in a delicate bird's nest, and her feet suffered in tight shoes. Whenever she went to fetch smoked eel or a quince pastry from the lavish buffet, she felt as if she were walking on broken glass, and it was difficult to breathe under the many layers of heavy material. How could all these so-called fine ladies squeeze themselves into such clothing night after night?

Even though Magdalena was less than comfortable, she did seem to make an impression on the men. More than once, one or another patrician or ambassador glanced at her. Silvio made it clear from the outset, though, that the beautiful stranger was under his personal protection, and whenever he could, he tried to be near her, exchanging small talk.

Magdalena quickly realized that this ball was only superfi-
cially about socializing. Its real purpose was politics, and thus
Silvio was busy most of the time discussing business alliances,
foreign exchanges, and, above all, the approaching congregation
of the Reichstag. The patricians and minor nobility flocked to
him like moths to a light. Though most loomed over him by
more than a head, the little Venetian was the focal point of nearly
every conversation. With his wide petticoat breeches, form-fit-
ting jacket, and wavy black hair, he exuded an aura of power that
others eagerly soaked up.

The few women there not only steered well clear of the
hangman's daughter but sent mean-spirited glances her way. In
their eyes Magdalena was just some prettied-up mistress the Venetian had likely picked up on the street. Only Silvio's presence
sheltered Magdalena from their ugly words — a fortunate thing,
as the hangman's daughter would likely have scratched the pale,
made-up faces of any of the fine ladies who dared insult her.

Magdalena sighed and continued sipping from her wineglass
that was almost as thin as parchment. She hadn't learned a single
thing that might help her father, and increasingly she felt like
just some pretty painted doll placed amid vases as decoration.
Just what had she expected? Here she was, nibbling on partridge
wings caramelized with honey while her father languished in
prison! It was time to put an end to this act.

She was about to hurry toward the door when someone
leaned against the wall next to her and raised his glass in a toast.
The elderly gentleman with thinning hair and a pince-nez
seemed strangely out of place in his simple black frock coat and
old-fashioned ruff, especially in the midst of all this finery. Having overheard his conversations with Silvio, she already knew he
was none less than the Regensburg city treasurer. In their negotiations concerning sweet Vin Santo and Venetian ravioli, the
men had mentioned sums of money that took Magdalena's breath
away.

And the very man who had just requested an additional credit of five thousand gold ducats now stood next to her and asked, "Have you tried the sweet almond paste? It's called marzipan. Divine!" The gentleman gallantly filled her glass with wine from a glass carafe.

Magdalena managed a smile. "If I'm honest, I don't care so much for sweets. I'd prefer a decent roast goose."

The treasurer chuckled. "Silvio Contarini already told me you're a real interesting woman. May I ask where you come from?"

"Oh, from around Nuremberg," Magdalena said, picking the first place that came to mind. "A relative of mine is the valet for the Elector's cavalry captain."

"I wasn't aware the cavalry captain had a valet."

"Well, only since very recently," the hangman's daughter explained without batting an eyelash. "His wife always complained that he never took off his boots, even in bed—that he went around looking more like his own horse's groom."

The treasurer frowned. "But doesn't the Elector's cavalry captain live in Munich?"

"He's moved. In Nuremberg there's more—uh—forest for hunting. You understand . . ."

Good Lord, what am I saying? Magdalena thought in despair. *Is there a hole somewhere around here I can crawl into?*

"Hunting can become a real passion. I hunt quite a bit myself." The patrician raised his glass to her with a smile. Magdalena had a growing suspicion the treasurer was toying with her. Had Silvio perhaps told him who she really was?

Or had he learned it from someone else?

As the treasurer continued speaking, he looked absentmindedly out one of the large windows. "Perhaps this cavalry captain just developed a distaste for city life, particularly now in the summer, when it stinks to high heaven and your clothes stick to your body—and then there's the constant, even imminent, danger of fire, as well." All of a sudden he looked at Magdalena straight on. "I expect you've already heard of last night's conflagration?"

The hangman's daughter's halfhearted smile froze on her face. "Of course. Who hasn't?"

"An awful affair." The old man nodded deliberately and regarded Magdalena through his pince-nez like an exotic beetle through a magnifying lens. "The word is that it was set by two arsonists—a man and a woman. We have quite good descriptions of both, and it looks as though the responsibility's fallen to me to deal with this wretched business. As if I don't have enough on my plate already . . . But here, I'm going on and on!" The treasurer instantly transformed into a kindly old man again. "I haven't even introduced myself yet. My name is Paulus Mämminger; I'm responsible for the financial matters in our great city." He made a small, stiff bow.

"Certainly an important job." Sweat was streaming down Magdalena's back now and surely seeping through her bodice. Her desperate attempt to keep up proper formal speech sounded ridiculous, even to her own ears, and she harbored no doubts the treasurer must have seen through her long ago.

Mämminger sighed and sipped from his glass. "At present not a soul in the council envies me this job. The coming Reichstag is costing us a fortune! And alas, I can't find enough suitable lodging for the ambassadors and noblemen!" He shook his head, giving way to a long pause.

"And why has the kaiser summoned a meeting of the Reichstag at all?" Magdalena finally asked in an attempt to keep the conversation moving. "I've heard it's about the war with the Turks. Is that true?"

The treasurer grinned. "Child, where have you been hiding? Of course it is! The kaiser needs money to wage war on his most hated enemy. We don't want those heathens laying siege to Vienna again, do we? So, Kaiser Leopold is passing the collection plate around, and we Regensburgers are stuck with the expense of playing host yet again to spoiled noblemen from all over the empire."

He sighed deeply, and Magdalena nodded in understanding.

"Just yesterday the Palatine Elector's quartermaster came to visit me," he continued, "and His Excellency is insisting on moving here into the Heuport House. But this is the residence of the Venetian ambassador, and he refuses to give up his home for anyone. Perhaps you'd be so kind as to speak with him? Contarini just may listen to you."

"I fear it's a hopeless case." Armed with a plateful of chocolates, Silvio had approached them unnoticed. He now placed an arm around Magdalena's sweaty shoulder and offered her some sweets. "Dear Mämminger, you'll never persuade me to abandon this wonderful domicile," he said with a smile. "Unless *la bella signorina* somehow persuades me to settle in Schongau with her."

Mämminger frowned. "Schongau? What do you mean, Schongau? I thought—"

"I'll leave you gentlemen to yourselves now," Magdalena said, curtsying awkwardly, as if she were a bit tipsy. "The wine has gone to my head—I need a bit of fresh air, I'm afraid." She held her hand in front of her mouth and yawned, then stepped gingerly in the direction of the exit, still deflecting the mean glares of the other women.

Head held high, she strode through the door and swaggered down a broad stairway into the deserted courtyard. Only then did she allow herself to collapse, exhausted, on a bench and take some deep breaths. No doubt the women were all in a tizzy now, gossiping viciously about the clumsy country wench. Outside, here under the stars, she could at least have a bit of peace.

Almost reverently, Magdalena looked around her at this little bit of paradise in the midst of the city. Scattered among the rosebushes and lemon trees were juniper bushes trimmed into geometric figures. As tall as a man, they looked like mythical creatures in the light of the full moon. None of the guests had ventured into the garden, so the sounds of laughter and music sounded far off. Somewhere in the bushes a nightingale was singing.

Despite her idyllic surroundings, Magdalena was close to tears. Mämminger seemed to suspect something, and it was quite possible that at that very moment he was telling Silvio all about it. What was she doing here anyway, amid all these vain old goats? She wanted to be back with Simon, back in her little world of Schongau, with its faded half-timbered houses, cheap taverns, and down-to-earth farm folk. Only then did it occur to her she could never again return to Schongau; she would never again hear the sometimes gentle, sometimes scolding voice of her mother or stroke the cheeks of her peacefully sleeping siblings. Schongau was at the other end of the world, and her father was here in Regensburg, rotting away in a dark hole, awaiting execution.

A bitter taste rose in Magdalena's throat. If only Simon were here with her! What would he say if he saw her made-up this way, in a hoop skirt and velvet jacket? The sordid mistress of the Venetian ambassador, a painted doll . . .

Her sobs were cut short by the sound of something creeping along the garden wall very close by.

Instinctively she slid down from the bench and crouched behind a juniper bush. From there she watched a black figure emerge from the window of a neighboring house and slip almost silently into the garden. When the stranger turned around to face her, she almost cried out.

It was the man from the coffeehouse, the same man who'd torn the Venetian ambassador's jacket and from whom they'd just barely escaped with their lives. As before, he wore a broad cloak with a hood drawn far down over his face and a rapier dangling at his side. His fluid movements reminded the hangman's daughter of a spider deftly closing in on a fly caught in its web.

Magdalena was about to turn and run when she realized the man hadn't even noticed her. He looked around warily before sitting down on a bench, as if he was waiting for something, and kept nervously scanning the broad staircase that led up to the patrician's house and the ballroom.

Magdalena backed farther onto the dewy lawn behind the juniper bush. She was so close to the bench that she could hear the man breathing.

As the cathedral bells struck midnight, a shadow descended the stairway. Magdalena lifted her head for a moment and froze.

It was the Regensburg city treasurer!

Paulus Mämminger walked purposefully toward the stranger and sat down beside him.

"We don't have much time," he whispered. "Contarini will become suspicious if I stay away too long. What's so urgent that we can't communicate in the usual way?"

"It's about the girl," the stranger said, slightly hoarse. "I think she knows something."

"Why do you think that?"

"She was at the bathhouse with the medicus. I saw them both there myself."

Magdalena's heart skipped a beat. He barricaded them in the well! And he set the fire! The men's voices were now so low she could hardly hear either of them, so she crept closer to the bench inch by inch.

"How could the girl have found anything more in the bathhouse than we did?" Mämminger wondered.

"I don't know. It's just a suspicion, but if she really does know something, it won't be long before Contarini learns of it, too, and then—"

A juniper branch cracked beneath Magdalena's foot, and though she froze, it was too late. The stranger had heard something.

"What was that?" he whispered, and stood up. Like a beast of prey trying to detect a scent, he turned his head in all directions.

"Damn you!" Mämminger whispered. "If someone has been eavesdropping on us, then God help you! I should never have agreed to meet with you here!"

"Wait." The stranger walked slowly toward the juniper bush behind which Magdalena crouched, trembling. Step by step he drew closer.

When he was nearly on top of the bush, Magdalena jumped up and threw a handful of pebbles in his face. Cursing, he swiped at his eyes, and in the ensuing confusion Magdalena ran toward some rosebushes growing up a wooden lattice on the wall of a nearby house.

"Damn it! That's the girl! Stop her!" Mämminger cried, but the hangman's daughter had already climbed up the shaky trellis of roses and wild raspberries to an open window. Ignoring the sound the red jacket made as it ripped and the thorns digging into her hands, she scrambled over the windowsill and tumbled into the room behind. Breathless, she saw she'd landed in the servants' quarters. Next to a battered wooden table and a chest was a narrow bed with a girl in it, a nightcap pulled down over her head. The girl sat up, rubbed her eyes, and when she saw the hangman's daughter began to scream.

"Excuse the interruption. I'm on my way out," Magdalena mumbled as she ran to a door on the opposite side of the room and onto the balcony behind it. The pitch of the screaming intensified behind her, and the sound of heavy steps followed. Her pursuer was close on her heels.

Magdalena carefully lowered herself over the balcony and

jumped the last few yards down. Her landing, broken by a bed of turnips and lamb's lettuce, was surprisingly soft. Without turning around she ran through the fresh garden soil, her pointed heels sinking into the damp ground like plowshares.

Damned women's stuff! Didn't I tell Silvio these tiny shoes would kill my feet?

She stopped for a moment to remove her shoes, then continued on, barefoot. The stranger had to be just a few steps behind her by now; she could hear his boots slurping as they sank into the wet ground. She tramped across the vegetable garden, dashed through a small orchard, and finally arrived at a little gate in the wall.

It was locked.

Desperate, Magdalena threw herself against the warped, rotting wood. The gate gave way with a crash, and she slipped through to find herself at a forking narrow lane. On a whim she ducked behind the open gate and held her breath. She listened in stunned silence as the stranger crashed through the gate and paused briefly before dashing off again. His steps echoed down the dark lane until she couldn't hear them at all.

Magdalena waited a bit before emerging from behind the gate. She ran in the opposite direction—it didn't matter where, just away from this place, away from the stranger, the ball, the smug nobles and patricians—all of whom seemed like traitors. Away from Silvio.

In her tattered red dress, bare feet, and velvet jacket reduced to rags, she looked like an angel cast out from heaven.

Amid the sacks of flour in the mill, Simon let the stiletto slip from his hand as he stared back at the robed man before him. His mouth gaping, it was a while before he could speak.

"You're here . . . with the freemen?" he stuttered. "But why—I mean how . . . ?"

The Regensburg raftmaster tossed his hood to the ground.

"Yes, it's me," Karl Gessner replied. "You won't give a man peace until you learn the truth. But don't say later I never warned you. You've still got time to turn back."

Simon shook his head in silence.

"That's what I thought." The raftmaster sighed, giving a sign to the other hooded men that they were no longer needed.

"Leave me alone with the doctor for a while," he told them. "I hardly believe he presents a danger to us."

"But master," one of the hooded men stammered, "you removed your hood. The man might betray you. Shouldn't we—"

"He won't betray us," Gessner interrupted, finding a seat on a bag of flour. "If what the beggar king told me is correct, then he's on our side. You may go now."

The men bowed and left the mill, murmuring. Simon sensed they weren't all in agreement with their master.

"And so you're the leader of the freemen?" the medicus said, impressed. "The Regensburg raftmaster? I expected to find a gang of outcasts, lawless . . ."

"Murderers and scoundrels?" replied Gessner, finishing his thought. "That's what the patricians say, but the truth is something else." He motioned for Simon to take a seat alongside him on one of the gray linen sacks. He pulled out a bottle from under his coat, took a long swig, and handed it to the medicus. Although Simon sipped cautiously from the bottle he burst into a coughing fit. This was high-proof liquor. All the same, he took another deep gulp. After all the frightening things that had happened, he badly needed something to calm him down.

"To the councilmen we're no more than a gang of criminals," the raftmaster continued. "But really they're the bandits."

"What do you mean by that?" Simon asked.

Gessner stood up and began pacing among the towering sacks of grain.

"Do you see this?" He slapped his palm on one of the bulging linen sacks. "This is good flour—harvested by farmers, ground by millers, and made into bread by bakers. It's a tremendous job that we workers do every day. We break our backs for it, and all profit goes to line the pockets of the fat merchants!" He spat into the flour dust. "In other cities the workers at least have a voice in their Inner Councils, but not here in Regensburg. Over the centuries patricians have forced us out of the council and taken all the important offices for themselves. Fifty families determine the fate of thousands, and for the last few years now only Protestants have been allowed citizenship!" The raftmaster had worked himself up into a fury. "Is that just?" he demanded, kicking over a pile of wood.

"Regensburg doesn't even have a mayor anymore!" Gessner continued angrily. "They simply abolished the office because it was filled by popular vote. Now the treasurer rules the council, and he's one of their own. In Regensburg money rules, not the people! And all that after we fought a long and bitter war to free ourselves from the duke and the bishop. The Free Imperial City of Regensburg—ha! We could be free, but instead we allow ourselves to be led around by the nose like a flock of sheep."

Gessner had come to the end of his speech. For a long moment there was silence, and then Simon cleared his throat.

"And what do your freemen intend to do about it?"

The raftmaster shrugged dismissively. "In England a while back they beheaded their king and founded a republic. The people won't let themselves be bossed around so easily anymore."

"So—revolution? Is that what you want?"

Sighing, the raftmaster sat down on the flour sacks beside the medicus and took another deep swig from his bottle. "We've tried peaceful means, believe me," he said softly. "We pleaded with the council to negotiate, but derision and punishment are all we got. Three years ago the patricians hanged some of our best men for treason and displayed their impaled heads at the city gates. Since then we've been working in secret, but my men have grown very afraid of being found out. Most of them have families."

"I've heard that the bathhouse owner Andreas Hofmann was also a freeman," Simon replied. "Is that why he was killed?"

Gessner nodded. "Hofmann was my deputy. The patricians must have found out and cut his throat, and his wife's, too, as a deterrent to the rest of us. But they needed a scapegoat, so—"

"And that was the Schongau hangman," Simon interrupted.

The raftmaster laughed despondently. "He ran right into their trap! The alleged letter from his brother-in-law, the forged will—it was all a setup!"

Simon bit his lip. "Is there no way to save him?"

"I'm afraid there isn't." Lost in thought, the raftmaster fingered the red kerchief he wore knotted around his throat. "The patricians will have the Schongau executioner put to death as quickly as possible, if only to cover up the murders of Hofmann and his wife. The only hope we have now is to find some clear proof to present to the council." Gessner looked at Simon questioningly. "Nathan told me you went to the scene of the crime. Did you notice anything suspicious?"

Simon cursed himself. He should have known the beggar king would talk. On the other hand, it didn't seem to matter much now that the raftmaster knew about their break-in. He decided to let Gessner in on everything.

"Hofmann's pharmacy was thoroughly ransacked," he replied. "But that may just as well have been a couple of guards hoping to find some coins and jewelry. What is certain is that someone tried to kill us while we were inside. We were nearly burned to death in there."

Gessner furrowed his brow. "Those were no doubt a few of the patricians' henchmen trying to cover their tracks. They were probably afraid you'd find something." The raftmaster sighed. "In any case, things look bad for your hangman."

"But we can't allow this to happen!" Simon exclaimed, standing up and pacing the floor. "Jakob Kuisl is innocent! We have to prove it!"

"And in so doing, prove the patricians' guilt?" Gessner laughed aloud. "Forget it. Nobody takes on Mämminger and his henchmen and walks away unscathed, unless he has absolute and incontrovertible proof. Go back home if you don't want to wind up like a drowned rat in the Danube. That would be the best thing for you and your girl."

Simon clenched his fists. "Didn't you just speak of resistance? Of struggle?" He had to rein in his rage now. "Didn't you just say you wouldn't tolerate the patricians' rule any longer? And now you're backing down! This isn't the way truly *freemen* act!"

The raftmaster's eyes became narrow slits. "Be careful how you speak to me, little doctor," he said. "You're talking about things you don't understand. Leave the battle to those who know how to fight it, you runty little quack!"

A short, ominous silence followed. Then Gessner smiled again, and his temper seemed to abate. "The time is coming, trust me." The raftmaster laid a powerful, tattooed arm around Simon's shoulders. "It's possible then that we'll need the help of people like you."

The raftmaster stood up and clapped his hands. Two hooded men emerged from behind the sacks where Gessner and Simon were just sitting; clearly they had been waiting there the entire time.

"If you and your girl insist on staying in Regensburg, concern yourselves with the poor and don't meddle in things you can't change," Gessner said, turning toward the exit with his guards.

Without another word, he disappeared among the sacks of

grain, and the clattering and grinding resumed as the mill lurched to life once more.

Magdalena wandered aimlessly through the narrow city streets. She didn't want to return to the Venetian's ball, and the hooded man was probably waiting for her at the Whale. He'd likely discovered by now where she was staying. Where could she possibly go?

Scared, she kept running along until the rows of houses on either side ended and the starry night sky opened above her. Without realizing it, Magdalena had ended up in the cathedral square. Like the fingers of an enormous, admonishing god, two steeples rose up into the night sky, towering over an architectural profusion of bays, turrets, balustrades, columns, and gargoyles. On the broad staircase leading up to an entrance some fifteen feet above, a number of dark figures loitered, evidently intending to camp out on the worn stone stairs overnight. Otherwise, the square was empty.

All at once the hangman's daughter felt extremely weary. Her feet hurt from running, her dress hung around her in tatters, and she'd cast off the red velvet jacket as she ran. She looked like a cheap whore fleeing her last customer after a couple of hours of hard work.

Without giving it another thought, she headed toward the steps of the cathedral in search of a spot where she could spend the night. More than once she had to step over snoring people huddled close together to ward off the cool night air. Some who were still awake eyed her distrustfully — beggars clothed in rags, many with soiled bandages on their feet and arms. Others had poorly healed stumps for legs and hobbled around on crutches. As Magdalena passed by, they scuttled toward her like huge beetles.

"Hey, pretty one," one of them simpered. His face was pitted with deep pockmarks, and he was missing his right leg. "How about doing an old soldier a favor and warming him up a bit? I'll give you some of my wages for it." He shook a little tin plate containing a few rusty coins.

"Leave her alone, Scarface," a toothless woman next to him chimed in, grinning at Magdalena through several layers of grimy rags. "The lady's much too fine for the likes of you. Aren't you, darling? You'll put out only for them fancy city guards." She cackled like a hen and thrust her hips suggestively. "Haven't you heard it's dangerous here in town these days for pretty whores like yourself? The reaper's makin' his rounds, pluckin' up your kind and draggin' them off in his cart."

Magdalena cursed herself for thinking she'd find a place to sleep around the cathedral, but now it was too late to run away. If she showed so much as a hint of fear, she didn't doubt these creatures would descend on her like a murder of crows. So she moved on silently.

"Stay here with us where it's safe!" the old soldier cawed hoarsely. "There's no harm in it. If I throw in another kreuzer, maybe you could keep the two of us warm at the same time. What do you say, Karl?"

A young fellow with a dumb stare giggled like a child as spit drooled out of the corner of his mouth. "Cou—cou—could be, Pe—Pe—Peter," he stuttered, sidling over to Magdalena on his knees.

"One more step, dummy," the hangman's daughter warned him, "and I'll slash your face so good you'll look like your pockmarked friend here. Now go away!"

"No way, darling," the veteran said. "Here's your chance to make some money." He reached for her dress and tried to pull Magdalena toward him—a miscalculation, as he learned all too soon. The hangman's daughter kicked the stump of his leg so hard he collapsed, whimpering and rolling around on the cathedral steps.

"She's attacked Peter Pockmark!" the old woman cried. "She's stuck a knife in his chest, the little slut!"

"Nonsense!" Magdalena shouted. "All I did was——" A brass plate struck her in the face, sending her staggering backward. Out of the corner of her eye she could see three more beggars running down the steps toward her now, swinging their crutches like halberds and not looking the least bit hobbled or lame. Magdalena leaped over Peter Pockmark, who still lay groaning on the steps, and ran through the cathedral colonnade. Perhaps she'd come across a doorway and find refuge inside the church.

She ran past stone columns, saints, and gargoyles. At every turn someone seemed to lie in wait, and she could hear footsteps rapidly approaching from all directions. She found a narrow doorway, but just as she grasped the door handle, she felt the heavy weight of a hairy arm on her shoulder. She spun around, prepared to fight to the bitter end, but a voice whispered in her ear.

"Don't move an inch, girl. I'll take care of this."

In front of her stood an older man with a bandage over his right eye, whom Magdalena instantly recognized as the blind beggar Simon had cured in the city square.

"I've been looking for you all night," he whispered, eyeing her reproachfully from head to toe. "The way you look, it's high time I found you. Your friend is worried sick."

He'll be even more worried when I tell him all I've been through these last few hours, she thought.

Meanwhile, Reiser turned to face the motley band that had gathered at the side door ready to attack the hangman's daughter with crutches, stones, and rusty plates.

"Listen up! This girl is one of us!" Reiser shouted. "She belongs to the young medicus who's already done so much to heal many of our brothers and sisters. And she stands under the personal protection of the beggar king——so leave her alone!"

"She——she nearly killed Peter Pockmark," the old woman retorted in a faltering voice. "And she offended us, the fresh whore!"

A murmur went up in the crowd, accompanied by a handful of stones that flew through the air.

"The little slut ought to be glad we're looking out for her!" replied a hunchbacked man on crutches. "Especially these days with a monster on the loose snatching up whores and ripping their bodies to shreds. She can at least lie down with us a while in thanks. It's only just!"

"You want to explain that to Nathan?" Reiser snarled, glaring at him menacingly. "Do you want to tell him what's just and what's not?" He turned then to the others. "Shall I tell Nathan you've no more interest in obeying his orders? Shall I do that?"

The hunchback cringed and crossed himself. "We didn't mean it that way. We just thought—"

"Now then—seems there's no problem after all." Reiser took the astonished Magdalena by the arm and led her slowly down the stairs. "I'm taking this girl to Nathan now," he informed them in a booming voice, "and I do hope no one attempts to interfere."

The beggars muttered and grumbled but stood aside, forming a passage just wide enough for Magdalena and her rescuer. Disgusted, the hangman's daughter noticed some of these wretched creatures licking their lips and gesturing obscenely, but no one moved an inch from his place as they passed.

"All right now, back to bed with you all," Reiser said to the crowd once the two of them had made their way down to the cathedral square. "And be quick about it before the guards come and drive you out of here with their pikes. Whoever's feeling sick or in pain can come to the guild house tomorrow, and the doctor will take care of you all, provided you keep your hands off his girl."

The old beggar pulled Magdalena into a narrow lane. For a time she could still hear the mumbling crowd behind her, and then the nightmare was over.

• • •

At that same moment, just a few blocks away, Satan was forcing Katharina's thighs apart, digging into her back with his claws. For more than a week now she'd been awaiting her fate in a daze. She'd long since lost the ability to distinguish between dream and reality.

Katharina felt sharp needles pierce her flesh; she could smell her own blood. She punched and she clawed, but the hairy, foul body bore down on her, pinning her to the ground until a searing pain spread between her legs. She could almost taste the oily, musky sweat of a rutting goat trickling down her body. For a single moment she opened her eyes to see three black-robed priests in her cell, pointing at her.

Unchaste woman . . . lustful woman . . . woman cursed by God . . .

Their eyes flashing like embers, the men metamorphosed into a trio of nude virgins before her eyes as they approached her, smiling. When one of them pulled back her lips, Katharina discerned the sharp fangs of a she-wolf.

"No! Go away, get away from me! You're nothing but an evil dream!"

The virgins, the priests, and the devil vanished, and all that remained was an empty room with a sweat-soaked Katharina lying on the cold floor. An itching sensation began to spread over her body, growing ever more intense until she had to rub her body against the wall like a wild boar. She couldn't suppress a giggle.

Like a wild sow in the woods . . . I'm turning into a wild sow. Soon I'll grow a snout and . . .

Her laughter became uncontrollable, convulsive; she struggled for air until she finally collapsed, the laughter turning to sobs that became softer and softer until they finally died away. For a single moment Katharina could think clearly again, and she struggled desperately to hold on to her reason, which she could feel gradually slipping away.

Is this purgatory? Am I dead?

There was a creak as the hatch opened and gloved hands delivered another round of delicacies—wine, white bread, veal still pink inside and drenched in a steaming cream sauce, with a side of dumplings and sweets dripping with honey.

Or is this paradise?

The eye stared at Katharina until she sopped up the last of the thick sauce with the warm bread. Then its owner turned and ascended the stairs, whistling.

The experiment was progressing nicely.

8

THE HOUR HAS COME, BAVARIAN. WE MUST BEGIN."

In the dungeon the Regensburg executioner bent down to Jakob Kuisl, who had fallen asleep on the grimy hard wooden floor, and gently shook him by the shoulder. When the Schongau hangman didn't stir, Teuber nudged him with his foot.

"Come on, now, pull yourself together. The authorities have decided to have you tortured," the executioner announced. "If you keep lolling around like this, we'll have to summon the guards and light a fire under your ass."

"It'll never burn, as wet and moldy as it is down here." Kuisl rubbed his bloodshot eyes. "Even back home in little Schongau, the condemned are better off than here in your fine Imperial City."

Teuber chuckled. "Just you wait. After the sentencing you'll go to death row, just like all the others condemned to die. There's at least a bit of sunlight there, and you're allowed visitors."

"I'm thrilled to hear it." Kuisl struggled to his feet and turned toward the door. "Let's go. Before I actually wake up."

Outside, four bailiffs waited for the Schongau hangman, a

mixture of fear and revulsion in their faces. To them he was the bathhouse monster who had sunk his fangs into the throats of two of their citizens — at least that was the word on the street. Because such a monster could even be expected to attack four guards armed to the teeth, the bailiffs lowered their halberds, ready to strike at any moment.

"Calm down," Kuisl said. "I'm not going to attack you."

Without paying further attention to the guards, he accompanied Teuber down the narrow corridor until they came to stairs leading down into a large room. Along the way they passed a brazier filled with glowing coals and a few pokers. The air was thick with smoke, sweat, and fear.

The Schongau hangman surveyed the torture chamber, impressed with both the equipment and the size of the room. On Kuisl's left stood a rack topped with a bloodstained roller spiked with iron balls. Behind it was the so-called Naughty Liesl, a wooden triangle attached to a cord, which the hangman used to hoist the offender into the air. Scattered around the room lay stones of various sizes, which were attached as weights to the victim's arms and legs as he swung from the device.

On the opposite wall were other torture instruments that Kuisl knew only by word of mouth, because the Schongau city council considered them too expensive. Among them were the Maiden's Lap, a chair with iron spikes covering the seat; the Spanish Donkey; and the Slide, an upright rack with four polished rotating wood triangles. Two white tallow candles gave off flickering light, and between them hung a crucifix: a solemn reminder that everything happening here was God's will.

"Well done, cousin. Nothing's missing here." Kuisl's gaze wandered to one side where a portion of the basement was closed off by a thick wooden lattice. From behind it came quiet murmurs.

"The three inquisitors are already here," Teuber whispered, pointing to the lattice. "We're just waiting now for the surgeon.

Until recently the bathhouse owner Hofmann played that part, but they had to replace him rather abruptly, of course. As far as I know, with the surgeon Dominik Elsperger." Teuber shrugged. "If you ask me, he's a real quack. But in here it doesn't really matter, now does it?"

"So, who are my three inquisitors?" asked Kuisl. He tried to make out anything behind the mesh but could see only moving shadows. "They're probably afraid I'm going to bite their heads off."

"All three are aldermen," Teuber said. "According to custom, it includes the oldest and the youngest members of the council. The third member is always someone different at each trial. Ah, here comes the doctor now."

The bailiff led in a timid little man who reminded Kuisl of the Schongau medicus Bonifaz Fronwieser. Dominik Elsperger wore a tattered jacket and, beneath it, a bloodstained linen smock. He held a large leather bag in front of him like a shield. When he caught sight of the Schongau hangman, he flinched.

"I—I'm supposed to examine you first," the surgeon stuttered. "To determine whether you're fit for questioning, you understand. Please remove your shirt."

Kuisl unbuttoned his shirt and pulled it over his head, revealing a hairy chest marked by a number of scars from old gunshot wounds. The little physician fumbled around, anxiously eyeing the guards. He looked Kuisl in the eye briefly as he felt for his heartbeat. Finding it calm and measured, the doctor nodded ceremoniously.

"The offender is more than fit for questioning," he said, looking toward the closed-off area. "Strong as an ox. He won't keel over so fast. In my estimation we can proceed."

Only a soft whisper could be heard from the niche behind the latticework. Finally Elsperger took his seat on a bench whose backrest, oddly, extended only half its length. Teuber noticed Kuisl's bemused glance.

"The other half of the bench is for me," the Regensburg executioner said with a grin. "We disreputable hangmen don't deserve a backrest. But I don't get to sit down very much anyway."

"That's right, Teuber," a harsh voice finally said behind the lattice. It sounded like an older man accustomed to being obeyed. "Enough chitchat. Let's begin."

Teuber nodded. "As you wish."

Once again the Regensburg executioner turned and whispered in Kuisl's ear. "Confess, Kuisl. I promise you a quick, clean death."

"Get to work, hangman," Kuisl growled. "Leave the rest to me."

A second voice with a strong Bavarian accent could be heard now behind the lattice, higher and brighter than the first. Kuisl assumed it belonged to the youngest council member. "Teuber, first show the man the instruments and explain their purpose. Maybe that will make him more cooperative."

"Save yourself the trouble," Kuisl said. "You know who I am. You don't have to explain to a hangman what he does."

Teuber sighed and led his colleague to the rack. With huge, callused hands he tied Kuisl's hands and feet to a roller at each end of the rack so not even the slightest movement was possible.

"Jakob Kuisl of Schongau," the harsh voice intoned once more from behind the lattice. "You stand accused of the murders of Andreas Hofmann and his wife, Lisbeth, née Kuisl, on the morning of the fourteenth of August in their very own bathhouse. Do you acknowledge your guilt?"

"As guilty as our Savior," Kuisl replied.

"Do not blaspheme our Lord," the young Bavarian replied. "You will just make everything worse."

"We have evidence, Kuisl," said the old man with the rasping voice. "We found the will. You had poison in your possession. For the last time, confess!"

"Good heavens, those were medicines!" Kuisl swore. "My

sister was deathly ill. I came to visit her to try to cure her, nothing more. This is a damned setup, don't you see that?"

"A setup?" asked the Bavarian, amused. "Now who do you think would have wanted to set you up?"

"I don't know myself," Kuisl muttered. "But when I find out, I'll—"

"Lies, nothing but lies," the old man interrupted. "This is pointless; we'll have to torture the suspect. Teuber, put the spike-tooth roller under him."

The Regensburg executioner lifted Kuisl's upper body until his back arched like a bridge, then inserted a roller covered in thin spikes between the rack and his body. When the executioner let go of him, Kuisl's back dropped onto the roller and the iron spikes bore deeply into his flesh. Kuisl clenched his jaw but didn't utter a sound.

"Now turn the wheel," the Bavarian ordered.

Teuber moved to the head of the rack and began turning a crank so that Kuisl's arms and legs were stretched in opposite directions. Bones cracked, beads of sweat appeared on Kuisl's brow, but still he remained silent.

Then a third voice sounded behind the lattice, quiet and throaty, of indeterminate age, but as sharp as a saw.

"Jakob Kuisl of Schongau," the man whispered. "Can you hear me?"

Kuisl shuddered. His back arched upward as if a fire had been lit beneath him. He knew this voice from his distant past. It had sought him out in the dungeon, and now it was here to torment him like something out of a nightmare.

How is this possible?

"Dear little hangman," the voice whispered. "I know you're a stubborn old bastard, but believe me when I tell you that we'll cause you more pain than you could ever imagine. And if you don't confess today, then you will tomorrow or the day after. We have time, plenty of it."

Kuisl pulled against the ropes with such force that the blood-
and soot-stained rack nearly toppled.

"Go to hell, damn it!" he screamed. "Whoever you are, go
back to where you came from!"

The guards seized their halberds, and the little surgeon
jumped up anxiously from the bench.

"Shall I bleed him a bit so he'll calm down?" Elsperger muttered. "With loss of blood, they tire quickly." But the Schongau
hangman's furious shouts drowned him out.

Teuber took firm hold of Kuisl's hands and bent down close
over him. "Damn it, what's the matter with you, Kuisl?" he
whispered. "This is just the beginning. You're only going to
make everything much, much worse."

Kuisl tried hard to breathe evenly.

Got to calm down . . . Have to find out who is behind the grille.

Again the third voice spoke.

"Teuber, it's time to show this monster how serious we are,"
the unknown man whispered with an enjoyment audible to
Kuisl alone. "He who refuses to hear shall feel. Put the blue fire
to him."

Kuisl turned his head in despair, but Teuber was already
outside his field of vision. Nearby he heard a sound he knew only
too well: a long, drawn-out hiss and sizzle, like the sound of fat
being dropped into a hot pan. Then the infernal odor of sulfur
wafted through the torture chamber.

Kuisl clenched his jaw. No matter what happened, they
wouldn't hear him scream.

Magdalena was stirring an ointment of butter, arnica, resin, and
chamomile in a wooden crucible. The pleasant aroma more or
less distracted her from the stench that permeated the space
around her.

Since the early-morning hours, more and more beggars had

been arriving at the underground hall with their various ailments. The hangman's daughter would have guessed there were almost two dozen now, but the exact number was hard to determine given the vault's irregular shape and the dim torchlight. The beggars lay, crouched, and leaned in corners and tiny niches. They came with scabies; open sores on their legs; hacking coughs; and *sudor anglicus,* English sweating sickness; and whatever their ailment, all wanted to be treated by Simon and Magdalena. By now it was almost noontime.

They had just finished treating an especially difficult case. The left leg of old Mathis was covered with festering wounds, some of them already infested with maggots.

"When the *principessa* finishes preparing her ointment, it would be nice if she could help me clean out these wounds," the young medicus said, glancing up from his work to Magdalena. "Of course, only if she doesn't find it beneath her dignity."

The hangman's daughter sighed softly. Simon was still out of sorts because she'd spent the prior evening with Silvio. A dozen times she reassured him she hadn't enjoyed herself at the ball at all, and that her curiosity had nearly cost her her life in the Venetian's garden. Still, Simon was in a huff. And though she could understand that somewhat at first, his fussing had begun to get on her nerves — mainly because she'd scarcely slept that night. At least the beggars had brought her her travel bag from the Whale; she'd put on a halfway clean dress, and in her linen skirt and gray bodice she felt once more like the simple daughter of the Schongau hangman. Yet none of that prevented Simon from treating her as if she'd just spent a fabulous and decadent night at a glittering ball.

"You can take your *principessa* and shove it," she snapped angrily. "And going forward, you can spare me your whining."

Sullenly, Magdalena took the salve to Simon and, with some tweezers, helped to pluck maggots from the leg of a snoring man she'd plied beforehand with a generous portion of brandy. Simon used a tattered cloth as a curtain to block off a niche that served as their examination room. He arranged some planks as a bed, as well as a wobbly chair and a table on which he laid out his few medical instruments and books.

"It's only because I worry," Simon whispered after a while, still cleaning the wound. "It's not a good idea for you to be gadding about Regensburg by yourself. You see what can happen when you get involved with a runty provincial aristocrat like him."

"Oh, I see, but you, sir, can march straight into a band of revolutionaries and listen to a raftmaster spout off all sorts of foolishness. *That's* a good idea?"

"At least now we know why this trap was set for your father," Simon replied.

Magdalena frowned. Simon had told her about his experience the night before with the freemen on Wöhrd Island. Nevertheless, she remained skeptical. There were just too many unanswered questions.

"I'm not sure I really understand it all," she said, laying the tweezers aside. "This freeman Gessner believes the Regensburg patricians lured my father here with some letter from his sister, forged a will, and then posted guards at the scene of the crime. All that just so they could frame him for murder? Why should they do that? They could just as well have framed some random person. These things happen in every big city. They didn't have to drag my father all the way from Schongau just for that."

Simon set a bowl of dirty water down on the table and began to bandage the beggar's leg with scraps of halfway clean cloth. "You're right; it's a roundabout way of doing it," he said. "But this way no one asked any questions. The patricians wanted to eliminate one of the freemen's leaders without arousing suspicion. They clearly succeeded in that."

"That just sounds too simple," Magdalena mumbled. "There's a catch here somewhere. Why, for instance, was the bathhouse under surveillance until just last night? Something important must have been inside."

"Hofmann's pharmacy looked like it had been hit by a tornado," Simon replied. He sat down on a stool, rubbed the sweat from his forehead, and tried to think. "Certainly someone was looking for something in there — "

"Perhaps there was some piece of evidence they wanted to destroy," Magdalena interrupted, "something that would have revealed the real reason for the murder. And now . . ."

"And now this someone thinks we know, too!" Simon continued excitedly. "They think we found something in the bathhouse that could implicate them." He sprang up from his stool. "That just might be it!"

"That would also explain the strange hooded man who tried to kill me twice yesterday," Magdalena said. "Once in the coffeehouse and later in Silvio's garden. The Mämminger fellow who spoke with the stranger is the Regensburg city treasurer, a patrician! I bet Mämminger hired him as an assassin to silence us both."

Simon nodded. "I'm certain this is the same man who locked us in the bathhouse basement and nearly burned us alive. As fast as possible we're going to have to — "

Magdalena put a finger to his lips. Without a word, she pointed to the curtain, then pulled it aside in a single motion. Behind it Nathan's grinning face appeared.

"Ah, I thought I heard someone calling for me," the beggar king said. "May I help you with something?"

Simon groaned softly. Nathan had probably overheard their entire conversation! Simon still wasn't sure how much he could trust the beggar king.

"I'm sure if we needed help you would have heard about it,"

the medicus replied, pointing to his sleeping patient. "In any event, this patient needs his rest, and so do we. We're nearly dying of hunger."

Nathan clapped his hands together. "Ah, well, it just so happens that I've gotten my hands on some delicious treats for you—under the table, so to speak. It's not much. The guards in Haid Square were especially vigilant today. But for a little lunch it'll do nicely."

He led Simon and Magdalena to the large table in the middle of the hall, where some bowls of bread, cheese, and apples, as well as a magnificent leg of pork, awaited them. Nathan's helpers had also managed to swipe a mug of foaming brown beer from right under the tavern keeper's eyes.

"Help yourselves!" the beggar king said. "You've really earned it today."

Simon bit into the pork and washed it down with a gulp of beer. Only now did he realize how hungry he was. Magdalena, too, hadn't really had much to eat since the night before at the Venetian's ball. She reached for the apples, which she devoured eagerly one after the other.

Nathan took a seat next to them and watched as they ate. He reminded Simon of a sly old crow patiently waiting for a crumb to fall from the table.

"I did, by the way, accidentally overhear your little discussion," Nathan said, picking his golden teeth. Then he turned to Simon with a conspiratorial look. "So do you really believe that Mämminger sent a hired assassin after you?"

The medicus just shrugged and continued chewing, but Magdalena nodded. "Everything points in that direction," she replied, reaching for a mug of beer. "The treasurer seems to think we've found proof of his guilt, and now he wants us out of the way."

Nathan snickered and took a bite of cheese. "Proof?" he finally scoffed. "And what kind of proof would that be? Perhaps

Mämminger dropped his signet ring somewhere in the bath-house? Or you found a bloody silver dagger engraved with initials in his kitchen drawer, or—"

"Nonsense," Simon mumbled. "It must be something serious, something that has to be kept hidden at all costs . . . some kind of secret."

Lost in thought, he ran his fingers across the tabletop, which was dusted in a thin layer of flour from the fresh-baked bread. Still pondering, he rubbed it between his fingers.

Flour?

Spinning around, Simon took Magdalena by the shoulder so abruptly she choked on her beer.

"The tracks in the cellar!" he exclaimed. "How could I have forgotten?"

"Tracks?" Nathan inquired, puzzled. "In what cellar?"

The medicus held out his right hand and placed his floury finger under the beggar king's nose. He looked around cautiously and lowered his voice. "There's a hidden storage room at the bottom of the bathhouse well. We found a few sacks of flour down there, which the rats had been nibbling. I had a closer look at them, and this flour . . ." Simon paused a moment to think. "There were tracks in it, big footprints, and they stopped directly in front of the wall. One of the tracks was cut off midway as if . . ."

"As if the trail continued on the other side!" Magdalena finished his sentence excitedly. "Damn! Why didn't you say something earlier?"

"I—I completely forgot," Simon stammered. "Just as I was going to take a closer look, the place caught fire and we had to run for our lives—or don't you remember? The tracks in the flour were just about the last thing I was thinking about at the moment."

Magdalena sighed. "Well, there's only one way to find out whether you're right," she said, standing up from the table.

"And what would that be?"

The hangman's daughter grinned. "We've got to go back to the bathhouse tonight and take a closer look."

"But the house was completely destroyed in the fire," Nathan said. "How can you expect to find anything there?"

"I hardly believe the fire made its way into the well," Magdalena said. "And the fire does give us one advantage. This time we don't need to worry about being locked inside a burning building. Thanks, by the way, for the meal."

An apple in hand, she returned to the makeshift ward to treat the next patient.

Jakob Kuisl lay on the wood floor of his cell and tried to forget his pain.

The Schongau hangman had retreated to his innermost being, where a bright sun sent its warming rays into the very tips of his fingers, filling him with pleasant thoughts.

A meadow of spring flowers, lilies of the valley with dew on their leaves, the bright laughter of the twins and Magdalena . . .

Kuisl knew from his own agonizing interrogations that people could bear a lot of pain if only their beliefs were strong, if they felt close to God, or if, like Kuisl, they were firmly convinced of their own innocence. His father once told him about an elderly woman who was tortured more than sixty times in the notorious Schongau witch trial. The stubborn old God-fearing midwife denied the accusations against her until she was finally released. Jakob Kuisl wondered how many sessions he could endure. Thirty? Forty?

The hangman groaned, trying to find a position that would minimize his pain. It was impossible for him to lie on his back because it was there the spikes had rolled through his flesh on the rack. Gaping black and red burn wounds covered his thighs, and he could scarcely move his arms. For over half an hour Teuber had turned the screws, and his thumbs, index fingers, and both

shinbones had turned blue and pulsed in pain as if an iron hammer were pounding them still.

Kuisl knew this was just the first stage of his torture. Early
the next morning they would start with stretching by ropes.
They would tie his arms behind his back and raise him from the
ground this way, attaching weights of as much as a hundred
pounds to his legs. The third voice behind the lattice had demanded all through the last session that they start the stretching
as soon as possible. Kuisl sensed the two other Regensburg aldermen were rather put off by their colleague's blatant hatred, but
they didn't interfere as the third man kept issuing increasingly
brutal orders.

The third man . . .

Kuisl had been racking his brain the last few hours trying to
remember where he'd heard that voice before, and though the
pain made it almost impossible to concentrate, he continued to
rummage through his memory. He recalled the hateful look of
the stranger on the raft. Could the third voice belong to him?
Something deep inside Kuisl told him he'd known the raftsman
long ago. But he couldn't possibly be an inquisitor. Teuber told
Kuisl that those selected to oversee the torture were always rich,
respected citizens; this raftsman, on the other hand, was a simple
man and probably not even from Regensburg.

Kuisl blinked and tried to guess the time. From far off he
could hear cries and laughter, and a dim light fell through the
hatch, causing the dust in the air to shimmer. Probably early afternoon.

At that moment he heard footsteps in the corridor outside
the cell. The bolt slid aside, and the Regensburg executioner entered. He carried a flickering torch and a linen sack, which he
opened now, arranging its contents on the floor. In the dim light
Kuisl could make out a few clay vessels, some rags, bouquets of
dried herbs, and a large bottle of brandy.

"Kuisl, Kuisl," Teuber muttered, handing the Schongau

hangman the uncorked bottle. "One thing is clear; the Regensburg aldermen tried everything: burning sulfur, the rack, thumb screws, and Spanish boots—all in one day! I've never seen anything like that before." He shook his head. "They want to see you hang, and sooner rather than later."

Kuisl nodded and took a deep swig of brandy. The alcohol seemed to wash through his entire body, rinsing away the worst of the pain.

"Well? Do you still believe I killed my own sister?" he asked, wiping his bloody, swollen hand across his lips.

Teuber opened one of the pots and spread a cooling ointment over a burn on Kuisl's thigh where, just a few hours before, he had applied burning sulfur.

"What *I* think is of no importance," he replied. "They told me to get you ready for tomorrow, and then we'll proceed. They don't trust the quack doctor to do it right, so it's up to me. Those damned patricians! Now turn around."

Kuisl rolled on his side so the Regensburg executioner could treat the wounds on his back. He had to hand it to Teuber—he was a master of his craft. He knew how to harm, but he knew how to heal as well. Years of experience working with burns, dislocated shoulders, and broken bones had made the Regensburg hangman an excellent doctor.

"You know, it's funny, Teuber," Kuisl said with his eyes closed. "First we hurt the people, then we nurse them back to health . . ."

"And in the end we kill them." Teuber nodded. "I've given up thinking about it. I do my work; that's all there is to it. Now your fingers."

Kuisl held his swollen blue thumbs out to the Regensburg executioner, who had crushed them only a few hours before. Now the executioner rubbed them with a fragrant yellow ointment that smelled of marigold and arnica. When he finished, he repeated this on Kuisl's legs, where Spanish boots—with iron uppers and spikes inside—had left colorful, shiny bruises.

"You know that I'm innocent," Kuisl whispered, clenching his fists to better endure the pain in his legs. "I've seen it in your eyes. You also believe that something's not right with one of the inquisitors. Admit it."

Pausing, Teuber stared at the man across from him for a long time. "Damn, you're right," he said at last. "The one alderman is spewing vitriol the way some people breathe fire and brimstone. Almost as if it was *his* sister whose throat you slit."

"For God's sake, I didn't . . ." Kuisl burst out, but he calmed down again, as there was no point in arguing now. The Regensburg executioner was his only ear to the outside world.

After a few deep breaths Kuisl asked, "Do you know the three aldermen?"

Teuber shrugged. "One of them is probably the president of the council, Hieronymus Rheiner. As far as I know, he's the oldest member of the council. Rheiner is also the president of the court that tried your case."

"Of course!" Kuisl interrupted. "The president at my trial the day before yesterday. How could I have forgotten?"

"The youngest one I recognized by his voice," Teuber continued. "That's Joachim Kerscher from the tax office, a little braggart whose father bought him the position."

Kuisl nodded. The chief of the tax office was responsible for municipal taxes and thus an extremely powerful man. Of course, the hangman was interested in someone else. "What about the third man?"

There was a long pause.

"Who is the third man?" Kuisl grew impatient.

Teuber shook his head. "I don't know. I've heard that voice somewhere before, but I can't say where."

"Can you find out for me who he is?"

By now the Regensburg executioner had bandaged Kuisl's back with clean cloth.

"Not even if I wanted to," Teuber replied. "The identity of the third inquisitor always remains secret, to ensure impartiality. He won't be named in any document, or found in any record either. So, that's the end of that."

He patted Kuisl lightly on the shoulder and started to pack the clay pots back into his bag.

"We'll see each other again tomorrow morning when I resume your torture," he said with a sigh, and turned to leave. "I'll leave the torch for you, since it's so gloomy down here."

"Teuber," Kuisl whispered. "Damn it, I've got to know who the third man is! I'm absolutely certain he has something to do with the murder. If I knew his name, I could send Magdalena to find out more about him, then maybe everything would end well after all. The judgment may not be passed until I confess under torture, but I don't know how much longer I can hold out. So don't let me down!"

"Hang it! I tell you I can't do it!" Teuber wrung his callused hands, unable to look Kuisl in the eye. "I have five children, and they all need their father. If I start poking around now, I'll end up on the scaffold right there with you. But in chains and minus my sword. Don't you get it?"

"I have children, too, Teuber," the Schongau hangman answered calmly. "Young twins, beautiful children. And my eldest daughter is somewhere out there trying to save my life."

Standing in the doorway, Teuber pressed his lips tightly together and clutched his linen sack as if trying to wring blood out of it.

"We'll see each other again in the morning," he said finally. "Try to get some sleep."

He slammed the door behind him and slid the bolt closed. Kuisl could hear his rapid footsteps retreat down the passageway. It almost seemed he wanted to run.

Kuisl stared pensively at the grimy cell wall in front of him. The torch Teuber left hanging on a ring was half burned down now, but by its light the Schongau hangman was able to get a clear look around his cell for the first time. The stinking chamber pot, the wedge of wood that served as his pillow, the scribbling on the wall . . . Kuisl studied the strange script that had troubled him so greatly the day before. It still glared out at him in the very middle of the back wall, directly under the line from the mercenary's song, which he'd carefully scratched out.

P.F.K. Weidenfeld, anno domini 1637 . . .

That was a quarter of a century ago. The hangman tried to remember what was going on back then, what the name and date brought to mind. Had he ever known anyone by that name?

P.F.K. Weidenfeld . . .

Back then Kuisl's colonel had already promoted him to sergeant, and even though he was only twenty-two years old, he commanded a large number of mercenaries. Many of the older, more seasoned soldiers objected on account of his youth, but after the first battle most didn't say another word. Kuisl taught them discipline and respect, two virtues the lansquenets knew about only through stories. Kuisl lived with the horror and terror of war, the nightmares of murder, robbery, and rape, all those years, but the memories grew within him like a poisonous mushroom. At least he had done what he could to stanch senseless bloodshed by his own men.

But what bloodshed was sensible?

P.F.K. Weidenfeld . . .

With torch in hand, Kuisl walked along the wall, trying to decipher the rest of the scribblings.

All of a sudden he noticed something.

The Weidenfeld inscription as well as some of the others were new! They had been carved into the wooden wall with a sharp knife, and they shone in a much lighter color than the older ones — so someone must have carved them just recently.

Just for him.

Softly the hangman began murmuring the names he'd been trying to forget all these years.

Magdeburg, Breitenfeld, Rain on the Lech, Nördlingen . . .

Familiar names from the Great War, battlefields where Kuisl served as a mercenary and where he pillaged, blasphemed, whored, and murdered. Images and smells came back to him now like dark storm clouds.

Good God!

The torch smoked in front of him, and another greater torture began.

This time it penetrated to his innermost being.

"Lord Almighty! Just look at what the fire has done here!" Simon whispered, pointing to what was left of the bathhouse, which had collapsed in a smoldering heap. A thunderstorm overnight had transformed much of the ruin into a muddy mountain of black, splintered beams. The walls had fallen in on three sides. Shattered tiles, scorched window frames, scraps of cloth, and broken pots were scattered all over the street, evidence that scavengers had already helped themselves. Only the chimney still rose up out of the devastation as a reminder that a stately building had once stood on this spot.

The medicus shook his head. "We certainly won't find anything here. Let's just go back."

Magdalena, too, looked sadly at the ruins. While she had to admit she hadn't expected to find her aunt's house so completely destroyed, she didn't want to give up so easily.

"How much time do we have?" she asked Nathan, who stood beside her now, gnawing on an old chicken bone.

The beggar king picked at something stuck between his gold teeth. "My boys will signal me when the guards return to patrol this area," he said. "At the moment the bailiffs are down at St.

Emmeram's Square, so it will probably be a while before they come back. I'll whistle when they do."

Magdalena nodded. She was happy to have Nathan and a dozen beggars along. The beggar king had advised her to wait to visit the ruin until the early-morning hours because the city guards would be nearing the end of their shifts, eager to be relieved, and thus patroling only halfheartedly. Although Simon had been against involving the beggars in their plans at first, it hadn't been hard to convince him: in a city like Regensburg it was never a good idea to wander about alone at night, but in the company of Nathan's colleagues they were as safe in the streets as Lazarus in the lap of Abraham. Here again it was evident how helpful the beggars guild could be. All along the Weißgerbergraben they posted lookouts to send word at the slightest sign of danger.

"Then let's not waste any time," Magdalena whispered.

With a lantern in hand, the hangman's daughter searched the pile of charred beams for an opening she could slip through.

"Magdalena," Simon whispered. "The place will collapse and bury you. Perhaps it would be better if we — "

"Just come along," she interrupted Simon curtly. "*I,* at least, am not going to let my father down."

She nudged a beam to one side, setting off a chain reaction that ended with a portion of the mountain of debris collapsing with a great crash. She jumped aside as a cloud of ash rained down on them.

"What did I tell you?" Simon whispered. "You're digging your own grave!"

Magdalena pointed to a new opening in the debris. "At least now we've found a way in," she said. "This is about where the boiler chamber with the well must have been."

She crouched down and crawled into the ruin, holding the lantern in front of her, and in just a few moments disappeared inside. Simon murmured a quick prayer and crawled in after her. If they were going to die, then at least they would die together.

"Good luck," he could hear Nathan call after him. "Don't worry. If the whole thing collapses, we'll dig you out, dead or alive."

"Thanks, that's very kind of you," Simon scoffed, though he knew the beggar king could no longer hear him.

The medicus could feel his back scrape against the charred beams, and a muddy layer of ash and dirt clung to his knees. They were making their way through a tunnel of masonry stones and large pieces of rubble when Magdalena's lantern brightened in front of him and the space around him opened up.

He rose to his feet carefully, realizing they'd in fact made it back into the bathhouse boiler room. Most of the equipment here was unrecognizable, though: the brick oven had burst into pieces, and the copper kettle used to heat bath water seemed to have completely disappeared. It took a while for Simon to notice shiny black pieces on the floor that reminded him of slag. The kettles had melted! What hellish temperatures must have prevailed here!

Meanwhile, Magdalena pushed aside a pile of bricks and gazed into a black hole directly beneath her.

"The well shaft," she said. "The rungs are still here. Now it gets interesting."

With these words she began her descent. Before long the medicus heard her call again. "Simon, you were right! This—this is unbelievable!"

When she fell silent, Simon leaned over the hole. "Magdalena, what's wrong?" he whispered. "Are you still there?"

"I'm here in the back." The voice of the hangman's daughter echoed strangely, as if she were now much farther away.

"Is there really a secret passageway?" Simon asked excitedly.

"It's best you come down and see for yourself."

Simon reached for the iron rungs, casting a quick glance at
the splintered beams and loose stones above him. If the roof
caved in now, they'd either drown or starve to death down in the
well. He couldn't imagine Nathan and his beggars taking up
shovels and digging them out.

Hand over hand, the medicus climbed down the rungs into
the shaft until he reached the opening. The flames had gutted the
hidden storage room, and the sacks and boxes they found there
on their last visit were reduced to ash. But Simon discovered
something else now.

Farther back there was yet another entryway, this one only
waist-high. Simon ducked into the low opening. The ground
was strewn with charred wood, some of it still marked with
whitewash. He had to smile.

*A secret wooden door painted white and hidden behind the sacks.
Hofmann was a clever fellow!*

Carefully he peered inside. In the large room before him the
fire had left its mark, though not so thoroughly as in the first
room. In one corner stood a charred table; a blackened shelf that
had fallen from the wall now lay on the floor. In the middle of
the room the chimney of a huge stone furnace rose up to the ceiling, and all around it were smashed pots and splinters of glass
that he suspected were once polished lenses.

Simon stepped over the broken glass and ran his hand along
the balance bar of a scale: still warm, scorched and twisted almost
beyond recognition by the heat.

"I'll be damned if this wasn't an alchemist's workshop," he
whispered. "Your uncle is looking stranger and stranger by the
minute."

"I wonder whether Hofmann's murderer searched this
room," Magdalena said.

Simon thought for a moment, then nodded. "It's quite possible he didn't. Your uncle kept his laboratory well hidden. I assume the fireplace is connected to the chimney in the boiler room

so no one would notice he was down here working with distillation flasks. A bathhouse operator has to always keep the water boiling, after all, and thus the chimney was always smoking."

"But what does that have to do with the patricians?" Magdalena picked up a piece of a glass lens and examined it as if this shard might hold the answer to all her questions. "Until now we've assumed the aldermen had my uncle killed because he was one of the leaders of the freemen—retaliation, nothing more."

"Apparently it's not that simple," Simon replied. "It's safe to say that someone was looking very hard for this secret room. The terrible mess in the apothecary's room on the second floor is evidence of that."

"Could Mämminger be behind it?" Magdalena asked.

"He has something to do with it at least."

The medicus continued reflecting on this as he made his way through the room, now and then picking up a fragment of pottery or a piece of melted glass. Underneath the toppled bookshelf he found a few scorched boards connected by thin bars, and then, as he continued rummaging around, he came upon a few small blackened bones.

Animal bones.

"It appears your uncle was keeping animals in cages down here," Simon said. "Not especially large ones. These bones could have come from rats or cats."

Disgusted, he tossed the bones aside and walked to a far back corner of the room, where a knee-high pile of ash still smoldered. Carefully he reached into the faintly glowing black mass.

Slowly he sifted the warm ashes through his fingers, letting them fall to the ground. There were bits the fire hadn't consumed entirely, which shimmered bluish white in the lantern light. Sniffing them, he recognized the same slightly sweet odor he had noticed a few days earlier while inspecting the moldy flour in the bathhouse supply room. Could this enormous pile of ash be simply burned flour? Or was this the remains of some alchemical powder he'd never heard of?

What the devil had Hofmann been doing down here?

He suddenly heard a loud crack and stones began falling to the ground. A moment later the world around them seemed to explode.

"Damn it, the house is collapsing!" Simon shouted. "I was afraid it would. Let's get out of here fast!"

Magdalena was already in the front supply room, scrambling like a cat up the rungs. Before Simon followed her, he frantically filled his purse with the bluish ash. Maybe he'd have a chance later to examine the powder more closely. Then he, too, rushed off toward the well shaft.

A loud thundering sound suggested the beams were breaking apart under the weight of the rubble. Up in the boiler room Magdalena stood amid the melted kettles while rubble and stones hailed down on her.

"The way out is blocked!" she shouted, pointing at the narrow tunnel now closed off by a mountain of bricks. The roof above them was creaking and starting to sag, and at any moment they knew they'd be buried beneath it.

"There has to be another way out!" Simon shouted over the deafening creaking and splintering.

Panicked, he looked around until at last, on the left, he discovered a passageway through the debris barely wide enough to pass through. He pushed Magdalena through the tiny opening, crawled in behind her, and found himself standing in what was once the bathing chamber. Here, too, the roof threatened to fall. The back part of the room had already collapsed completely, but in front, where the door had once been, a new hole had just opened up in the wall.

After nudging Magdalena through the hole, Simon scrambled through behind her. Just seconds later the entire ruin collapsed behind them with a terrible roar, and a cloud of dust rose up into the sky.

Coughing and panting, Simon and Magdalena lay on the ground, unable to speak. When the dust had drifted away, they could see Nathan and the other beggars standing nearby.

"Well done," the beggar king said, tipping his hat. "Most of my fellows bet you wouldn't make it out. It sounded out here like a whole load of gunpowder—"

"Shut your damn mouth!" Magdalena burst out, apparently having regained her voice. "We were nearly killed and you're taking bets on it! Are you insane? You didn't say a word about *helping!*"

"What could I have done?" Nathan replied meekly in a subdued voice. "I wanted to warn you, but the timbers were already cracking." Then, lowering his voice, he continued. "By the way, you should quiet down a bit unless you want the entire neighborhood to come running."

Simon noticed now that some windows had already opened in nearby houses and curious eyes were watching their little group.

"I would have called you soon in any case," Nathan whispered. "There's something I want to show you. It appears you weren't the only ones to visit the bathhouse tonight."

Taking Simon and Magdalena by the arm, the king of beggars led them to the other side of the burned-out building, where they crouched behind a collapsed stone wall. He pointed to a figure in a black cape who was clinging to the wall of a neighboring house like a bat.

"My boys didn't even see him at first," Nathan whispered. "He must have been prowling around here the whole time, and I think he had the same plan you did. Well, he sure won't find anything now."

"Oh, God, Simon!" Magdalena whispered. "That's the

stranger who was in the garden at Silvio's house! The man who tried to kill me! He's coming toward us!"

Nathan raised his hands reassuringly. "Don't worry; you have me and my boys here now."

"Your *boys* are blind, crippled old men," Simon sneered. "Just what are they going to do?"

"Well, see for yourself."

The beggar king pointed to the doorway of a house, where two of his men loitered on the steps. As the stranger approached the ruin, presumably to get a better look, they lurched toward him. Simon noticed one of them was Crazy Johannes, Nathan's right-hand man.

"My good fellow, a pittance for an old soldier who lost his sight in the Battle of Rheinfelden," Johannes croaked, looking very much indeed like a down-and-out mercenary. "Just a kreuzer for a cup of mulled wine."

"Away with you!" shouted the stranger. "I have no time for your twaddle!"

In the meantime the other beggars had reached the man and were jostling him. As the stranger faltered, Crazy Johannes raised a crutch and rammed it between the man's legs, causing him to fall with a startled cry. Seconds later two more beggars on crutches emerged from the shadows of an entryway and began flailing away at the figure on the ground.

In one fluid motion the stranger jumped to his feet and pulled out his rapier. The beggars surrounded him like a pack of ravenous dogs, each waving a crutch through the air to hold the man at bay.

Unexpectedly the man lunged to one side, feinted to the left, then attacked from the right. Johannes let out a loud cry as the blade cut into his shoulder.

The cloaked stranger took advantage of the momentary confusion to jump onto a dung cart beside a nearby house. The beggars attacked the cart and tried to overturn it, but the man scrambled up to an open window in the second story, climbed inside, and disappeared. Moments later a woman's scream was followed by heavy footsteps on a stairway. Simon looked up to see the stranger squeezing through a hatch in the roof, then dashing across neighboring rooftops in the direction of the Danube.

"Damn!" Nathan shouted. "We almost had him!"

Beggars arrived now from all directions to help their injured companion. In his sooty jacket Simon, too, rushed over to Johannes, whose wound, he saw immediately, was serious. The blade had pierced Johannes's right shoulder clean through. The medicus was relieved to see that the blood seeping from the wound was dark in color rather than light, meaning the lung hadn't been injured.

"Give me a hand!" he shouted, gesturing to some of the beggars. "We'll carry him carefully to the catacombs, and I'll see if there's anything I can do for him there."

Magdalena was still standing behind the collapsed wall, peering out over the roofs of Regensburg, where the red sun was just beginning to rise. She was so lost in thought she didn't notice a boy standing directly in front of her. He was about ten years old, had strawberry-blond hair and a face so covered with freckles it looked as if he'd been splattered with mud. At first she presumed he'd come to see the collapsed house, but then she realized he was addressing her.

"Are you—uh—Magdalena Kuisl?" he asked fearfully. "The daughter of the Schongau hangman?"

"Who wants to know?" Magdalena snapped, scrutinizing him carefully. "You sure don't look like a city guard."

The boy shook his head shyly. "I'm Benjamin Teuber, the son of the Regensburg executioner. My friends and I have been looking for you everywhere. I have something to give you," he replied, handing her a folded piece of paper. "It's a letter from your father."

Incredulous, Magdalena took the note. "From my father?"

Benjamin nodded and rubbed his toes together bashfully. "He gave it to my dad and asked him to find you and give it to you. And then I have a message for you from *my* father."

"What's that?" Magdalena asked.

"That your dad is a thick-skulled, pigheaded, low-down bastard."

The hangman's daughter smiled. There was no greater compliment anyone could give her father.

9

THIS MORNING THEY BEGAN WITH THE RACK straightaway.

In silence the Regensburg executioner removed Kuisl's bandages and bound his arms behind his back. Perceiving shadows behind the wooden lattice, Kuisl knew the doctor and the three inquisitors were already present. He fixed his eyes on the lattice as if by sheer force of will he might see through it to finally get a look at the man who'd set this awful trap for him.

Since Teuber had visited the cell to care for his wounds, only a single, agonizing night had passed and Kuisl had slept little. Instead, he'd spent the whole time brooding over the name Weidenfeld and where he might have heard it before. It was clear now that the third man whose face was hidden behind the lattice was an avenging angel risen out of his past. The same stranger had made all the inscriptions on the cell wall to remind the hangman of a time he'd long ago banished to the remote corners of his memory. The ghosts of the war had risen again, and the worst among them was hiding here, in the torture chamber in Regensburg behind a wooden lattice. Who was it? And why was he pursuing him?

P.F.K. Weidenfeld . . .

Kuisl moaned softly as the executioner strapped him to a modified ladder rack. The herbal ointment Teuber had spread on his wounds was a blessing but in no way a cure. Now Teuber tied Kuisl's hands, already bound together behind his back, tightly to an upper rung of the rack. Sharply filed wood pyramids bored into his wounded flesh while the weight of his body pulled him inexorably downward along the rungs, prying his shoulder joints apart as he slid. Still, that wasn't the worst: Teuber tied a noose around Kuisl's legs, then attached it to a roller at the bottom of the instrument. When the executioner turned the roller, the victim's arms would be pulled farther and farther upward, behind his back, until his shoulders would at last rip from their sockets.

"We begin the second interrogation," the older man intoned from behind the lattice, a voice Kuisl now knew belonged to the president of the council, Hieronymus Rheiner. "Kuisl, you can save yourself a lot of pain if you simply confess that—"

"To hell with you, you dirty bastards!" Kuisl shouted. "Even if you cut me to pieces and throw me into boiling water, it wasn't me!"

"It's quite possible we'll do just that," the third voice replied sardonically. "But first we're going to try the rack. Teuber, turn the crank."

Drops of sweat appeared on Teuber's brow, and his lips pressed into a thin line. Nevertheless, he moved the roller about a quarter turn, just enough for Kuisl's bones to crack audibly.

"Don't make this unnecessarily hard on yourself," admonished the youngest inquisitor, presumably Joachim Kerscher from the Regensburg tax office. "The evidence is overwhelming. We all know you committed the murder, but by Carolingian Law we need your confession."

"It wasn't me," Kuisl muttered.

"Blast it, we caught you red-handed! Right alongside the

two corpses!" Hieronymus Rheiner fumed. "God knows you are guilty! He's looking down on you now!"

Kuisl laughed softly. "God isn't here. Only the devil's present in this room."

"This isn't working," the third man said icily. "Teuber, keep turning. I want to hear his bones break."

"But Your Honors," Teuber spoke up cautiously. His face looked pale and bloated in the torchlight. The merry sparkle in his eyes had disappeared, and he seemed to have suddenly aged by years. "Were I to proceed too quickly, Kuisl might pass out, and then—"

"Who asked your opinion, hangman?" the third inquisitor snarled.

Doctor Elsperger, who until that point had been sitting silently on the wooden bench, now stood up and cleared his throat.

"Teuber isn't entirely mistaken," he said. "From appearances the accused may indeed become unconscious. Then we'd have to terminate the procedure prematurely."

"Elsperger, you're right," old Rheiner responded from behind the lattice. "We must proceed slowly. Teuber, just a quarter turn again, no more."

The Regensburg executioner, who was leaning silently against the rack, didn't seem to hear the inquisitor at first.

"Pardon, Your Honor. A quarter turn, as you command."

As Teuber cranked the roller, Kuisl could feel his arms about to be wrenched from their sockets. This pain only intensified as the pyramid-shaped wedges dug ever deeper into his back. Kuisl closed his eyes and hummed the old nursery rhyme he'd first heard in an army encampment outside Breitenfeld long ago. Soldiers' wives hummed it in their children's ears to soothe them while villages burned on the horizon. Kuisl himself had sung it to send his little sister, as well as his own children, off to the land of dreams.

"Ladybug, ladybug, fly away home . . ."

"Kuisl, stop this foolishness and confess!" young Kerscher warned him. "It's over for you."

"Your house is on fire . . ."

"Good Lord, confess!" Rheiner shouted.

"Your children will burn . . ."

"Confess!"

Kuisl spat at the lattice. "Go to hell, you potbellied little pricks."

For a moment everyone fell silent, and the only sound was Kuisl's labored breathing.

"A lovely song," the third inquisitor said finally in a malevolent tone. "Unfortunately you'll never again sing it to your children. You do have children, don't you? And a beautiful wife, as well. What's her name? Anna-Maria, I believe."

He repeated the name, pronouncing each syllable slowly, almost lustfully. *"An-na-Ma-ri-a."*

The Schongau hangman struggled to get up, while his bones cracked and his left shoulder snapped out of its socket. This devil knew his wife? And his children, too? What did he have planned for them? Had he already taken out his vengeance on them for some crime their husband and father committed decades ago? Though the pain almost caused Kuisl to faint, he spat a stream of bile in the direction of the wooden lattice.

"You goddamned swine!" he screamed. "Come out here and show me your goddamned face so I can rip the skin off it!"

"You're a bit confused," the third man calmly replied. "You're the one whose face we're going to tear to shreds in a little while."

"I implore you to show a bit more respect, colleague," Rheiner scolded. "This is an interrogation. One might almost think the accused has somehow wronged you personally . . . Elsperger?"

The gaunt surgeon sprang up from the bench. "Your Honor?"

"Is the subject still fit for interrogation?"

Elsperger approached the Schongau hangman and examined his crippled arm in the dim torchlight.

"His left shoulder seems to be dislocated," he said finally, "but the right one still looks in good shape."

"Respiration?"

Elsperger nodded. "He's still breathing. This man is as strong as an ox, if I may say so. I've never seen —"

"Nobody asked for your opinion," Rheiner said. "Esteemed colleagues, may I suggest the left arm be untied and we continue with the right? And as far as I'm concerned, we might as well get started with the hot poker. I'm certain we'll have our confession soon. Teuber, take down the left arm, and we'll continue with the right. For God's sake, Teuber, what's the matter with you?"

The Regensburg executioner wiped the sweat from his brow as his gaze went blank. "Pardon, once more," he stammered. "But I believe the man has had enough for today."

"Another person determined to have his say!" the older councilman groused. "Where are we? In a ship of fools? Now hurry up and do as we've ordered, or I'll cancel the two guilders you're to be paid for the day's work."

When Teuber loosened the shackles, Kuisl's arm collapsed like an empty wineskin. Then the executioner reached again for the crank.

"Good Lord, confess, will you!" Teuber whispered in Kuisl's ear. "Confess, and it will be over!"

"My dear, sweet twins . . ." Kuisl whispered, on the verge of passing out. "Lisl, my Lisl, come and I'll sing you to sleep . . ."

"Teuber, crank the damned roller at once," the third man snarled. "Or must I come out and do it myself?"

With a clenched jaw, the Regensburg executioner once again

began turning the crank, as Kuisl continued singing the nursery rhyme over and over.

The melody would echo in Teuber's mind the entire night.

Simon and the beggar carried Crazy Johannes through the dark, deserted streets toward Neupfarr Church Square while Magdalena scouted ahead to make sure their strange ensemble didn't encounter any watchmen who might have some unpleasant questions to ask. Having finally arrived back in the catacombs, they bedded the injured man down in the niche they were using as a sick bay.

Just as the medicus had assumed, the blow hadn't pierced the lungs. And though the blade had passed straight through his shoulder, the wound was clean. After Simon applied some moss to stanch the bleeding, he treated it with an ointment of arnica and chamomile.

"You'll have to dispense with your crazy Saint Vitus' dances for a while," he told Johannes as he tentatively pressed the edge of the wound, whereupon the beggar let out a shout of pain. "How about trying to earn some honest money the next few weeks?" Simon continued. "Just lie down by the cathedral and hold out your hand."

"That's not half as much fun," Johannes said, trying to grin despite the pain.

In the meantime Magdalena handed Simon clean water, cloths, and bandages, always keeping an eye on the ragged bunch crowded behind the dirty sick-bay curtain. By now she'd come to know some of the beggars: the crippled and sick, the disbanded mercenaries, stranded pilgrims, cast-off wives, prostitutes, and abandoned orphans—a motley mix of outcasts just like Magdalena. Looking over their faces, she felt a strange bond with them all.

I'm one of them, she thought. *A city within a city, and I'm part of it.*

The previous night she and Simon had gone for a walk through the winding subterranean passageways, counting almost forty cellars all connected to one another. Many were empty, but the beggars had stashed food and furnishings in some. Musty drapes and trunks, even a child's toy here and there, all suggested whole families called these damp, dark vaults home. Beneath some of the cellars Simon and Magdalena came upon even deeper cellars by way of staircases or narrow, winding corridors. Here they found Latin inscriptions on the walls, and tucked away in one corner they even discovered a small bronze pagan statue. Were these the remains of an even older Roman settlement predating the Jewish ghetto above?

Here, deep in the bowels of the city, far from the beggars, they found themselves alone together for the first time in a long while. They made love in the dim, sooty glow of a lantern and promised each other not to give up. Magdalena still believed they could save her father. What might come next, though, she refused to consider now. Would she return with Simon to Schongau, where she could expect nothing but mockery and shame? Where Alderman Berchtholdt and his cronies would make their life hell? And where they could never expect to build a life together?

In spite of it all, Magdalena missed her mother and the twins desperately. Perhaps the little ones were ill or her mother was spending sleepless nights worrying over the disappearance not only of her husband but of her eldest daughter as well. Wasn't it Magdalena's duty to return to report her father's fate?

A sharp cry brought her back to the present, where Simon had just finished sewing up Johannes's wound and given the beggar a friendly slap.

"That's it!" he said, helping the beggar back to his feet. "As I said, no tricks for the next few weeks. And lots of wine; you've got to get your strength back."

Despite his pain, Johannes forced a smile. "Now that's a

medicine to my liking. Is there an illness for which peach brandy is the cure?"

Smiling, Magdalena packed the bandages and salves into a leather bag. She found it hard to imagine she'd ever feared the beggars. For a while now they'd felt to her like one big family.

At that moment she remembered the letter from her father that the hangman's son had given her. She hadn't even gotten around to opening it! So once she'd helped Simon wipe the bloodstains from the sickbed, she retired to a quieter niche and with trembling fingers unfolded the crumpled piece of paper. What did her father have to tell her? Had he found a way to escape?

Looking down at the letter, she stopped short. The faded note consisted of a single line:

GREETINGS FROM WEIDENFELD . . .

Magdalena held the paper close enough to the candle that its edges slowly started to curl, but there was nothing else legible in the note.

GREETINGS FROM WEIDENFELD . . .

Was her father trying to tell her something that no one else was supposed to know? Was this a secret clue something only she was meant to understand?

Then Magdalena realized this letter couldn't possibly be from her father.

It was in someone else's handwriting.

The boy had told her the letter came from her father, so someone was lying. Deep in thought, Magdalena folded it up and returned it to her skirt pocket.

"What's wrong?" Simon, who had returned to her side, looked at her with surprise.

"The letter from my father . . ." she began hesitantly. "Someone else wrote it." She told Simon about the mysterious text.

"Well?" Simon asked. "Do you know anyone by that name?"

Magdalena shook her head. "Unfortunately no." She bit her

lip, thinking. "This letter must have come from the man who's out to get my father. I'm pretty sure there's more behind this than the patricians retaliating against the freemen." Magdalena collapsed onto the straw, rubbing her temples. "Someone has it in for my father—maybe someone he crossed a long time ago, someone who is sparing no pains to pay him back now."

"Does your father have lots of enemies?" Simon asked hesitantly.

Magdalena laughed. "Enemies? My father is the hangman. He has more enemies than the kaiser has soldiers."

"So the murderer could be a relative of someone he once executed?" the medicus persisted.

Magdalena shrugged. "Or someone he broke on the rack until he got the truth out of him, or someone he whipped or whose ear he cut off, or someone he put in the stocks or banished from town . . . Just forget about that! It won't lead anywhere."

"What bad luck that the bathhouse ruins collapsed!" Simon said. "Now we'll probably never learn what was going on in that secret alchemist's workshop."

"But the stranger who's apparently on our trail won't learn anything, either," Magdalena replied. "And don't forget, we have an advantage: *we* know what was down there."

"Though we can't make any sense of it." Sighing, Simon sank down in the straw beside Magdalena and stared off into the gloomy hall. Nathan sat at the massive table amid a number of other beggars and sipped from a mug of watery beer. Though the beggar king seemed to watch them out of the corner of his eye, he made no attempt to approach them.

"Let's go over what we know again," Magdalena said, chewing on a piece of straw. "The bathhouse owner, Andreas Hofmann, and his wife, my aunt, were killed. They were members of the freemen, who are rebelling against patrician rule and whose leader is the Regensburg raftmaster, Karl Gessner. Hofmann was Gessner's second in command, and when his cover got blown, he had to die—the patricians' act of revenge and a deterrent to the other revolutionaries."

"Your father was the scapegoat," Simon added. "He received a forged letter about his oh-so-sick sister, traveled to Regensburg, where he was arrested at the scene of the crime to divert suspicion from the patricians. So far, so good. But in the bathhouse cellar there was a secret alchemist's workshop, and apparently someone was looking for it—the stranger with the rapier who tried to kill us and who, it seems, is taking orders from none less than the Regensburg city treasurer."

Magdalena nodded. "Paulus Mämminger. He must be at the center of everything. And he's the only lead we really have. We'll have to follow him."

"And how do you intend to do that?" Simon inquired. "Shadow one of the most powerful patricians in Regensburg around the clock? It won't be easy. You'd need an army."

Magdalena grinned. "You forget we have one." She pointed at the beggars Nathan was now toasting jovially with his mug of beer. "They're just itching for someone to send them into battle."

Philipp Teuber shuffled home from the torture chamber as if he were on his way to his own execution. He'd spent the entire morning torturing Jakob Kuisl and in the afternoon was to begin again. Teuber felt as if he'd aged years in a matter of hours, and not even the prospect of a hot dinner at home could change that.

The Regensburg executioner's house was located on Henkersgässchen, Hangman's Lane, in a rundown part of town south of the old grain market. Amid muddy roads, crooked, warped roofs, and dilapidated houses the tidy property seemed a bit out of place. It was freshly whitewashed, the well-tended garden behind it was full of fragrant roses and lavender blossoms, and a newly renovated barn next door housed cattle and carts. Teuber wasn't poor; in a Free Imperial City like Regensburg, the hangman made a decent living. And almost every day people came to him to purchase some medicine or talisman, among them well-to-do citizens who hid their faces as they passed through the rank lanes of this part of town.

The hangman, stooped and pale, opened the door to his home and was immediately surrounded by a crowd of cheerful children. Under normal circumstances he would lift his five little children high into the air one by one and hug them against his broad chest, but today he quietly pushed the rambunctious group aside and sat down at the table, where his wife, Caroline, had already set down a steaming bowl of bone-marrow broth and tripe. As usual, everyone waited for the hard-working father to take the first spoonful; only after he had taken an unenthusiastic taste did the five children pounce on the food like hungry wolves. Lost in thought, Teuber watched his family eat, while he himself could only stir his spoon around in the bowl.

"What's wrong, Philipp?" his wife asked, holding the bawling youngest child on her lap as she fed him. "If you keep this up, you'll be nothing more than skin and bones. You haven't eaten a thing for days. Is it because of this hangman from Schongau?"

Teuber nodded and stared vacantly at the wooden spoon in his bowl, where a gleaming glob of fat floated on the surface. He remained silent.

"Papa, can I have your tripe?" his oldest son asked. It was the redheaded Benjamin who'd taken the letter to Magdalena early that morning. When his father didn't answer, the boy pointed to the few gray scraps floating in the soup and repeated his question. "Papa, can I—"

"For God's sake, leave me alone, all of you!"

Teuber pounded the table so hard with his fist that the bowls clattered and the startled youngsters fell silent. "Can't we *just once* have peace and quiet in this house!"

He got up from the table and stomped into the main room, slamming the door behind him. Alone at last, Teuber bent over a wash basin and splashed cold water on his face, as if that could wash away his worries. He shook himself off like a dog and slumped onto a rickety stool in a corner. Then, folding his hands across his broad chest, he stared at a long executioner's sword on the wall in front of him.

Fitted with a leather grip, its blade was nearly as long as a man is tall. Regensburgers had gruesome stories to tell about it. Market women whispered that the sword quivered for three days before every execution and could be appeased only with blood. Others claimed the steel rattled whenever a death sentence was pronounced. Teuber knew all this was nonsense. It was a good sword, passed down through many generations and carefully forged by human hands to bring a quick and painless death. It was solid handiwork; there was nothing magical about it. Engraved on the blade was a saying the Regensburg executioner often repeated quietly to himself:

ABIDE WITH ME, ALMIGHTY GOD

Although this line was intended for the condemned man, Teuber had the feeling it referred to him now, as well.

After a while his wife opened the door cautiously and sat down beside him. Outside, the children could be heard giggling and roughhousing. They seemed to have gotten over the incident.

"Would you like to talk?" Caroline asked after a while. Silence fell over the room, and only the children's muffled laughter could be heard from outside.

"He's just like me," her husband finally said. "He has a wife and a few children, he does his job, he's a damn good executioner, and he's innocent."

Caroline gave him a skeptical sidelong look. Her once-delicate face was gaunt now, fine lines spread from the corners of her eyes and mouth, and her blond hair had turned gray in many places. Together the Teubers had seen their fair share of hard times. Countless sleepless nights before executions, the screams of the tortured, the disapproving looks of narrow-minded citizens in the street—over a lifetime all this had left its mark, not just on the Regensburg executioner but on his wife as well.

"How do you know he's innocent?" the executioner's wife asked finally. "Doesn't every petty thief claim that?"

Teuber shook his head. "He really is innocent. Someone set him up. The third inquisitor . . ." He hesitated briefly before continuing. "The dirty swine insists I torture Kuisl more mercilessly than I've ever done. He seems to know things about Kuisl that he couldn't reasonably know. The fiend wants him dead, not because Kuisl has broken the law but because of something that happened between them long, long ago. And I'm his instrument."

His wife smiled. "Aren't you always? The instrument, I mean?"

Teuber slapped his broad, muscular thigh in frustration. "Don't you understand? This time is different! By torturing an innocent man, I'm assisting in someone else's revenge while the real murderer runs around free! And even more men may die because of it!"

Caroline sighed. "What can you do? If you refuse to torture him, they'll only replace you with another executioner. The knacker's son has been waiting for his chance a long time now. And they'll drive us out of town. Is that what you want?"

Teuber shook his head. "God, no! But maybe there's another way."

His wife looked at him sharply. "What do you mean? Tell me!" A light flashed in her eyes, even as they narrowed to little slits. "You don't intend to . . . ?"

Without a word, Teuber headed for a huge pharmacy cupboard, which was as tall as a man and took up half the back wall. He opened it, pulled a rusty bunch of keys from a hidden drawer, and held the ring out like a monstrance, letting the keys jangle softly.

"The key to the cells in the city hall," he said softly. "The late mayor, Bartholomäus Marchthaler, God rest his soul, had them made for me many years ago because he was too lazy to accompany me to the torture chamber each time. Since Marchthaler is long gone now, it's unlikely anyone knows about this set of keys except me—and now you."

Caroline stood up and took the keys from her husband's hand. "Do you know how dangerous this is?" she asked. "There are still the guards to consider. If even the slightest suspicion falls on you, they'll hang you, whip the children and me, and drive us right out of town."

The Regensburg executioner took his wife by the shoulders, then stroked her cheek clumsily with his huge hand. "We've always made our decisions together," he whispered. "I would never do this if you were against it."

For a long time all was silent except for the crying of the youngest child, on the other side of the door, who obviously wanted his mother.

"The children adore you," his wife said abruptly. "If something were to happen to you, they would never forgive you."

Teuber brushed a lock of hair from her forehead. "They would also never forgive me for being an unconscionable, cowardly dog." He smiled awkwardly. "And you? Could you love a man like that?"

Caroline gave him a quick kiss on the cheek. "Be quiet, you silly old bear. Is he really innocent?"

Teuber nodded. "As innocent as you and I."

Caroline closed her eyes and took a deep breath. "Then do it quickly. The sooner we get this behind us, the better. Now let me go back to the children."

As she pulled herself from his embrace and left the room, Philipp Teuber watched her brush away a single tear on her cheek. Moments later he heard her in the kitchen scolding the children, who had apparently raided the honeypot.

Teuber stood motionless, turning the keys over in his sweaty palm and balling his fist so hard around them he almost bent the rusty key ring in half. He loved his wife and his children more than anything in the world, but this time he had to follow his conscience.

Once more he glanced at the inscription on the sword:

ABIDE WITH ME, ALMIGHTY GOD

Reciting the words like an incantation, he turned back to the cupboard, where bunches of herbs and aromatic pouches hung along shelves overflowing with little clay pots. He scrutinized the inventory. He'd need some additional ingredients and would have to speak with a few people. There were bribes to be paid and tracks to be covered. All this would take at least a day or two, perhaps even longer if his plans didn't work out at first.

Teuber hoped fervently that he could finish his work before the Schongau hangman finally broke.

The eye stared at the nearly lifeless body of the prostitute who had spent so many days in the basement of this house. Katharina hadn't moved for hours; her breathing, spasmodic at first, had become weaker; and now her chest scarcely moved. Her head lay framed in a pool of blood, drying shiny like sealing wax.

The experiment was coming to an end.

The eye had recorded in great detail the decline of Katharina Sonnleitner, veteran Regensburg prostitute and the daughter of a linen dyer. After exactly seven days and four hours of torment, she at last began to tear the clothing from her body and scratch at her skin until she exposed the underlying flesh in places. Katharina had examined the bruises all over her body with fascination, and then she'd tried to bite her fingers off. She'd run from one corner of the room to the other, banging her forehead against the wall and flailing her arms about, as if trying to drive off invisible spirits. She'd screamed and cursed and, in the very next moment, nearly choked in a sudden fit of laughter. Katharina had whirled through her little cell like a gyroscope until, finally, she smashed head-on into the wall and fell motionless and bleeding onto the ground.

At that moment the eye had blinked almost imperceptibly.

He ought to have suspected it! How aggravating! This was the fifth time now that something had gone wrong! Usually the doses were simply too high. Once a girl had thrust a fork into her chest and bled to death, and another time a prostitute had thought she could fly and fell to her death from the second-story window. Thank God it had been night and he was able to hide the battered body without being seen. Aggravating, very aggravating . . .

The eye turned away.

Next time he would pad the walls with fabric and cut back the dosage a bit. The only thing still missing was the girl.

Fortunately, he already had an idea. Why hadn't he thought of her sooner?

In the two days that followed, Magdalena and Simon saw just how well organized the ostensibly lazy guild of beggars really was. Nathan was willing to set his spies on Paulus Mämminger, provided Simon would continue caring for the sick and injured in the catacombs.

Mämminger's house, located on the wide, paved Scherer-gasse where many patricians had their mansions, was an awe-inspiring building complete with a seven-story tower with embrasures on top. The beggars kept the house under surveillance by hobbling up and down the well-traveled road and loitering across the street behind a manure cart until a bailiff inevitably came to drive them off. In this way a dozen of them took shifts every day.

Magdalena was amazed to learn all the vocations represented in the brotherhood. The *Stabüler,* along with their ragamuffin children, begged for alms; the *Klenkner* crawled about on their knees, pretending to be cripples; the *Fopper* were allegedly insane; the *Clamyrer* dressed as pilgrims stranded on their way to Rome; and the *Grantner,* who claimed to be epileptics, chewed on soap so that foam would run from their mouths. All had practiced and played these roles as well as any actor, and they were proud when their performances brought them even a few rusty kreuzers. Some beggars endlessly fine-tuned the details: the right accent for a pilgrim who'd traveled the world, for example; or an especially miserable facial expression; or the perfect, most gruesome color to paint the fake stump of a limb. Especially ambitious beggars rubbed their underarms with clematis juice to cause inflammation and blisters and thus inspire compassion.

While Simon was caring for his patients, Magdalena would often stroll down the Scherergasse to watch the beggars pass secret signs back and forth and converse in a strange language she couldn't understand. They called their pidgin Beggars' Latin, a hodgepodge of German, Yiddish, and incomprehensible scraps of words. So far Magdalena had been able to glean only that *bock* meant hunger, *behaime* idiot, and *baldowern,* apparently, to scope out the house of a patrician. Whenever the beggars spotted Magdalena, they just nodded to her, then continued harassing passersby who atoned for their sins by offering small gifts and hurrying off ashamed and disgusted.

At first it seemed nothing would come of all this watching and waiting. On the first day Mämminger did nothing remarkable whatsoever. He attended church with his wife and grown children and went to one of the bathhouses around midday. Otherwise he remained in his mansion and didn't venture out again. On the second day, however, the beggars reported that several aldermen, one after the other, visited the patrician. Behind the panes of bull's-eye glass on the second floor the merchants were engaged in rather heated debate, apparently in disagreement over one particular point. Though the beggars couldn't understand what was being said, the men's violently shaking heads and wild gesticulations made at least this much clear.

Not until early evening of the second day did the last of the aldermen leave the house, whispering to one another. Unfortunately neither one-legged Hans nor Brother Paulus, who was disguised as a mendicant monk, got close enough to understand what they were saying. And as night fell rapidly over the city, it seemed nothing else unusual would happen for a while.

Then, long after midnight, the securely locked massive portal of the patrician's mansion suddenly opened and Mämminger himself scurried out into the street, wearing a cape and a hat drawn down so far over his face the dozing beggars almost didn't recognize him.

But once they did, they promptly notified Simon and Magdalena. It was clear even to the most dimwitted vagabond that a patrician sneaking through Regensburg in the dead of night, and without a guard, must have something to hide.

And soon enough they'd find out what.

Kuisl, confess! . . . One more turn of the crank . . . Confess! . . . Put more sulfur matches under him . . . Confess! . . . Tighten the screws . . . Let him feel the lash . . . Confess! Confess! Confess!

Jakob Kuisl tossed and turned as pain surged through his body in waves. Whenever pain subsided into a dull ache in one place, it resurfaced somewhere else with a vengeance: an all-consuming fire that ate away at him, wormed its way into his dreams even now, in the middle of the night, as he lay in a stupor in his cell.

The Schongau hangman knew all methods of torture and had applied most of them himself at one time or another. He'd seen pain flash in hundreds of pairs of eyes, but now he felt that pain in his very own body.

He thought he would have been able to endure more.

He'd suffered three days of torture now. On the second day they stopped just before his right arm was wrenched from its socket—not to spare him, Kuisl was certain, but to let his body

recover for the torture yet to come. This morning they began
with the Spanish Donkey, a vertical board whose sharp upper
edge he had to straddle while his legs were weighted with stones.
In the afternoon the Regensburg executioner repeatedly applied
thumb and leg screws and forced burning matches under Kuisl's
fingernails.

Kuisl had remained silent. Not a whimper crossed his lips,
not even once; he threw all his strength into the curses he shouted
at his prosecutors. And from behind the lattice the voice of the
third man could still be heard, taunting him.

*You have children, don't you? And a beautiful wife as well . . .
Tighten the screws . . . Confess!*

The man knew about Kuisl's family; he knew the name of
his wife. He knew all about him. And yet he remained a mere
shadow behind the wooden lattice, a monster from the past that
Kuisl couldn't place.

Who was this man? Who was Weidenfeld?

On the morning of the third day they introduced the Maid-
en's Lap, a chair covered with sharpened wooden spikes on
which the victim had to sit for hours with bare buttocks while
the spikes dug into his flesh. In the afternoon Teuber put him
back on the rack and almost finished the work of dislocating his
right shoulder.

It was during this part of the torture that the unknown third
man delivered his next blow. So casually that the two other inquisitors didn't notice, he whispered a few words, more pointed
than any of the rest, that cut Kuisl to the quick.

*Don't believe for a second that your daughter can help you
now . . .*

These words pulled the ground out from under Kuisl's feet.
The third man not only knew his wife; he also knew his daughter! And he knew she was here in Regensburg! Had he intercepted the letter? Had he already abducted her?

Despite the fetters, Kuisl almost succeeded in breaking himself free of the rack now. The combined strength of four city guards was needed to force him back down on the board and tie him up again. Kuisl didn't speak another word, and the bailiffs finally took him back to his cell. It took three men to do so since, with his shins crushed, Kuisl could no longer walk. His left arm hung limp at his side, and his hands, bright purple now, had swollen up like pig bladders.

As he lay there in his cell and drifted off into a half sleep, an endless nightmare played over and over in his mind. When the pain woke him again—as had so often been the case in the last few days and nights—it took him a while to get his bearings again. To judge by the darkness, it was already night. Moaning, he pulled himself up to a wall until he crouched in a halfway bearable position on the floor.

All of a sudden he heard a soft scraping sound. It took a while for him to realize it was the bolt to the cell door sliding back slowly. Silently, the door swung open and a dark figure stood in the entry.

"Have you come to get me again, you wretched swine?" the Schongau hangman rasped. "The sun isn't even up yet. Decent people are asleep at this hour. Be so good as to come back in an hour or so."

"Hurry up, you blockhead," the figure in the door whispered. Only now did Kuisl realize this was no bailiff but Teuber. "We don't have much time!"

"What in the world . . . ?" Kuisl started to straighten up, but as soon as he got to his feet, he collapsed again like a sack of grain. Pain surged once more through his swollen legs, and despite the cool night air he was feverish and bathed in sweat.

Cursing softly, Teuber bent down to the injured man. He pulled a long set of pliers from his bag and, with one vigorous snap, cut through the rusty chain.

"Keep still now."

He struggled to pull the Schongau hangman back to his feet

again, laid Kuisl's good arm over his own shoulder, wrapped his own arm tight against Kuisl's chest, and dragged the heavy body into the hall.

"What—what are you doing?" Kuisl said, shivering. "Where are the damned guards?" He winced as a fresh wave of pain rolled through his body.

"I sent them off to dream for a while," Teuber whispered. "It took me two days to make the potion, but the virtue of that patience is that they won't taste it in the wine now, especially with just a few drops in each gallon." He grinned as he continued to lug Kuisl toward the exit. "And in case you're wondering about the bailiff in the corridor, he's shitting and vomiting up everything in his body as we speak. That's what good old Christmas rose can do. Oh, well, he'll survive."

They arrived at the low vaulted room where five soldiers lay snoring among two empty wine jugs. With only a few torches flickering dimly on the walls, the room was blanketed in near total darkness. Along one side cannons and coaches were dimly visible.

"Why . . . are you . . . doing this?" Kuisl stammered, clinging tightly to the Regensburg executioner who, despite his powerful arms, struggled to keep Kuisl on his feet. "They'll . . . flay you alive when they find out what you've done."

"*If* they find out." Teuber pulled a large bunch of keys from his jacket and opened the door leading out into the city hall square. He pointed to the guards snoring behind them. "I prepared the sleeping potion so that it would look as if a heavy bout of drinking knocked them out. The guard in the hall got a bad tummy ache, and a stupid bailiff must have been so drunk he didn't close the door to your cell properly. *I* certainly had nothing to do with it." He smiled coolly as he steered the nearly unconscious Kuisl toward a cart nearby, but Kuisl sensed a slight trembling in his colleague's voice.

"But in case any of them become suspicious, they're welcome

to put me on the rack," he said softly. "The fine patricians can dirty their own hands for once."

By this point Kuisl was lying in a cart that smelled of decay and human excrement. Teuber spread a few old rags and a load of damp straw over the Schongau hangman, then took his seat on the coach box and clicked his tongue. His old gray mare set off, pulling the cart into a nearby lane.

"I hope the stench doesn't kill you before your wounds," Teuber said. Grinning, he cast a backward glance at his load of animal carcasses, rotten vegetables, and excrement. "But I can carry you safely through town on the knacker's wagon. I hardly think the city guards are interested in what exactly is rotting under there."

"Where . . . are we going?" Kuisl groaned. He saw dark roofs and façades pass by overhead while the wagon rumbled over the cobblestones—a jolting reminder of the innumerable contusions, broken bones, and burned flesh he'd suffered in recent days.

"We can't go to my house," Teuber said. "That's the first place they'd think to look for you. Besides, my wife's against sheltering a murderer. But I know a good hiding place. You'll like it there. The proprietress of the inn takes good care of . . ." He hesitated before going on. "Let's say she keeps a very close eye on her guests, most of them men."

Simon and Magdalena slunk from house to house, always keeping their distance from the hooded figure in front of them. Nathan was by their side, as well as Hans Reiser, who had since recovered. The four followed Mämminger's small lantern through little back alleys until he turned off Scherergasse and headed south. At one point they encountered a foul-smelling cart with a sinister broad-shouldered man sitting on the coach box, but both Mämminger and his pursuers retreated into dark doorways as the phantom passed.

Simon sensed Mämminger intentionally chose a roundabout way to avoid pursuit. Only after a full quarter-hour did the treasurer arrive at the cathedral square. Mämminger's steps echoed across the pavement as he hurried along the right side of the church, turning at last into a graveyard behind the cathedral. Simon and the others ducked behind a cluster of weathered headstones and watched the patrician make his way cautiously down a row of freshly dug graves, cursing softly whenever his leather boots stuck in mud left by the recent thunderstorm. On a column at the edge of the graveyard a light flickered, and in its faint glow Simon saw Mämminger climb over another burial mound and sneak toward a low back door that led into the rear of the cathedral. Within moments he'd disappeared inside.

"It will attract too much attention if all four of us follow him," Magdalena whispered from behind one of the gravestones. "I suggest Simon and I go in after him. Hans can wait here while Nathan creeps around to the main portal, in case Mämminger tries to escape that way."

The beggar king frowned. "Not a bad plan . . . for a woman. But I'd like very much to know what His Excellency the treasurer expects to find in there. So Simon and I will go and—"

"Oh, no you won't," Magdalena interrupted. "It's *my* father's life at stake, so *I* will go."

"We'll tell you all about it later over a nice glass of wine, Nathan. I promise," Simon added. "Now let's go, or Mämminger will slip through our fingers."

Nathan was about to protest, but then he waved his agreement and disappeared among the gravestones. Simon and Magdalena approached the little door and opened it quietly. Inside, under an enormous cupola, a few flickering candles provided as much light as they did shadow, and except for a bit of moonlight falling in through the stained-glass windows, it was almost completely dark inside.

They entered the cathedral from the right of the apse. From there Simon and Magdalena could make out the huge columns of the nave, which rose straight up to disappear in the darkness of the cupola. From altars on all sides saints glowered down at them, and from a stone arch on their left a silver chain dangled over a well. An immense bronze sarcophagus stood in the center of an aisle ahead of them, and a life-size statue of a cardinal knelt before the crucifix on top.

Simon, who noticed that every step they took was echoing from the walls, signaled to Magdalena to stop moving and remain still beside the altar.

Soon, from the south aisle, they heard a soft creaking sound of iron scraping on iron. A moment passed; then they heard the shuffle of leather-soled shoes receding. To the west, where the main portal was located, a small crack appeared and a narrow bar of light shone in, contrasting with the deep darkness of the interior.

"Damn!" Simon whispered. "He's escaping through the main entrance! He must have a key, and now we can only hope that Nathan's following him."

"Shouldn't we go after him?" Magdalena asked.

Simon shrugged. "I think there's no point. If we leave through the main portal, he'll be able to see us from the square or he'll have disappeared already. What luck!"

He stamped his foot angrily. The sound carried through the vault like a thunderclap, startling the medicus.

"We can at least try to find out what he was doing here," Magdalena consoled him. "Come, let's have a look."

They ran to the south aisle, from where the rasping sound had come, Simon lighting the way with a votive candle he'd taken from a side altar.

"Look!" he whispered after a short while, pointing to muddy footprints on the floor. "This is where Mämminger must have walked. You can still see the tracks!" Unsure what to do next, he scanned the chapel. "But what, for heaven's sake, was he doing here?"

His glance landed on a small recessed altar displaying a triptych dedicated to Saint Sebastian. A middle panel showed the martyr lashed to a tree and pierced with arrows. And on the altar stood a gilded statuette holding a purse in one hand and an arrow in the other.

It took Simon a while to notice what was strange about the figure.

While all the other proportions were correct, the arrow was much too long and too thick, looking more like a spear or a silver tube. Bending down to examine the arrow in the candlelight, Simon noticed the arrow wasn't firmly attached to the hand, and in the top third there was a groove, as if the spear consisted of two parts screwed together.

Screwed together?

Simon turned to Magdalena. "The scraping sound!" he exclaimed. "I think I now know what—"

Once again a small strip of light shone through the crack at the main portal, and shortly after, they could hear the door close softly. Magdalena pulled Simon away from the altar and behind a column.

"It looks like Mämminger's come back," she whispered excitedly. "Do you think he forgot something?"

Simon shook his head. "I think someone is coming to pick up the message."

"The message?" Magdalena asked. "What message?"

Simon put his finger to his lips, silencing her as they observed a dark figure tiptoe down the center aisle and approach the niche. When the stranger reached the altar, Magdalena had to put her hand over her mouth to keep from screaming. It was the man who had tried to kill her! At his side he still carried the deadly rapier, but now that he'd taken off his hood, she was able

to see his face—narrow and ferret-like with tiny eyes that nervously darted back and forth and just faint thin lines for eyebrows. His head was like an enormous balloon, its size emphasized
by his baldness and disproportionate atop an otherwise small
frame. He was dressed inconspicuously in knee breeches, leather
boots, and a short coat over a mouse-gray shirt. He looked
around in every direction, his gaze passing over the very column
behind which Magdalena and Simon were hiding. The hangman's daughter quickly drew back, hoping the man hadn't seen
her.

When they heard the scraping sound again, Magdalena
looked out from behind the column to witness the stranger un-
screwing the little silver arrow. He removed a thin, rolled-up
document, smiling briefly as he unfolded the letter and began to
read.

A hiding place for messages! Magdalena realized. *Mämminger
leaves notes in the cathedral for his hired assassin!*

She remembered how indignant the treasurer had been
when the stranger had asked to speak with him in Silvio's garden. What had Mämminger said to him then?

What's so urgent that we can't communicate in the usual way?

This was the usual way. A brilliant hiding place! No honorable city financier had to dirty his hands in direct contact with
less reputable personages. Presumably they could exchange messages in the dark niche even during the day.

And presumably the stranger would now place his response
to Mämminger in the tube. Then she and Simon could quite easily—

Something startled her out of her thoughts. At first she
couldn't figure out what, but then she was conscious of a soft
sound—more the hint of a sound than anything. The stranger
seemed to notice it as well. Again he turned his monstrous, hairless head in all directions like some kind of snake, but when he
detected nothing suspicious, he held the note over an altar can-

dle, and a blue flame shot up, reducing the secret message to ashes.

Suddenly Simon seized Magdalena by the shoulder. She turned around, terrified, while the medicus pointed frantically at a shadow cast against the cathedral wall. Enlarged to gigantic proportions, the form scurried from column to column, but as it moved farther from the altar and out of range of the candlelight, the shadow disappeared as quickly as it had come. It was a while before Simon and Magdalena noticed the man just a few steps away, lurking behind the pews with a drawn dagger. He was far smaller than the shadow suggested. It was Silvio Contarini.

The trip in the knacker's cart through the city's back streets seemed endless. The Regensburg executioner kept stopping to shovel more feces, dead rats, and garbage onto his cart. Even though it was against the law to be out on the street in Regensburg after dark, an exception was clearly made for the hangman. The few night watchmen they encountered looked aside and made the sign of the cross once the wagon had rumbled by. It brought misfortune to look a hangman in the eye, especially at night when people said the souls of the damned he'd executed accompanied him through the streets.

When they finally reached their destination, Kuisl struggled to raise his head. Before them stood a fortress-like building consisting of three towers and a courtyard at the center. In contrast to the surrounding houses, light still burned in the windows of the tower to the right, and Kuisl could hear the distant laughter of women.

"Peter's Tower," Teuber whispered. "The city guard has a garrison of a dozen soldiers billeted here." He winked at the hangman. "If you want to hide someone, the best place is where the enemy least expects. That's an old mercenary saying. Wait here. I'll be right back."

Kuisl watched Teuber approach the tower on the right and

pound on the door. The Schongau hangman was seized by momentary panic. Did Teuber intend to hand him over to the soldiers? Didn't he just say a garrison was billeted here? And now this idiot was knocking at the door of the lion's den!

Then he noticed a woman in a bright dress in the open doorway. On her head was a red and yellow cap just like those the mercenaries' whores used to wear. He estimated she was about fifty years old, even though her broad hips and full breasts made her look considerably younger. Though she was overweight and her hair graying, she was strangely attractive, and Kuisl supposed she must have been stunning in her day.

The woman spoke briefly with the Regensburg executioner; she then cast a glance at Kuisl, who tried to sit up a bit amid the piles of rags and manure. Only now did he notice she wore a patch over one eye. With the other eye she squinted at him suspiciously.

"A stinking excuse for a man you're bringing me," she said loud enough for Kuisl to hear. Her voice had something sharp to it, like that of one accustomed to giving orders. "Not worth much more than the carcasses lying next to him in the cart. You know that if the bailiffs catch me with this monster, they'll put the shrew's fiddle on me and chase me out of town — but only if I'm *lucky*. If I'm not so lucky, well . . ." She sighed. "But for the Holy Virgin and because it's you, Teuber, bring the poor fellow in. Just make sure my guests don't get wind of it."

"I . . . can walk . . . by myself," Kuisl grunted. "I . . . can do it."

He slid off the cart and staggered toward the doorway. Kuisl hated it when women caught him in weak moments. And this woman didn't look as if she'd have much sympathy for whiners.

When he arrived at the door, the woman looked up at him disdainfully. Kuisl was almost three heads taller than she.

"So this is the devil of Regensburg?" she said. "If you ask me, he looks more like an abused circus bear who's had his claws ripped out. How tall are you anyway, eh? Six feet?" she asked in a snide tone and laughed. "Be careful you don't bash your forehead when you enter my modest home. By the looks of you, a whore's fart would blow you over right now."

"It wasn't him, Dorothea," Teuber replied. "I had to torture him until the blood came out of his ears. I swear by God he's not the one."

"Leave God out of this"—Dorothea had already turned to go back inside—"or lightning will strike the tower."

They entered a low, dark anteroom illuminated by a single torch. A winding staircase led down to a cellar and up to the floors above. From here Kuisl heard laughter and voices and, now and then, a sharp cry followed by a deep masculine groan.

"You see, my honorable guests are enjoying themselves splendidly tonight," Dorothea said to the Regensburg executioner as they walked down the spiral stone staircase together. "I wouldn't want to disturb them, above all because among them are a few aldermen who really mustn't know about our surly murderer here. I have a nice hiding place down in the basement storage room, and he can stay there for the time being."

"That's fine, Dorothea," Teuber replied. "We won't bother you anymore, I promise."

After a few more steps they reached the cellar, where sacks and crates were scattered around several large wine barrels. Dorothea hurried over to a barrel in the middle.

"Push that out of the way, Teuber," she said, "or is that too much for you? You look a bit worn out. Won't your wife let you into bed anymore?"

Silently the executioner placed his arms around the wine barrel and, straining, moved it a bit to the left. Behind it a low doorway led into another dank storage room not much bigger than the cell where Kuisl had spent the last few days.

"He can stay here for the time being," Dorothea said. "And

now excuse me. Upstairs I'm entertaining a close confidant of the bishop, and I don't like to keep the church waiting."

Without another word, she winked briefly with her good eye and left Kuisl and the Regensburg executioner alone. Once the sound of her footsteps died away, Kuisl finally collapsed, sliding down the wall and rolling into himself like a sick animal.

"Can . . . we . . . trust her?" he wondered, half asleep.

"Dorothea?" Teuber nodded. "Fat Thea is the procuress of the whorehouse here at Peter's Gate. Actually, such houses are illegal, but—oh, the flesh is weak. Even the honorable aldermen's . . ." Grinning, he lit another torch and spread out some wool blankets he'd brought along on the floor of the tiny room. "The patricians know about this place, but they leave Thea alone, and in return they get special favors. The soldiers garrisoned next door are of course regular guests, and for a few hellers I make sure the guests don't get out of line and hurt the girls. If the fellows misbehave, all I have to do is grab them by the scruff of the neck, and the next morning they're bowed over in church saying the Lord's Prayer a hundred times because they think my touch has brought an evil spell on them." He bent down to Kuisl, who was still doubled over on the floor. "Do you need anything else?"

"Why?" Jakob Kuisl asked, half asleep.

"Why what?"

"You didn't have to help me. It's . . . dangerous. Your family . . ."

Teuber was silent a long time before replying. "You're one of us, Kuisl," he said at last. "Just as much an outcast as I am. You have family, just as I do, and I know you're innocent. Someone's out to get you, some rotten bastard of an alderman got it into his head to do this, and now I'm supposed to carry out his dirty work for him. They think I'm stupid, but we hangmen aren't stupid, are we, Kuisl? We may not have honor, but we're not stupid."

The Schongau executioner had already dozed off.

Teuber spread a blanket over him, ducked through the low entryway, and pushed the wine barrel in front of the opening again. He would return early in the morning with herbs and medicines that would help Kuisl bear at least the worst of the pain.

Teuber stomped up the steps and out into the cool night air. A moment later Dorothea appeared beside him and squeezed his hand; her cold, calculating manner seemed to have vanished now as they looked up into the clear, starry sky together.

"So you really believe he's innocent?" Dorothea finally asked.

Teuber nodded. "I've never before been so sure of anything. He doesn't have to stay long, I promise. Perhaps only a few days, until he's able to take a few steps again."

Fat Thea sighed. "Do you realize what you're saddling me with? Tomorrow half the council will be here, to say nothing of the soldiers at Peter's Gate. If just one of them catches sight of this monster—"

"Thea, I beg you." Teuber brushed a gray lock out of his friend's face and looked at her earnestly. "Just this once."

The Regensburg executioner knew he could count on Dorothea, but it was also clear just how dangerous the matter was for them both. Teuber had known Fat Thea for almost twenty years. She started out as a simple streetwalker but for the last few years had run this house at Peter's Gate, becoming the most powerful prostitute in the city. Nevertheless, it would take just one word from the aldermen, one slip-up, one false accusation, to send her back to where she came from.

Back to the gutter.

"How's your daughter?" Teuber asked abruptly, trying to change the subject. "Is she still as beautiful as I remember?"

Dorothea smiled. "More so, and she knows it. I have to hide her from her suitors, or they'll drive me crazy." Her face became serious again. "I want Christina to have it better than I did. Tomorrow, when the councilors come here, their purses will be jangling. Who knows, maybe I'll just up and quit, marry a good-looking bookbinder, and spread my legs for him alone after that."

Teuber grinned. "Consider that carefully. In a few months the Reichstag is coming to Regensburg, and the ambassadors will be pounding at your door. You'll earn so much you'll be shitting gold."

All at once he had an idea. "Tomorrow when the aldermen visit, can you do a little snooping for me?"

Dorothea eyed him crossly. "Don't you think one favor is enough? What else do you want?"

"There were three inquisitors present when Kuisl was being tortured," Teuber mused, "and all three are members of the council: Rheiner, the president of the court; young Kerscher from the tax office; and a third one I don't know. Can you find out who that was?"

Dorothea shrugged. "If it was an alderman, it's possible he'll be with the group tomorrow night as well. Almost all of them intend to come. I even had to bring a few girls in off the street, since at least two of the noble gentlemen will most certainly want to be whipped . . ." She made a disgusted face. "It will be a tough job, but I'll see what I can find out."

"Thanks, Thea, I don't know how —"

"One of my girls missed her monthly menstruation," she interrupted crossly. "Take care of her and give her a few of your herbs. I have no use for a child around here."

Teuber nodded. "I'll see what I can do —"

"And find the madman who's been killing my girls out in the streets these last few weeks," Dorothea interrupted again. "He's knocked off half a dozen already. Something's not right. Someone's lurking around out there, and I can only hope it isn't the monster I've got in my cellar now."

Without another word, she disappeared into the tower,

where giggles and an occasional moan could still be heard. Alone now, Teuber stood outside the door and watched a falling star shoot across the sky.

Dear God, see that my family gets through this unharmed . . .

He took a deep breath, trying to shake the fear that had been raging inside him like a wild beast since the previous night. If the aldermen could find even the slightest piece of evidence against him, a new hangman would drag the old one off to the scaffold, and his wife and children would be driven from town to live out the rest of their days in the forest. The little ones would slowly die of hunger, asking their mother again and again why their father had done this to them.

The Regensburg executioner climbed into his wagon and set out for home. Dense fog crept in through the city streets and beneath his coat and trousers, causing a shiver to run up and down his spine.

He knew the shaking didn't come from the cool night air alone.

"Do you know what your little Venetian friend might be looking for here?" Simon whispered, pointing to Silvio Contarini, who still crouched behind the pews.

"First, he's not *my* little Venetian, and second, I have no idea," Magdalena replied in a low voice. "But if you absolutely have to—"

"Shh!" Simon put his finger to her lips, but it was too late. The stranger by the Saint Sebastian altar seemed to have heard something, for he quickly screwed the secret tube together and placed it back in the statue's right hand. Then he reached for his rapier and tensed up. Step by step, holding the blade in front of him, he approached the column behind which Simon and Magdalena hid. Beads of sweat broke out on Simon's brow, and he held his breath, hoping the intruder wouldn't see them. The footsteps paused, and just when the medicus thought perhaps the man had turned to look elsewhere, the stranger's monstrous head darted out from behind the pillar.

The stranger seemed just as surprised as Simon and Magdalena. For a moment it looked as if he wanted to say something, but before he could, a shadow rushed toward them from the left. Silvio Contarini leaped over several pews, knocked over a few chairs, and finally threw himself at the intruder. Their blades clashing, Silvio drove his opponent farther and farther back toward the sarcophagus.

In a movement so fast it was nearly imperceptible, the stranger feinted to the side and then struck Silvio's upper torso, ripping the entire length of his velvet coat from top to bottom. The attacker thrust his rapier a second time, and the little Venetian foundered and fell to his knees. A cold smile spread over the stranger's face as he raised his weapon to deliver a *coup de grâce* to the heart. The blade sloped down like the head of a venomous snake.

"No!" Magdalena screamed. "You—you monster!"

Instinctively the hangman's daughter grabbed the silver statuette of Saint Sebastian from the altar and flung it toward the stranger.

With a dull thud the heavy figurine struck him on the back of the head.

The man reeled, flailing his arms, then crashed to the floor like a fallen angel. He lay there so long Magdalena thought he might even be dead, but moments later he struggled to his feet again, breathing heavily. Like a drunk, he reached for his rapier, staggered, and tried to find something to hold on to. In this manner he made his way step by step down the center aisle. Even disoriented he somehow seemed as dangerous as ever.

Simon and Magdalena were about to run after him when they heard someone moaning nearby. Silvio. The Venetian seemed more seriously injured than it first appeared. He was bleeding from his left arm and chest, and a bright red gash ran across his right cheek. He struggled to get up, panting, but then tipped back over on his side and lay motionless on the floor.

"My God, Silvio!" Magdalena rushed to the ambassador. For a moment Simon was tempted to pursue the stranger, but the man had already disappeared, and all Simon could see was the fog creeping in through the open church portal.

"Grazie," Silvio gasped. He leaned against the sarcophagus, breathing heavily. "If you hadn't thrown that statue, then . . ."

"I owed you a dress," Magdalena said, inspecting the Venetian's wounds. "Let's just call it even."

"What kind of a dress?" Simon asked with some irritation as he stepped out from behind the column. "What's this Venetian got to do with your dress?"

Magdalena sighed. "It's not what you think. He gave me—"

"I lent her a gown from my dressing room to wear to the ball," Silvio interrupted, struggling to his feet and wiping blood from his face with a white lace handkerchief. "She looked positively charming in it, a real *principessa!*"

Simon raised his eyebrows. "A gown to wear to the ball. I see. You didn't tell me about that, *principessa.*"

"Damn it all," Magdalena cursed. "Because it wasn't important!" Her voice was so loud it echoed throughout the cathedral. "There are murderers running around in here, my father will probably be drawn and quartered, and you have nothing better to do than act like a spoiled, jealous child!"

"Me, jealous? Ridiculous." Simon, affecting a hurt expression, ran his hand through his hair. "A man should at least be allowed a question when he learns his girl has been out tarting herself up for strangers in some foreigner's dressing room."

That was the last straw. "Tarting?" she snapped. "You're one to talk, you dandy!" Her voice cracked with emotion. "And just what do you mean by *girl?* Not once have I heard a proposal from you. Only excuses, excuses! When have you ever given me a dress, or even a lousy engagement ribbon, huh? I'd let that pass,

but *now,* you little overeducated wimp, you want to tell me
—*me*—how to live my life! Get away, you wretch!"

Her final words echoed through the cathedral, then faded
into an awkward silence.

Simon bowed stiffly. "I understand. I wish you both a pleasant good evening." He turned on his heels and headed toward
the main portal, where the priest had just arrived to prepare for
morning prayers. Leaving the cathedral with his head held high,
Simon stumbled on the door frame and had to grab the astonished priest to keep from falling.

"Someone back there is in need of confession, Father," the
medicus said. "Pride and wrath, two mortal sins. Don't let the
lady go until she recites the Lord's Prayer a hundred times."

Before the startled priest could reply, Simon disappeared
into the foggy night.

Back in the niche, Silvio sighed and looked up to the ceiling.
"O *Invidia!*" he lamented. "Your *amico* is jealous. That's not what
I intended."

"Oh, don't worry; he'll come back down from his high
horse," Magdalena said, but there was a twinge of doubt in her
voice. Perhaps she'd gone a bit too far. She knew that Simon
suffered from not being able to offer her the life they both
longed for.

"He's probably waiting for us right outside the door," she
said, trying to console herself. "Why don't you tell me what in
the world you came looking for here in the church? You haven't
been stalking me, have you?"

Silvio shook his head in horror. "*Madonna!* Never would I do
anything like that! I was following that man! I was coming home
from the Whale when I saw him sneak across the square in front
of the cathedral—the same man who ambushed us before! So I
followed him and—well, you know the rest." He smiled. "You
see, it's really up to you to explain what you're doing here. By the
way, it was disgraceful how you abandoned me at that boring *soi-*

rée. In return you should at least offer me another invitation."
His eyes started to glaze over and he reached for his left arm.
Only now did Magdalena notice that Silvio's shirt was drenched
in blood.

"Oh, God, with all this fuss, I completely forgot you're injured!" she exclaimed. "Quick, I'll take you to Simon. He'll—"

"I don't think that's such a good idea," Silvio lamented as he
leaned against a column for support. His face was as pale as a
ghost. "No doubt your *amico* would let enough blood from me to
paint the whole cathedral."

Magdalena smiled. "You might be right about that. Well,
then, I'll have to see to your wounds myself. Let's go—fortunately your house is just across the way."

She supported Silvio under his arms as they left.

"What a wonderful feeling to be carried by you," the little
Venetian rejoiced. "I hope to require your help a long time."

"Stop talking such nonsense," Magdalena replied sharply. "A
few bandages and herbs from the market to stanch the bleeding,
and you'll be your old self again. The wounds aren't as bad as I
thought. Now quit making such a fuss and try walking a bit. You
men are all such sissies!"

Cursing under his breath, Simon stomped across the cathedral
square, nearly swallowed up in the fog that had descended over
the city in the last hour. In vain he looked for Nathan, who was
supposed to have been waiting there for them. Had the beggar
king secretly run off?

Simon didn't dare call out, so he just quietly looked about the
square, then slipped away into the first small street he came to.
He had to clear his head! Just what was the matter with him?
He'd lost control of himself, and now Magdalena really believed
he was jealous.

And worse: this Venetian fool thought so as well.

With a deep sigh, Simon had to admit that his jealousy was

not entirely imagined. Contarini had more possessions than Simon could ever dream of as a poor medicus—money, fine clothes, influence, power . . . things Simon would never be able to offer Magdalena. Without a single certificate from a recognized university, he was just an insignificant quack. And now that he'd fled Schongau, he'd lost whatever respectability he had left!

Simon looked down at himself. His jacket and shirt were mud-stained and torn; he had no money and was sleeping in dank basements with beggars; and his girl was spending her time in the dressing rooms of foreign men to whom he'd never be able to hold a candle.

This was the end.

Simon was so distressed he didn't notice the two guards armed with spears until he literally stumbled into them.

"Well, well, who do we have here?" one guard sneered, grabbing Simon by the scruff of the neck like a naughty child. "A night owl, eh? Don't you know it's forbidden to go out in the streets at night? And right now I think it's about . . ." He and his colleague pretended to look up in the sky for the moon. "Well, let's just say it's not a good time for you to be out here, eh?"

Simon nodded respectfully, trying desperately to think of a way out of this situation. He had to assume all the guards had received descriptions of the alleged arsonists. And though this pair hadn't recognized him yet, that could change at any moment.

"Went down by the river for a drink," he slurred, in the hope the two guards would be fooled by his affectation. "It jush got a lil bit late . . ."

"Speak up," the second night watchman said threateningly as he held a lantern in his face and sized him up distrustfully. "For people like you we have a nice little pub room. A bit drafty, but it'll clear your head fast."

He gave Simon a shove, and they all set out toward city hall square, the medicus attempting to stumble along appropriately. After a short while they arrived in the square, which looked quite different in the early-morning hours than during the typical daytime hustle and bustle.

The fatter of the two men pointed his spear at a rusty cage sitting on the ground and chained to the wall of city hall. It looked like a gigantic birdcage.

"The House of Fools," the night watchman said. "You'll stay here for the next few hours. You should have lots of fine company."

"But everyone will see me in there!" Simon croaked, temporarily forgetting his role as a drunk and falling out of character.

The tall, thin night watchman holding the lantern nodded. "Correct. The people need something to gawk at. Everyone we pick up at night winds up in the House of Fools—drunks and drifters, but also honorable citizens and men of the church. Once we even locked up an alderman, since the fine gentleman couldn't pull together the money to buy himself out. Oh, and don't you try to hide in a corner or we'll chain you to the bars up front where it's hard to dodge the rotten vegetables that'll come flying at you."

Simon's heart began to race.

When morning comes, all of Regensburg will see me in there. If even one person takes a close look, I'll be keeping Kuisl company on the scaffold, as an arsonist.

"Can't we perhaps . . . come to some other arrangement?" Simon simpered.

The fat night watchman nodded, thinking. "Do you have money?"

The medicus shook his head silently.

"Then I have good news for you," the bailiff responded. "Food and lodging are free at the House of Fools."

He poked Simon in the back with the point of his spear and pushed him along toward city hall.

10

SIMON BUTTONED UP HIS TATTERED JACKET TO ward off the cool night air that was worst now as dawn was breaking. He closed his eyes, then opened them again, but the scene around him remained bleak as before.

A trio of drinking buddies next to him were snoring so loudly it sounded as if they were trying to saw through the bars of their drafty dungeon. Two of them were presumably traveling journeymen who'd spent far more than they could afford that night making the rounds of the city taverns. They wore ragged trousers and linen shirts but had apparently forgotten their hats at the last tavern. Purses fastened to their belts hung down weightless and empty. Simon guessed that after a lash or two of the whip, the two day laborers would be banished from the city in the morning, but that would be all. These traveling journeymen offered very little to interest the crowds that would start arriving at city hall square before long. The city guards rounded up such specimens every night of the week.

The third reveler was a different story. To all outward appearances he looked like a Franciscan monk whose brown frock was pulled tightly across a remarkably fat belly. Innumerable blowflies flitted about his fresh tonsure and greasy, flushed cheeks, feeding on sweat that streamed down his face despite the cool morning air. In his pudgy hands he held a dirty linen sack that he pressed to his chest from time to time like a nursing infant, murmuring something incomprehensible in his sleep. Each time he was about to belt out another snore, his whole body quivered as if he were in the throes of death. Then, at other moments, he stopped breathing altogether, only to start in again all the more violently minutes later.

Of these cellmates Simon hated the fat monk the most.

The medicus had tried again to convince the guards not to lock him up, but they just laughed and wished him a pleasant night's rest. Now he sat on a hard wooden bench, wedged between the two snoring workmen, and watched night slowly recede from the square. From time to time one of the journeymen's heads would fall onto Simon's shoulder and he would smack his lips peacefully, no doubt dreaming of the expensive roast goose he had enjoyed for dinner the night before—probably the last he'd have for a long time, Simon imagined. The medicus couldn't bring himself to waken the journeyman, so he just pushed the workman's head back gently.

Simon closed his eyes again and tried to concentrate—not easy given the loud snoring all around him. In no more than an hour shopkeepers would start opening their doors, maids would stroll across the square, and every person who passed would have a look into the House of Fools. Simon was sure it was only a matter of time before someone recognized him as the bathhouse arsonist. The description of him and Magdalena had been rather precise, and the guards surely possessed a warrant by now. Simon considered cutting his finger with his stiletto and rubbing blood over his face in the hope of passing himself off as the unfortunate victim of a barroom brawl. But he couldn't change his height or his clothing, and those alone were probably enough to give him away.

Unless he had something else to wear.

Simon glanced again at the two workmen and the fat Franciscan, who still clutched his linen sack like a doll.

The linen sack!

Simon's heart began to pound. He could at least turn that into a hood, and—who knows?—perhaps there was more clothing inside it! The medicus rose quietly and stepped toward the monk, who lay like a corpse on a bench across from him. Inch by inch he gingerly reached for the sack in the Franciscan's arms. Although Simon fumbled with it, he felt the bundle coming free. He'd almost extricated half the sack from the monk's grip when he heard a deep snarl.

Simon froze as the monk's bloodshot right eye opened and glared back at him suspiciously.

"Are you trying to take my wine away, you damned son of a bitch?" the cleric growled. "That's wine for mass, the blood of Christ. If you do that, they'll boil you in oil, you damned heretic . . ."

The eye closed and the man resumed snoring loudly. Simon exhaled, waited a while, and then reached out confidently a second time.

Now the monk's fingers closed around Simon's wrist like a vise and pulled him close. The stench of wine on the monk's breath almost knocked the medicus out.

"No one steals from Brother Hubertus," the monk bellowed. "No one, do you hear?"

Looking for all the world like an overgrown bat, the Franciscan rose up and hit his head on the low top of the cage.

"Ouch, damn!"

Only now did the monk seem to comprehend where he was. Looking at his cellmates, then onto the city hall square, he let out an endless stream of curses. "In the name of the unholy trinity, that goddamned band of blockheaded bailiffs has locked me up *again!* Worthless philistines!" He shook the bars of the cage so hard Simon thought he might actually tear them apart at any moment. "Only because I tried to lead those poor stray virgins back into God's grace!" he continued.

"Virgins?" Though he was afraid, Simon couldn't resist asking.

The Franciscan, evidently Brother Hubertus, looked back at the medicus with some irritation, as if he'd only just now noticed him. Apparently he'd already forgotten Simon's botched robbery.

"Yes, virgins!" he barked. "They hang around the brothel down at Peter's Gate waiting for someone to come and read the Bible to them."

Simon nodded sympathetically. "And you were so selfless as to take on that thankless job."

A grin broke across the brother's face. "What was it Saint Augustine said?" He began in a professorial tone, though his tongue was still too thick to pronounce some of the words. "'If you suppress prostitution, capricious lusts will overthrow society.'" Hubertus shook his finger. "We cannot therefore hinder the prostitutes, but we can still bring them closer to God."

Simon chuckled. "A noble undertaking and a necessary one. I remember Thomas Aquinas saying, 'Remove prostitutes from the world—'"

"'And you will fill the world with sodomy,'" Brother Hubertus interrupted. He nodded his fat head in agreement. "I see you're a true scholar. Very few know this passage by the great Dominican. May I inquire what brings you to your unfortunate present situation?"

The medicus saw his chance but paused a moment before answering. "I was engaged in a passionate dispute concerning our Savior's poverty and the trenchant observations of Wilhelm von Ockham when the night watchmen came and rudely inter-rupted us. My disputatious interlocutor was able to flee, but the bailiffs caught me and locked me in this drafty hole."

The monk shook his head in indignation. "And thus schol-arship goes to the dogs! We must continue this conversation at my house."

Simon eyed him with astonishment. "I beg your pardon?"

Brother Hubertus was already knocking loudly on a door that led into the city hall. The two workmen continued snoring, unperturbed.

"Just let me take care of it," the monk said. "I know these barbarians."

After a while a key turned in the squeaky lock and the scrawny night watchman stuck his nose through the doorway.

"Have you slept it off then, Brother Hubertus?" He grinned.

"Don't be fresh, Hannes"—the monk shook his finger—"or there will be consequences, believe me. I'll talk to the bishop about this."

The night watchman sighed. "That's what you always say, but you know just as well as I do that we have the right to detain even honorable society if they defy the curfew and—"

"Yes, yes, very well," replied Brother Hubertus, nudging the bailiff aside and pressing a few coins into his hand. "You don't have to preach it from the rooftops. And he's coming with me," he said, pointing to Simon.

"Him?" The night watchman gave Brother Hubertus an as-tonished look. "But he's nothing more than a lowlife drifter; he's not even from around here. You can hear it in the way he talks."

"And I can hear when someone has nothing inside his head but stinking straw like you. He's a learned man, but you numb-skulls don't have any understanding of that."

"Ah, I see, a *scholar*." The night watchman looked skepti-cally at Simon. "I've seen this scholar somewhere before, but I just can't remember—"

"Nonsense," Hubertus interrupted. "The man is coming with me, and that's that. Here, this is for your expenses."

He put two more coins in the bailiff's coat pocket and led Simon into a guardroom adjacent to the House of Fools. The scrawny night watchman, grinding his teeth and glaring, wouldn't take his eyes off the medicus.

"It'll come to me," he mused, then drew close to Simon again. "Don't show your face around here again, *scholar*," he sneered. "Next time you won't be stuck with a fat monk who believes your blatherings. Then we'll take our clubs and beat the learning out of you." He smiled smugly and waved goodbye to the monk, who was already storming through another door and out of the building.

"Until next time, Brother Hubertus." The night watchman sighed. "It was nice doing business with you." With that, he glared at Simon and ran his index finger across his neck in warning.

The medicus staggered into city hall square where tradesmen were just opening up shop. In the east the sun was rising over the rooftops of Regensburg.

Magdalena ripped the Venetian's shirt in two and began washing the blood from his chest. Silvio lay on a four-poster bed that took up half an enormous bedroom on the second floor. Here, as in the dressing room, mirrors were hung throughout the room, as well as paintings of biblical scenes with all sorts of fat little cherubs — all framed in what appeared to be pure gold.

"*Santa Maria,* I think I'm in heaven," the Venetian sighed, closing his eyes. "This must be paradise, and you must be an angel sitting at my side."

"Just hold still, damn it!" Magdalena cursed, dabbing the wounds with a wet cloth. "Or you'll really be seeing angels soon."

Silvio was injured below the right nipple. Although a rib

had, fortunately, deflected the blade, the wound bled profusely, as did the cut on Silvio's left upper arm.

Magdalena went about her work in silence. She found some fine fustian in a bedroom trunk, which she tore into long strips to bandage Silvio's chest and forearm. To help him recover from his loss of blood, she also heated some water on the hearth in the main room, then added honey and the juice of the little green and yellow fruits she found in Silvio's garden. She poured the steaming brew in a cup by the bed, but the Venetian just shook his head in disgust when Magdalena handed it to him.

"I prefer a strong Tokay," he said. "You'll find an excellent vintage over there in the cupboard——"

"Oh, no," Magdalena objected. "This is a sick visit, not a little tryst. If you don't do exactly as I say, your little angel will fly right away. Understood?"

Silvio sighed meekly and opened his mouth so that Magdalena could spoon-feed him the concoction. Between doses he pummeled her with questions about what had happened since her sudden flight from his garden a few days back. Magdalena refused to answer at first but, upon further consideration, decided to let Silvio in on at least some details. As the Venetian ambassador, he could be a powerful ally in her attempt to free her father. She was, simply put, in no position to reject such help.

"My father . . ." she began haltingly. "He's locked in the city dungeon for two murders he didn't commit."

Silvio looked at her questioningly. "Do you mean the murders of the bathhouse owner and his wife that the whole town is talking about?"

Nodding, Magdalena recounted the remarkable events of the past few days—their arrival in Regensburg, the break-in at the bathhouse, and the cryptic letter naming a certain Weidenfeld.

"And now you believe this Weidenfeld cooked all this up

just to see your father hang?" Silvio inquired incredulously between spoonfuls of the warm brew.

Magdalena shrugged. "The beggars believe the patricians
had both Hofmanns killed because my uncle was one of these
freemen, but that seems too simple. Then there's the letter the
hangman's boy brought me, which isn't from my father at all.
Somebody's trying to pay him back for something."

Silvio leaned back in the bed. The loss of blood had weakened him, and his face was still as white as wax.

"I'd be glad to help you," he whispered. "But I don't know
what I can do."

"What do you know about Mämminger?" Magdalena asked
abruptly.

"Mämminger?" Silvio looked surprised. "The Regensburg
city treasurer? Why do you ask?"

"He's involved somehow," Magdalena replied. "He met with
this murderer, in your own garden."

The little Venetian whistled through his teeth. "Paulus
Mämminger, ringleader of a conspiracy to murder? *I miei osse-
qui, signorina.* My compliments! When that gets out, heads will
roll in Regensburg, and I don't mean your father's."

Magdalena nodded excitedly. "Exactly. Can you find out
more about Mämminger? You have influence with the city council, don't you?"

Silvio sat up in bed, twirling his mustache. "I'll see what can
be done. But let's not talk anymore about politics; let's talk instead about . . . *amore.*"

He pulled Magdalena to him and kissed her gently on the
cheek.

The hangman's daughter recoiled as if bitten by a snake and
gave the Venetian a firm slap in the face.

"What do you think you're doing?" she shouted. "Do you
think you can just buy me with gowns and balls and connec-
tions? I'm a midwife, not a prostitute."

Silvio's face blanched a shade whiter.

"*Signorina,* I beg your forgiveness. I thought the two of us—"

"*Signorina* nothing! If you think I'm your mistress, you're making a big mistake. I may be the daughter of a hangman—a dishonorable and dirty person who hauls shit away from the streets—but I'm no whore. Remember that, you drunk old Venetian ass!"

She stood up and marched to the door, her hair flying behind her. Holding the door handle, she turned around and glared at him, her eyes flashing.

"Drink a glass of that stuff three times a day, you understand? And call one of your mistresses to help you change that dressing by tomorrow morning at the latest. I hope it hurts like hell when she tears it off your skin. Get well soon!"

She slammed the door and left Silvio staring open-mouthed at his own dumbstruck image in the mirror.

His brown robe billowing behind him, the Franciscan monk walked along so fast that Simon had trouble keeping up. Hubertus stopped only now and then to take a drink from his wineskin and share his latest philosophical musings with the medicus.

"Naturally Wilhelm von Ockham was correct in asserting that Jesus and his disciples owned no property," he panted, wiping red wine from his lips. "But just think what that means for the church! If the shepherd had no money, then his followers should have none either. All the pomp and ceremony would be nothing but idolatry!" He pointed at the magnificent façade of the bishop's palace, which they were approaching now. Directly adjoining the Regensburg cathedral, it was a little empire to itself, surrounded by high walls separating it from the city, the kaiser, and the Elector.

"Hasn't the church also done much good with its money?" Simon gasped, trying to keep pace with the fat monk.

Brother Hubertus gestured dismissively. "A huge collection of paintings framed in gold but gathering dust in the monastery archives? Altars and statues so magnificent they overwhelm the beholder? For my part I'd rather be outside with the simple folk. God resides in the whorehouses, as well! But try telling the bishop that! Oh, well, at least he'll let you argue with him without burning you at the stake."

The Franciscan strode toward a tremendous archway flanked by two of the bishop's halberd-wielding soldiers. He looked back impatiently at Simon, who hesitated at the entrance.

"What's the matter?" Hubertus inquired. "You wouldn't decline a breakfast of freshly boiled sausage and a mug of cold beer, would you?"

Simon's stomach growled, reminding him that it had indeed been some time since he'd eaten last. And so, with trepidation, he followed the Franciscan monk. What did he have to lose? Magdalena was probably having a fine time with that little fop, so he might as well take his time dining at the bishop's residence. The danger of being recognized was no doubt lessened in the company of a Franciscan monk. Besides, Simon was curious what position Hubertus actually held in the church; whatever it was, the fat monk seemed to have quite a reputation in town.

Greeting Brother Hubertus with a nod, the guards allowed both men to pass through. The Franciscan returned their greeting with a smile.

"From this point on, we're safe from the city guards," he said conspiratorially. "This is the bishop's territory, with its own court and prison. That lousy gang of night watchmen can't do anything to us here."

"Really?" A faint, almost imperceptible smile spread over Simon's face. His unexpected visit to the bishop's residence was taking a new turn. "Suppose a — let's say a thief or an arsonist were to seek refuge here?" he inquired cautiously.

"Then the bishop would probably grant him asylum," Hubertus replied. "If only to annoy the city. But the guards out there keep a damn close watch to see that no suspicious person enters here. Otherwise things could get out of hand."

"Naturally." Simon nodded.

They passed beneath a stone archway and found themselves in a finely cultivated, shady inner courtyard extending a full five hundred feet to the east and surrounded by stately buildings. To one side the cathedral loomed over the bishopric walls, and the entire area looked like the inside of a fortress. Brother Hubertus quickly crossed the courtyard and, after turning left, came to a stop in front of a heavy wooden door. The air was filled with an unusual odor that Simon couldn't place at first — sweet and heavy, like old beer that had been in the sun too long.

The Franciscan pulled a large key from his robe, unlocked the door, bowed slightly, and gestured for the visitor to enter. "My empire. Please make yourself at home."

Simon entered a room whose vaulted ceiling rose up out of sight. From several huge copper vats steam rose toward the ceiling. Wooden barrels, each inlaid with the bishop's coat of arms, were stacked high along the walls, and in the room's center stood a hot brick oven with a huge copper pan on top. The air was so humid the medicus's shirt instantly clung to his body.

"A brewery . . ." he said, astonished.

Brother Hubertus nodded proudly. "The bishop's brewery. We had it built just this past year atop the ruins of an ancient Roman gate. And I venture to say that we brew the best damn beer in all of Bavaria."

"And you are . . ." Simon began.

"The bishop's brewmaster," Hubertus finished for him. "And incidentally the best damn brewmaster the bishop could find. His Excellency loves beer, especially mine." Grinning, he poured them each a mug from a wooden keg. "Perhaps that's the reason I can take a few more liberties than the other servants. The bishop would give up his Sunday mass before his morning pint. Cheers!"

He held up his foaming mug as Simon tasted the beer, his eyes widening in pleasant surprise. The beer was excellent—cold and smooth, with just the perfect hint of hops.

"Good, isn't it?" The Franciscan winked. "Wheat beer, but don't tell a soul. In Bavaria only the Elector is allowed to brew it. But why should he alone have the privilege of such an excellent brew, hmm? It's a sin not to share." He took another deep gulp and burped loudly.

"But have a seat and tell me what brought a scholar like yourself to Regensburg." Brother Hubertus gestured to a rickety table and two stools alongside a steaming kettle. "I must tell you that when I'm not brewing beer, I like to dabble in other sciences and theories: Wilhelm von Ockham, Thomas Aquinas, but the worldly scholars, too, like Bacon and Hobbes." He sighed. "I'm surrounded here by drunken fools! It's good to talk with a like-minded individual. So what brings you here?"

Simon sipped his beer and decided to tell the truth, at least in part.

"I'm a medicus in search of employment," he said.

"Aha, I see, a medicus." Deep folds appeared on the fat monk's brow. "And where did you study, if I may ask?"

"In . . . Ingolstadt." Simon didn't mention he'd broken off his studies after just a few terms—out of laziness, a gambling addiction, and debt.

"It's not easy to establish a position for oneself among the guilds as a doctor," the medicus continued after a short hesitation. "The old ones drive off the new ones. I'm waiting to be tested by the Regensburg collegium."

"Do you have references?"

"I . . . well . . ." Simon fumbled nervously in his jacket pockets as if he could magically produce such a document. Though no miracle, he did feel a disgusting, granular lump in his coin purse.

The powder from the alchemist's cellar!

In all the excitement he'd never gotten around to examining it more carefully, and now he lacked the necessary instruments and books to do so anyhow. He'd never be able to solve this riddle with what he had to work with in the beggars' catacombs.

Then an idea came to him. He pulled out his little leather purse and handed it to Brother Hubertus.

"Unfortunately I don't have any references with me, but the venerable members of the guild assigned me a little task prior to my examination." Simon adopted a scholarly air. "By next week I'm supposed to identify this powder. Do you have any idea what it could be?"

The monk poured a bit of the powder into his huge hand and sniffed it.

"Hmm," he replied, scratching his bald head. "A musty smell, bluish, mixed with ash . . ."

"At first I thought it might be burned flour," Simon continued. "But I suspect it's something else now."

Hubertus nodded. "It is. I have a hunch, too."

"You know?" Simon jumped up from his stool. "Then tell me, please!"

The Franciscan placed the pouch back on the table. "Not so fast, young friend. It would be a pity if I was mistaken and caused you to fail the collegium." He shook his head, thinking. "Besides, it's your test, not mine. I'll do you this favor, but I'll need a little time."

"How long?" Simon asked impatiently.

Hubertus shrugged. "One or two days. I just want to be certain. In the meantime I look forward to an intelligent, scholarly discussion or two."

Simon shook his head. "I can't wait that long."

The monk sipped his beer thoughtfully, then brushed the foam from his lips. "You're welcome to stay here with me for the time being. I have a room next to the brewery that's empty, and now that it's summer I don't have much to do around here. I'm always happy for the company. Besides"—he winked—"didn't you yourself say that it's a week until your examination? So don't be so impatient. I'm a thorough person—and not just in brewing beer."

Simon sighed. "All right, I'll wait, just not here. You do promise to tell me as soon as possible, don't you?"

Brother Hubertus grinned broadly. "You have the word of the bishop's brewmaster."

He opened a drawer in the table and extracted a stained piece of paper, ink, and a goose-quill pen.

"I'll prepare something in writing for you, so that the next time you come to visit you can get past the guards. We don't want those dolts to leave you standing there." Brother Hubertus scribbled a few words on the paper, placed the bishop's seal on it, then rolled it up and handed it to Simon.

"Anyone who falls out of favor with me also falls out with the bishop. Those fools have figured out that much at least. Without his beer His Excellency grows irritable. But now let's have ourselves a taste of those boiled sausages."

He went over to a steaming kettle, opened it, and pulled out a chain of plump pink sausages. As steam enveloped the monk, he looked as if he were standing on a cloud.

"A brewer's kettles are good for all sorts of things, aren't they?" Hubertus inhaled the scent of tightly packed sheep intestines. "So tell me, what do you think of this fashionable new rascal Descartes?"

Jakob Kuisl woke to the sound of pebbles crunching. He sat up, in pain, with no idea at first where he was. Except for a small crack of light that grew brighter and brighter on the other side of the room, everything around him was black.

With the pain, memories came flooding back. He'd escaped; the Regensburg executioner had brought him to this dungeon under the brothel at Peter's Gate. Were bailiffs standing just outside, ready to carry him back to his former cell? Had that woman Dorothea betrayed him?

A stooped figure entered the little room. It was Philipp Teuber, who set a large sack down in a corner, groaning.

"Everything's still calm out there," he said. "No doubt they're keeping your escape a secret for now and accusing one another for the slip-up." Teuber laughed softly. "An escape from the city hall dungeon! That hasn't happened for hundreds of years! But the shock will pass quickly, and the big manhunt will no doubt begin today, so it's best for you to stay here the next few days and lie low."

"I've got to find Magdalena . . ." Kuisl whispered, trying to stand, but the pain in his legs was so crippling he slid down the wall with a moan.

"First you've got to get better," Teuber said, rummaging through his bag, then pulled out a knuckle of pork, some bread, a piece of cheese, and a corked jug of wine. "This will help you get your strength back. Let's have a look at your leg."

While the Regensburg executioner rubbed Kuisl's lower thigh with salve, Kuisl bit into the pork knuckle, letting the fat run down into his beard. After days of watery soup and moldy bread, the tough meat seemed like manna from heaven. He could already feel strength returning to his abused body.

"My son found your daughter and gave her the letter," Teuber said as he rubbed Kuisl's legs.

Kuisl stopped chewing. "How is she?" he asked. "Is she in trouble?"

Teuber laughed. "It's funny you ask." He shook his head

with a grin. "Things are evidently going very well for her. My son met her in the company of a medicus and several beggars down by the burned-out bathhouse. It seems they've discovered something."

"And where is she now?"

The Regensburg executioner shrugged. "I don't know, but if she's in with the beggars, I'll learn of it. I've thrown my fair share of them into the stocks, then either burned them or beaten them and driven them out of the city. But I've also let a few of those poor bastards escape, and they owe me."

"Damn! What the devil did you put in this ointment?" Kuisl asked, turning up his nose. "It stinks like bear fat that's sat out for three years."

"A family recipe," Teuber replied. "If you think I'm going to reveal the ingredients, think again."

The Schongau hangman tried to grin despite his pain. "I'd rather drink dandelion soup for a year than try out your recipe, you old knacker. In Schongau I don't even rub down cattle with stuff like that."

"I've already figured out that of the two of us, you're the bigger smart aleck," Teuber grumbled. "Now turn over so I can have a look at your arm. Does it hurt bad?"

Kuisl took a long swig of red wine before answering. "What a stupid question! You wrenched it from the socket! Now, horse doctor, show me that you can at least do something useful and shove it back into place."

"If I were you, I'd take another swig first, so the guards down at Jakob's Gate won't hear you scream."

"Not necessary." Kuisl bit his lip.

"Or perhaps wedge a piece of wood between your teeth?"

"You son of a bitch," Kuisl cursed. "Just do it."

The Regensburg executioner grabbed Kuisl's left arm and pulled hard. It crunched and cracked like a tree branch snapping. Kuisl grimaced and ground his teeth a moment, but otherwise an almost eerie silence prevailed. Finally, Kuisl rolled his shoulder cautiously, then nodded approvingly. With just one strong tug, Teuber had set the arm back in its socket.

"Good job, Teuber," Kuisl whispered, blanching as he leaned against the wall and beads of sweat ran down his face. "I couldn't have done better myself."

"You'll have to go easy on the arm for a few days," his colleague reminded him. "I'll leave the ointment here for you. Be sure to rub some of it on every day . . ."

"Yes, yes, fine." Kuisl turned aside and took a deep breath. "I myself know what I have to do. I always have."

As silence spread through the room, only the Schongau hangman's deep breathing was audible.

"Do you still believe someone set you up?" Teuber asked at last.

Kuisl nodded, staring at the wall in front of him. "Some bastard from years ago. He covered the walls of the cell with the names of old battlefields, so this must go all the way back to the war. He knows every battle I fought, and he knows my wife." He pounded the wall with his good arm. "How the hell does this devil know my wife?"

And where have I heard the name Weidenfeld? The thought flashed through his mind. *Damn it!*

"You were a mercenary?" Teuber asked. "Why didn't you stay a hangman? I've heard about you Kuisls. You're a tough breed. A whole tribe of executioners all over Bavaria bears your name. Why didn't you just stick with what your father taught you?"

Kuisl was silent a long time. Not until the Regensburg executioner stood up and made ready to leave did he begin to speak.

"My father is dead," he said. "They killed him when I was fourteen. They stoned him to death because he showed up drunk to perform an execution one time too many." Kuisl stared off into space. "It was the third time he was unable to handle his sword and turned the scaffold into a bloodbath. His drinking before every execution finally did him in."

A shadow passed over his face.

The onlookers' shouts . . . A single ear lying on the ground in front of the scaffold . . . Father staggering, falling as the crowd swallows him up . . . Mother at home crying for days until Jakob can take it no longer . . . He follows the sound of the drummer without once looking back . . .

"Hey, are you still in your right mind?" Teuber grabbed the Schongau hangman, who appeared to be drifting into unconsciousness. Like a wet dog, Kuisl shook his head vigorously, trying to drive away bad thoughts.

"I'm all right. Just need a little sleep." He closed his eyes for a moment. "The damned war. I just can't get it out of my head."

Teuber looked at him, lost in thought. "Kuisl, Kuisl," he said at last. "Whoever is behind this affair has been more successful than he can imagine. There is an agony in your eyes greater than any rack could inflict." He sighed as he rose to his feet. "I'm going to leave you alone now. Try to sleep, and tomorrow I'll bring you some food and drink."

Stooping, he left the little room and rolled the barrel in front of the entry behind him, where Kuisl still lay in darkness.

Though he could see nothing, his eyes were wide open.

The master baker Josef Haberger lay stretched out on a wooden bench, moaning with pleasure.

Daily dough-kneading made his muscles as stiff as old leather, and it was high time he paid Marie Deisch in the bathhouse another visit. No other woman in Regensburg was so skilled in handling a hard-working man's worn-out muscles. Her hands were as strong as a butcher apprentice's and as tender as a tight-lipped whore's. Now, Haberger grunted and closed his eyes as Marie's nimble fingers moved up and down his back.

"To the left," he moaned. "The shoulder blade. Those damn dough troughs are so heavy they'll pull me into the grave yet."

Marie's fingers scurried up his back again and, with a few targeted blows, began loosening the most painful places.

"Here?" the bathhouse worker asked in her deep, throaty voice. As big around at the hips as a medium-size wine barrel, she could leverage that heft behind her movements.

Haberger grunted in satisfaction. He loved strong women, women he could grab hold of, sinking into their warm, tender breasts like a pillow as they made love. His own wife was a bony, anemic shrew whose ribs stuck out like knives and who hadn't been intimate with him since he fathered their last son five years before. But who needed a spouse when you had Marie Deisch? Haberger was glad to pay a half guilder every week for his trip to the bathhouse, which included bloodletting, beard trimming, and cupping with leeches. When he was young, there were many more of these blessed institutions in Regensburg to choose from, but the curses of French disease and sullen Protestants had turned these paradises on earth into temples of sin, and only a handful of bathhouses remained.

And now that the Hofmann house on Weißgerbergraben was gone, there was even one fewer . . .

The massage diverted the master baker temporarily from worries that had pursued him like demons the past few days. But now, with his eyes closed and the soft hum of the bathhouse woman in his ears, they returned. He felt as if his heart were in a vise and knew that the best massage in the world wouldn't relieve this pain.

They'd gone too far; that much was clear. The plan was not only dangerous but megalomaniacal, and if they weren't careful, they would bring the whole city down around them. The bathhouse owner, Hofmann, had been right in trying to convince the others of the plan's madness and, then, in simply refusing to go along with it. But what good had it done? He lay dead in Saint Jakob's Cemetery now, a putrid sack of maggots, just like his wife, the fresh little bitch. It was probably she who put the idea of stopping it into his head.

But they couldn't be stopped.

After Hofmann's death Haberger made a mistake that he regretted now more than anything else in his life. In despair he pointed a finger at the others, accused them of murder, while they met him with silence, letting his accusations ricochet off them as off a rock wall. At that moment he realized he'd crossed the line. Their convictions were cast in stone, and they would carry out the plan to its bitter end.

With or without him.

It quickly became apparent that with his rash assertions he'd become a liability, and now he imagined assassins around every corner, the clicks of crossbows behind every door. Death could be waiting for him under his bed or in the privy. Still, they needed him! They couldn't do without him . . . or could they? No, not without the most important master baker in the city with customers at city hall, at the Reichstag, and among the most important patricians.

In retrospect the whole plan seemed an outrageous, scandalous crime, a crime so devilish that everyone involved would roast in hell forever. Haberger considered turning on the others, but his fear of their vengeance was too great. And besides, what would happen to him when everything finally came to light? He heard that traitors were often hanged before they were gutted and quartered. Could the same fate await him?

Preoccupied with his fears, he didn't notice that Marie had stopped humming. Her fingers, too, had disappeared. Surprised, Haberger was about to get up when he felt hands on his back again. He sighed in relief. The bathhouse worker had likely just gone for some more olive oil and was now preparing to massage the right shoulder blade. Haberger closed his eyes and tried to suppress bad thoughts and concentrate only on the present massage.

The hands worked their way up his back until they reached the shoulder blades again. For an instant Haberger had the premonition that these hands were somehow stronger than before, that they lacked Marie's delicate, feminine touch and their grip on him was harder.

Much harder.

As if they were trying to mash his muscles to a pulp.

"Thanks, Marie," Haberger moaned again. "But that should be enough. I can't feel anything in my shoulders anymore."

The hands didn't stop, though, but moved higher until finally they reached Haberger's throat.

"What the devil . . . ?"

Haberger tried to stand up, but unrelenting muscular arms forced him back down to the bench. When he attempted to scream, he felt fingers tighten around his neck, squeezing the life from his body bit by bit.

The master baker quivered and flailed about like a fish out of water. He tried to slip free, but the strong arms held him down, pressing him hard against the wood like a piece of raw meat. His face turned red first, then blue; his tongue stuck out of his mouth like a slug; then, with a final gasp, he collapsed.

Just before the world went black, Josef Haberger glimpsed right before his nose an arm with powerful protruding sinews. He saw close-up—almost as if magnified—a mass of curly hair, and he smelled sharp manly sweat.

Strange. I don't feel pain anymore, Haberger thought.

Then he passed into a dark tunnel ending in ethereal light.

Still enthused by his conversation with Brother Hubertus, Simon left the bishopric around noon with the beer-stained invitation from the bishop's brewmaster in his pocket.

They had discussed Descartes, whose *Discours de la méthode* he read as a university student in Ingolstadt. Simon was especially taken with the revolutionary idea that a rational explanation could be found for everything. The Franciscan had kept Simon's glass brimming with cool, splendid wheat beer, and the medicus felt tipsy now as he wondered how Descartes would have solved the double murder in Regensburg. Presumably the philosopher would have found a simple answer for every riddle. Sighing, Simon had to admit he didn't have Descartes's divine intelligence. Just the same, he tried to order his thoughts — though the accursed alcohol kept getting in the way.

All that beer, however, had one benefit: Simon had temporarily forgotten his quarrel with Magdalena. But now the nagging thought returned that the love of his life was possibly still hanging around with that Venetian dwarf. But then again she might have returned to the catacombs by now, worrying herself sick about him. It served her right! What business did Magdalena have in the dressing room of that vain fop? Simon looked down at his torn, hastily patched jacket, his shredded breeches, and muddy boots and had to admit he himself wished he could spend half a day in a filthy-rich ambassador's dressing room. But for an unmarried girl that was completely inappropriate! And who knew what else the two had been up to amid all those mirrors, linens, and clothing? Whatever the case, everything would have to be cleared up tonight.

The marketplace at the cathedral square was filled with noisy, chattering market women, cursing stable boys, churchgoers deep in conversation, and blasé patricians. Although the medicus assumed he wouldn't attract undue attention in the bustling crowd, he pulled up his jacket collar and lowered his eyes nevertheless. He didn't want to give the bailiffs a second opportunity to identify him as the Weißgerbergraben arsonist.

Despite his three or four mugs of wheat beer, Simon tried his best to concentrate. There had to be some connection between the Hofmann murders and the trap set for Magdalena's father, something he just hadn't thought of yet, a logical scheme that would bring together all the disparate and bizarre little incidents. Simon hoped fervently that Brother Hubertus could help him analyze the strange powder. By now the medicus was convinced it wasn't just burned flour. Perhaps it was the key to solving the other riddles.

A bathhouse owner as rebel and alchemist . . . What was Hofmann experimenting with anyway?

Simon suddenly realized there was yet another person he hadn't spoken with about the matter: the raftmaster, Karl Gessner! The bathhouse owner, like Gessner, had been a leader of the freemen, so it was quite possible Gessner knew something about Hofmann's alchemical experiments. When they last met on Wöhrd Island, Gessner hadn't said anything about it, but perhaps that was only because Simon hadn't brought it up.

The medicus decided to pay a visit to Gessner at the raft landing. While there was some danger in going down to the Danube, where so many city bailiffs were afoot, he was willing to take the risk.

Simon turned around, hurried northward past the bishop's court, and entered a labyrinth of small lanes. Finally, between two buildings, he spotted the river flowing lazily by. At the noon hour there was almost no activity on the raft landing. Most freight had been unloaded in the early morning, and the raft attendants and laborers were dozing now in the shadows of crates, bales, and barrels, waiting for the sweltering noon heat to pass. A single rope hung down from a wooden crane over the Danube, swaying calmly back and forth in the breeze. The air smelled of fish, river water, and freshly cut firs, and the stench of the city was not quite so strong here. Simon felt he could breathe freely for the first time in a long while.

He asked one of the dozing workers where he might find the raftmaster and was directed to Gessner's office in a small building next to the lumber-loading dock. As he strolled along the fortified jetty, Simon noticed for the first time just how vast the Regensburg harbor actually was. This stretch of river that ran along the city wall extended from the boat landings east of the Stone Bridge almost as far as the western boundary of the city. On his way down to the lumber dock Simon passed the wine-loading dock, dotted with respectable middle-class inns; salt-storage depots as big as barns; and innumerable mooring posts encrusted with mussels. Finally, huge piles of boards and timber came into view. A dozen day laborers were busy stacking planks and wet pieces of driftwood, some as long as a yard, that they had fished out of the Danube. Not far from here stood the raftmaster's house—a low, lopsided shed built directly onto the jetty that looked as if at any moment it just might collapse.

Simon was about to knock on the door when he noticed it was already ajar. He carefully pushed, and it swung inward without a sound, revealing a rough-hewn table covered with an assortment of stained documents in the middle of a pleasantly cool room. Shelves built into the back wall overflowed with sealed, rolled parchments. But there was no sign of Gessner.

Simon was turning to leave when he heard a sudden clatter, a loud crash like the sound of a crate falling. The noise came from the other side of the shelves; evidently there was another room somewhere behind the office, a kind of storage room, he supposed, but inaccessible from the office directly.

Was there perhaps an entrance around the back of the building? Puzzled, the medicus left the way he came in and walked briskly around the little house. Gessner had to be working in the adjoining room, and when he finished stacking his crates, he'd surely be able to answer a few friendly questions over a glass or two of wine. All of a sudden Simon felt incredibly thirsty. The heat was bringing on a hangover—Brother Hubertus's wheat beer must have been stronger than Simon first assumed. He had to get out of the sun, now! Where was the other damned entrance? Could he have overlooked it? To be sure, he walked around the building again, with the same result.

There was no other entrance.

Simon hurried back inside. Only now did he realize that the size of the little office didn't correspond to the exterior dimensions.

It was considerably smaller.

Simon held his breath, listening closely. He could definitely hear the muffled sound of crates being moved around.

What in the world . . . ?

As Simon cautiously approached the wall on the other side of the room, he noticed a gap between two shelves. He reached in, pulled on one of the boards, and to his surprise the entire left wall — with its shelves and everything on them — swung silently away, revealing a windowless room piled high with crates and sacks. Gessner stood with his back to the entrance, building precarious towers of some large containers. By the light of a lantern on the floor Simon could see that some of the crates had been opened. Inside, dried brown leaves were gathered into bundles and tied with fine thread. The medicus instantly recognized the bundles' scent as one he knew so well from the Schongau hangman's house, though Simon had never before smelled it as strongly as here.

Tobacco.

Now Gessner turned around, his look turning quickly from frank astonishment to outright anger. "What in hell's name are you doing here, you nosy little quack?" he snarled, reaching for a hatchet on his belt. "I don't recall having invited you."

"Uh . . . excuse me," Simon stuttered, "I was looking for you, and the door was open . . ."

"Certainly you don't mean this door." The raftmaster pushed him rudely aside and slammed the wall of shelves shut behind

him. The darkness in the room was now almost palpable, miti-
gated only in part by the small lantern on the floor. By its flickering light Gessner's otherwise sympathetic features now appeared
very threatening.

"You'll keep this little secret to yourself, won't you?" the
raftmaster whispered. "One hand washes the other, as they say. I
told you about the patricians' plans, so *you* won't say a word
about this room. To anyone. Understood?"

Simon nodded eagerly. Despite his fear, he couldn't resist
looking around with curiosity. When Gessner noticed Simon's
gaze, he reached into a box for a few of the brown, curled leaves.
He crushed them between his fingers and held his hand out to
Simon to smell.

"Expensive West Indian tobacco," the raftmaster said, taking
a seat on one of the large wooden crates. With an impatient gesture, he motioned for Simon to do the same. "There's no better
ware to smuggle right now. Tariffs are higher than ever, and
therefore so are my profits." He shrugged apologetically. "A Regensburg raftmaster struggles to make ends meet. Taxes are eating me alive, lumber thieves steal the privy seat right out from
under my ass, and just two years ago a blasted flood washed my
whole house clear away. So, I've had the new one built to order,
so to speak, exactly the way I wanted." He winked, gesturing toward the wooden partition.

With a sudden creaking sound, the secret door opened a
crack. In the dazzling sunlight Simon could make out only the
outline of a very large figure.

"Is everything all right in there?" a deep voice barked.

Gessner raised a reassuring hand. "We have a visitor, big fellow. But don't worry. I've got it under control. You may leave."

"You sure?"

The raftmaster nodded impatiently. "Yes, I'm sure."

With another soft creaking sound, the door closed again.
Gessner reached into another crate and fished out a bottle of

brandy, which he proceeded to uncork with his teeth. He took a long swig before offering the bottle to Simon, whose hangover had started bothering him again.

"No, thanks," the medicus mumbled. "My head . . . is a bit thick today."

The raftmaster shrugged and took another slug.

"This is contraband, too," he muttered, licking his lips. "But tobacco is better — easier to stash away, and there's more profit in it."

He cast a suspicious side glance at the medicus. "Do you have any idea how lucky you are? If I hadn't recognized you right away, you'd be nailed up inside a barrel, floating down the Danube by now. What are you doing here, anyway? Didn't I tell you you'd be better off back in your little Bavarian cow town with that little girl of yours?"

Simon sighed deeply. "As it turns out, that girl of mine just happens to be the daughter of the Schongau hangman, who's due to be hanged, broken on the wheel, or even drawn and quartered right here in Regensburg. Magdalena is hell-bent on doing everything to save him."

"And you, too, I suppose? This girl has you on a pretty tight leash." Gessner grinned and poked Simon in the chest. "But you can forget about all of that — Kuisl is as good as dead."

"There may still be a way out," Simon said. "Something's not quite right with your assumption that the aldermen are behind all this."

"I don't see the problem," Gessner said. "It's obvious. The patricians want their revenge on us, the freemen, so they had Hofmann stabbed to death and went looking for a scapegoat. And then Kuisl came along at just the right time."

"All this trouble to get the Schongau hangman to Regensburg — the letter, the forged will, the trial. Why would the patricians do all that, cook up something so elaborate?" Simon persisted. "Just for revenge?"

"So what do *you,* in your infinite wisdom, think happened then?" Gessner asked peevishly.

Simon shrugged. "I don't know. Someone who's obviously trying to get revenge on Kuisl must have set this all up. I have no idea who—perhaps it's this Weidenfeld who keeps sending these cryptic letters . . . or perhaps some other complete lunatic. Who knows? But there are still a few things I don't understand. Did you know, for example, that Andreas Hofmann had a secret alchemist's workshop?"

"An alchemist's workshop?" Gessner frowned.

The medicus nodded. "We found a secret room in his cellar where some kind of alchemical experiments were taking place. There were traces of a strange-smelling bluish powder that unfortunately, just like everything else down there, has by now been reduced to ash. Did you know about this room?"

The raftmaster was silent for a long time; he took a long swig of brandy before finally replying. "Hofmann actually was dabbling in alchemy," he said. "I wasn't aware of the secret room, but I suspected something of the sort. For years Andreas had been in search of this . . ." He paused briefly. "Well, of this stone they've all been trying to produce."

"The philosopher's stone," Simon whispered.

Gessner nodded. "Exactly. He thought he was getting close to being able to turn iron into gold. Naturally, none of us believed him, and truthfully we even made fun of him a bit. It was just such a crazy idea, though perhaps there really was something more to it. A few days before he died he was hinting that he would very soon be a very wealthy man—"

"So maybe that's what happened!" Simon leaped out of his chair and paced the little room excitedly. "Hofmann is on his way to creating something very valuable in his workshop—perhaps the philosopher's stone even. Whatever it is, the Regensburg patricians are very eager to get their hands on it. They question him, but when he doesn't give them what they want, they kill him and his wife—or have them killed. It's a delicate matter—there may even be others we're not aware of, all of whom are after the same thing. So the aldermen have to see to it that not even the slightest suspicion falls on them. That would explain why they lured Kuisl to Regensburg. They have to ensure everything looks like an ordinary robbery-murder. The whole thing really has nothing to do with the freemen at all!" Simon was worked up now. "Once the Hofmanns are dead, the patricians have the whole house ransacked. But they can't find the philosopher's stone, because Hofmann hid it down in his workshop!"

"So?" Gessner asked curiously. "Where's this stone now?"

Simon settled back down on the crate and sighed. "We'll probably never find out. Perhaps the stone is still down there; perhaps Hofmann hid it somewhere else. The bathhouse is no more than a heap of rubble and no one's going to find anything there now. But I'm sure the strange powder has something to do with it."

The raftmaster thought it over, nodding as he fumbled with his red bandanna. "You may be on to something, and I just may be able to find something in those ruins yet. I have my sources..." He fingered his jet-black beard. "If I learn anything, I'll let you know. Are you still staying at the Whale?"

Simon shook his head. "That was too dangerous . . . for various reasons. No, for now we're living with the beggars guild."

"The beggars guild?"

"I have an agreement with the beggar king," Simon replied curtly. "I heal his sick, and in return he guarantees our safety."

"Hmm," Gessner mused. "Not that it's any business of mine, but does the beggar king know about the alchemist's workshop?"

"We told Nathan about it," Simon replied. "Why do you ask?"

The Regensburg raftmaster clicked his tongue. "If I were in your shoes, I wouldn't trust him further than I can spit. Nathan will do anything for money. How else do you think he and his people can tramp about here in Regensburg without anyone bothering them?"

"Do you think . . . ?"

"I don't think; I *know*. More than once I've seen Nathan turn someone over to the city officials or pass information to the guards. And you'd better believe some people would pay a pretty penny for such a stone."

"I never thought of that." Simon frowned. "Perhaps you're right and we should really consider a change in our accommodations."

"You could hide out here at my place, if you like." The raftmaster pointed behind him. "It's as safe in here. No one will ever find you."

"Thanks, but I think I have an even better solution," Simon replied in a soft voice as he stood up.

"As you wish." Gessner opened the bookshelf door. Light streamed into the room, nearly blinding Simon, who could only stand still for a moment, blinking.

"If you hear any news, by all means let me know," the raftmaster said as he stood there bathed in the sunlight. "And as far as this room is concerned—" He pulled Simon close. "—you know nothing. Clear?"

Simon felt Gessner's hot, brandy-soaked breath on his face. "My lips are sealed. Promise."

"Good," Gessner replied, patting the medicus on the shoulder. "Perhaps I'll send you a crate of tobacco. Do you smoke?"

Simon shook his head with a smile. "Not me, but I know someone who would be more than happy with such a gift. First, however, we've got to save his life."

II

THE STUFFY AIR IN THE BROTHEL'S HIDDEN ROOM
was keeping Kuisl from getting the sleep he very much needed.
Teuber had left him only a few hours ago, but the Schongau
hangman felt as if he'd been in this hole an eternity. It didn't
stink of urine or excrement like the cell in the city hall, but there
was no light here and no air, just Jakob and his thoughts.

He sighed and groped around him on the floor until he finally found a solid object. A carafe of wine! He almost knocked
the vessel over but at the last moment was able to grab hold of it.
Carefully he brought it to his lips, and as the cool, invigorating
liquid wet his parched palate, fresh strength seemed to flow
through his body. The wine was watery but nonetheless strong
and numbing enough to make him drowsy.

Just as he was drifting off to sleep, a scraping sound echoed
outside the room. The wine barrel blocking the entrance was
being pushed aside, and by the light of the lantern the Schongau
hangman saw Dorothea's face, dripping with sweat. The fat procuress, who had evidently moved the makeshift barricade aside
all by herself, was peering down at him now with a mixture of
skepticism and curiosity.

"Just wanted to make sure you were still here," she whispered. "And since you are, it couldn't have been you then after all."

"What?" Kuisl croaked, lifting himself to a seated position against the cool, damp wall of the tiny chamber. "What couldn't have been me?"

"The murder in the bathhouse this morning," Dorothea replied. "Or *did* you have something to do with it?"

Kuisl blinked in the harsh light of the lantern. "This morning? I don't understand . . . Lisl and Hofmann . . . that was days ago . . ."

"You ninny," the procuress replied. "I don't mean Hofmann's bathhouse but the bathhouse on Hackengässchen Street. The master baker, Haberger, was strangled there, and the bathhouse mistress, Marie Deisch, was found in a wooden washtub with her throat slit. So it really wasn't you?"

The hangman shook his head silently.

"From the looks of you it's actually pretty hard for me to imagine it," Fat Thea said. "I don't think you could even cut your own throat right now." She placed the lantern on the floor and entered the dark chamber. "Lots of people sure would be happy if they could find someone to blame for all the murders happening around here of late. My girls don't even dare set foot in the streets since this stranger's been out on the prowl."

"What stranger?" Kuisl asked hesitantly.

Fat Thea gave him a suspicious look. "Are you truly that dumb, or is this an act? For the last few weeks prostitutes have been disappearing all over the city. You must have heard about that!"

Kuisl shook his head, and the procuress sighed deeply.

"No matter," she continued. "All hell has broken loose over in the garrison. Every bailiff in Regensburg is out looking for you now, and the city gates are so well guarded you'd think the devil himself were on the loose! They want to pin all the murders of the last few weeks on you. It's like they're hunting a wild animal!"

"How do you know all this?" Kuisl whispered.

"One of the soldiers at Peter's Gate let me in on it," Dorothea replied. "They tried to keep your escape under wraps because they were so embarrassed, but now, after Haberger's murder, all the bailiffs are on full alert. The public still doesn't know anything; the bailiffs are probably trying to avoid a general panic. But word is sure to spread fast. They'll be inspecting every last mouse hole, and I have the council coming here tonight, damn it all to hell!" She kicked the wall so hard that some of the plaster came fluttering down, then took a deep breath and glared at Kuisl with her one eye.

"I promised Philipp that you could stay here, but I didn't say for how long. It's bad enough I'll have a house full of aldermen and soldiers tonight, but now I have a monster living in my wine cellar, too." She hesitated a moment. "It's too risky. You can stay tonight, but you'll have to leave in the morning. I'll pack up a few things for you — clothing, bread, everything you'll need. Can you walk?"

Kuisl nodded. "I can manage."

Dorothea sighed. "Don't be angry with me, but I have a daughter — you understand — and . . ."

"I have a daughter, too." The hangman sighed. "I understand. Tomorrow I'll be gone."

"Good. Then we've said all there is to say."

The procuress went out into the cellar and returned with a cold piece of roast and a full jug of wine.

"Here," she said. "It'll help you get your strength back. You can put these new clothes on now. They may be a bit snug, but they'll do." She tossed him a little bundle. "Linen shirt, trousers, and simple leather shoes; you'll look just like any other ordinary stable hand. Leave your old rags here, and I'll bury them."

"God bless you." Kuisl bit into the roast greedily.

Fat Thea sat and watched him eat. "What's your daughter's name?" she finally asked.

The hangman hastily swallowed a mouthful of food. "Magdalena. A real devil of a girl. If I ever see her again, I'm going to give her one hell of a whipping."

Dorothea smiled. "Just as long as you don't slit her throat."

Lost in her own thoughts, the procuress took a sip from the jug of wine she had brought the hangman. "Don't be too strict with your daughter," she said, with some concern. "Growing children are like foals. If they're not given room to run, they'll lash out in every direction."

"That's no excuse for her to go gadding all about this godforsaken city with her good-for-nothing sweetheart and leave her mother and our children all alone at home, the ungrateful little brat." Kuisl wiped his hand across his mouth. "The little ones are likely crying their eyes out while the fine *mademoiselle* is making a show of herself around town."

But his real fear went unspoken: that Magdalena might at this very moment be in the hands of some lunatic, a lunatic bent on torturing *her* to get revenge on *him*.

Dorothea whistled softly through her teeth. "Magdalena seems like a real little minx. What sort of mischief has she gotten herself into?"

"Well, at the moment she's trying to save me from the gallows," Kuisl said. "I only hope nothing's happened to her — her and that daft charlatan."

Curled up in the subbasement of the catacombs, Magdalena stared morosely at the flickering oil lamp in front of her.

Shadows darted across the ancient foundation stones that still bore a few faintly legible Latin inscriptions. Simon once told her that long ago the Romans had built a settlement on this spot. Over the course of many centuries the city had grown up around these ruins: the Jewish quarter was established on this spot, and

after the Jews were driven out, Neupfarrplatz, or Neupfarr
Church Square, with its Protestant church, had been built. Here,
deep underground, buried in its history, Magdalena felt as if she
could hear the heart of Regensburg beating, and beating so
loudly it drowned out the anxious pounding of her own heart. In
this place she felt as safe as if she were in her mother's womb.

Mother . . .

Magdalena closed her eyes. How could she have left her
mother and the twins all alone, all for the sake of a tawdry dream
of a new life in this strange city? Magdalena had been thinking
only of herself, and of Simon, and now she'd failed everyone.
Her father was still wasting away in a death cell, the victim of
some conspiracy. Soon the Regensburg executioner would haul
him up onto the scaffold, and she and Simon would be forced to
watch the hangman break his bones. What would Mother say
when Magdalena finally returned home?

Could she ever go back?

Magdalena's thoughts also lingered on Simon. Where in the
world could he be, and was he still angry at her on account of the
Venetian ambassador? What had caused her to snap at him like
that? Once again she'd bolted from him like a wild mare. Why
couldn't she control her temper?

After her second visit to Silvio's house, Magdalena knew she
would never fit into his glittering, gaudy world. There was an
insurmountable wall between Silvio's life and her own, and she
had now experienced firsthand the city's cruelty, how mercilessly
it dealt with anyone who didn't belong. There were the *citizens*
and then there was everyone else — the human dross, the beggars, whores, and street performers, the knackers and the hangmen . . .

She would always belong to the dregs of society.

Someone came running down the crumbling staircase now,
startling Magdalena out of her reverie. She was just about to extinguish the light to hide in the darkness when she recognized

the figure standing before her. Simon! She leaped up and ran toward him.

"Simon! I'm so sorry, I shouldn't have . . ."

Not until that moment did she notice the grave expression in his eyes. She stopped in her tracks. "What's happened?"

With his finger to his lips, Simon led her to the farthest corner of the old Roman vault.

"Forget everything that's happened up till now," he whispered. "There's something much more important we've got to deal with. We have to get out of here, tonight if possible."

"What are you saying?" Magdalena's voice echoed through the room.

Simon cringed, clapping his hand over her mouth. "For God's sake, be quiet!" he gasped. "I have the feeling that all of Regensburg is conspiring against us now."

In a whisper he told Magdalena of his meeting with Gessner and of his suspicion that Nathan was in league with the city. He also told her about the philosopher's stone.

She listened with a furrowed brow. "So you think my uncle really did discover this stone?" she asked at last, a bit skeptical. "But isn't it just some fantasy the alchemists peddled to their princes and sponsors to ingratiate themselves with them?"

Simon shrugged. "Who knows? The stone is more a symbol than a real object. Paracelsus wrote about it; I attended a medical lecture on it at the university in Ingolstadt. Some people really believe some substance exists that can transform base metals into gold or silver, while there are others who speak of a powder that, when mixed with wine, will bestow health and eternal life. *Aurum potabile,* liquid gold, is what they call it."

"So it's a medicine . . ." Magdalena nodded thoughtfully. "That's something a bathhouse owner like Hofmann could really have used."

"Do you remember the mountains of burned flour down in

the alchemist's workshop?" Simon asked. "I've been thinking it over; I'm pretty sure it wasn't flour. It may have been the very powder Mämminger was looking for. I pinched a sample as we were leaving." He pulled Magdalena close to him. "We have to get away from here. I get the feeling Nathan's been sounding us out for a while now. Do you remember how he insisted on coming with us into the cathedral? After that he disappeared, just like Mämminger and the murderer. And he was eavesdropping on us down in the catacombs as well. Gessner's right! We can't risk having Nathan follow us everywhere, only to have him call the bailiffs when he thinks we're getting too close."

"But where do you want to go?" Magdalena asked. "Don't forget we're still wanted for arson. There's no place up there where we'd be as secure."

Simon grinned. "I know a place where the guards can't get to us."

The hangman's daughter raised her bushy eyebrows. "And where would that be?"

"The bishop's palace," Simon said, triumphant. "I even have an invitation." The medicus reached into his pocket and fished out the beer-stained document Brother Hubertus had given him and waved it under Magdalena's nose. Before she could say a word, he went on.

"I met the bishop's brewmaster this morning—a wise, well-read monk. I left the powder in his care so he could examine it."

"Are you out of your mind?" Magdalena had to get hold of herself to keep her voice from rising. "You gave the only possible piece of evidence we have to a complete stranger? Why didn't you just scatter it to the winds from the balcony of city hall? No doubt you also told this bishop's servant about the alchemist's workshop!"

Simon raised his hands, trying to calm her down. "Don't worry. He doesn't know a thing. And, that said, I'm not going to

ask about all the things you may have blabbed to that old Venetian goat. You trust your dwarf just as much as I trust my fat
brewmaster. Understood?"

"Keep Silvio out of this, will you?"

"*Silvio?* Aha!" Simon sneered. "At least we have the first two
letters of our names in common. But never mind that . . ." He
turned serious again. "I think Brother Hubertus would have no
objection to our lodging at his place. Nobody will think to look
for us in the bishop's palace."

"And how do you think you'll . . ."

Magdalena broke off when they heard footsteps on the stairs.
Torchlight filled the doorway, but it took a while for them to recognize Nathan's dimly backlit face. The beggar king wore such
a broad grin that his golden incisors sparkled like crown jewels,
even in the half light.

"Ah, there you are, my dears," he said. For a brief moment
Magdalena feared Nathan had been eavesdropping on their entire conversation and had come over only because he wanted to
silence them. Instead, he just stood stock-still, his hand extended
cordially.

"I've looked for you everywhere," he said, sounding somewhat peeved. "I was worried when I didn't see you leave the cathedral this morning."

"Oh, but we left," Magdalena replied curtly, trying to conceal her initial fear. "The one who never showed was you!"

Nathan cocked his head to the side. "Then we'll have to
blame the damned morning fog. Who knows?" As he turned to
leave, he said, "Upstairs there's a little boy with a very high fever
and a cough. Could the Herr Medicus have a look?"

Simon nodded silently, and together they climbed the crumbling narrow stairway up to the rooms above. Nathan lit the way
for them with his lantern, pausing at every low doorway to bow
slightly and wave Magdalena ahead of him. Such gestures had

just recently seemed witty, even comical, to her; but now she found them obsequious and insincere.

"Our brother Paulus rescued an abandoned barrel of brandy from the street," Nathan told them with a grin as they hurried through the passageways. "It was just standing there in front of the Black Elephant Tavern. In his boundless mercy Paulus decided to take the barrel in. If you hurry, there may still be a drop or two left."

When the beggar king rounded a corner and disappeared, Simon pulled Magdalena close.

"This is our chance!" he whispered. "Once they're all drunk, we'll pack our things and clear out."

Nathan's face suddenly reappeared from around the corner. A glint of suspicion shone in his eyes. "Why are you whispering?" he snapped. "We don't have any secrets between us, do we?"

Magdalena put on her sweetest smile. "Simon was just telling me how nice it might be to be alone together tonight. I'm sure you don't want to know the details."

"Young lovers!" the beggar king exclaimed, rolling his eyes theatrically toward the ceiling. "They're always thinking of just one thing. But first you'll have to fill me in on what happened this morning in the cathedral."

"Later, later," Simon replied. "The little sick boy comes first."

He squeezed Magdalena's hand, and together they hurried through the narrow, crumbling corridors and archways toward the large subterranean hall. The beggars' catacombs didn't feel so much like home anymore.

After countless hours in near total darkness, Jakob Kuisl had the feeling the roof was closing in on him. This room was slightly larger than his cell in the dungeon, but he still felt as if an iron vise were clamped around his chest, squeezing him tighter and tighter.

Kuisl was a man reared on sunlight and forests. Even as a child, he'd never been able to endure being cooped up. Sunlight and green moss, birdcalls and the rustle of pines and beeches — all these were as essential to him as the air he breathed. It was in the dark, then, that the shadows of the past lurked. In the dark the Great War reached long, shadowy arms out to seize him . . .

Blood trickling down onto the furrowed field like a light summer rain, the screams of the wounded, the muffled sound of cannon fire, the sharp odor of gunpowder . . . Germans, Croats, Hungarians, Italians, Frenchmen, Spaniards, all united in a shrill, monstrous chorus. In the vanguard, men with pikes over five paces long; behind them, musketeers and dragoons, sitting high atop their horses and thrashing away at the surging mob in front of them.

He is Jakob, the hangman's son, the man with the two-handed sword. In his pack he has stowed a certificate validating his mastery of the longsword. As a "double mercenary," he receives twice the pay of an ordinary soldier. A sergeant, their leader.

He is one of them.

When they are encamped before the gates of the city, the surrounding countryside is like a festering wound. The villages are scorched and deserted, the farmers are dead or have long since fled into the forests and swamps. His men now and then capture a ragged figure and hang the poor wretch by his feet over the fire. Where are your cattle? Out with it! Where have you stashed your silver? Where are the women? Speak! *They force a tube down the farmer's throat and fill it with urine and feces until he chokes.* Spit it out! Talk! Die, you bastard! *They take whatever they lay their hands on, then set the shabby cottages on fire.*

How often has he watched this from afar? How often have his men ridden back into camp with bloodstained coats and a mad light in their eyes? He never asks. He keeps silent because that's war. Be-

cause men have a gnawing hunger and a desire for women, and the long wait inflames them. Because he knows they respect him only for his strength and his courage. Because he fears punishment . . . Because . . .

Because he's afraid?

Kuisl couldn't take it anymore. He had to get out of here. Gasping, he struggled to his feet and leaned against the barrel blocking the low entrance. It was just yesterday that Teuber had wrenched Kuisl's shoulder back into its socket. It throbbed now with pain, and the wounds on his arms and legs felt as if they were on fire. From outside the room he probably could have rolled the barrel aside, but from here all he could do was try to push with all his strength against the hundred-pound barrier. He braced his legs and bore down with his bandaged back against the wooden surface, biting his lip to avoid crying out in pain.

There was a soft scraping sound, and a crack of faint light appeared between the barrel and the wall.

Again the hangman pressed against the wooden barrier until the crack was at last wide enough to slip through. On the other side he collapsed on the floor, breathing heavily as the room around him began to spin. He closed his eyes and waited until his dizziness subsided.

The effort of moving the wine barrel had robbed him of much of the strength he'd gathered in the past few hours. But at least he was able to get to his feet and walk around unassisted now. He stood up straight and looked around the damp cellar. A smoking torch near the stairway cast a dim light over the room. Lined up along the walls among wine casks were barrels of sauerkraut. Smoked sausages and legs of pork hung from the low ceiling, and dried cherries, onions, and withered apples from the previous year lay in straw-filled baskets. Kuisl took an apple and bit into it.

It tasted wonderful.

While the hangman ground the apple's flesh in his teeth, he pondered his next move. Outside it was probably night now. He could walk straight up the stairs, out the front door, and disappear into the darkness. But how far would he get once he was out there? If Fat Thea was right, if Kuisl was actually being sought for two more murders, every bailiff in the city would be looking for him. The gates would be under strict surveillance. He could possibly flee across the Danube; Kuisl was a good swimmer and the summer current wasn't as strong as in springtime. He might even be able to break out over the city wall. But something held him back; something kept him from fleeing at once.

Magdalena.

Where was she hiding? Could she already be in the clutches of this madman? Was he torturing *her* now that his adversary had escaped? Kuisl couldn't leave this city until he knew Magdalena was safe.

He felt warm juice running down his pant leg. Unwittingly he'd crushed the apple to a pulp in his palm.

He heard a sudden commotion from the ground floor above. Someone was pounding on the front door. The voice of Fat Thea answered.

"Yes, yes, gentlemen! Please be patient! My girls are absolutely wild to get their hands on you. No one's going anywhere, believe me!"

Kuisl cringed. The aldermen! He'd completely forgotten about them. He heard the door creak softly and shortly thereafter, laughter and a loud chorus of voices. The procuress hadn't lied. It did seem in fact as if half the town council had joined the party.

"Come right on in, gentlemen!" Fat Thea's voice boomed from the top of the stairs. "There's something here for everyone. Hey there, girl, let's take it upstairs, please; there's nothing of interest downstairs anyway."

The hangman instinctively withdrew as he heard footsteps

on the cellar stairs, but the sound receded soon and was lost in the upper reaches of the house. Evidently someone had just taken a wrong turn.

After a while he heard giggling and shouting upstairs, indicating the girls were receiving their guests now. There was a sound of breaking glass and of doors opening and closing, a sign that the men were withdrawing to the rooms with their playmates. Kuisl was just about to hide behind the wine barrel again when he heard someone knocking on the front door — no doubt a late arrival.

"Just a moment, I'm coming!"

Fat Thea opened the door to greet the new arrival.

"Oh, what an honor!" she purred. "I haven't seen *you* here for a long time."

"I've been rather busy of late," the man replied. "I hope you haven't forgotten the whip."

"Of course I haven't, silly boy. But this time don't hit so hard, you hear? Or it will cost you a guilder extra. The girls have complained."

The man chuckled softly to the sound of coins dropping into a purse.

"Then here are two more guilders right off," he whispered. "Because believe me, this time it's going to hurt. There's a rage in my belly, and it'll take more than one girl to fix that. Let's go."

As he crouched on the cellar floor, the Schongau hangman's blood froze. Only after the stranger's footsteps began to fade away did Kuisl's mind spring back to life again.

He knew this voice. He knew it better than his own by now. He'd heard it all too often these past days and nights, even in his nightmares.

It was the voice of the third inquisitor.

Just after dusk Simon and Magdalena tiptoed through the subterranean hall, around the beggars, who had drunk the barrel of brandy down to the last drop and were now sprawled all over the cellar floor, sleeping it off. Every now and then one would moan and roll over in his sleep, mumbling something incoherent. Simon threaded his way through a litter of gnawed bones, smashed cups, and pools of vomit, careful not to stumble over any of the beggars. Nathan was slumped in a corner, his chin to his chest, cradling a clay mug. For a moment Simon thought the beggar king might still be awake, but then, with a long rattling snore, he toppled over and lay motionless on the ground.

"Quick," Magdalena whispered. "Let's get out of here. Who knows when one of them will wake up?"

Simon squeezed her hand. "Just a moment."

He hurried over to the curtained niche that had served as a sick bay the past few days and began to pack his medical utensils. Meanwhile Magdalena kept a nervous eye on Nathan, who was twitching in his sleep, licking his lips now and then. At some point he reached across the floor as if in search of the clay mug that had slipped out of his hand.

"Hurry!" she whispered. "I think he's coming to!"

"I'll be right there." Simon was frantically gathering his books and stuffing them into the bag when a heavy volume of Dioscorides slipped from his sweaty fingers and fell to the floor with a crash.

"Damn!"

Bending down to retrieve it, he noticed out of the corner of his eye that one of Nathan's eyes had opened a crack. He seemed to be dreaming, but Simon had the feeling the eye was staring at them disapprovingly. The next moment Magdalena was by Nathan's side, placing the mug back gently into his hand. Murmuring, Nathan clutched it to his chest like a doll, rolled onto his side, and was soon snoring away calmly and evenly.

"Your damned books!" Magdalena whispered. "One of these days I'm going to make a bonfire of them. Now move!"

Simon hefted the heavy sack onto his shoulder and groped

his way toward Magdalena, who was waiting for him impatiently by the exit. They ran along the narrow corridor until they came to the stairway leading up to the rear courtyard. As they hurried up its slick, moss-covered steps, they heard a sudden cry behind them—*Nathan!* Evidently he'd pulled himself together and had followed them.

"Hey, wait, where are you off to?"

Simon and Magdalena didn't reply but continued on up the steep staircase. When the beggar king realized they intended to flee, he sprinted after them.

"What in God's name is this all about?" he shouted. "Is this any way to say goodbye to your friends?"

Despite his drunken state, Nathan was astonishingly fast. He raced up the stairs, taking several steps at a time, and just managed to catch Magdalena by the hem of her skirt. Instinctively the hangman's daughter kicked Nathan square in the face with her left foot. An awful crunching sound was followed by a shriek of pain. Magdalena had apparently knocked the two golden teeth right out of her pursuer's mouth.

"Damned hangman's bitch," Nathan shouted, his voice sounding strangely garbled. "You'll pay for this! My teesh, my bschootiful teesh!"

His curses turned to a wail as he stopped to gather the broken pieces of his precious teeth from the floor. Simon and Magdalena took advantage of the extra time to push a moldering cart in front of the opening.

"Sorry!" the hangman's daughter called meekly. "They were crooked anyway. Simon will make you a new set, I promise!"

Outside, night had already fallen but clouds concealed the stars. The pair climbed over piles of foul-smelling garbage, then ran through the back courtyard toward a narrow passageway.

Soon they'd disappeared in the dark little streets of the city.

• • •

Jakob Kuisl stood motionless in the middle of the brothel cellar.

He was certain that his nemesis was directly above him! The third inquisitor had disappeared into one of the rooms upstairs and was amusing himself there with the prostitutes.

There's a rage in my belly, and it'll take more than one girl to fix that.

Kuisl would never forget that voice.

What now? His enemy wasn't alone up there. No, half the city council kept him company, along with some soldiers from Peter's Gate and a number of noisy prostitutes. If Kuisl went upstairs now, he'd almost certainly be caught.

He closed his eyes and tried to imagine what would happen after that. The bailiffs would drag him back to his cell in chains, and this time darkness, torture, and ultimately the scaffold would be inevitable. On the rack he'd probably be forced to confess who had helped him escape, and every turn of the crank would bring the Regensburg executioner closer to his own demise.

And my daughter will be helpless, at the mercy of this madman . . .

Kuisl knew he didn't want to risk all that, but he also couldn't stay here, not with the devil incarnate having his way with the girls just two floors above him. The sound of those voices alone would drive him mad.

And so he had to leave, at once. But where could he go? The only refuge that came to mind was the house of the Regensburg executioner. Aside from Teuber, there was no one in Regensburg he trusted. Perhaps he could stay in the hangman's house long enough to assure himself of Magdalena's safety.

Kuisl tried rotating his newly adjusted shoulder and stretched his back. He still felt as if he'd fallen from the roof of a house, but thanks to Teuber's bandages and the ointment, the pain wasn't so bad. If he didn't run too quickly, if he paced himself along the way and hid in doorways and niches to rest, he'd make it to Teuber's house all right. Fortunately the executioner had mentioned the name of his street in the course of one of their conversations. He'd even boasted about his pretty house, his wife, and his five darling children. Now Kuisl would have a chance to meet them.

Carefully placing one foot in front of the other, the hangman groped his way up the stairs until he was standing at the heavy front door. Softly he pushed back the bolt and looked out into the cloudy night. Despite the pleasant cool temperature, the air still reeked of garbage and sewage, but the scents of wheat, meadows, marshland, and forests were here as well. Soon he'd be out in them again.

He was just about to step out into the street when he heard a door slam upstairs.

"Hey, Thea, more wine! This cheeky tart here drank it all up herself. I'll wring her neck for that."

The door upstairs slammed shut again, and Kuisl held still with his right foot on the doorsill.

It was that voice again, the voice from his nightmares.

As if compelled by a mysterious force, he closed the door and tiptoed up the stairs. He had to see him; he had to look this man in the eye, if only for a moment, or the ghosts of the past would never release him.

After two dozen steps the spiral stone staircase ended in a white plastered foyer illuminated by a single torch. Four doors opened onto the foyer, and behind each one giggles, shouts, and soft moans could be heard. Another stairway led up to the third floor, where some raucous celebration was taking place.

Kuisl hesitated. The voice had definitely come from the second floor. The man he was looking for was behind one of these four doors.

Evidently Fat Thea hadn't heard the stranger's call, as neither she nor any of her girls had brought a fresh pitcher of wine. Carefully Kuisl put his ear to the first door. He could hear labored breathing and short, shrill cries, but no one was speaking.

He turned to the next room and put his ear again to the thin wooden door. He couldn't quite make out what was being said—a lovers' oath, perhaps? This couldn't be the man he was after, could it?

As Kuisl tried to catch a glimpse through the keyhole, the door swung open and smacked him right in the nose. Reeling, the hangman fell backward.

"Who the hell . . . ?" The young man stood over him with his pants around his ankles and his shirt open so that his pale, hairless potbelly jiggled above Kuisl's head. The man's thinning ash-blond hair tumbled down over his face, and he gasped for air like a big fat fish out of water.

"I must have the wrong door," the hangman mumbled, straightening up. "No offense intended."

Kuisl realized he didn't exactly look like a drunken alderman—drunk perhaps, but by no means a smug, well-fed patrician about to have an orgasm. But perhaps this client was tipsy enough himself not to notice that.

The man closed his mouth and stared back in fear at the man in front of him. His pale face was an expression of pure terror.

"You—you—are Kuisl, aren't you?" he whispered.

Blood dripping from his nose, the hangman grew silent. This much was certain: this character before him wasn't the third inquisitor; his voice was different. In fact, he might have been a rather decent fellow, unlike the man Kuisl was seeking. Still, there was something familiar about him. It was finally his Bavarian accent that gave him away.

It was Joachim Kerscher, one of the two other inquisitors.

"Oh, for the love of the Virgin Mother, please don't hurt me," Kerscher stuttered, awkwardly trying to hide behind the thin wooden door. "I'm just an ordinary councilman. I didn't approve of the torture, believe me. Why did you flee . . . ? We were going to—"

"Who was the third man?" the hangman snarled menacingly.

"The third?" Kerscher had retreated almost completely behind the door now, and only his pallid face peered out through
the crack. "I don't understand—"

"The third inquisitor, jackass!" Kuisl whispered through
clenched teeth, holding his bloody nose. "Who was it?"

The hangman took a deep breath. The pain in his shoulder,
the burning in his arms and legs, the shooting pains in his
back—this all came back now like a hammer blow. He felt suddenly sick to his stomach.

Kerscher nodded obsequiously. "The third inquisitor, of
course. Such a bastard. I can understand why you'd want to get
back at him. It was—"

At that moment a piercing scream came from the floor above.

Kuisl turned to find Fat Thea coming down the stairs with a
pitcher of wine, which slipped from her grasp and shattered on
the floor.

Suddenly it felt to Kuisl as if the entire house were beginning
to sway beneath him. Everything seemed to happen at once—the
pitcher breaking, the commotion on the floor above, the doors
opening all around him like portals to hell. Men stared at him,
but their faces were strangely blurred, and they all seemed to be
shouting at him at once. Was *he* shouting, too? Kuisl couldn't
say. Everything around him had become a muffled roar.

He shook his head to clear his mind a bit. Someone approached and tried to grab him, but Kuisl flung the figure aside
like a rag doll and stumbled toward the stairs. *Out!* He had to get
out, he had to get away from here before he collapsed once and
for all. Again he felt someone grab him by his injured shoulder.
The hangman crouched, rolling the man over his back and sending him tumbling down the stairs, screaming.

Kuisl could hear himself scream, too; he raged like a

wounded bear backed into a corner by a pack of hunting dogs. Again he reached out with his good right arm and pulled one of the men close, smashing the man's nose against his forehead. Kuisl felt the man's warm blood on his face and heard him howl as he tossed him aside like a straw puppet. His pain and fear lent him one last burst of energy before unconsciousness threatened to overcome him.

Half crazed, he staggered down the steps, kicked the front door open, and dashed out into the fresh air. He inhaled deeply, and immediately his mind began to clear. Holding his throbbing shoulder, he hobbled toward a low wall and climbed over. On the other side he collapsed in a garden overgrown with thorny blackberries and wild rosebushes.

Kuisl was finished. Leaning against the crumbling wall, pricked on all sides by thorns, and raging with pain, he waited for his pursuers to find him and drag him back to his cell.

He closed his eyes and listened as the sound of excited voices approached.

Among them he heard the voice of his most hated enemy.

Simon and Magdalena heard the shouts just as they were sneaking across the cathedral square.

Catching their breath, they pressed their backs against the front of a patrician house and watched as a dozen city guards rushed past, heading south toward Neupfarr Church Square. Only a few minutes had passed since they fled the catacombs. Could Nathan already have betrayed them to Mämminger? Was the city treasurer's power so great he could summon the entire city guard in an instant, just to pursue them?

Simon heard alarm bells begin to ring all over town, as if all of Regensburg were being called to Easter mass. The beggars had told him that each quarter of the city kept its own company of guards—a civilian militia called upon only in times of war or fire or other grave catastrophe. The militias were summoned to duty by the ringing of church bells. When another dozen soldiers came running from the old grain market through the cathedral square, the medicus feared the worst.

"Where could they all be headed?" Magdalena whispered, pressing herself even closer to the wall as the bailiffs marched south, just a few yards away. "They can't all be looking for us, can they?"

Simon shrugged. "I don't think so, but I also don't see any signs of fire, and it's unlikely war's broken out. Perhaps they're going to smoke out the beggars' hideaway. That's more or less the direction they're headed."

"Something's fishy here," Magdalena muttered, taking Simon's hand and leading him out onto the now-deserted cathedral square. "Come on; let's follow them and see."

"That's much too dangerous!" Simon said. "Believe me, the bishop's palace is the only safe place for us right now. We've got to find the fastest way—"

"Oh, come now," Magdalena interrupted. "Life's dangerous. Let's go."

Simon followed her with a sigh as the haven of the bishop's residence disappeared behind them in the darkness. They turned into Judengasse Street, which ended in Neupfarr Church Square with its austere Protestant church. Just as they were about to step out into the open square, they noticed a group of perhaps thirty city bailiffs at its center, gesticulating wildly toward the south. The shrill alarm bells were still ringing, and many citizens had by now opened their shutters to gape at the spectacle below from the safety of their balconies.

"I have to know what the guards are up to," Magdalena whispered. "Let's creep up a little closer."

Simon knew his friend well enough now to sense it was pointless to argue. She had a wrinkle in her brow that meant there was just no stopping her. So he knelt down beside her on the dirty cobblestones spattered with horse manure, knowing it would ruin his last decent pair of trousers. Under the cover of darkness they crept toward the light of the torches.

The men in front of them were not trained soldiers but common citizens, some still in nightshirts and bathrobes beneath hastily donned cuirasses. Their hair was disheveled, their faces pale and frightened. In their hands they held rusty pikes, daggers, and crossbows that seemed like survivors from an earlier century. They were bakers, carpenters, butchers, and simple linen weavers, and to judge by their appearance, the last thing in the world they wanted to do was stand here in the middle of the night, listening to a speech by the captain of the guards.

"Citizens, listen up!" a bearded, elderly man exhorted them. In contrast to the others, he looked at least halfway battle-tested. In his right hand he clutched a halberd over ten feet long with a point that glittered menacingly in the torchlight. "As many of you perhaps already know, the Schongau monster, the throat slitter and bloodsucker, broke out of his cell last night. But that's not all. Yesterday, the murderer strangled Master Baker Haberger and gruesomely slaughtered Marie Deisch in her own bathhouse—"

An anxious whisper spread among the men, and the commander of the guards raised his hand for silence.

"Fortunately the man has been found. He's lurking somewhere down by Peter's Gate, and with your help we'll send him back to hell today once and for all! Three cheers for our strong and mighty city!"

The old officer had evidently expected some enthusiasm—or at least a response—but the men in the crowd before him remained strangely silent and whispered among themselves.

Then a young boy in a stained old mercenary helmet raised his hand hesitantly. "Is it true that the monster bites his victims' necks and drinks their blood?"

The old officer, who hadn't expected that question, stood still for a moment with his mouth open. "Ah . . . as far as I know, he used a knife, but—"

"They say this Kuisl is a werewolf, that he turns into a beast at night and eats little children," someone else added. "He's already ripped apart five prostitutes and drunk their blood. How are we going to hunt a demon like that with our rusty old swords and crossbows? He'll probably just take wing and fly away!"

Those standing around him clamored in agreement. At the crowd's edge a few anxious men seemed about to turn around and go home.

"Nonsense!" The captain pounded his halberd on the ground as a call to order. "This Kuisl is a man like any other, but he's a murderer. And for that reason we'll capture him today and bring him to justice. Do you understand? It's your goddamned duty as citizens!" His threatening eyes wandered over the assembled company of pale, unshaven men. "You can, of course, buy your way out of this obligation, but believe me, I'll check with the president of the council to see that you pay dearly."

The citizens didn't seem convinced, but they permitted the captain to divide them up into groups.

"Turmeier and Schwendner, you'll go over to the Ostner Quarter," he began in a voice accustomed to giving orders. "Poeverlein and Bergmüller, you'll take the Wittwanger Quarter. The rest of you . . ."

Magdalena stopped paying attention now and turned to Simon, who had listened to the captain's speech with his mouth as wide open as hers.

"Thanks be to the saints above! Father actually managed to escape!" the hangman's daughter whispered. "But now they want to charge him with two more murders!"

Simon frowned. "And if he really . . . ? I mean maybe this master baker got in his way, or—"

"And he slaughtered the bathhouse mistress for good measure?" Magdalena snorted. "Sometimes I believe you really think my father is some kind of monster. I don't believe a single word of what that pompous guard said! As long as my father's here in this city, they'll accuse him of practically anything!" Lowering her voice, she added, "He's probably hiding in a shed or a vacant lot somewhere. It's very likely he's injured. We've got to help him at once!"

"And how do you intend to do that?" Simon replied quietly. "We don't know where he's hiding any more than the guards do. Do you plan to run around calling for him by name?"

Magdalena thought for a moment; then her face lit up with a smile.

"That's not such a bad idea," she said. "Listen, this is how we'll do it." In a hasty whisper she explained her plan.

Jakob Kuisl sat against the low, crumbling wall, trying to fight off an impending blackout. The fresh air had revived him, but he'd reached the end of his strength. His escape from Peter's Gate had required every last ounce of it, but he'd shaken his pursuers, at least for the moment. The men had run right past him. Among their voices he heard that of the third inquisitor and for a brief moment considered jumping up and strangling him with the one good hand he had left. Thank God he was too weak to try.

Now he was crouched in an overgrown lot somewhere in Regensburg, trying to pull himself together. All was not lost. He could still go to Teuber's house if only this damned dizziness would pass!

When the alarm bells sounded, Kuisl knew at once they were for him. Bailiffs in every quarter would be alerted and in no time would be after him like dogs after a young fox. He tried to stand up but collapsed again immediately. On the third try he finally managed to pull himself halfway upright and set off, carefully placing one foot in front of the other.

Kuisl climbed over the low-lying wall overgrown with rosebushes and tried to orient himself. He knew that Peter's Gate,
which rose into view over the rooftops, was in the southern part
of the city, and that Teuber's house therefore had to be to the
north, in the Henkersgässchen, or Hangman's Lane. Beyond this
he knew nothing. Until now he hadn't given a single thought to
how he might find the hangman's house. He could hardly ask
someone for directions, and there were no street signs in this
damned city. The only option he had was to wander the streets in
the hope that his nose would lead him there.

What a bloody ridiculous plan!

Kuisl cursed his own stupidity. Why hadn't he questioned
Teuber more closely about the location of his house? All Kuisl
could do was hope he might run into a shady character like himself in the middle of the night who might take pity on him and
help him out.

And turn me over to the bailiffs at the first opportunity . . .

Hunched over and peering in every direction as he went, the
hangman slunk through the part of town neighboring Peter's
Gate. The houses here were small and low, the gardens unten-
ded, and he came upon house after house that had been reduced
to ashes — evidence of the Great War and the last Plague, a few
years ago. When the inhabitants went off to the former — or suc-
cumbed to the latter — their homes had fallen to ruin. From
where he was he could hear the alarm bells still ringing and far-
off shouts that signaled pursuit.

They were hot on his trail; he didn't have much time left.

Just as Kuisl was seeking a hiding place next to a nearby
house, two guards turned a corner and headed toward him. The
men, armed with halberds, seemed just as surprised by him as he
was by them. The younger of the two was so taken aback that his
helmet fell off; the other reached nervously for an ancient wheel-
lock pistol with a patina of verdigris that hung from his belt.
Kuisl could only hope the weapon wasn't loaded.

"Over here! Over here!" the younger one shouted, "We got him! The monster is right here!"

The older man fumbled with his pistol, which had snagged on his belt. When a shot rang out, the man shouted and fell to the ground, clutching his right boot and wailing. He'd shot himself in the foot.

Kuisl took advantage of the general confusion to run back out into the street, but he didn't get very far before two more bailiffs appeared from the other direction. One shouldered a crossbow at eye level. A moment later a bolt whizzed by, just a hair's breadth from Kuisl's right ear.

The hangman decided to risk it all: shouting at the top of his lungs, he ran toward the two newly arrived guards in the blind hope that the second man had neither a loaded crossbow nor a pistol. The bailiffs awaited him with their pikes pointed straight ahead, and Kuisl detected a mixture of fear and bloodlust in their eyes.

"Everyone to the Pfaffengasse!" one shouted. "He's in the Pfaffengasse! Over here! He's —"

Kuisl gathered all his strength and, with a single leap, soared headlong over the pikes, landing a punch in the face of the screaming guard that knocked the man down like a felled tree. The other dropped his spear and pulled out a large hunting knife. He lunged for the hangman, but Kuisl bucked like a wild horse. With a kick to the gut, the man collapsed, moaning.

The hangman turned to discover more and more guards streaming into the lane. Panicked, he spotted a low archway on his left that seemed to lead off into a narrow path. Without a moment's hesitation, he fled through the archway and down the path, arriving soon at an interior courtyard surrounded on three sides by tall buildings.

A dead end.

Turning around, Kuisl saw three or four bailiffs approaching through the archway with their halberds raised. Cold smiles played across their lips, and their eyes gleamed. They were clearly now in no hurry. They had cornered their prey at last, and now they'd finish him off.

Someone tossed a torch into the middle of the courtyard, casting a larger-than-life shadow of Kuisl on the wall behind him. In the flickering light the hangman made an easy target.

A crossbow bolt splintered on the plaster wall behind him, then another. Out of the corner of his eye the hangman looked all around for a way out. There wasn't a single door in sight; the windows were all on the second story and therefore out of reach, with no trellises or trees to climb. In one corner of the yard a two-wheeled oxcart was parked and loaded with hay. The cart had a heavy, waist-high shaft with iron fittings. The hangman hesitated. Then an idea hit him.

The hay . . .

Doubled over, he ran toward the wagon as arrows rained down around him like hailstones. With his good right arm he grabbed the wagon shaft and turned the vehicle so that the rear was now facing the soldiers. Kuisl knew his strength was about to give out; this was his only chance.

Taking a deep breath, he ran to the middle of the courtyard, grabbed the burning torch from the ground, and threw it at the cart. In a flash the dry hay was ablaze, and the wagon an enormous fireball. Disregarding the brutal heat, Kuisl picked up the shaft again with his good arm and pushed with all his might. The burning wagon rolled backward toward the guards—the only way out. The bailiffs screamed and leaped aside, but burning hay bales fell on them, setting their hats and jackets on fire.

The wagon now began to gain speed. At last Kuisl reached the archway and headed straight for the narrow exit.

I have to make it . . . Oh, stubborn, irascible God, please, for Magdalena's sake . . .

The wagon squeezed through the exit and rolled out into the Pfaffengasse. Kuisl gave the cart a final shove so that it veered to the left, crashing into a doorway, where it exploded. Burning hay and glowing splinters rained down as the flames began to spread.

Wheezing from the smoke, the hangman ran down the Pfaffengasse, looking back one last time. By now the fire had spread to the building's ground floor and the shop window on the floor above. Everywhere citizens were shouting and running to the public well with buckets to get water. In spite of his pain, Kuisl couldn't suppress a grin. This would keep the guards occupied for a while at least.

The hangman ran on a few yards, finally turning into a little side street, where he found a pair of old splintered barrels. One of them lay on its side, and with the last of his strength Kuisl folded up his legs and squeezed himself in so that he was no longer visible from the outside. Numbed by his fever and the wine fumes inside, he felt half dead as the shouts of the crowd gradually moved away. He closed his eyes and resisted the urge to fall asleep. He had to get out of here, at once. Where was Teuber? Where was his house, the safe house of the executioner, his friend . . . ?

When Kuisl heard singing, he thought he was dreaming at first. The song was definitely not of this world, but from a time long ago.

Ladybug, ladybug, fly away home . . .

He listened in astonishment. The singing wasn't coming from just anywhere, but from the street to the immediate left of where he was hiding. And it was no figment of his imagination but reality, pure and simple.

Your house is on fire, your children will burn . . .

Now the voice was right beside him, both off-key and very familiar.

"Do you really think we're going to find your father this way?" Simon complained. "So far we've only managed to avoid being hit by a chamber pot—twice. And frankly, your singing leaves something to be desired."

"It's not about how well I sing, just that I'm singing," Magdalena snapped. "The main thing is it's loud enough for Father to hear me."

Simon laughed. "Well, loud you are, all right. You're even drowning out the alarm bells."

They were moving slowly south from Neupfarr Church Square, winding through little side streets. Three times already they'd encountered bands of armed city guards, who on any other ordinary night and without a second thought would have thrown Magdalena and Simon into the House of Fools for disturbing the peace. But the pale, anxious guards were otherwise occupied now and simply peered intently at the strange couple before setting off again. Simon and Magdalena could hear the shouts of guards from every direction and then a far-off but very loud explosion.

"Let me think," Magdalena whispered, already going hoarse from singing *Hans, Hans, has fancy pants. . . The night of winter's over. . .* "I'm running out of songs. Can you think of another one?"

As a child, the hangman's daughter often sang with her father. Now she hoped he might recognize her voice and the songs she chose. In this way, at least, she looked a lot less suspicious than if she were running around calling out his name. For the watchmen, as well as the curious onlookers who stared out at them from behind shutters, she looked like just another drunken prostitute staggering through the streets with a client.

Magdalena was struggling to think of another song when her face brightened in a flash.

"I have one more," she said. "I can't believe I didn't think of it sooner!"

She started singing a lullaby her father always hummed to

her just before bed. And as she did so, memories of her father passed through her mind in fragments.

The scent of sweat and tobacco as he bends down to me. Piggy-backing on the shoulders of a giant who protects me from an evil world—strong, invincible, the god of my childhood . . .

Tears ran down her cheeks, but still she kept on singing.

"Ladybug, ladybug, fly away home . . ."

Suddenly a ghost emerged from a rotten wine barrel in the gutter and staggered to its feet. The enormous figure wore tattered trousers and a bloodstained linen shirt, its arms and legs covered with bandages and its face dusted with cinders. Magdalena knew at once who stood before her.

"Father, my God, Father!" she screamed, nearly hysterical, not giving a single thought to whether guards might be nearby. Quickly she covered her mouth with her hand and whispered, "Holy Saint Anthony, we've really found you. You're alive!"

"Not for much longer if you keep on singing like that," Kuisl replied as he staggered toward his daughter. Only now did Magdalena realize how severely wounded he was.

"We have to . . . get away . . . from here," he stammered. "They're . . . on our . . . trail. The third inquisitor . . ."

Magdalena frowned. "The third inquisitor? What are you talking about, Father?"

"I thought he'd caught you," he said in a low voice. "He knows you and the name of your mother. The devil is out for revenge."

"It's got to be a fever," Simon said. "Hallucinations that—"

"Weidenfeld!" Kuisl shouted through his pain. "He's out for revenge!"

"My God!" Magdalena put her hand over her mouth again. "There's that name again. Who's this damned Weidenfeld?"

The alarm bells were still ringing, and over them the guards' voices sounded suddenly much closer than before, only a few streets away now. A window opened directly above the little group, and a toothless old man in a nightcap glared down at them suspiciously.

"Quiet, goddamn it! You good-for-nothing drunks! If you want to have a good time, take your woman somewhere else!"

Simon grabbed the nearly unconscious hangman by the shoulder and led him quickly behind the barrels.

"The bishop's palace," he whispered to Magdalena, who knelt down next to him. "We have to go there and ask the church for asylum. That's our only chance! We certainly won't make it out of town tonight."

"And do you really think the bishop will grant asylum to a suspected murderer?" Magdalena asked skeptically.

Simon nodded enthusiastically. "Asylum in the church has been sacred since time immemorial! Only the bishop has the power to make and enforce laws on lands belonging to the church, so once your father makes it there, the city guards are powerless."

"Isn't that just wonderful!" Magdalena rolled her eyes. "The bishop himself, rather than the city, will have the personal privilege of breaking my father on the wheel. What a relief!"

"At least we'll gain some time," Simon replied. "I'm sure once we know what your uncle's alchemical experiments were all about, we'll get a better handle on what the big secret is. Then maybe we can start to prove your father's innocence."

"And if not, then all this will have been for naught!" Magdalena shook her head. "Out of the question! My father's free now. Why would I put him right back in danger again?"

"Just look at him!" Simon pointed at Kuisl, who crouched behind a wine barrel, his head hanging down to his chest, breathing heavily. "We'll be lucky if we can even make it to the bishop's palace. But if we do, at least your father will get the care he obviously needs."

All of a sudden the voices of the guards sounded very close, their footsteps pounding on the hard-packed clay soil. Magdalena watched as two of them charged around the corner and into the narrow lane. She held her breath; she could feel her exhausted father leaning hard against the barrel, and the barrel itself was now threatening to topple under his weight. Mustering all her might, she hugged her father close, hoping to keep both him and the barrel upright. The bailiffs raced past and soon disappeared in the darkness.

"Very well," Magdalena whispered. "We'll do as you say. But if they harm so much as a single hair on my father's head, you'll be sleeping alone for many years to come!"

Simon smiled. "Believe me, that's the last thing on my mind at this point. Come on, now; let's wake the sleeping giant."

They gave Jakob Kuisl a few brisk slaps in the face until he came at least partway to, then each took an arm and led him away.

"We'll get you to the cathedral square as fast as we can," Simon whispered. "I hope the people will just figure we're lugging a drunk friend home."

"Get . . . your . . . hands . . . off me," the hangman growled. "I can . . . walk by myself."

"Don't make such a fuss, Father," Magdalena said. "It'll do you some good if you let your daughter help you out a bit from time to time. You're not a young fellow anymore."

"Snotty little . . . bitch." Kuisl gave up, collapsing into Simon's and Magdalena's arms. The hangman's daughter doubted he had any idea what they planned to do with him.

"Let's go now!" Simon urged. "Before the guards show up again."

He and Magdalena stumbled through the dark city, shouldering the hangman's dead weight between them. Kuisl collapsed again and again, forcing them to stop each time. Twice they encountered guards too busy to be bothered by a trio of revelers as they frantically poked their torches into every last nook and cranny in search of their convict. They had better things to do tonight than be distracted by a handful of drunks.

After an anxious quarter-hour Simon and Magdalena finally came to the deserted Krauterermarkt Square, where the entrance to the bishop's palace was located. They were disappointed to find that the doors, nearly fifteen feet high, were locked.

"Damn!" Magdalena said. "We might have expected something like this."

From a distance the heavy, iron-studded portal seemed about as inviting as the gates to hell. It rose above them darkly, ending at the top in a pointed arch and alcove displaying several coats of arms. In the left wing of the door they spotted a small porthole, also shut tight.

"How do you intend to get in?" Magdalena asked. "Just knock?"

"You forget I have an invitation from the bishop's brewmaster."

"Yes, for yourself. But does it include permission for a hangman's daughter and a fugitive murderer?"

Simon rolled his eyes. "Must you always be so petulant? Before, we followed *your* plan; now, we're going to follow *mine*. Is that all right?"

"So, then, what is it exactly you intend to do, smart aleck?"

"Let's put your father down somewhere first. My arms feel like they're about to fall off."

They carefully led Kuisl to a little recessed area between two houses where he would be invisible to most passersby. The hangman's face was ashen, and beads of sweat stood out on his forehead, but he was somehow able to keep more or less upright against the wall.

"Do you think you can walk a little ways by yourself?" Simon asked.

Kuisl nodded, teeth clenched, as the medicus quietly explained the plan. Then Simon approached the portal and gave a few loud knocks.

It was a while before they heard shuffling steps on the other side. With a creak, the porthole opened on the pinched, unshaven face of a bishop's guard.

"There'd better be a good reason for knocking on my door at this godforsaken hour," the guard growled, "or you just may be living out the rest of the summer in our modest little dungeon. Without water."

Gravely Simon produced his invitation from the brewmaster. "His Excellency Brother Hubertus has summoned me here," he said, without batting an eye. "He's expecting me right away."

"Now?" The soldier scratched his lice-ridden scalp. "After midnight?"

"I'm Simon Fronwieser from the Spital Brewery," the medicus improvised. "Your brewmaster is having problems with the fermentation of the wheat beer, and if we don't do something about it right away, the beer will taste like horse piss by tomorrow and your bishop will be high and dry."

The guard frowned. The thought of being held in any way responsible for the irascible bishop's thirst made him queasy.

"Hey, Rupert!" he shouted to someone behind him. "Wake that fat monk in the brewery. He has a visitor."

Suddenly they heard hundreds of boots marching toward them from the direction of the cathedral square. A large contingent of guards was returning to their quarters. Simon could only imagine what might happen were they to discover him here.

"Ah, would you mind opening the door?" the medicus asked. "It's drafty out here, and I could stand to get off my feet."

"Hold it," the soldier barked. "The monk will be here in a moment."

They could now hear distinct voices approaching from the south. Simon turned his head to see at least a dozen bailiffs armed with pikes advancing toward them from the cathedral square.

"What difference does it make if I wait out here or wait inside?" He offered a strained smile. "Besides, I have a stomachache. The mashed peas I had for lunch must have been a bit rotten, so just open the door and —"

"Silence, I said!" the guard interrupted. "First we'll see if the brewmaster in fact knows you. Many others have made their way here before you, hoping for asylum."

Now the city guards were no more than thirty paces from Simon.

Maybe they won't recognize me, he thought frantically. *But they'll ask questions nonetheless. A man, all alone in the middle of the night, before the door to the bishop's palace — that's suspicious in and of itself...*

"I'd really like to know what in hell is going on out there," the guard said, poking his head out the porthole for a better look. "All that shouting and the bells clanging — as if the Turks were at the city gates. Well, we'll find out soon enough, I suppose."

Now some bailiffs were in fact approaching the bishop's palace. One soldier pointed his long pike at Simon and shouted something to the others. The men seemed to be moving more quickly now in his direction. Beads of sweat broke out on his forehead. Should he run? If he did, he'd have squandered his last chance.

"Hey, you there!" cried one soldier, hurrying toward him. "What are you doing there by that door?"

Just then a familiar voice boomed out from inside the palace. "Simon Fronwieser! Have you come to make confession or are you just dying for another sip of my heavenly wheat beer?"

The medicus took a deep breath. Brother Hubertus had finally gotten out of bed.

"I have good news!" his voice thundered from behind the porthole. "I now know what the powder of yours is! But let's discuss that in peace over a mug of beer or two. Good Lord, won't you damned numbskulls let my friend in?"

His last words were directed at the bishop's guards, who finally slid back the heavy bolt and opened the gigantic portal.

"Now!" Simon cried suddenly. "Run!"

At this instant several things happened all at once.

Two figures emerged from the shadows on the other side of the square. Magdalena had explained to her father that as soon as Simon called for them, Kuisl would have to run for his life. He managed to pull himself together enough to run in great strides with his daughter toward the open portal. Simon, meanwhile, leaped over the threshold and pushed aside the guard, who struggled desperately to shut the door again as horrified city bailiffs approached from the right, crossbows loaded and pistols drawn as it dawned on them that the hangman was here.

"The monster!" one shouted. "The monster is trying to escape into the bishop's palace!"

Bullets and arrows crashed into the masonry, and armed men ran shouting toward the portal with pikes and halberds raised. The bishop's guard had by now freed himself from Simon's grip and with his colleagues was trying to push the door closed. Magdalena watched the opening narrow as she ran toward it. The door was closing inch by inch, slowly yet inexorably. At the last moment she and Kuisl slipped through into the courtyard and fell gasping to the ground.

The heavy door crashed closed, and from without came angry shouts and insistent pounding.

Brother Hubertus stood gaping over the tangle of people at his feet, which slowly began to unravel itself.

"What in God's name is this all about, Fronwieser?" he asked, pointing to Magdalena and her father, who lay panting at the doorsill.

"Grant . . . us . . . asylum," Simon whispered with his last bit of strength. "Jakob Kuisl . . . is innocent."

Then a bishop's guard delivered a blow that knocked him out.

12

DO YOU REALIZE THE TROUBLE YOU'VE CAUSED
me?" Brother Hubertus shook his head. His face, flushed with
outrage, glowed like an oversize radish. Not even a third tankard of beer seemed to calm him down much. Trembling with
fury, he pointed a finger at Simon and Magdalena, who sat at a
table in the muggy brew house, staring at the ground like two
defendants on trial.

"I trusted you, Simon Fronwieser," the Franciscan continued to berate him. "And what do you do? You bring the most
wanted man in all of Regensburg into my house — the man
they're calling a monster, a man who's being sought for multiple
murders! The bishop has been screaming at me all morning — my ears are still ringing. We're giving asylum to a monster! And all this at a time when His Excellency has enough
trouble with the city already over the construction of the walk-
ways above the road in town. I could rip you to shreds, Fronwieser!"

"Jakob Kuisl is an innocent man," Simon insisted once more.
"You have my word."

"That's the only thing standing between you and immediate

expulsion," Brother Hubertus said, dabbing the sweat on his forehead.

Simon wrapped both hands around his tankard and stared down into his beer, as if somehow he might find the solution to all his problems there. Of course, his wonderful plan had ended in a fiasco. Why on earth had he thought Brother Hubertus would welcome them with open arms? Last night the Franciscan had thrown a fit when he learned how much he'd been deceived. That's when Simon laid all his cards on the table. He told Brother Hubertus about Kuisl and the intrigue against him. He told the monk where the powder came from, as well as his suspicions about the philosopher's stone. For the most part Brother Hubertus took it all in in silence, his lips tightly pressed. Not until Simon mentioned the floury dust in the storage room and alchemist's workshop did the brewmaster interject a few questions. He seemed mostly interested in the quantity of powder Simon and Magdalena had found down there.

Hubertus appeared to have calmed down a bit in the meantime, but though he continued to sip his wheat beer, he really didn't seem to enjoy it.

"At least it looks like your father's feeling better," he said, looking over at the hangman's daughter. "He has the constitution of an ox; give him a few days and he'll shake those shackles right off. I'll have to assign a guard to his bedside soon enough."

"Does that mean my father can stay here in the bishop's palace?" Magdalena looked hopefully at the Franciscan. Until now she'd kept silent for the most part, leaving the explaining to Simon. But this concerned the fate of her family. "You won't turn him over to the city, will you?" she inquired. "You'll grant him asylum?"

"How can the bishop deny asylum to such a battered man?" Hubertus replied. "That is our damned duty as shepherds of the Lord, even when upholding this duty may — er — conflict, shall

we say, with other concerns." This last sentence he added with a
sigh.

Simon breathed a sigh of relief. Magdalena's father was safe
for the time being. The night before, they had taken Kuisl to the
brewmaster's chamber and applied fresh bandages to his wounds,
and he'd been sleeping like a baby ever since. Simon had briefly
examined his wounds, burns, and bruises. Neither he nor Magdalena could imagine all the suffering he'd been through in the
past few days.

"But don't get your hopes up too much," the fat monk continued. "I was able to persuade the bishop to allow you to stay
here for only three days." He turned to both Simon and Magdalena and held three fat fingers up to their faces. "Three days, no
more. That's all the time you have to prove this man's innocence.
Thereafter he'll be turned over — and you along with him — to
the city guards. To be clear, the only reason you have even this
much time is because I interceded on your behalf. If it was up to
the bishop, the whole lot of you would be rotting away as we
speak in the dungeon at city hall."

Simon nodded timidly. "I can't tell you how grateful I am.
I'm sorry I so shamelessly abused your trust."

"Oh, come now!" Brother Hubertus took a big gulp from his
tankard. "Enough of this pompous talk — let's get to work."

"You're right," Simon declared with a firmer voice. "Time is
precious, and so it's all the more urgent now that you tell us what
you've learned about the powder. Last night you implied you'd
found the secret — so put an end to the suspense. What is it?"

The Franciscan looked thoughtfully at Simon for a long
while before answering. "Actually, I wanted to tell you yesterday
what nasty stuff that powder is," he began. "But tell me the truth,
Fronwieser. Can I really trust you? How do I know that you're
not looking for more of this evil stuff yourself? How am I supposed to know you're not lying to me again? You, a doctor in the
Regensburger Collegium? Bah!"

"I give you my word as a doctor," Simon stammered.

"Your word's worth nothing here," Hubertus retorted. "Believe me, this powder is much too dangerous for me to depend on the word of any old quack who comes along." He rose to his full, imposing height. "I'll tell you what. I'll make some more inquiries, and only when I'm convinced this stuff can't cause any greater damage than it may have already, then I'll let you in on the secret."

Simon stared back at him, his mouth open. "But—but then how are we supposed to help Magdalena's father?" he stuttered. "We need to know what—"

"Whatever you need to know or do, it's all the same to me," the brewmaster interrupted. "Early tomorrow morning I'll have more to tell you. But until then the matter is too delicate. This secret could drive us all out of our minds, and if what I think is true . . ." His expression clouded over. "Just tend to your future father-in-law, or he may die even before his time here is up."

With these words, he turned to leave the brew house, teetering as he slammed the door behind him.

The medicus sighed and drummed his fingers on the rutted tabletop.

"And now?" asked Magdalena. "What shall we do now, you know-it-all?"

"You heard him," Simon replied gruffly. "We take care of your father. That's something I know how to do at least."

He rose abruptly and walked past steaming vats to a little wooden door in the back of the vaulted room. It opened into a low room furnished with a simple bed and a trunk with metal fittings. This would ordinarily have been the brewmaster's bedroom, but Brother Hubertus had made it up yesterday for Jakob Kuisl, who now lay snoring loudly on the bed, bare from the waist up. Simon leaned down and put his ear to Kuisl's powerful hairy chest. A few hours earlier he'd given Kuisl a bit of the opium poppy extract he carried around in his bag, and as a result

the hangman's breathing was calmer now and even. Magdalena
had also been keeping watch at her father's bedside, periodically
spooning hot chicken broth between his chapped lips. The medicus carefully checked the hangman's bandages.

The bishop's bailiffs had tied the hangman to the bed with
ropes, but Simon very much doubted these fetters could hold
him there for long. The Schongau executioner had the constitution of a bear and, in keeping with that, seemed to have fallen
into a deep winter's sleep. The wounds on his back, arms, and
legs no longer festered, and the inflammation had begun to go
down overnight. Simon was hopeful Kuisl would be well on his
way to recovery within a few days.

Just in time for his next torture session, he thought gloomily.

He felt a hand on his shoulder. Magdalena gave him a sympathetic look.

"I'm really sorry about what happened earlier," she said
softly. "I know you meant well. We've always found a way out.
Let's wait and see — we just might again."

Simon smiled wearily and nodded. "You're right. We'll
make out, all three of us." But his voice sounded strangely hol-
low. For the first time since their arrival in Regensburg he
couldn't shake the feeling that their situation might be hopeless
after all.

"At least he probably won't remember a thing about all this."
The hangman's daughter gestured toward her father, whom she
hadn't seen for such a long time. Kuisl slept as sweetly as if he
were back home in his own bed.

"One thing is clear," Magdalena continued. "We can't escape
with him now, not in his present condition. And as long as we sit
around here in the bishop's palace, we'll never find out what
there is to know about this powder. This fat monk is just putting
us off."

Simon frowned. "At least I was right in thinking that there
was something special about the stuff. It may hold the key to all

our questions—and it's dangerous. Brother Hubertus seems to have great respect for it. *A secret that could drive us all out of our minds . . .*" He quietly pondered the brewmaster's strange words. "Just what in the world could Brother Hubertus have meant by that?"

"It's already starting to drive me out of my mind." Magdalena sighed. "A powder that the Regensburg patricians are chasing after as they would a murderer—or God knows who else! What on earth could it be?"

"Perhaps it really is something like the philosopher's stone," Simon whispered. "But what exactly this stone is . . ." He shook his head. "This kind of thinking won't get us very far. Let's wait until morning to see whether Hubertus lets us in on his secret. If not, we'll try to escape with your father before the bishop has him locked up in the dungeon."

"And how do you think we're going to manage that?" Magdalena asked incredulously. "The guards in the courtyard outside rattle their sabers every time I so much as poke my head out the brewery door."

"No idea. But there's no point in sitting here twiddling our thumbs. We might as well start looking around here." Shrugging, Simon headed back into the brewery, waving cheerfully through the window at the suspicious bailiffs outside. "There's got to be more than one exit in this whole place," he mused. "We just have to find it."

The Danube flowed past the city like a sluggish ribbon of black slime. Dead fish, cabbage stalks, and shredded fishnets bobbed up and down along the rotting posts of the pier. Not a breath of air stirred in the midday heat, and the stench hung heavily over the pier, permeating the shutters of every building around the harbor.

On the pier, hidden behind shipping crates piled high, two men were seated atop two large wooden tethering posts. They didn't even smell the infernal stench. The hatred within them was so great it blocked out everything else. Their hatred was a poison that had eaten away at them year after year, leaving room in their hearts and their minds for only one thought.

Revenge.

"But how could that happen!" one of them complained, cracking his knuckles so loudly the sound echoed across the deserted waterfront. "We were so close, and then he slipped away like a mouse into a hole. Now he's feasting at the bishop's palace and pleading for asylum! What a goddamned disgrace!"

"The bishop can't let him stay there forever," the other calmly replied. His voice was prickly, cold, like the dead of winter. "He won't dare let a mass murderer loose."

"How did Kuisl even manage to escape the dungeon in the first place, huh? There's something not right there. They say the guards fell asleep. Bah!"

The other nodded. "I have a suspicion about that; if I'm right, Teuber just may have the pleasure of torturing his children with his very own hand. But first things first . . ." Vacantly, he watched the bloated carcass of a wild duck float by. After a pause he continued, his voice impassive. "Sooner or later the bishop's going to have to turn Kuisl over, and then we can pick up where we left off."

"And if he doesn't?" snapped the other. "These priests love to play games with the city. It's quite possible Kuisl will remain there until pigs grow wings and fly. I can't wait that long! I've been waiting for this moment for years. I want my vengeance. I want—"

"Silence!" the man with the cold voice interrupted, slapping his companion's face so hard he nearly fell headlong into the harbor. "You're like a child, and someone's taken your damn toy away. Do you think I don't want revenge, too? He read the inscription on the cell wall, and I got him to the point where he almost recognized me down in the torture chamber—and no doubt in his nightmares as well. . ." His lips curled into a thin smile; then he grew serious. "But we have to be careful, or the others could start asking questions. I have worked a very long time to make sure no one in Regensburg would recognize me or my old name. At the inquisition I was a little too . . . ardent, and that was a mistake. We've got to remain calm — both of us. Also on account of the other matter."

The second man whimpered and pinched his nose as a mixture of blood and green snot dripped into the Danube below. As so often, anger swelled within him. Why did he put up with this man? Why didn't he just snap his neck? Instead, the second man swallowed his rage, just as he had his entire life.

"So what would you suggest, then?" he asked.

The man with the icy voice spat into the water. "You're right," he said. "We don't know when the bishop is going to release him. Besides, his daughter and that smart aleck, the quack, are with him. They're working hand in glove with the fat brewmaster. And they know about the Holy Fire . . ."

"Goddamn it! How do you know that?"

"The little weasel told me. The blasted little schemer knows everything about those two and thinks we ought to come up with some kind of a plan as quickly as possible." He grinned. "But don't worry — I have something in mind."

"What?" the second man asked hopefully. He admired how the other man could throw together a plan. He was cunning, so damned shrewd!

But the other man hesitated. When he did begin to speak, his speech was clipped. He had thought it all out very carefully, and now they just had to be sure they didn't make any mistakes. "We have to lure the mouse from its hole again," he whispered. "With some kind of bait. But we have to find a way to get at him first."

"You want to go *into* the bishop's palace?"

The man nodded. "I know a few of the guards there, so that shouldn't be difficult. I'll leave a little note for Kuisl that he won't forget as long as he lives." Again, the corners of his mouth twitched into a thin smile. "We'll have to bring him back to where it all began. We should have done that long ago, just him and us. That's how it has to be."

The second man nodded enthusiastically. "Just the two of us—and him! Like before! Kuisl will wish he was back in the torture chamber!" Suddenly he scowled. "But suppose the fat brewmaster already knows too much; suppose the others have explained the Holy Fire to him?"

The man with the icy voice spat in the river again and stood up in a single motion. "Leave that to me. We'll catch both of them—the mouse as well as the fat rat."

Jakob Kuisl woke to a stomach growling as loud as a bear. He was overwhelmed by hunger.

Good, he thought. *If I'm hungry at least I know I can't be dead.*

He opened his eyes and stared into the darkness. It was night; alongside his bed a beeswax candle flickered atop a trunk. Next to it some kind soul had placed a jug of wine, a bowl of soup, and a loaf of bread. Kuisl vaguely recalled how his daughter had fed him like an infant just a short while ago. A wave of relief passed through his body: the third inquisitor hadn't gotten his hands on Magdalena! What else had happened? They had fled together through the streets of Regensburg and sought refuge at the bishop's palace. Young Simon had mentioned something about asylum, and shortly after that Kuisl had passed out again. In brief waking moments he remembered Magdalena, her voice shaking, speaking about the inscriptions in the dungeon, about the third inquisitor, and about his escape.

And then there was something else, too: he thought he remembered a man bending down over his bed at some point during the night. The stranger, whose face was hidden in shadow, had passed his fingers over the hangman's throat and whispered just one word.

Weidenfeld.

Kuisl blinked as a shudder ran through his body. The impression was so vivid, he believed he'd even *smelled* the man. Kuisl had felt a hand on his sweaty shirt. Evidently his nightmares had followed him to this place as well, but for the moment they were mostly drowned out by hunger and thirst.

He was about to sit up and reach for the bread when he felt the strap across his chest. Surprised, he looked down to find leather bonds on his arms and legs tying him to the bed. He cursed softly. The bishop's guards had apparently locked him in this room and tied him to this bed. Panicked, he pulled at the straps, but they didn't give even the slightest. After a few minutes of struggle fat beads of sweat broke out on his forehead, and his hunger and thirst were starting to make him crazy. Should he call for help and beg the guards to loosen his bonds, just for a moment? He didn't want to give them the satisfaction. Perhaps they'd allow his daughter to come feed him again like a toothless old man on his deathbed. That made him shudder. He'd rather die of thirst than degrade himself like that.

So he kept tugging at the straps, thrashing back and forth until he felt the strap around his left foot begin to loosen. The hangman shifted his legs until, at last, he could slip first his right and then his left foot out of the bonds. Although he'd worked his way at least partially free, the straps around his chest and arms were as tight as if they'd been riveted to him. Kuisl threw himself so violently to the side that the bed tipped over with a crash, pinning him beneath it.

With bated breath he lay still on the ground and listened.

Had the guards heard him? All was quiet. Perhaps the bailiffs were asleep in another wing of the bishop's palace, assuming he was still too weak to break free.

After a few minutes Kuisl tried to get upright in spite of the bed strapped to his back. He struggled to get a look around the room. He needed something sharp to tear the straps, but the room was empty except for the bed and the trunk. He'd have to look elsewhere. Swaying and grunting, he got to his feet like an animated wardrobe; the bed on his back made him even broader across than he already was. With his right hand he grabbed the door handle and pressed down cautiously. Perhaps . . . ?

Creaking softly, the door swung outward.

Kuisl grinned. The bishop's bailiffs had indeed forgotten to lock him inside! Stooping, he staggered through the doorway and groped around in the darkness before him like a clumsy giant. He had to be careful not to stumble or he'd wake up the entire palace. Step by step he moved quietly through a vaulted room with a stone ceiling and high windows letting in moonlight. In this dim light Kuisl noticed large copper buckets atop brick ovens and sacks of wheat and hops, some of them open, scattered across the floor. But it was the aroma that told Kuisl definitively this was a brewery.

The fragrance of malt and hops made his thirst almost unbearable. He had to free himself at once! He could just dunk his head into one of the beer tubs and take a long draught. He could —

The hangman stopped short. In the moonlight it looked as though someone else had the same idea. Directly in front of Kuisl, in one of the large brewing kettles, he could just make out the figure of a man pitched head over heels into one of the vats, with only his legs sticking out — looking for all the world like an enormous stirring spoon. His brown cassock had slipped open, revealing two pale, massive thighs.

Kuisl could only stand there with his mouth open in a grimace. In a moment all thoughts of thirst and hunger had vanished. The man in the beer kettle had clearly drowned in the brew.

There are worse ways to die, the hangman thought regretfully.

A sound from behind caused him to wheel around. Only a few steps away Simon and Magdalena stood, fully dressed, though their faces were dirty and sweaty, as if moments before they'd been hard at work.

"Papa!" Magdalena scolded. "What's all this noise? You mustn't . . ."

Then her eyes happened upon the corpse in the beer vat. She froze. Simon, too, was at a loss for words.

"My God, that's Brother Hubertus!" the medicus shouted finally, raising his hand to his mouth in horror. After a moment of silence he looked suspiciously at Kuisl, still staggering around with the bed on his back. "Did you do anything to . . . ?"

"You fool!" Kuisl spit. "How could I have done anything like that with forty pounds of wood on my back!"

And for the first time the couple noticed the bed tied to the hangman's back. Despite the dead monk in the vat, Magdalena had to bite her lips to keep from laughing out loud.

"For heaven's sake, Father! When Simon told you to stay in bed he didn't mean for you to carry the bed around with you."

"Be still, silly woman, and help me cut off these straps," Kuisl said. "There's a dead man in front of you, so please pull yourself together."

Simon hurriedly cut through the leather bands with his stiletto. Careful not to make a sound, they lowered the bed to the floor before turning to deal with the corpse whose head was still submerged in the mash. With their combined strength they pulled the monk from the vat.

Brother Hubertus's eyes were frozen open in horror. Slimy green catkins stuck to the fringe of hair that ringed his tonsure, and his face was even more bloated now than it had been in life. Magdalena pulled the wet cassock, which reeked of stale beer, over his ankles while Simon mouthed a silent prayer. Kuisl nudged him, pointing to a purple bruise that ringed the brewmaster's neck.

"He was strangled," he concluded. "No easy task, especially considering what an ox of a man the clergyman was. A strong man did this, one who knew how exactly how to go about it." He peered down into the brown liquid sloshing around in the vat. "In fact, I'm pretty sure it must have been two men. One to hold him over the edge while the other strangled him."

"Good Lord!" Simon closed his eyes for a moment. "I'm sure it was on account of the powder. The good monk wanted to make some more inquiries, and he clearly went to the wrong person!"

"The baldheaded murderer!" Magdalena whispered. "I bet he bribed the guards to get in. We've got to get out of here as quickly as possible!"

Kuisl frowned. "Powder? Murderers? What the hell is going on here, for Christ's sake?"

"That's what we'd like to know." Simon gave the dead Franciscan monk at their feet a look of pity. Then he explained to the hangman in brief, halting words all that had happened the past few days.

Kuisl listened in silence and finally shook his head. "What a cesspool of iniquity we've gotten ourselves mired in! The story gets more colorful by the minute!" On his fingers he ticked off what he'd learned: "We have a secret alchemical workshop where you find a strange powder. My brother-in-law gets himself killed for producing it, and in addition he's supposedly a member of this secret freemen group." He shook his head incredulously. "And who are they anyway?"

"They're a secret affiliation of tradesmen opposing the patricians," Simon explained. "The raftmaster, Karl Gessner, is their leader, and your brother-in-law was his deputy. At first we thought the patricians wanted to make an example of him, as a warning to others. But that can't be the answer. There's more behind it than that . . ." He drew his finger absently through the brown beer suds. "Gessner told me yesterday that Andreas Hofmann was apparently seeking something like the philosopher's stone in his secret workshop. Whether that's true or not, I believe this powder goes right to the heart of the matter. That would explain why the culprit was so intent on covering up his motive in the bathhouse murders."

"Philosopher's stone? Bah!" Kuisl spat into the vat. "I always knew my brother-in-law was an idle dabbler. But that's complete nonsense! Alchemy is just a hobby for bored noblemen and the pampered sons of the patricians. And even if there's anything to it, it can't be motive enough for the murders — or the third inquisitor wouldn't have been so aggressive. That wasn't any decent kind of torture; it was revenge, pure and simple." He pointed his finger at Magdalena, who looked back at him with wide eyes. "The dirty bastard knew the name of your mother, and he knew about you. Philosopher's stone or not, someone's out for revenge. But I'll give him so much to chew on he'll choke!"

"For heaven's sake, not so loud!" Simon whispered. "There have to be guards out front, and if they hear us, we might as well just hop into the kettles and boil ourselves to save them the trouble!"

Kuisl bit his lip and kept quiet.

"What happened with my letter, by the way?" he asked finally, in a markedly softer voice. "The message I sent you through Teuber? I asked you to find out more about this Weidenfeld fellow. And — did you find anything?"

Magdalena shrugged. "I received a letter, but it wasn't from you. *Best wishes from Weidenfeld* is all it said. I imagine the third inquisitor must have intercepted the message and had a little fun at our expense."

"Damn it!" Kuisl kicked the brew kettle so hard that brown liquid splashed over the side. "If only I had something to smoke, I'm sure I'd remember where I know that name."

He searched frantically in his linen shirt and pants pockets

for a few buds of tobacco. Then he froze, pulling out a little roll
of paper tucked in his breast pocket. He apprehensively unrolled
the soiled scrap of paper and had to squint to read the words.

In the next moment he turned as white as a sheet.

"Father, what's wrong?" Magdalena asked anxiously.
"What's on the paper?"

Slowly, as if in a trance, Kuisl shook his head.

"It's nothing." He crumpled the paper and returned it to his
breast pocket. "Just a scrap of paper, nothing more."

His daughter gave him skeptical look. "Are you sure?"

"Yes, for God's sake!" he snapped. "Don't give me any back-
talk. I'm still your father."

Magdalena raised her hands in appeasement. "Of course. Everyone has his secrets. I only wonder—"

"Let's deal with that later," Simon interjected. "First we have
to dispose of the dead monk. If the guards find him, they're going
to blame us."

Kuisl nodded, though his expression had since turned stony.
He absent-mindedly stroked his breast pocket. "Very well," he
announced. "Let's get to it."

Together they lifted the fat monk's corpse, carried it back to
the beer kettle, and watched as his body sank, gurgling, into the
brown brew. But his head kept bobbing to the surface, dotted
with hops catkins. Only after Kuisl dumped a few bags of grain
on top of him did the monk disappear in the brew.

Satisfied, Kuisl used his trousers to dry his hands, which
were by now so bloodstained and dirty it looked as though he'd
just dragged a dead cow to the knacker. Simon shuddered. He
kept forgetting his future father-in-law was a master of killing.
As a hangman, Kuisl had probably seen more corpses than there
were apples on any given apple tree. And the vacant look in
Kuisl's eyes continued to trouble Simon. Just what was written
on that piece of paper he'd so hurriedly hidden away in his
pocket?

The medicus suddenly recalled why they were awake at this hour of the night in the first place.

"We have to get away from here as quickly as possible," he whispered. "At once, if we can. I suggest we leave the bishop's palace and find a place to hide in the ruins in the west of the city; they look as if they've been abandoned since the Great War. When things have calmed down, we'll try to get out of town."

"The bishop's guards will hardly see us off with a party," Kuisl mused. His face was still pale and his mind in some far-away place.

Simon grinned. "Well, I do have some good news, for a change. Magdalena and I spent the past day exploring the bishop's palace in search of escape routes. In the back of the brew house we came upon a walled-up door that evidently dates from Roman times." He pointed to the rear of the vault, where beer kegs were stacked almost to the ceiling. "The door directly borders the main road north of the bishop's palace. We removed a few of the stones and felt a draft come through. It looks as if this door just may lead out of the compound."

"Show me," Kuisl said.

Magdalena and Simon led him into a corner of the brew house behind a stack of barrels, where they saw the outline of a doorway barely wide enough for a man to pass through. Some stones had been removed, and through the tiny opening a faint stench of garbage and excrement wafted in. Never in his life would Simon have imagined he'd find such a stink so pleasant.

The smell of the city.

"Get your things together," Kuisl said. "Meanwhile, I'll remove these stones, one at a time so nobody will hear a thing."

"Will that be too much of a strain, Father?" Magdalena asked anxiously. "Simon thinks you should take care of yourself and—"

"When I need a nursemaid, I'll let you know," the hangman

groused. "As long as I'm able to break a man's bones, I can break down a little wall."

Magdalena grinned. Her father was clearly well on his way to recovery.

"I was just asking," she said. "We'll be right back. Don't be too hard on the stones, all right?"

Together she and Simon hurried through the vaulted room and slipped through a small passage into the brewmaster's kitchen. Outside, the moon shone brightly enough that Magdalena could see a guard leaning wearily on his pike. But the guard was thankfully too far from the kitchen window to recognize her. Smoked sausages and fragrant legs of pork hung from the ceiling on hooks, and baskets of fresh fruit and bread lined the windowsills alongside handwritten cookbooks and an old book on herbs.

"The fat brewmaster must have been a gourmand; he really seems to have known his way around a kitchen." Magdalena nodded approvingly as she plucked a few sausages from a hook. "I'm really sorry about what happened to him; I'm sure he was a really decent fellow."

Simon sighed. "He was. I regret having gotten him mired in this. I should never have — "

"We haven't got time for regrets right now," Magdalena interrupted in a whisper. "Save your prayers until we get to Saint Michael's Basilica in Altenstadt, or light a votive at church back in Schongau, if you prefer. Right now, though, this is a matter of life and death for us and for my father, and that's my first concern."

"You're right." Simon filled a wineskin with dark Malvasian wine from a little keg next to the hearth. "Right now what worries me most is your father. What in the world was on that piece of paper? When he read it, it was as if someone had whitewashed his whole face."

"Who can tell what's going on with my father?" Magdalena replied softly. "Sometimes I think not even Mother knows all his secrets. He's never once spoken of his experiences in the war, even though that's when the two met."

"Wait, your mother isn't from Schongau?" asked Simon, astonished. "I always thought—"

Magdalena shook her head. "She comes from around here. But whenever I've asked about my grandparents, or the time before I was born, she just falls silent."

"Do you think that damn Weidenfeld fellow dates back to that time, too?"

"Maybe, but that's just a hunch." Magdalena shouldered her bundle. "We'll probably never know for sure. You're right, you know. We've got to get out of this loathsome city as fast as we can. My mother even said that Regensburg is cursed. Let's forget about all these secrets and just get back home to Schongau."

Without another word, she hurried out into the brew house. Simon packed one more wedge of cheese in his bundle and followed. As he left, he took a last look into the kettle, but Brother Hubertus hadn't resurfaced; his body was still drifting somewhere down below in the cloudy brew.

Drowned in his drink, Simon thought. *A fitting grave for a brewmaster.*

When the medicus arrived back at the walled-up doorway, he stopped short. Magdalena, too, stood there looking around helplessly.

A good portion of the stones had been cleared away and stacked neatly along the wall, leaving a dark hole just large enough for a man to pass through.

There was no trace of Jakob Kuisl.

For several minutes neither of them budged. Then Magdalena started running among the barrels, calling out her father's name in a tense, frantic voice. But there was no response.

"Forget it!" Simon whispered. "He's gone; he's taken off—can't you see that?"

"Yes, but to where?" Magdalena asked in despair. "Why did he leave us behind?"

The medicus knit his brow. "It must have something to do with that paper in his pocket. After reading it, he was like a different person."

"That may very well be," Magdalena said, "but that's no cause for him to abandon us. What are we supposed to do now?"

"We'll just leave without him," Simon suggested. "It's possible he didn't want to put us in danger unnecessarily. For the guards we're small fry. *He*'s the one they're really after."

"But if that was the case, he would have told us." Magdalena stared vacantly into the darkness. "To just up and disappear like that is not his way."

"Be that as it may, we've still got to get out of here ourselves. It'll be morning soon, and the guards will be making their rounds." Simon began removing more stones from the entry. "Come on, help me!" When no answer came, he turned around angrily.

Magdalena just stood there, her arms folded and her lips clenched in defiance. "My father's in trouble, and all you're concerned with is saving your own hide!" she scolded. "You're nothing but a coward!"

"But Magdalena, that's not the least bit true!" Irritated, Simon put down a stone and straightened up. "Your father clearly didn't want our help. Believe me—he'll make out just fine by himself. And what we have to do now is get out of here as fast as we can. If you have something else in mind, please tell me."

"I do in fact have something in mind," she replied stubbornly. "We'll hide out at Silvio's place."

Simon's face fell. "At the house of the Venetian dwarf? Why there, for heaven's sake?"

"He likes me, and he has influence. We can hide there until the coast is clear. We'll be better off there than in some stinking barn or pigsty," she added smugly, "and from there we can keep up our search for my father."

"And who's to guarantee your beloved Silvio won't immediately turn us over to the city guards, huh?" Wiping the dust from his hands with his jacket, he narrowed his eyes. "Has the smart *mademoiselle* considered that possibility?"

"Silvio would never do that. He's Venetian. City affairs don't concern him. Anyway, he fancies me."

"Aha, so that's how the wind is blowing!" Simon was annoyed. "You're flattered by the attention."

"He's a gentleman. What's wrong with that?"

"Well, if that's how you feel, let your gentleman go out and buy you a new wardrobe." Exasperated now, Simon struggled to control his voice. "Should the opportunity arise, you two might take a nice coach ride to the Piazza San Marco in Venice, or maybe even to Paris. Just don't expect me to play the part of your footman!"

"Don't get yourself all worked up, you old goat. Remind me, way back when, who was it who fell all over that Benedikta woman? You bowed and scraped so foolishly you were an embarrassment to behold!"

Simon rolled his eyes. "That was almost two years ago, and I don't know how many times I've apologized for that—"

"Forget it," Magdalena interrupted gruffly. "Your brilliant rescue plan is dead in the water, or shall we say dead in the beer tub? Your brewmaster is dead, so let's give my Venetian a try. It's as simple as that."

"'*My* Venetian'?" said Simon mimicking her. "Do you think I don't notice that dwarf fawning over you? You women are all the same—give a woman a new dress and she can't tell up from down anymore."

Her palm met his face so hard the slap echoed through the domed vault.

"Do as you please, you wretch," Magdalena shouted. "Go sleep in a pigsty or boil yourself in beer suds, for all I care. I, for my part, am going to Silvio's. He at least has manners and can probably help my father somehow." She cast him an angry glance. "More than you, at any rate."

Without another word, she pushed her bundle through the hole in the wall, heaved herself through it, and, within moments, disappeared into the darkness.

The dark space behind the door smelled of mildew and damp wood. Under her breath Magdalena cursed herself for not bringing a torch, but she could hardly turn back now. How would that look to Simon? Just thinking of him made her blood boil. What a jealous, self-absorbed little toad! Why couldn't he see that her plan was better, plain and simple? At Silvio's house they'd be safe, at least for the time being, and they might even be able to keep an eye out for her father. Magdalena sensed he was in danger. Never in her life had she seen her father turn so pale and shaken as just a short while ago. He needed her help, even if he'd never admit it.

Sometimes Simon got so jealous he couldn't see, let alone think straight. Doubtless once he cooled down, he'd see the error of his ways and catch up with her. Perhaps she ought to wait here in the dark for him and scare the dickens out of him when he came after her. The bastard deserved that, at least!

She was so lost in thought she didn't notice the wooden wall until her head slammed into it. Her face contorted in pain, she placed her hand on her throbbing forehead. Blindly she reached out in front of her and discovered this wasn't a wall at all, but a huge fermenting vat as tall as a man. To the right and left of it stood other enormous wooden containers. Desperately she tried to push the vat aside, and just seconds later her hands broke through the rotted barrel staves. Tumbling forward, she tried to catch herself on a rusty barrel ring but fell instead into a dusty storage cellar located behind it. Ahead she could make out a slim ray of moonlight through a crack in the wall. Junk of all sorts lay scattered across the hard-packed dirt floor—broken wagon wheels, millstones, old crates and barrels, which had probably been moldering away down here for years. Ages ago someone must have walled up the entrance to the bishop's palace, and as the years progressed, the storage room behind it had been forgotten.

Magdalena looked around, blinking. By now her eyes had grown somewhat accustomed to the dark. Carefully, silently, she climbed over broken boards and bricks until she stood before a wooden shed. Some of the siding appeared to have been removed very recently, revealing a well-worn staircase that led up to a wide road.

Magdalena recognized three covered arches that spanned the street ahead: she'd surfaced in a part of town just north of the bishop's palace. These "flying bridges" arched over the street and ended at the bishop's warehouses along the river. Not a single guard was to be seen, even though Magdalena could only imagine how eagerly the city bailiffs were waiting and watching, ready to pounce the moment any one of their three faces peeked out of the bishop's palace. Apparently, though, the guards had reckoned only with an escape through the main entrance or the cathedral.

Magdalena looked behind her into the darkness. Where was Simon? She was convinced he'd follow her, fuming and fussing, but at least halfway cooled down, having realized the sense of her plan. The medicus, who knew all about her occasional temper tantrums, was never angry with her for long, nor she with him. Should she turn back to look for him? Again she scanned the still-deserted lane. How long had her father been gone? Ten minutes? Fifteen? Perhaps he was hiding just a few yards away, in some yard. Magdalena could feel her breath quicken. The longer she waited here, the farther away her father would be.

Simon or her father?

She looked back again, but there was no sign of the medicus, and time was running out. She made up her mind at last: Simon knew where she planned to go, and he could just as well find her at the house of the Venetian ambassador. Her father, on the other hand, she now risked losing forever.

Cursing softly, Magdalena squeezed through the crack in the boards, tiptoed to the street, and disappeared into the night.

Without a single thought as to whether someone might hear him, the medicus hurled a sack of grain hard against the wall. The sack split open on impact and the grain burst out, falling to the ground like a sudden heavy rain shower.

Simon raged. What was that impertinent wench thinking, talking down to him like that? He knew his plan to flee the city with the help of the bishop's brewmaster had failed. But was that his fault? Was he somehow responsible for the fact that Brother Hubertus had wound up bobbing up and down like an overgrown apple in a vat of beer? The very thought of asking the arrogant Venetian for help was absurd! Well, maybe not completely absurd . . . Silvio probably had influence and could offer them a place to stay, but for Simon it was out of the question. How did Magdalena imagine it would play out? Would Simon stand calmly by as this dwarf made advances to her? Even if Silvio did manage to smuggle them both out of the city, did she think Simon would play the willing cuckold?

As he got ready to toss the next sack of grain against the wall, Simon had to acknowledge he was in fact jealous.

Magdalena was probably right; Silvio was their last hope. With a sigh he lowered the sack to the ground and sat on a pile of stones next to the secret doorway. From the room behind he heard a splintering sound and assumed Magdalena had knocked something over. He considered calling to her but decided against it. He'd give the girl a chance to figure things out for herself, for once. If she needed help, she could always come back.

Simon picked up a handful of grain from the ground and sifted it through his fingers. The last half-hour had rattled him. Just when all three of them had managed to reunite after such a long struggle and to plan their escape at last, they were all running off on their own again. It was enough to drive a man out of his skin! The kernels passed through his fingers, one by one, slowly at first, then faster and faster.

Like sand through an hourglass, he thought, *time goes by. If I don't hurry, I may never catch up with Magdalena again.*

But something held him back, a sudden premonition he couldn't quite place. He contemplated the rye in his palm: yellow and firm, the little pearls popped open if you squeezed them long enough between your fingers, revealing a damp white flour inside.

But some of the grains were different—they had a bluish sheen—and when Simon rubbed them, they gave off a musty, sickly sweet odor.

He knew this odor.

The medicus held his breath. This was the odor he first detected in the bathhouse storage room and, later, in the underground alchemist's workshop, where he and Magdalena had come upon the burned powder. Several hundred pounds of the stuff must have been stored down there.

The powder! My God . . . !

What had Brother Hubertus said shortly before his death?

This secret could drive us all out of our minds . . .

Simon slapped his forehead. For a moment he forgot the dead monk in the brewing vat; he forgot Kuisl; in fact, he even forgot Magdalena. Was it possible? Could *this* be the philosopher's stone? He had to be sure, but how? Suddenly he recalled the little herbarium on the kitchen windowsill. His heart pounding, Simon ran through the brew house, opened the kitchen door, and reached for the tattered book. He lit a tallow candle with trembling hands and sat down at the table. In the flickering light he flipped through the pages until he came to one illustration in particular. Below it a few lines were written in cautionary red ink.

The medicus almost burst into hysterical laughter, but fear seized him first. The idea was so monstrous, so insane, that at first he couldn't believe it, but bit by bit the scattered tiny tiles of the mosaic began coming together; an image was beginning to form. He tore the page out of the herbarium and stuck it in his jacket pocket.

Finally Simon thought he knew what this damned powder was and where he might find more.

Much more.

Magdalena took the scarf from her shoulders and wrapped it around her head. She walked stooped over so that from a distance she'd look to passersby like a harmless old woman. She knew full well this disguise wouldn't help much. After all, it was the middle of the night, when even old women were forbidden to be out in the street. All the same, she felt safer this way.

She scurried westward under the arched bridges but decided to avoid the main entrance of the bishop's palace, where guards were likely still on the lookout for her. She took a detour instead, approaching the cathedral square from the opposite side.

At last she came upon the Heuport House. The building, grim and menacing, rose up before her with nothing of the charm and nobility it emanated in the light of day. In the darkness it looked more like an impregnable fortress.

Magdalena rattled the handle of the towering double door, if only to make sure it was locked, as she expected. Hesitantly she reached for a bronze knocker molded in the shape of a lion's head and pounded with all her might. Once—twice—three times, the knocks echoed in her ears like a blacksmith's hammer. If she kept on, she'd wake all of Regensburg.

A window on the second floor finally opened on a maid's pinched face. She wore a white nightcap and squinted wearily down at Magdalena. This was the same maid who'd looked at her so crossly on her last visit. When she recognized the hangman's daughter on the street below, the maid's eyes flashed.

"Go away!" she sneered. "There's nothing for you here, my dear."

She thinks I'm a whore, Magdalena thought in despair. This cut her to the quick. *Do I really look like a whore?*

"I must speak with the ambassador," she replied, trying not to sound overbearing. If the maid didn't let her in or alerted the guards, all would be lost. "It's an emergency; please believe me!"

The servant girl eyed her skeptically. To Magdalena the woman's gaze was nearly palpable; she could almost feel the woman's eyes looking her up and down. "The master isn't home," she replied finally, but less condescendingly this time. "He's over at the Whale playing cards, as usual. Don't waste your time—he's likely found someone else to sit in his lap." She spoke the last sentence with a certain smugness.

Magdalena sighed. She should have figured as much. Naturally Silvio was camped out at his favorite tavern.

"Thanks," she said, turning to leave. Suddenly she turned back around. "Uh, if I don't run into Silvio, could you please—"

The shutters banged closed.

"Silly old goose," the hangman's daughter grumbled. "No doubt your master's thrown you out of his bed more than once, you flat-chested, bitter old broomstick!"

But the cursing didn't help. The window remained closed, and with a sigh, Magdalena set out for the Whale.

The tavern lay east of the little bridges, not far from the bishop's palace, so again she decided on a detour through one of the unguarded back alleys. At last the warm, inviting lights of the tavern appeared in front of her. With candlelight emanating into the street through its bull's-eye windows, the Whale was like a guiding light in the dark—the only place in Regensburg with any life at this hour. Magdalena surmised the innkeeper had to pay the city a pretty penny for that privilege—an investment that paid for itself, if the loud singing and laughter inside were any indication. The door swung open and three raftsmen lurched out, evidently having spent their last hellers on drink. Babbling noisily, they staggered off in the direction of the raft landing.

Magdalena bit her lip. Did she dare set foot in the lion's den? There probably wasn't another woman in the place, with the exception of the innkeeper. Were she to go prancing in, she'd surely attract everyone's attention, not least that of the guards, who might in fact already be waiting for her inside. All the same, it was a risk she had to take.

She tightened the black scarf around her head once more, took a deep breath, and opened the door. A warm wave of all kinds of odors assailed her: sweat, brandy, tobacco, smoke, and the stale residue of some kind of stew. Every last seat in the sooty low-ceilinged taproom was occupied. Raftsmen, workers, and young bull-necked journeymen sat, foaming mugs before them, singing, playing cards, and throwing dice. In back, in his usual stove-side seat, the Venetian ambassador was busily rolling dice with three rather coarse men. Compared to his simply clad companions in their linen shirts and leather vests, the Venetian was nothing less than a colorful bird of paradise. He wore a red shirt decorated with white ribbons and a very high collar; wide, flared trousers; and, on his head, a dashing musketeer's hat complete with a plume of feathers. Silvio was either winning at the moment or so deeply engaged in his game he didn't seem to see the young woman in the doorway.

The other men, however, hadn't failed to notice Magdalena. Some of the workers stared at her lustfully, while others whistled or ran their tongues over the dark stumps of their teeth.

"Hey, sweetheart!" a potbellied, curly-haired raftsman bellowed. "Not satisfied with the day's earnings? Then come have a seat here with me and give my beard a stroke or two."

"Let her have a stroke of something else, Hans!" his companion shouted, wiping his fat lips with his shirtsleeve. "Come over here, girl. Take that ugly scarf off and show us what you've got!"

"Off with the scarf, off with the scarf!" some men at a neighboring table began to shout. "We want a better look at the lady, ha-ha!"

A loud crash and the sound of breaking glass interrupted the jeers. The crowd grew silent and turned toward Silvio, who stood now on the stove-side bench and looked almost meditatively at the broken bottle in his hand. He raised the bottleneck to the dim overhead light so the rough, razor-sharp edges sparkled menacingly.

"*Con calma, signori!*" he said softly. "The gentlemen will not lay hands on a *signorina*. Especially not when *la bella signorina* in question stands under my personal protection." He smiled at Magdalena and pointed to the chair next to him. "I implore you, have a seat and make yourself—*come si dice*—at home."

"Hey, dwarf!" growled a fat raftsman struggling to his feet. "Who the hell do you think you are . . . ?" Two other men restrained him, whispering something in his ear. The fat man turned white and sat back down quietly. Evidently his comrades had explained just who the hell indeed the ambassador was.

"*Grazie* for understanding, everyone." Silvio bowed slightly. "And now, innkeeper, a barrel of brandy for the entire house! To the *signorina*'s health!"

Guarded cheers came from the tables, and the threatening mood dissipated quickly like an unpleasant odor. The brandy made the rounds, and over and over the men toasted Magdalena, whom they had to thank for this welcome gift. Silvio's three roughneck companions carried on their card game without him, drinking freely of the brandy, apparently having quickly lost interest in the beautiful new arrival.

"Nice to see you again," Silvio whispered, still smiling at the crowd, very much like a little king graciously accepting the homage of his subjects. "I thought you might forever be angry with me on account of that kiss. I shouldn't have done that, but where I come from—"

"Forget it," Magdalena interrupted gruffly. "To be brief, Simon and I need your help. May we stay a while at your house?"

The Venetian grinned from ear to ear. "I would be delighted! I never understood anyway why a *bella donna* such as yourself elected to sleep in the gutter with beggars and thieves. Is your proud little companion in agreement with this, then?"

Magdalena didn't hesitate. "He has no choice."

Silvio smiled. "*Ho capito.* You are wearing the pants, it seems—that's the expression, isn't it?" Then his face turned serious. "But I can see in your face that something's the matter. Tell me, what's happened?"

"The baldheaded murderer," she whispered. "He's on our heels, all on account of a powder!"

"Powder?" Silvio squinted at her, perplexed.

"We found some powder in the bathhouse owner's secret alchemist's workshop," she whispered. "Half of Regensburg is apparently trying to get their hands on it. And the baldheaded man wants to silence us because he thinks we know too much! We need a place to hide—you're our only hope!"

"And your father?"

"He's already . . ." Magdalena stopped short. A premonition told her they were being watched. She raised her head to look around. Most of the men seemed to have forgotten Magdalena and were back to playing cards and drinking. In a far corner of the room, however, a cloaked figure stood out from the rest of the men.

The man, who had pulled his cowl down over his face, sat sipping from a little tin cup. As he wiped his thick lips with his sleeve, his cloak slipped back a bit to reveal a bald head. On the back of his head he wore a white bandage.

Magdalena flinched. It was the same man she'd hit over the head with the statue of Saint Sebastian in the cathedral!

"Look!" she whispered to Silvio. Throwing caution to the wind, she pointed at the stranger. "I'll be damned; the bastard's followed me!"

Now the Venetian recognized the man as well. Their eyes met; the stranger rose and slowly moved toward their table. His movements reminded Magdalena of a deadly poisonous snake.

"Let's get out of here!" Silvio whispered, standing up abruptly from the table. He pulled Magdalena along, and together they made their way through the boisterous crowd. The stranger followed, jostling men to his right and left to catch up with them. Several drunk patrons shoved him in return, and an uproar broke out. For a moment the stranger fell to the ground, out of view, but he appeared again like a ship's sail on a rough and stormy sea.

By now Magdalena and Silvio had reached the exit. Turning around for one last look, the hangman's daughter saw the bald stranger drawing his rapier. With loud shouts the men scattered, opening a path through which the man came running toward them.

"Quick, let's go!" Silvio shouted, pulling her out into the alley. "We have no time to lose!"

The stranger followed just a few steps behind and seemed to be calling something out to them, but Magdalena couldn't hear anything over all the noise.

Breathlessly she staggered into the street.

Despite the almost impenetrable darkness, Silvio found his

way through the city as if he were a native. He led Magdalena into a narrow side street, which they ran down together while, behind them, they could hear the stranger's pounding footfalls on the hard-packed ground. At some point Magdalena thought she heard at least two more sets of feet, and it sounded as if they were gaining on them. Had their pursuer called for reinforcements? In their last two encounters with this man she and Silvio had escaped by the skin of their teeth. If he had help this time, they didn't stand a chance.

But there was no time for reflection. Silvio turned into ever-narrower streets until, at last, the odor of fish and sewage told Magdalena they were approaching the boat landing along the Danube. Between buildings she spotted the jetty, stacked high with crates and barrels. Behind these, small boats bobbed along the shore, and the dark outline of a wooden crane rose up from the quay wall. Silvio ran in great strides toward the jetty.

Magdalena turned to find that the stranger was now only a few paces back. She cursed softly. Why had Silvio brought them to this godforsaken place? They would have been safer if only they'd stayed at the Whale! The stranger wouldn't have dared attack them in front of all the patrons, but here they were alone and helpless. Again she heard the sounds of several more pairs of feet behind them; apparently they would have to fend off a number of pursuers.

Silvio jumped into an empty rowboat tied to the jetty and beckoned to her to follow. As she stepped in, she felt the nearly ten-foot-long boat begin to pitch. How did the Venetian intend to use an unsteady boat like this to his advantage?

With a great leap the stranger landed in the boat with them. His voice was high and shrill, almost childlike. "In the name of—" he began, but Silvio stopped him with a shout. The Venetian charged his pursuer, drew his rapier, and attacked. His opponent skillfully parried the blow, and they crossed swords again and again, moving from one side of the boat to the other. Time and time again, the men jumped over coils of rope and slippery wooden benches as the boat pitched and tossed, demanding a great deal of skill of the combatants.

Magdalena meanwhile cowered in the back of the boat to watch the men slash away at each other, sweat pouring down their foreheads. Silvio was an excellent swordsman, but the bald-headed stranger was so skilled with his rapier one might believe he was born with it in his hand. Again and again he found gaps in the Venetian's defenses, and each time Silvio was only able to parry the blow frantically at the very last moment.

Silvio was now backed into the bow of the tiny vessel, his leather boots slipping on the wavering rail. The stranger thrust once more at Silvio, almost sending him overboard, but with feline agility Silvio sprang upward to grab a rope dangling from the crane directly above him and swung over the stranger's head. When he landed in the middle of the boat, the vessel rocked so violently Magdalena feared it might capsize.

The stranger struggled to keep his balance as he swayed from left to right as if intoxicated. When he finally managed to stabilize himself again, he swung his blade in a perfect semicircle, catching Silvio's shirt with the tip of his rapier. With a nasty ripping sound, the shirt tore open and blood came seeping out. The little ambassador staggered, stumbling on a coil of rope and collapsing against the railing with a moan.

Smiling victoriously, the stranger bent over him, holding his rapier to his opponent's neck, where a small rivulet of blood was forming. Silvio's expensive hat had slipped from his head, and he stared up wide-eyed at his opponent, expecting the final blow at any moment.

"It's over, Silvio Contarini," the bald man gasped in a high-pitched voice. "In the name of the kaiser—"

He fell silent, his mouth forming a silent *O* as blood poured from his lips. For one last moment he stood there, swaying back and forth, before his eyes turned up to the breaking dawn. Then, with a loud splash, he fell over the railing into the water, where his body bobbed gently in the current.

"What happened, Silvio? Is he dead?"

As Magdalena leaped up with relief, she saw a crossbow bolt protruding from between the stranger's shoulder blades.

"Food for the fish," the Venetian panted. His gaze rested a moment on his opponent's corpse drifting away face-down; then he turned toward the shore.

"It was high time, wasn't it?" he shouted into the slowly brightening gray of morning. "*Maledetti!* Why didn't you shoot sooner?"

"Couldn't have done it, master!" a deep voice replied from the other side of the quay. "I might have hit you, with all the running back and forth."

In the very next moment three figures appeared out of the darkness, one holding a heavy crossbow. Magdalena caught her breath. They were the three roughnecks who'd been playing cards with Silvio at the Whale. Now she understood why she'd heard all those footsteps behind them as they fled. Evidently these three fellows served the ambassador and had followed their master only to save his life at the very last moment.

But why had they all fled the safety of the Whale in the first place? And why did the stranger speak of the kaiser just before he was killed?

Silvio approached Magdalena, smiling. He gently brushed a lock of hair from her face.

"*Mea culpa,*" he whispered. "I never should have put you in such danger. You're too valuable. *Madonna,* what a waste that would have been!" His eyes glistened sadly as he ran his fingers through her thick black hair. "But you're not only beautiful, you're also clever. Too clever. And we need someone for our experiment anyway."

"Ex—experiment?" she stammered. Then her voice failed her.

Silvio just nodded. "I'm really anxious to see how it will turn out this time, Magdalena. After all our failures, it's high time we made a success of it."

A blade flashed, and Silvio held up a lock of her hair. "Allow me this souvenir." He bowed gallantly.

Meanwhile the three men had boarded the unsteady boat. To the east the sun was just cresting the horizon, a glowing red ball.

"What are we going to do with her?" the man with the cross-bow growled. "Throw her overboard?"

Silvio sighed. "*Grande stupido!* You'll have to bind and gag her. She's unruly, and we don't want our experiment to end up . . . um . . ." He frowned, searching for just the right word. "Dead in the water? Isn't that what you say?"

Magdalena was speechless. Not until the three grinning, bull-necked monsters began to approach her with anchor ropes in hand did she pull herself together.

"What — what's this all about?" she whispered.

Silvio shrugged. "You'll get an explanation, just not here and not now. I know a nice quiet place where we'll have all the time in the world to chat. So just keep still a little longer . . ."

"Take all the time you like, you dirty foreigner, but it will be without me."

Like a slippery fish, Magdalena disappeared over the railing into the filthy, putrid green Danube. Dark waves passed over her as she swam away, but when she'd nearly escaped, powerful hands reached out and dragged her back on board. She struggled and kicked, but the men were too strong. In no time she found herself on the bottom of the boat, tied up like a bale of cloth, a moldy piece of linen stuffed in her mouth. She struggled against her bonds, moaning.

"If you promise not to scream, I can remove the gag," Silvio offered sympathetically. "Believe me, it would be better for your complexion."

When Magdalena nodded, one of the men took the cloth from her mouth. She spat out stinking river water and saliva.

"Who . . . ?" she finally whispered. But she had no strength to finish.

"Who was he?" The little Venetian stared downstream, where the stranger's body was now little more than a distant speck.

"Heinrich von Bütten." Silvio nodded respectfully. "The kaiser's best agent, a superb swordsman. He was the only one who could have helped you." A wan smile spread across his face. "And you beat him half to death in the cathedral. How ironic!"

He looked out over the Danube, whose water reflected the blood-red light of the rising sun. "It's high time for our experiment," he said, addressing his servants. "Let's push off, shall we?"

Slowly the boat started to move.

13

THE SILHOUETTE OF JAKOB'S GATE ROSE UP BEfore Jakob Kuisl. Dawn was already brushing the top of the tower while night still reigned down below.

It had taken the hangman almost two hours to get here from the bishop's palace; over and over he'd come across groups of guards and had to take cover. He'd walked in circles through narrow back alleys and wound up several times in the dead end of a courtyard. At one point two guards marched past just inches from where he cowered in an entryway; later he had to dive behind a pile of manure when, out of nowhere, guards appeared in front of him. Now he stood before the same city gate through which, an eternity ago, he'd entered and by which he now had every intention of leaving. Teuber had told him Jakob's Gate was what most farmers used when they entered the city with their wagons, and now Kuisl hoped to stow away in one of them, hidden among crates, bales, or barrels.

From behind a fountain Kuisl watched the early-morning changing of the guard. The soldiers saluted one another, but their movements seemed sluggish, and some of them stretched and yawned. Kuisl grinned and cracked his knuckles. At least he wasn't the only one who'd had a long night.

A huge bolt the size of a wooden beam was pushed aside, the towering gate creaked open, and the first farmer came lumbering into the city in his cart. He was followed by ragged day laborers and peddlers with packs of merchandise slung over their backs, men who'd evidently waited the entire night outside the city walls. Cocks crowed and church bells rang as Regensburg came to life.

After closely observing the gate's activity for some time, Kuisl decided to scrap his original plan. It was simply too dangerous to smuggle himself out of the city this way. However tired the bailiffs appeared, they were still keeping a close watch on everything, and everyone intending to leave the city met with careful inspection first. Again and again guards stuck their pikes into sacks of flour or broke open barrels of wine, seemingly indifferent to the complaints of the merchants and farmers.

"Shut your damned mouth," one guard shouted when a clothier complained too loudly about having to untie every single bale. "Do you think I'm doing this for fun? We're looking for that monster from Schongau, jackass! Be happy we're taking care that the werewolf doesn't sneak up on you from behind and cut your throat as you go about your merry way."

"Bah!" the merchant snapped, peevishly packing up his cloth again. "This monster is leading you on a merry chase! You let him escape, and now it's we who have to pay. If you weren't always drinking when you were supposed to be at work —"

"Watch what you say!"

As the clothier moved along, Kuisl tried frantically to think of another way to get out of town. He gazed northwest over the city wall, where smoke was rising from the chimneys of several houses. On his arrival in Regensburg the hangman had noticed that the damage from the Great War in that part of town hadn't all been repaired. The fortifications outside the city were in dreadful shape. Gaps and cracks yawned in the stone, and grass grew thick and wild over the ruins, an indication that the city didn't have the money to rebuild at present. Perhaps there was even a gap somewhere in the city wall itself . . .

Just as Kuisl was preparing to leave, he heard the sound of crunching gravel behind him. Darting aside, he lost his balance and fell painfully onto his shoulder. Once he'd picked himself up again, he saw a small stooped figure in front of him, holding his hands up as if in surrender. The man wore ragged trousers and a shirt so soiled its original color was now impossible to discern. He was barefoot and as gaunt as a mangy dog, and over his long, stringy hair he wore a straw hat held together by a single leather band.

"For the love of the Virgin Mary, please don't hurt me!" the little man pleaded, squeaking like a ferret. "I mean you no harm. Teuber sent me!"

"Teuber? How in the world . . . ?" Only now did Kuisl notice that the tattered creature in front of him reeked like a manure pit. And at once it became clear to the hangman what color the man's shirt actually was: the man must have literally bathed in manure.

"And how would Teuber know where to find me, huh?" Kuisl growled, raising his hand menacingly. "Tell me the truth or else . . ."

The little ferret cringed. "We've been watching you since you left the bishop's palace. By order of the hangman. He said we're to bring you to him."

"But I'm . . ." Kuisl began.

The ferret winked his cagey little eyes. "You almost got away from us. Thank God one of us saw you down by the bridges. An interesting passageway, that one. We—"

"Make it brief," the hangman interrupted. "Just tell me who you are."

For the first time the little man grinned. He was almost toothless; only a single rotted black stump was visible behind his chapped upper lip. "Me? You mean *we*," he said, with a shallow bow. "We are the gold diggers, if you please."

Kuisl stood still for a moment, his mouth hanging open. "The gold diggers . . . ?"

The ferret turned away. "Come along; you'll see."

Kuisl hesitated before following the stooped little creature. The hangman thought it highly unlikely this was a trap. No one knew about his connection with the Regensburg executioner, and a simple shout or wave would have sufficed to summon the guards. Why would this stinking ferret take the trouble to lie to him?

Kuisl's companion scurried northward along the city wall, looking cautiously in every direction as they progressed. Few people were about at this early hour of the morning, but every single one of them gave this dirty little man a wide berth.

After a while Kuisl noted that the houses they passed looked poorer and poorer. Most, in fact, were no more than makeshift cottages nestled close to the city wall. Garbage piled up in the streets, and sewage flowed in broad streams through the ditches dug into the street for precisely that purpose. From time to time Kuisl and his strange companion had to wade ankle-deep through the mud and manure where skinny, ragged children were using pebbles for a game of marbles. A cart loaded with animal carcasses and manure, driven by another dark figure, passed by. The ferret turned to Kuisl and winked.

"This has never been a good part of town, down here by the city wall, but ever since the war folk like us have had it all to ourselves." He giggled and pointed at his nose "We'll be there in a second. Just have to follow the scent, ha!"

At long last they reached the far end of the city. Here the western and northern city walls met in a sharp angle. Kuisl was relieved to notice a breach in the wall not far away, which had been filled in with something recognizable only on closer examination—something that caused Kuisl involuntarily to hold his breath.

A mountain of putrid wet garbage at least fifteen feet high.

Recoiling, Kuisl held his hand over his mouth and nose. He could make out the decaying carcasses of chickens, cats, and dogs scattered among the garbage—there was even an entire pig here with fat white maggots crawling out of its empty eye sockets.

On the top of the mountain of garbage stood Philipp Teuber, arms akimbo, grinning.

"So we meet again, Kuisl," his voice boomed. "No doubt you've never in your life seen so much trash." The Regensburg executioner carefully climbed down the slippery slope, his boots sinking in almost to his knees. "It's not like this in your little Bavarian village, is it?"

"Something to be proud of, you old knacker!" Kuisl turned away, disgusted, but with a thin smile on his lips. His former torturer had become a true friend. "I should have known you'd never leave me in peace."

Kuisl looked around cautiously to make sure no one had followed him. Out of the corner of his eye he spied a few men with soiled scarves over their mouths standing not far from him and shoveling excrement from a cart. The ferret was among them. Alert gazes seemed to be watching him with interest.

"You can trust them," said Teuber. "If any of them betrays you, I'll break every bone in his body and toss his corpse onto the pile like a dead animal to rot alongside the others." He smiled. "And besides, you're one of us, a hangman without honor, just like the whores, beggars, street performers, and knackers. We all ought to stick together."

Kuisl pointed at the slimy mountain, from which pieces kept breaking off and sliding to the ground. "What are you going to do with all that stuff? Bury it?"

Teuber shook his head and pointed behind him. "From here the rubbish goes right into the Danube, a few cartloads of it every day. The city pays us well for our work."

"Us?"

The Regensburg executioner spat noisily. "All I do is bring it here. The real work is done by the knackers and the gold diggers. They empty the sewers and bring the mess here."

Kuisl looked down at his feet, where iridescent yellow sewage ran over his leather boots.

The gold diggers . . .

So that's what the ferret meant!

"Pure gold," Philipp Teuber added, pointing at the pile of garbage fermenting in the rising sun. "I think it was a Roman kaiser who once said that gold doesn't stink. Believe me — without my men the city would choke on its own filth."

"How did you find me?" Kuisl asked abruptly.

"After you fled Fat Thea's place, city hall really gave me hell," Teuber said. "I think the noblemen know it was me who helped you break out of the jail, but they can't prove it." He tapped Kuisl on his bandaged left shoulder. "It's all better, isn't it? I told you, my remedy —"

"Be quiet you wise-ass," Kuisl interrupted. "Finish your story."

Teuber caught one of the many bluebottle flies that buzzed around the trash heap and crushed it between his fingers. "The whole city knows you were hiding out in the bishop's palace," he finally said. "It was clear that you'd have to get out at some point, so I asked my gold diggers to keep an eye out. They see more than any soldier does; plus they manage to keep out of sight themselves." He wiped the sweat and dirt from his forehead. "But that won't do you any more good than it's done already. You've got to get out of here, and fast."

"There's one thing I have to do first," Kuisl replied.

"I know what you have in mind, and that's why I brought you here." Teuber looked Kuisl in the eye before he continued; his words were measured. "I now know who the third inquisitor is. Fat Thea told me."

Kuisl's gaze wandered aimlessly over the city wall as if he sensed something lurking behind it.

"Since last night I believe I know, too. If it's who I think it is. But it's not possible . . ." He hesitated. "He sent me a letter—a letter from a dead man."

"Weidenfeld?" Teuber asked incredulously. "But . . ."

"Weidenfeld, ha!" Kuisl took out the crumpled note he had discovered in his breast pocket just two hours before. "The bastard was inside the bishop's palace! At first I thought I was dreaming—until I found this letter." Gingerly he held up the paper as if it were poison. "He must have brought it to me while I was sleeping. He probably bribed the guards and managed to slip in unnoticed. Or he's a ghost." His face darkened. "This man is dead. I killed him with my own hands. It's impossible he's alive."

"Ghost or no ghost," Teuber retorted. "If vengeance is what he's after, why didn't he simply slit your throat while he was inside the bishop's palace?"

"He wants something more. He wants to torment me as long as he can. Look." Kuisl handed the paper to Teuber. Squinting, the Regensburg executioner read the few lines, whistling softly between his teeth.

"Is it true what it says here?"

Kuisl's lips became as narrow as the edge of a knife. "I—I don't know," he said finally. "To find out I'll have to pull out each and every one of the bastard's fingernails, one by one. And if he's indeed a ghost, I'll whip him straight back to hell."

Teuber frowned. "But where are you planning to look for him? You have no idea where this damned Weidenfeld could be.

Besides, I still don't understand what this name is supposed to mean. That's not the third inquisitor's name. He goes by — "

"You idiot! You dumb ass!" Kuisl exploded. "You still don't get it? Weidenfeld is not the name of a *man;* it's the name of a *place!*"

Silence fell between them; only the shoveling of the gold diggers behind them was audible.

"A . . . place?" Teuber shook his head in disbelief. "But . . . ?"

"Look here." Kuisl pointed to the first line on the tattered sheet. "'Greetings from Weidenfeld,' it says, just as in the first letter he sent to Magdalena. It's a greeting from a *place!* The names of all the battlefields I ever fought in were scratched on the walls in that cell: Magdeburg, Breitenfeld, Rain on the Lech, Nördlingen . . . and Weidenfeld. He's the one who inscribed them down there to torment me. He even gave the *dates,* damn it!" Kuisl closed his eyes as if he were trying to remember something. "P.F.K. Weidenfeld, anno domini 1637. How could I ever forget that day! It's the day he died."

"So Weidenfeld is a battlefield?" the Regensburg executioner asked.

Kuisl gazed absently into space. "Not a battlefield, but a bad place, a wicked place. I tried to banish it from my mind forever, but it has been haunting me for years; I buried it but couldn't banish it. When I opened the letter last night, it all came rushing back."

Teuber's eyes widened. "By all the saints, I think I'm beginning to understand. The second line of the letter — "

"I must go," Kuisl interrupted gruffly. "At once. He'll be waiting there for me."

He began to climb over the muck toward the hole in the city wall but slipped suddenly and landed again on his injured shoulder.

"Damn!"

"Wait!" Teuber ran after him. "You're injured, you have no weapon, and you don't even know your way to Weidenfeld from here. If you——"

"Let me go! You don't understand!" Kuisl drew himself up and continued to march to the top of the trash heap. Behind the ruins of the wall the Danube sparkled like a green ribbon in the sunlight, and soon the Schongau hangman disappeared through the ivy-covered breach in the city wall.

"I don't *understand*? You damned thick-headed fool! Who do you think you are? My priest?" Teuber picked up a handful of rocks, then debris, and flung them through the hole in the wall. "You shameless good-for-nothing! Just how do you think you're going to fight this devil all by yourself? He'll tear you to pieces before you can utter an Ave Maria. Don't you see you're playing right into his hands?"

But no answer came from the other side. Teuber sighed, then hesitated a moment before ascending the pile of garbage.

"You'd better not believe I've risked the life of my entire family just to watch you die now, you bastard! Just hold on; I'm coming, too!"

Moments later he disappeared from sight.

The gold diggers shook their heads, picked up their shovels, and got back to the work of ridding the city of trash. Today was shaping up to be sultry and foul.

Simon stood in the shadow of a huge salt warehouse next to the boat landing, waiting nervously for the Stone Bridge to open. His heart was pounding as he watched the bridge guards slowly open the gate.

Just like Jakob Kuisl and his daughter after him, Simon had made his way through the hidden corridor into the storage room and out into the city from there. He had hoped he might find Magdalena somewhere in front of the bishop's palace, but she was long gone. Only a short while ago this might have infuriated him, but now he was relieved. He knew where he could find her — at the home of that smug Venetian dwarf. There, at least, she'd be safe. And, considering what he now had in mind, it was best he acted alone.

Simon took the quickest way he knew through the city to the place he figured he could pick up the trail of the mysterious pow- der. The streets were still completely dark and deserted at this hour. Now, as he stood at the gateway to the Stone Bridge, wait- ing what seemed an eternity for it to open, his patience was put to the test.

While Simon drummed his fingers against the stone wall, he studied irritably the guards who calmly slid open one bolt after another. Why couldn't these bastards hurry up? The fate of the city probably stood in the balance, and these half-drunk provin- cial constables couldn't get their asses moving! Now Simon no- ticed he'd been chewing his fingernails for some time.

Ultimately the medicus had to admit he was happy Magda- lena had gone to stay with Silvio. The situation was just too dan- gerous, and no one could predict who or what really awaited him where he was headed. Simon could only hope it wasn't too late. Still, he couldn't be the only one who'd come to this conclusion, could he? The ramifications of this powder's existence were so great, so monstrous, so obviously horrible, that he couldn't pos- sibly be the only one to whom it had occurred by now. Simon breathed a sigh of relief. Evidently the conspirators hadn't yet set their plan into motion. Of course, he first had to make sure his assumption was correct. If he was right, he'd go straight to the powers that be and . . .

Simon was painfully aware that city treasurer Paulus Mäm- minger was one of the most powerful men in Regensburg. Whom could Simon trust, then? It still wasn't clear what Mämminger's role was in this game, to say nothing of Nathan or the baldheaded murderer! For that reason Simon hadn't taken the secret tunnel under the Danube. Nathan and his henchmen could very well be lying in wait for him there, their pockets lined by powerful men to whom Simon was no more than a pesky bug to be squashed.

The medicus bit his lip. He had to figure out whether his hunch was right before he could determine just whom to trust.

At last the guards managed to open the gate, and along with a dozen shopkeepers, farmers, and day laborers, Simon headed across the Stone Bridge. With fifteen arches, it spanned the river to the other side, where the Electorate of Bavaria began. In the slowly lifting morning fog, the medicus could see that the customs barrier on the other side was now raised. Walking briskly, his head bent, he hurried past the guards. The day before, Simon had found in the brewmaster's room a brown felt hat, which he now drew down over his face. He could only hope the guards were too tired to look closely.

It seemed to work. He didn't hear anyone call out after him, so, breathing deeply, he continued over the bridge, glancing over the railing at eddies that formed between the artificial islands. Rafts and fishing boats glided under the arches and then passed by the Lower Wöhrd Island.

His goal was almost within reach.

About halfway across the bridge Simon caught sight of a wooden ramp that led to the larger island, the Upper Wöhrd. A little house with a clock tower stood at the entry to the ramp. Here a city official leaned back on a bench, eyes sleepy and small, taking pleasure in the first rays of morning sun.

Simon slowed his pace to avoid arousing suspicion.

"What business do you have on the Wöhrd?" the bearded guard asked gruffly. "You don't exactly look like a miller or carpenter." He squinted beneath his helmet as he eyed Simon. "You look more like a pen pusher to me."

Simon nodded. "That I am." He casually produced the tattered page he'd torn from the brewmaster's herbarium. In the shadow of the gate's parapet, it was just about impossible to make out anything on the page. Simon held his breath and prayed the guard would fall for the cheap trick. "The Wöhrd miller is behind on his taxes, and I'm here on behalf of the city."

"Let me see that." The bailiff tore the paper from Simon's hand and studied it carefully.

My God, he's going to call the guards! Simon thought. *They're going to lock me up, and all will be lost! All of Regensburg will—*

"Fine. You may pass." The bailiff pompously handed the paper back. "Looks all right to me."

Simon nodded respectfully, suppressing a grin. This man was illiterate! Not even the drawings on the back had aroused his suspicion. Bowing a few times, the medicus took leave of the grim watchman and proceeded down the ramp. He waited a few yards before he dared to stand up straight.

At that moment he heard banging and pouncing across the water. Not far from where he stood, mill wheels turned in the swift current, powering huge hammers and millstones inside the island's several buildings and sheds. Clattering sawmills stood side by side with rattling grain, fulling, and paper mills. The island was a single rumbling beast, and Simon could almost feel its vibration underfoot.

The mill . . .

His goal was in sight. Now he only hoped his hunch was right.

The island was overgrown with low bushes, and it took Simon some time to orient himself in the daylight, but he finally recognized the big wooden gabled building to which Nathan had brought him that night. He slackened his pace, still uncertain what he might find inside. Was the mill being guarded?

On the spur of the moment he decided to avoid the main door and first take a quick look inside through one of the windows. He clambered up onto a stack of wood against the side of the building until he reached the sealed window shutters. Bending a slat to one side, he stared into the half darkness.

There wasn't much to see. Just as last time, sacks of grain and flour were scattered throughout, and at the rear an enormous millstone creaked and groaned, driven by a water wheel on the building's shore side. Simon was about to turn away when he spotted an especially large sack that had fallen from a larger pile and now lay by itself in the middle of the large room.

The sack was moving.

Simon blinked and took another look. Indeed, the big sack quivered and shook. Only now did the medicus realize it wasn't a sack of grain at all but a person tied into a tight bundle. When this person rolled to the side and Simon saw her face, he had to suppress a scream.

It was Magdalena!

Her hair wet and tousled, her face pale, she trembled from head to toe. Nevertheless, her eyes flashed with anger, reminding Simon of a captured lynx.

Seconds later several figures emerged from the shadows inside the mill. Two were hefty thugs with broad shoulders and the fixed gazes of men accustomed to carrying out orders. Simon thought he recognized at least one of them from the raft landing. The third was different—small, he wore a red shirt with white ribbons and, on his head, one of those chic musketeer hats Simon so wished he could afford.

The man was Silvio Contarini.

Crossing his legs, the Venetian took a seat on a sack of grain and scrutinized the quivering bundle in front of him. During the whole trip on the river Magdalena had struggled in vain to free herself from her bonds. In the meantime she seemed to have tired, and her movements had grown weaker. Silvio shook his head regretfully.

"It's really such a shame that our relationship had to come to this." He sighed. "But the ways of the Lord are inscrutable. Believe me, I adore you all the same—your courage, your intelligence, and, of course, your beauty."

"You miserable dwarf!" Magdalena barked as she tried to get up. "I'll cut off your tiny little prick if you so much as touch me again!"

"*Scusate,* but that's unavoidable," Silvio purred. "After all, I need you for our experiment. But if you prefer, I'll see that from now on, only these charming *cavaliere* — " He gestured to the two grinning behemoths at his side. " — that only their hands touch you. Would you prefer that?"

"What kind of damned experiment?" Magdalena snapped, a hint of uncertainty resonating in her voice. "Give it to me straight for once."

Silvio settled onto his sack of grain as he might a chaise longue, folding his arms behind his head and looking around the mill as if for the first time. Wholly satisfied, he turned back to Magdalena.

"So tell me, what do you think all this is here?"

"Grain. Flour. What else?" the hangman's daughter snapped.

Silvio nodded. "*Esattamente.* But flour from a very special grain." With a flash, the Venetian thrust his sword into one of the bags on which he'd sat just a moment ago like a king atop his throne. Rye trickled through his fingers and spilled across the floor. Almost half of the grains were blackish blue in color as if they'd begun to mold.

"Freshly harvested and threshed from fields I leased around Regensburg," he continued. "We've taken great pains to produce grain so pure. In fact, the color comes from a simple fungus that grows on the grain during warm, wet summers. The farmers fear it, but its effects are truly astonishing. You could almost say these grains are blessed by God. They give humankind the *ignis sanctus,* the Holy Fire." Looking into Magdalena's eyes, he added, "But you midwives probably know it better by the name Saint Anthony's Fire."

"My God!" Magdalena panted. Her face turned a shade whiter. "Saint Anthony's Fire! Then inside all these grains is . . ."

Silvio nodded. "Ergot. Indeed. God's poison. It offers man a vision of Judgment Day. Those who partake of it behold a vision of heaven . . . and hell. It's said the grain is as old as humankind." Again the grain trickled through his fingers. "Entire villages have given themselves up to the Almighty God after a taste. Men who've eaten bread baked with ergot-laced flour have gone into ecstasies, identifying witches and devils in their midst and destroying them. Twitching and dancing, they move through the streets singing our Savior's praise. A purifying poison! I can proudly say that never has such a great amount of ergot been produced by the hand of man." He gestured grandly at the sacks piled up all over the mill as a rapturous smile spread across his lips.

"Enough for an entire city."

From his hiding place Simon watched the Venetian stand up and stride down the line of sacks like a commander inspecting his troops. Simon's heart was racing. They should have guessed this from the start! Bluish, musty powder. Ground ergot! This fungus grew not only in rye but in other types of grain as well—and on more than one occasion it had infected entire grain fields, resulting in mass intoxication. People who ate contaminated bread went mad, and many even died. Only in very small quantities did it have any healing power, and even then it was primarily used to induce labor or abort a pregnancy. Now this madman intended to poison an entire city!

Simon cursed himself for not having considered this possibility before. Just the day before they'd left for Regensburg, the baker, Berchtholdt, had poisoned his maid, Resl, with ergot. The medicus had never seen the stuff in Schongau, so his father must have been storing it secretly. Before that Simon's last experience with it was at the university in Ingolstadt.

He remembered the bathhouse owner's illustrated herbarium, in which some types of grain had been highlighted. In his secret alchemist workshop Hofmann must have been producing an especially pure form of ergot. It had been right in front of Simon's eyes all this time!

Desperately Simon tried to think of a way out, for himself and for Magdalena. The Venetian's two hulking henchmen had withdrawn to a corner of the mill below and were taking turns drinking from a clay jug that—to judge from their blissful expressions—must have contained some high-proof brandy. All the same, the medicus was sure the thugs were still sober enough to present a real danger. What should he do? Alert the city guards? By the time the blundering bailiffs made it here from the bridge, Silvio would be long gone, and Magdalena with him. And who was to say that the patricians weren't in on it themselves? Hadn't Mämminger tried to get a hold of this powder, too? Hadn't he hired a murderer to do just that?

At that moment Simon heard movement behind him. When he turned around, he was horrified to find another of Silvio's servants climbing the woodpile like a cat. So there were three of them! This one had apparently been keeping watch by the door.

When the servant realized Simon saw him, too, he uttered a loud curse and reached for Simon's foot a few inches away. The medicus kicked frantically and struck the man in the face. The servant tumbled back with a scream, bringing down some logs with him. As the whole pile started to shift, Simon could feel logs slipping beneath him and knew that at any moment he could be crushed among them like grain in a millstone.

He straightened up, trying to regain his balance atop the tumbling logs, and just managed to save himself with a daring leap to the side. With a loud crash, the logs on which he'd just been standing toppled to the ground. He watched the servant desperately try to crawl out from under the thundering chaos. In the next moment, however, a heavy trunk, which surely weighed a ton, crashed down on the man, silencing his cries abruptly.

The timbers were still rolling down all around Simon. A

sudden, heavy blow to his shoulder knocked him down, and a long timber rolled over his thigh, pinning him to the ground. He shifted back and forth, pushing against the wood with all his might, but was unable to free himself.

When, moments later, the logs stopped falling, he could hear soft footsteps approach. He tried to turn his head, but a shadow appeared above him, and he closed his eyes, afraid of what he would see. When he dared to open them again, the Venetian stood directly above him.

Silvio cocked his head to the side, smiling, and drew his rapier slowly across Simon's trembling chest, inch by inch, toward his neck.

"Well, well, look what we have here," the ambassador whispered. "The loyal, jealous lover. *Che dramma!* At least now you have a good reason to dislike me."

Jakob Kuisl and the Regensburg executioner sat silently in a rotten little rowboat heading east down the Danube.

They'd found the worm-eaten boat floating just behind the landing dock and for just a few hellers had talked the ferryman into lending it without any unnecessary or embarrassing questions. At first Kuisl was anything but enthused that the Regensburg executioner had followed him, but when he noticed Teuber's grim, determined look, he reached out to shake his hand. Whatever was compelling Teuber to help him, Teuber was a friend. And a friend was something Kuisl badly needed at the moment. Pain still throbbed in his left shoulder, and his arms and legs burned red hot one minute, ice cold the next.

"You don't have to do this," the Schongau hangman said softly. "I'll get through this without—"

"Shut your mouth before I change my mind." Teuber plunged the oar violently into the water as if he were trying to slay a monster in the depths. "I'm not quite sure myself why I'm helping a thick-headed, stubborn old fool like you. And now be quiet and just pretend you're mending your fishing net. The raftsmen over there are already looking askance at us."

Kuisl chuckled and reached behind him for a tangle of nets, which reeked of fish. On his lap he began busily unraveling them. As the boat passed the Upper Wöhrd Island and floated through the whirlpool under the Stone Bridge, the two passengers lowered their heads, but none of the guards on the bridge above gave them so much as a glance. To the bailiffs the men in the soiled jackets were just a pair of fishermen headed downstream to cast their nets. For a moment Kuisl thought he saw a small figure on the bridge that reminded him of Simon, but that was surely just his imagination.

For most of the trip the Schongau hangman kept his eyes closed, lost in the images playing out under his eyelids, images from the past that had returned with a vengeance. It seemed his fever had revived all the memories he'd buried so long ago.

"We were here, in this region," Kuisl mused, as the eastern city wall receded behind them. "I'd almost forgotten. In the distance there was a castle atop a hill, a ruin." He opened his eyes and looked at Teuber. "It was big, and it overlooked a burned-out market town on the Danube. Is there anything like that around here?"

Teuber nodded hesitantly. "That must be Donaustauf, just a few miles downriver. The Swedes set fire to the castle a long time ago, just after the occupiers ran off with an entire load of salt. Did you have anything to do with that?"

Kuisl looked out over the Danube winding through the forests like a muddy green monster. A mill stood on the right-hand bank, but otherwise there were no buildings in sight.

"We were there a few years afterward," he said, closing his eyes again. "The castle had been destroyed sometime before that, but our winter encampment was somewhere very near there. In the spring we were supposed to go back to Bohemia again for yet another murderous campaign." He spat into the water. "By God, for every one of them I'll roast in hell a hundred years."

Teuber dipped the rudder below the river's glassy surface. A flock of ducks scattered and flew off, quacking.

"You were in the war a long time, weren't you?" Teuber asked finally.

"Far too long."

For a while neither spoke. The boat drifted gently down-river as the sun rose over the eastern treetops and burned down on the backs of the men's necks.

"What did you do in the war?" Teuber asked. "Pikeman, swordsman, musketeer?"

"I was a sergeant."

Teuber whistled through his teeth. "A hangman sergeant — well, isn't that something! You must have been a good soldier to have risen so far above your station."

"I know a thing or two about killing."

They were silent once more, until at long last, around a bend in the river, a dreary little city came into view with a hastily re-paired castle perched atop a hill. A crooked jetty lined the shore, where a number of boats and rafts were docked. As they drew closer, Kuisl could see that many of the buildings were in ruins, their roofs collapsed and walls black with soot. The wall that once surrounded this city had been eaten away like a piece of old cheese.

"Donaustauf," said Teuber, steering the boat toward a mud-splattered pier. "Used to be a pretty little market town, but once the Swedes were done with it, Plague and hunger ravaged it only further. No doubt it'll be a while before they can rebuild it, and the next war will come along." He laughed softly and tethered the boat to a rotted post. "So, then, where did your dreams tell you to look?"

Kuisl held his nose in the air as if trying to catch a scent. "Don't know. Weidenfeld . . . was a little village, actually more like a hamlet, just a few miles from our winter quarters. More or less that way." He pointed uncertainly toward the castle on the hill. "We could see that ruin from there."

"Great," Teuber said. "Behind that hill the forest begins. That won't get us very far. Wait here."

He approached the jetty, where a few ragged fishermen had spread out their morning catch. They eyed him warily at first but didn't seem to recognize him as the Regensburg executioner. When he asked about the town, they shook their heads and pointed toward the other side of the hill.

In a few minutes Teuber returned. "I have news — some good and some bad," he reported. "Your Weidenfeld is in fact back in the forest over there — a little hamlet. The older men can still remember it. But there isn't much left of it. Everything's ruined and overgrown, and nobody lives there anymore. Why don't you finally come out with it and tell me about this Weidenfeld?"

"Later." With a deep sigh, Kuisl stood up in the boat and climbed onto the shore. "There's no time now. Let's get this over with."

"Wait." Teuber pulled a two-foot-long boat knife and a nicked rapier from under the rowing bench. He clamped the rapier onto his belt and handed Kuisl the other weapon. "We'll need these. I talked the old fisherman who lent us this rotten boat into letting me have them. The old fellow was probably in the war himself."

Kuisl stopped to think for a moment. "I'd prefer a good old larch-wood cudgel," he said. "And if it's a ghost we meet, even the sharpest blade won't do us any good."

"If it's a ghost, you won't need a club either," Teuber said. "And now stop fussing and take the damned knife!"

Kuisl took the weapon. As he ran his fingers along the rusty blade and the discolored greenish handle, his eyes glassed over. "I've always fought with a two-hander or a shortsword," he said. "That'll rip open a stomach like paper. This here is nothing more than a toy. But what difference does it make?" He turned to leave without looking back. "Come on."

They left Donaustauf and entered a narrow lane behind the village that led into a dense forest. Soon tall beeches and firs surrounded them, and the path was bathed in an almost surreal green light. Apart from the rustling trees and a jaybird call, an oppressive silence prevailed. Down here on the forest floor it was shady, almost cool, and their boots sank into the swampy ground an earlier thunderstorm had left in its wake. From time to time broad wheel treads were visible in the mire.

"This road continues on to a hammer mill," Teuber explained, looking around intently. "Just before it a small hidden path ought to branch off to the left. The fishermen in town said it's mostly overgrown now, so we'll have to keep our eyes peeled."

"That won't be necessary—look!" Kuisl pointed to fresh prints in the swampy ground that trailed off further down the path. "These are fresh, not three hours old."

Teuber bent down to study the prints. "There's not just one of them—evidently your ghost has a helper."

Kuisl nodded. "I wouldn't be surprised if it turned out there were three. They always come in threes . . . three men, risen from the dead."

"Quit that, or I'll be seeing ghosts, too." The Regensburg executioner crossed himself and made another sign to ward off evil spirits. "You'll drive a man crazy with your superstitious blathering."

All of a sudden he stopped. To their left a narrow, overgrown path—more like a deer trail—led off into the forest. They'd almost overlooked it. On closer inspection they spied a border stone among the leaves and rotting branches. And next to that, half rotted and buried in foliage, were the remains of a wayside cross.

Kuisl picked up the splintered crucifix and leaned it almost reverently against the stone.

"Weidenfeld," he murmured. "We're on the right track."

They headed down the path, making their way with difficulty through fallen trees and dense undergrowth. Freshly broken branches indicated someone had recently passed this way. The air filled with the odor of mushrooms, decay, and rotting wood, and all they could hear now were their own footsteps and muffled breathing.

After a good quarter-hour the forest brightened and a sunny clearing with tall bushes and young trees opened before them. It took Kuisl a while to realize this grove concealed the remnants of houses. Nibbling on a hazelnut bush that grew out of a crumbling well, a deer caught sight of the two intruders and bounded away, leaving behind it a deep silence that took Kuisl's breath away.

Weidenfeld . . .

His mind awash in memories, the hangman looked around. Roofs had collapsed, scorched beams rose out of the ground; all that was left of the houses were piles of stones among which blue forget-me-nots were growing. In the town center a street was now overgrown with ferns and wild grain, and a little tower rose up over a pile of stones in the distance. Crooked mossy gravestones reminded Kuisl that at one time a village church must have stood there.

High in the tower, in a burned-out window, a man sat, legs dangling over the ledge. He beckoned to them, but instinctively the hangman took a step backward.

How is this possible? From what hell has he returned?

The man who sat there cackling like an old hag, his lips twisted in a wolf-like grin . . . this man had been dead for almost thirty years.

Almost prancing, the Venetian ambassador circled Simon and Magdalena, who were both bound with heavy ropes on the floor of the mill.

"Simon, Simon," Silvio Contarini said, dabbing the sweat on his forehead with a white lace handkerchief. "You put me in a difficult position. You tell *me* what I should do with you now. I most certainly have a use for your charming companion—but for you?" He shook his head. "All three of you ought never to have left Schongau—you, honorable medicus; the *bella signorina;* and her hulk of a father, as well. But now isn't the time for regrets. How did you ever find out about our hiding place? Speak up now. Or will I have to fill your throat with flour to get you to talk?"

Simon tried to pull his arms free, but the boat ropes were as tight as iron clamps. He turned his eyes to Silvio's servants, seated in a corner of the mill drinking brandy. In the meantime three enormous fellows had joined them. Like their comrades, they wore soiled leather vests and trousers spotted with mud, and Simon thought he'd seen one or the other before, working as day laborers on the boat landing.

All five cast fierce looks at the medicus who'd killed their friend. Simon was sure an excruciating end awaited him if he couldn't come up with something quick. What in the world had he gotten himself into?

"It was just a guess, but it turns out I was right!" he panted, red with effort. Despairing, he stared up at Silvio, who still regarded him like some annoying insect. "Where else could you have milled such a huge quantity of grain?" He struggled to loosen the fetters, then sank back onto the floor.

"When I realized the milled powder was ergot, I remembered just how much of it we saw down in the little bathhouse laboratory," he continued. "Of course, it was nothing but ash by the time we found it, but there must have once been hundreds of pounds of it. To grind so much flour, you'd need a big mill, and someplace out of town, where you could go about your work undisturbed. The mill on the Wöhrd!"

"Hmm, not bad." Silvio considered him with interest. "But couldn't it have also been a mill somewhere outside of town, in a suburb perhaps?"

"The sacks gave you away." In spite of his desperate situation, Simon almost laughed when he saw the Venetian bite his lip. "I was here not long ago, and the linen sacks in the bathhouse cellar were the same as the ones here—gray-white and tied with black rope. And only this morning did the thought occur to me . . . What have you done with the Wöhrd miller? Did you bribe him, or kill him?"

Silvio shrugged. "That wasn't necessary. He is one of us, and in our blessed brotherhood each of us has his duty." Now he counted off with his fingers: "The bathhouse owner, Hofmann, was responsible for growing the pure ergot; a few loyal farmers cultivated it; the miller on the Wöhrd ground it; and the baker mixed it into his dough. Each among us knows his place."

"But it's unfortunate that Hofmann and Haberger had their sudden qualms of conscience," Simon replied defiantly. "So they had to be eliminated."

Silvio scowled. "Sad, yes, but those were precautionary measures and couldn't have been avoided. Our cause is much too important; there's no place among us for ditherers." The Venetian ambassador bent down to stroke Magdalena's hair. "The only thing we were missing was a test subject for the ergot. We tried it out on rats and cats at first." He smiled. "And, admittedly, with highly satisfactory results. The animals began to quiver and run in circles, though unfortunately some died. I then found some young girls willing to sacrifice their bodies for science."

Magdalena shuddered. "The prostitutes who vanished," she gasped. "That was you! You fed them more and more ergot until they died! You probably locked them in your cellar and fattened them up like cattle."

Silvio frowned. "What an ugly thing to say. Honestly, I didn't want to see them die. Insanity is enough for us; we'll happily leave mass murder to the military. It's just that we haven't yet fine-tuned the dose; though this time around I'm sure we'll get it right." He stroked Magdalena's hair. "One final experiment and we'll have it."

Simon remembered the strange cages they'd found down in the alchemist's workshop, the buckets of dirt in the courtyard, the herbarium upstairs in the pharmacy . . . Hofmann's house had been one gigantic laboratory! Simon wondered whether the bathhouse owner had known anything about the experiments on prostitutes. Perhaps that was the real reason Andreas Hofmann wanted out.

"You cloven-hoofed devil! You're completely mad!" Magdalena spat in Silvio's face, causing the rouge on his cheeks to run. "You hope to poison a whole city—men, women, and children! Who are you? Some kind of religious zealot? A groveling papist who can't live with the fact that Regensburg is a Protestant city? Or maybe you've dipped into the ergot yourself."

"The time of the nobles and the patricians is over," the ambassador began smugly, wiping the spit from his face with his lace handkerchief. "The time has come for free working people, the workers and peasants." He raised his voice so that even his men across the room could hear him. "The prophets have proclaimed the year 1666 the year of Christ's return, and we shall prepare a dignified reception for our Savior. When the entire city has gone mad, we freemen will take command of Regensburg, and soon—"

But Simon didn't allow him to finish. "Enough of this foolishness!" he spit out. "The return of Christ! Free working men!

Nobody's going to believe that! You're a smug little nobleman yourself, and you're proposing the freemen wipe all nobles off the face of the earth. You can't be serious! You've got something else in mind, Silvio Contarini." His lips twisting into a grimace, Simon looked the Venetian up and down. Silvio's face was now strangely rigid.

"I saw through you long ago," Simon continued. "You don't give a rotten fig for religion, for ordinary, hard-working people; it's all politics for you, or at least whatever you consider politics to be."

"So, if he's not one of the crazy freemen, or some heretic who's out to get the rich," Magdalena began disbelievingly, "then what—"

"The Reichstag!" Simon interrupted. When once again the monstrousness of Silvio's plan became clear to him, he shuddered. "He wants to poison the entire Reichstag!"

Magdalena's mouth fell open. "Poison the Reichstag?"

The Venetian ambassador glanced quickly at his five helpers. The brandy was still making its rounds among them, and they didn't seem to be paying particular attention to the conversation across the room. "Nonsense!" Silvio whispered. "Nonetheless, I'd be very much obliged if we might continue our discussion in a somewhat softer tone. The men here are simple raftsmen who don't take any special interest in politics."

All of a sudden Simon thought he saw his chance. "If we promise not to tell a single soul about your real plans, not even your men over there, will you let us go?" he asked hesitantly.

Silvio shrugged, absent-mindedly toying with the rings on his fingers. "We'll see about that. First you can tell me what you think I'm up to. If the story you've concocted amuses me, I might let you go. Who'd believe a suspected arsonist, anyway?"

Simon swallowed hard, then, in a soft voice, began: "In a few months the Reichstag will meet in Regensburg. Representatives from across the German Empire will travel here—princes, dukes, bishops, perhaps even the kaiser. The most powerful men in the land will convene, making Regensburg the ideal place to inflict damage on the German Empire. You won't find such a collection of noblemen anywhere else in the world."

"Not bad," Silvio whispered. "Go on . . ."

"The bathhouse owner Andreas Hofmann was experimenting with an especially pure ergot in his secret workshop," Simon hurried on. "In the courtyard behind the bathhouse we found row after row of pots filled with soil. You probably leased fields outside the city, where you transferred this fungus from Hofmann's garden on a massive scale. You milled the grain here and stockpiled the flour in sacks." By the look on Silvio's face Simon could tell he was right. "The master baker, Haberger, is the sole supplier to the old city hall, where the Reichstag will convene, and I assume he was supposed to bake the poisoned flour into bread. But then Haberger got cold feet and had to be eliminated . . ." Simon frowned. "But now you've lost your means of making bread from the flour and of delivering it to the conference—but surely you've thought up something else by now."

"Haberger's son is perfectly clueless," Silvio replied. "We'll offer him the flour at such a good price he'll be unable to refuse."

Simon nodded. "And so your poisoned bread will make its way at last onto the plates of the noblemen and ambassadors, after all. At each meal they'll ingest a bit more of the ergot. The consequences will be dire! Hundreds will turn stark raving mad. They'll stagger through the streets in a state of rapture, plagued by visions and terrible nightmares. Negotiations will be impossible, and it's likely most of the emissaries will leave the city in a panic. The entire Reichstag will be thrown into chaos and brought to a standstill!"

"And thus the German Empire, as well. *Bravissimo!*" Silvio clapped loudly, genuine enthusiasm on his powdered face. "My compliments! What splendid work! It's too bad, you know—in another life, at another time, we might have made very good use

of someone like you." He spoke the last words somewhat regretfully. "You would have made an excellent agent, just like Heinrich von Bütten. What a waste! He, too, unfortunately chose the
wrong side."

"Heinrich von Bütten?" Simon asked in confusion. "I don't
understand . . ."

"The baldheaded assassin," Magdalena interrupted. "He
was an agent of the kaiser!" She sighed. "He probably wanted to
warn me all along about this scheming dwarf. Silvio killed him
this morning."

Simon opened his eyes wide. "But that means that Paulus
Mämminger . . ."

"He's a well-behaved little patrician in cahoots with the kaiser trying to cut us off." Silvio nodded. "But he had only suspicions, nothing more. Heinrich von Bütten was trying to learn
more about our plans."

Magdalena's eyes narrowed. "Who are you? The devil? Who
else comes up with a plan as demonic as yours, to drive an entire
city to the brink of madness?"

The Venetian was silent, but Simon picked up the thread.
"Why don't you just come out with it, then? Why so coy? It's obvious anyway."

"I really don't know what you're talking about," replied Silvio, still playing with his rings.

"Then let me guess, if I may," said Simon. "You're working
on behalf of the Turkish Grand Vizier. The Ottoman Empire is,
after all, the greatest threat to the German Empire."

"Of course!" Magdalena cried out. "Mämminger told me
himself at the ball at Heuport House that the kaiser intends to
collect money at the upcoming Reichstag to arm the Germanic
lands against the Turks. If the Reichstag dissolves into madness,
the Grand Vizier will have an easy time of it."

The Venetian's expression told them they were both correct.

"What a dastardly plan," the medicus said, impressed. "The

city hall, where the negotiations take place, is heavily guarded, but no one would give a second thought to the bread — why would they? The Reichstag would collapse in chaos, all to the advantage of the Turkish Empire." He pointed at the raftsmen, who were still wholeheartedly absorbed in their bottle of brandy. "You make fools of your cronies here and pretend to be the bold defender of the poor. I'm sure you've made them promises of heaven on earth. The Venetian ambassador, a freeman — what a joke! Nobody must have the slightest suspicion of your connection with the Grand Vizier. Isn't that so?"

The ambassador's lips pressed into a thin, bloodless line, just the hint of a smile playing across them.

Simon turned to Magdalena. "Have you noticed how our dear little Venetian can suddenly speak perfect unaccented German? All along he's been playing the part of the clumsy, innocent, love-struck Silvio, and you fell for it! He may be the official ambassador from Venice, but clearly he's working for more than one side!"

Silvio drew his rapier with a soft *whoosh* and ran it lightly across Simon's throat.

"Give me one reason why I shouldn't slaughter you like a pig right here and now!" he hissed. "Nobody's going to listen to your cute little conspiracy theories. Not even the raftsmen right over there! So tell me why I shouldn't kill you right now."

"Kill me as you did the bathhouse owner, his wife, the baker, the bishop's brewmaster, and all the others?" Simon gasped, his eyes fixed on the point of the sword at his throat.

Silvio's eyes glassed over. "The . . . brewmaster?" His voice was suddenly uncertain. "*Maledizione!*" he growled. "That was someone else. And the other murders, too." He closed his eyes and took a deep breath before continuing. "I never should have gotten involved with that one. He's the reason my entire plan is in danger! The fool! He could have lived out his life in the lap of luxury, but he acted impetuously!" Silvio spat angrily on the

ground, and his makeup began to run, revealing a face full of hatred beneath.

Simon held his breath.

So there was someone else . . .

Someone else who was responsible for killing Magdalena's
aunt and uncle, someone involved in Silvio's plans! Someone
who had been doing Silvio's dirty work. Who? Was it the same
man who wanted revenge on Magdalena's father? Evidently the
Venetian was clueless about what had happened in the bishop's
palace the night before. Feverishly, Simon tried to think of a way
to use this knowledge to his advantage.

The little ambassador turned to Simon once more, letting
the point of his sword wander slowly across his prisoner's chest.
"All right, then, I'll worry about that later. I'll attend to you first,
you little quack, too smart for your own good!"

"The city council knows about this," Simon gasped suddenly.

Pausing, Silvio looked down at his victim with pity. "You're
lying; this is just a cheap trick to prolong your pathetic life a few
moments."

Simon shook his head desperately. This was his last chance.
If the Venetian saw through him now, he'd slit him from belly to
throat like livestock in a slaughterhouse. Then he'd force Magdalena to eat the ergot.

"Then how do you think I know so much about your plans?"
Simon said as self-assured as possible, his voice as solid and regular as a well-oiled clock. "Your irascible crony broke into the
bishop's residence last night. He murdered the brewmaster, then
was captured by the guards. He confessed everything on the
rack! I listened through the door but ran off before the others because I feared for Magdalena's life." He grinned broadly at the
ambassador. "In half an hour or less the city guards will be
knocking down the door, and then, by God, your entire plan will
go up in smoke!"

It was such a bald-faced lie even Simon didn't think he'd get away with it. Yet the Venetian hesitated.

"Even if that were true," Silvio said at last, "what reason would that be to let you live?"

"I can divert the guards!" Simon sputtered. "I'll go to city hall and tell them you're already half crazed from the ergot and holding Magdalena hostage. If it works, you can let her go."

Clearly the Venetian would never let them both go at the same time, but this just might buy Simon some time until he could come up with something better. At least now Silvio had sheathed his rapier and seemed to seriously consider the offer.

"So they've caught him . . ." Silvio said, more to himself than to anyone in particular, shaking his head, clearly still undecided about what to do next. Finally he spoke. "What you've described is entirely possible. He has been my concern from the start. He is so full of hate; I knew one day it would be his undoing. I never should have involved the hangman in this matter," he said, angrily kicking a bag of grain. "A single, swift blow in some dark alley would have been the end of the bathhouse owner! But *he* had to have his revenge. And now the whole thing's gone sour."

The ambassador stood up and began to pace silently among the sacks of grain. Then, in a flash, he turned to gaze thoughtfully at Magdalena. His voice, muted now, was laced with fear.

"By all the saints in heaven, Karl Gessner is a real devil. Sometimes I wish your father had sent that man straight back to the hell he arose from all those years ago."

From up in the Weidenfeld church belfry, raftmaster Karl Gessner looked down scornfully on the two hangmen below. His jet-black hair was tied back in a ponytail, and he wore the colorful, loose-fitting costume of a foot soldier and an old, threadbare coat over that. Behind one shoulder rose the glittering pommel of a shortsword strapped to his back by its scabbard. Only his red bandanna signaled this was the same man responsible for the daily shipments of goods moving through the Regensburg raft landing. The Gessner so well liked by about everyone had changed almost overnight into a deadly warrior eerily risen from the past.

He's dead, thought Kuisl. *I killed him with my own hands. This can only be a ghost . . .*

After Gessner's shrill laughter had died away, he wiped his eyes as one might after a particularly funny joke.

"Jakob, Jakob," he said, as if addressing an old friend. "Who would ever have thought we'd meet again in this miserable little town? It's a pity you didn't come alone. I'm afraid our history will only bore the Regensburg executioner."

He gestured at Teuber, who stood beside Kuisl with his rapier drawn, looking upward with fury. "Seems age has made a coward of you," he continued. "Oh, well, we all get older, and weaker."

"You can be sure this concerns only the two of us," Kuisl said. "I packed you off to hell once before, and I'll do it again."

Gessner closed his eyes as if lost in a dream. "Do you know what I've enjoyed most? Watching you writhe on the rack like a blathering cripple, your despair at not knowing who brought this misery upon you. I'm almost offended you didn't recognize my voice, seeing how we've been through so much together." He clicked his tongue. "It's a shame you're always running from me, first in the torture chamber, then in the bordello. We should have split the girl between us. Just as in the old days."

"*He* is the third inquisitor!" Teuber exclaimed. "I wanted to tell you from the start. As the Regensburg raftmaster, Karl Gessner is a member of the Outer Council. Fat Thea heard from her 'customers' in city hall that he did everything possible to be present at your torture."

Gessner nodded, dangling his legs from the window ledge.

"Wasn't all that easy. Those fat patricians will defend their privileges tooth and nail, but they did relent at last. I do have some influence with those simple people, after all."

"I might have figured as much when Simon told me about the freemen—and that you, of all people, are their leader," Kuisl replied. "Stirring people up has always been your forte. And then this story about the philosopher's stone. Only you would come up with such nonsense!"

Gessner shrugged. "I had to do something to distract that conniving little medicus, or he would have figured out what our special powder really was. He fell for my little ruse, and now he'll come running to me with everything he learns." He smiled. "The little quack isn't quite as clever as he'd like to think."

"What do you have to do with this powder?" Kuisl asked.

"Nothing that concerns the two of us, Jakob."

All of a sudden Gessner leaped from the window opening, landing on a burial mound thickly overgrown with ivy. His sinewy body tensed up like a cat as he bent his knees to absorb the impact. With powerful strides he approached the two hangmen, who watched him warily.

"But since you asked, I just happen to have an answer," he continued. "The powder is poison. Poison enough for an entire city."

Kuisl kept his eye on the pommel of the sword that jostled at Gessner's shoulder with every movement. It was a last-resort kind of weapon, a *katzbalger*, or shortsword, with a cross guard in the form of a snake and a wide, tapering blade. In hand-to-hand combat this sword was highly prized, and pikesmen and cavalry often carried it as backup. It was capable of delivering a lethal wound.

Especially when your opponent carries only a rusty dagger, Kuisl thought.

Gessner reached over his shoulder, unsheathed the katzbalger, and regarded his reflection in the polished iron blade.

"An influential man was in need of my help," he said softly. "I met him in the course of smuggling goods down the Danube. He was very pleased to learn that I, as a leader of the freemen, command a small secret army." Gessner smiled, running his thumb along the katzbalger's blade. "For years I've been trying to figure out how to break the backs of those fat patricians and smug noblemen. Now, the struggle that began with the great Peasants' Wars over a hundred years ago will finally come to a close. A new age is dawning! Once this is over, I'll be richer and more powerful than the entire Regensburg city council."

Gessner swung his katzbalger through the air. Though he was approaching fifty, he was as agile as a man thirty years his junior. His eyes flashed blue, and his teeth were a dazzling white.

Nothing changes, Kuisl thought. *He certainly hasn't. Evil and crazy as a rabid dog—except now he goes by another name . . .*

"Philipp Lettner!" the hangman whispered. "Years ago I strung you up from an old gnarled oak right here in Weidenfeld. You can't be alive. Who—what are you? A ghost?"

The man who was once Philipp Lettner grinned. "You're right, Jakob. Lettner is dead. But on that very day twenty-five years ago Karl Gessner was born. Karl, just like my little brother whom you strung up beside me. Gessner, a fat, rich riverman whose raft I stole a few days later after I'd slit his throat. I took his raft and his wares and came to Regensburg."

He ripped the bandanna from his neck, where a red scar seemed to have eaten a ring into the skin all around his neck.

"Take a close look! This here is the beginning of my new life," Gessner yelled. "I should actually thank you for all that happened back then. Karl Gessner is much richer, much more powerful and evil, than Philipp Lettner ever could have been. From a mangy mercenary to a respected raftmaster! I've come a long way, Jakob."

As the raftmaster drew menacingly closer, Kuisl's world became a blur and he cursed softly, realizing he was starting to sway. The fever had returned, not strong, but enough to bring cold sweat to his forehead in spite of the stifling heat.

"You botched the job back then, hangman," Lettner whispered. "You should have waited just a bit longer until our bodies had quit twitching in the branches. But you were in such a hurry to make off with your sweetheart. It was too late for Karl, but not for me. I was still breathing; I was still salvageable."

Gradually Kuisl felt a chill settling in.

Cold, just like back then . . .

The warped old houses seemed to straighten up again before his eyes. In the center, around a well, was the hard-packed dirt of the village square. The rooftops on fire, the crackling of the flames, the cries of the women and children.

And in the middle of it all, Lettner, his second in command. The bloodsucker. The bane of his existence.

Everything around him began to spin. Kuisl closed his eyes as the images came pelting down around him like a heavy rain.

The screams . . .

So very long ago, half a lifetime. It's a cold November day somewhere near Regensburg. The air is fresh, and snowflakes shimmer among the trees like little stars. A good day for hunting, a very good day in contrast to the murderous boredom of a mercenary's life whiled away between battles. New troops have enlisted, eager young farm boys, setting out with the old battle-hardened men in the direction of Lothringen. Fresh blood that soon will quench the dry, thirsty fields. Jakob has already seen so many die. In the end they all call out for their mothers.

Even now, on this November day, he's surrounded by pimple-faced, hot-blooded youths, as well as a handful of scarred old veterans he knows he can trust. He promises them all a boar hunt, just as in the old days before the war. Most of these new recruits, though, know no other world; "before the war" is little more than a tale told around the campfire.

The screams come from far off. At first like the chirping of angry birds. Only as Jakob and his men draw near can he distinguish the people's desperate wails. He pushes his way through branches to stare down at a burning village. Fire is eating through the roofs of the houses, acrid smoke fills the air, and twisted bodies lie scattered on the ground in pools of blood. Cowering in the center of the village square are the women—old, young, pretty, ugly—all wearing thin shirts and trembling, screaming, crying.

Around a crackling fire a few men are roasting chickens and laughing.

Jakob's men.

They're throwing dice. Cheers go up, then one mercenary grabs a woman by the hair and disappears with her behind the burning houses. There's a long, drawn-out scream, a quiet whimper, then silence.

Another round begins. A new game, a new winner.

A moment later an overgrown black-haired man stands and lets out a shriek of laughter as he holds up the dice cup triumphantly. He pulls a girl toward him and grabs her breasts. He's the double mercenary Philipp Lettner, Jakob's second in command. Like Jakob, he's paid double for his service, not on account of his skill with a two-hander but for his ruthlessness at the front. Jakob knows at once that Lettner is the leader of this gang; for years the man has been drinking blood, and all too often Jakob has let him get away with it.

Jakob's gaze wanders to the recruits at his side, who stare down at the bloodbath in horror. This is war, and now they're in the midst of it. They may still want to vomit at the sight of it now, but soon enough they, too, will be plundering villages and raping women with the rest. How can they be expected to know what's right and what's not? Who is supposed to show them?

Jakob closes his eyes for a second, then gives the men at his side the sign to attack. They storm out of the forest, shouting; there's a brief struggle, curses, swearing, and then the band of murderers is overwhelmed and disarmed. His eyes cold and scornful, Lettner looks at

*Jakob. Next to Lettner stand his two brothers, fat Friedrich and
scrawny Karl—little Karl, who is still just a child, and a monster.
How many of the new recruits at Jakob's side will turn out like Karl?*

"What's this all about, sergeant?" *Lettner asks.* "Just having a
little fun, that's all. Let us go."

"You were throwing dice for the women . . ."

"Why not? They're only peasants. Who cares?"

"You threw dice for them, raped them, and then killed them . . ."

"There's still some left. Help yourself, Jakob."

*Lettner grins, his white teeth shining like a wolf's in the light of
the fire. How often Jakob has seen this grin in the midst of battle, how
often has he closed his eyes to it! Cowering in front of Lettner is a
black-haired girl, her eyes glassy with fear beneath bushy eyebrows, a
silent plea shining in them, her lips formed into a soft prayer.*

She would have been next.

*Jakob is overcome with fury like never before. From his pocket he
fetches the dice carved from bone and presses them into Lettner's
hand.*

"You're on."

"What do you mean?" *Philipp Lettner looks at him in disbelief,
his clear blue eyes flitting back and forth. He smells a trap.*

"You're going to play for your lives. Every third man hangs."

"You goddamned bastard!"

*Fat Friedrich jumps up to plunge his dagger into Jakob's stom-
ach. But the young sergeant dodges and strikes the fat combatant in
the face with the pommel of his sword. He hits him over and over.
Friedrich staggers toward a burning house, flailing his arms, trying to
find something to hold on to, until at last he stumbles over the threshold and falls screaming into the raging inferno. Timbers begin crashing to the ground, and then there's only silence.*

*Turning, Jakob approaches the campfire and points his sword
first at Philipp Lettner, then at the dice.*

"I said play."

Suddenly he feels the black-haired girl looking at him. Her eyes

*are deep, murky whirlpools; they're pulling him down, and he can't
tear his eyes from hers. A fire burns in the pit of his stomach, far hotter
than the flames on the rooftops.*

*Only later, when the last bits of life twitch in the dangling legs as
they sway gently in the breeze, when the final horrid scream has been
carried off on the breeze, when he's ridden away with her, far away,
homeward, where there's no more war — it's only then, when he's decided he'll never be a mercenary again, that he learns her name.*

Anna-Maria.

She will be his partner for life.

"Damn, Kuisl! What's the matter with you? Wake up!"

The pain in his left shoulder brought Jakob Kuisl back to the
present. Teuber had grabbed him and was now shaking him
roughly.

"Wake up before that bastard rams his katzbalger straight
through your stomach!"

Kuisl shook himself until his vision cleared. He looked up to
find Philipp Lettner just a few steps away, his sword upraised
and a smile still on his lips.

"Let him be, hangman," Lettner purred almost tenderly.
"It's the memories taking hold of you, isn't it, Jakob? All the
dead who've paved your walk through life. Did you really think
you could live happily ever after with your pretty farmer's daughter in Schongau? No!" His voice suddenly turned sharp and
cold, just as it had days ago in the torture chamber. "I swore revenge! I knew I would get a hold of you one day, and now that
day has come!"

The hangman wiped the sweat from his forehead. The sun
was now directly above the little village, and its rays stung him
like needles. His pain returned, bringing nausea with it.

"Why did you kill my sister?" he whispered. "Lisl did nothing to harm you."

Philipp Lettner laughed out loud. "You fool!" he cried out.

"You still don't see, do you? It was your sister who led me to you! When it became clear her husband would have to die, I had to figure out how best to manage it. Only then did I come upon her maiden name, *Kuisl*." He spat the name out like a mouthful of dirt. "So, naturally, I got a little inquisitive. The little woman was really fond of you; she loved to talk about you — your darling daughter and your oh-so-beloved Anna-Maria. After a while I realized the Lord above had given me a gift, an honest-to-God gift from heaven — you!" Lettner broke into shrill, almost feminine laughter as little tears sparkled in the corners of his eyes. But in the next moment he regained his composure.

"I am your destiny and your undoing," he continued in a sharp voice. "*I* sent the letter to Schongau to lure you to Regensburg; *I* cut the throats of your sister and brother-in-law and devised this trap. *I* was the third inquisitor, and now I'm death staring you in the face." He bowed like a tacky street magician and lunged with his katzbalger.

"Murder always takes two," growled Teuber, who'd listened in silence till that point. "You'll no doubt have an easy time of it with a sick man like Kuisl, but you forget you also have me to deal with."

Lettner feigned astonishment. "Ah, so true, little hangman, I'd almost forgotten all about you."

The raftmaster raised his left hand as if in a tentative greeting. Kuisl noticed a shadow in the church-tower window, then heard something whir through the air. A bolt from a crossbow struck Teuber in the chest and sent him tumbling backward, flailing his arms like a drowning man, his mouth wide open in a mute scream. He fell at last, like a tree crashing to the ground, and lay still, his huge chest rising and falling, staring quizzically up at the sky.

"Now it's a fair fight, isn't it, Jakob?" Lettner whispered. "Just you and me. Here in Weidenfeld. I hope you don't mind if my brother Friedrich watches up there. He's thought about you a lot these past years."

Kuisl looked up to see a figure standing in the burned-out window of the ruined tower. The man, tall and broad, held a crossbow in his hands like a toy. This was the stranger he'd seen almost two weeks ago on the raft heading for Regensburg, his face deeply pitted and scarred.

It took Kuisl a while to realize that one of the scars was in fact his grinning mouth.

Simon struggled to breathe. The dirty rag Silvio Contarini had stuffed in his mouth stank of mold and mouse droppings, and his nose was congested with flour, causing him to sneeze over and over. Only with great effort was he able to turn his head enough to see what was happening around him.

Beside him lay Magdalena, also bound and gagged. A ways off, through clouds of chaff and flour, he saw the Venetian's five helpers loading sacks onto a wagon parked in front of the mill. They'd spent the past few hours grinding the rest of the ergot to destroy all the evidence. Now, in the early afternoon, it was an oven inside the mill and the men's shirts were soaked through with sweat. Clean and sharp in his red doublet, jacket, and hat, only Silvio seemed not to be sweating. He sat on a millstone biting his lip, looking increasingly nervous.

"I'm starting to think you're right, Fronwieser," Silvio said as he chewed thoughtfully on a piece of straw. "Even a clever little quack such as yourself couldn't possibly have divined my plans, certainly not in so much detail. Gessner *must* have blabbed. Why in the world did I ever get involved with such an idiot! I curse the day I met him on my way to Vienna!" He turned his head to make sure none of the raftsmen were listening, then he whispered, "These freemen are nothing but a pack of crazy jackasses! And Gessner is the craziest of them all."

All of a sudden the damp flour blocked Simon's nostrils. Struggling for air, he drew frantic shallow breaths. He twitched and floundered until a sack of flour fell to the ground beside him. Surprised by the noise, Silvio glanced over at him but didn't seem in any hurry to remove the gag. Instead, he sat still, observing Simon's struggle with interest.

"How long can a man get by without air? What do you think, hmm? I should just let you suffocate here like a fish on dry land. Ever since you and *la bella signorina* came to town, everything's been going to pieces. But I won't allow you to destroy my plan!" He pounded on one of the sacks, sending up a white cloud around him. "Not you, and not that crazy Gessner, either!"

Simon couldn't get any air at all now — the flour had completely plugged his nose. His eyes bulging, he started to turn blue while the Venetian stared off into the distance, seeming to have forgotten all about his prisoner for the moment.

"Gessner's greatest achievement was talking that bathhouse owner, Hofmann, into joining in our cause," he muttered. "A brilliant alchemist! He'd been studying poisonous plants for years, and without him we never could have produced such pure ergot!" The ambassador was almost gushing now. "Somehow that modest little bathhouse owner managed to get the fungus to coat almost the entire head of each plant. It was fantastic! But Hofmann's conscience suddenly got the better of him, and he was about to spill the whole story to the city council." Silvio took the straw from his mouth and ripped it into pieces. "We should have just slaughtered him like a dog in an alley! Quick and painless. A robbery that turned into a murder — no one would ever have suspected anything! But no, it had to be something elaborate . . ."

The medicus felt himself slowly losing consciousness as iridescent vapors swirled through his head. He could comprehend only fragments of the Venetian's speech now.

"Gessner only learned by chance that Hofmann's wife was

the sister of his archenemy," Silvio continued. "After that it was like he became a different person. He insisted that we write a letter to lure Kuisl to Regensburg, that we forge a will and pin the murder on him. God knows what the Schongau hangman did to Gessner during the war, but it was certainly enough to have turned him into a raging angel of vengeance all these years later. He talked me into it, spoke of his ingenious plan, but then the two of you showed up and—oh, is something wrong?"

"Mmmmmmmmhhhhh . . ."

As his consciousness faded, Simon tipped over onto a pile of flour alongside him, enveloping himself and Magdalena in plumes of dust that rose toward the ceiling. Silvio, irritated at first, stood up, sighing, and walked over to his captives.

"What do you think?" he said, turning to the hangman's daughter, who stared up at him, her eyes wide with fear. "Shall we rid the world of this green-eyed little smart aleck? Or shall we allow him to pester us a bit longer?"

Magdalena writhed wildly. Gagged as she was, she seemed to be cursing fiercely.

"I'll take that as a yes," Silvio said, gingerly removing the cloth from Simon's mouth. Immediately the medicus gasped like a man saved from drowning, inhaling huge quantities of air. As the color slowly returned to his face, he lay on the floor, wheezing and unable to speak a word.

"Don't think for a minute that you've thwarted my plans, Fronwieser!" the Venetian snarled. "A man like Silvio Contarini always has another card up his sleeve. Now I'll just have to go back to my original plan. I didn't care for it so much at first because it seemed it would call for many more lives to be lost, but now, unfortunately, I see no other choice." He pointed to the five raftsmen, who had now loaded almost all the sacks onto the wagon. "At least Gessner left his men for me. We'll take the ergot to a safe place until we can find a way to use it. And we'll take *la bella signorina* along with us and destroy the remaining evidence." Silvio smiled. "I'm sorry to say, you're a piece of evidence. *Arrivederci!*"

He clapped his hands and turned to his helpers. "Hurry, before the guards show up! Aren't you finished yet?"

The men nodded respectfully. Evidently the ignorant raftsmen were still convinced by Silvio's plan. Simon assumed the Venetian had promised each a seat on the city council and at least his weight in gold.

"Now let's bring this show to a close, *il grande finale!*"

Gesturing dramatically, Silvio approached a large wooden box attached to the wall at eye level and filled with flour. He slid open the bottom panel, emptying flour onto the floor and sending up an enormous cloud of dust that soon engulfed the entire mill. Simon could see only the Venetian's shadowy outline next to the box, like a ghost enshrouded in fog. Two raftsmen grabbed Magdalena's flailing form and carried her outside.

"Flour is wonderful stuff," Silvio gushed. "You can bake bread with it, poison people, and even turn it into a bomb. The tiniest spark will cause this dust to explode. What you see here should be enough to blow up half the island. But, little bookworm that you are, you surely already knew that, didn't you?"

Through the cloud of dust Simon watched the Venetian fetch a small trunk from behind a millstone. After opening it, he pulled out what at first glance looked like a long rope, but only after Silvio unrolled it did Simon realize what it really was.

A fuse.

"I found this thing right here, a while back," Silvio said as he slowly laid the cord out along the floor and backed toward the door. "Along with a whole trunk of gunpowder and a dozen muskets. I assume soldiers must have left them here during the Great War. How nice that I've finally found a good use for them."

From the doorway the Venetian looked back at his prisoner a last time.

Simon, meanwhile, had regained his speech. "Where—

where are you taking Magdalena?" he gasped. "Where are you . . . taking all those sacks?"

Silvio smiled. "Well, man lives not by bread alone, isn't that so? But I'm afraid you have other more pressing concerns at the moment."

He fetched a box of matches from his pocket and shook it gently.

"At least you won't suffer," he said. "I can promise you that. The instant the spark touches this dust, the whole place will go up with a bang. And with all the gunpowder, it should put on a fireworks show for all of Regensburg." He bowed slightly. "Enjoy your flight."

Stepping outside, he gave the raftsmen the order to depart. The wagon groaned under its weight as it began to move forward. And as the sound of the wagon faded away, a softer sound reached Simon's ears.

The hiss of the burning fuse.

14

THE RAFTMASTER'S ATTACK WAS SO SUDDEN THAT Kuisl didn't turn aside until the last moment. The sun was shining straight into his eyes, forcing him to squint and rely on instinct alone. As Kuisl dodged to the left, he felt the katzbalger whiz by just inches from his face. At his feet lay Teuber, the bolt through his chest, his shirt soaked in blood, staring glassy-eyed at the two combatants.

Kuisl reached for the old, beat-up rapier on his belt. From the corner of his eye he could see Lettner preparing for another attack. The hangman unsheathed his weapon just as the raftmaster came at him from the left, where Kuisl was exposed. The rapier and the katzbalger met with a loud clatter in the air, and the battle raged back and forth.

Kuisl could feel sweat streaming down his back, fever pulsing through his body, and his left arm hanging down like a dead tree branch. Had he been in better condition, he might have been a match for Philipp Lettner. Kuisl had always been the stronger of the two, but his former second in command was known to compensate for this deficiency with excessive cruelty.

Now, weakened from torture, however, the hangman was hopelessly outmatched. The last twenty-five years hadn't softened or fattened Philipp but had made him as sinewy and hard as a polished walnut. To make matters worse, his brother was still lingering up in the steeple, his eyes flashing down on the two opponents. His crossbow lay in arm's reach on the windowsill, and Kuisl assumed the enormous man could load it again in no time.

"Does my brother frighten you?" Philipp Lettner bared his white teeth. Relentlessly he forced Kuisl toward the church with his katzbalger. "Don't forget, Friedrich is a monster of your own creation. You thought he'd burned to death back then in that farmhouse, didn't you? But my brother is strong—strong and tough, just like all Lettners. He fought his way out of the smoking ruins and pulled me down from the tree, after your hasty departure, that is. But for Karl, our youngest, help came too late. *This* is for Karl."

Kuisl didn't notice Lettner draw a dagger from his belt and prepare to strike the hangman's stomach. Only at the last moment did Kuisl knock the blade aside with his left arm, causing severe pain to return to his shoulder. When Kuisl's vision went black, he had to kick blindly at his opponent, striking him in the stomach. Moaning, Lettner staggered backward, stumbling over the crumbling ruin of a farmhouse wall.

Without pausing, the hangman took advantage of the unexpected reprieve and ran toward the ruined church. If he was to stand any chance at all against the mercenary, it would be with a surprise attack. Perhaps there was a hiding place in the church ruins, somewhere he could seek cover.

The ruins were enveloped in a muted light that filtered through partially collapsed roof beams, where swallows and pigeons had come to nest. Ivy wound like a venomous snake around what remained of the nave's left aisle. The right wing was in better shape; a charred, life-size wooden cross still hung on the wall there. But there, too, the church windows were like lifeless black eyes, overgrown with blackberry bushes that allowed only a glimmer of light to penetrate. Moldy leaves fluttered down from the ceiling, and Kuisl could hear bees buzzing about somewhere.

Toward the front Kuisl discovered a stone altar that, absent its altar cloth, Eucharist monstrance, and gilded finery, looked like the sacrificial stage for some pagan rite. The hangman ran and crouched behind it to catch his breath, his back tucked against the side facing away from the pews.

Soon Kuisl heard footsteps, though he didn't realize at first that they came not from the entrance but from the church spire. Pressed tight against the altar's edge, he peered into the right aisle, toward the crumbling door of the steeple ruins, just as an enormous figure emerged from behind a pile of moss-covered rocks.

It was Friedrich Lettner.

The man aimed his loaded crossbow straight at the altar. Kuisl ducked as a bolt whizzed within millimeters of his nose, boring into the wall next to him and sending shards of stone flying in all directions.

"You know something, Kuisl? My brother shouldn't get to have all the fun for himself, now should he?" Friedrich's deep voice echoed through the ruined church. "I'll nail you to the cross with these bolts, then burn the eyes out of your head. Too bad the Regensburg executioner won't be able to watch. I'll bet he's never seen a torture technique like that." Kuisl heard a soft creak — one he'd heard many times before — the sound of the crossbow crank as Friedrich Lettner loaded a new bolt.

"How long I've waited for this moment, Kuisl!" Friedrich said as he casually turned the crank. "Philipp didn't think I should take the raft back to Regensburg with you; he thought you might recognize me. But someone had to deliver the letter, after all. And besides . . ." His laughter was harsh, almost a rattle, as if the flames from that farmhouse long ago had scarred his throat as well. "The way I look, my own mother wouldn't even recognize me."

"Shut your mouth, Friedrich! You talk too much!" It was the voice of Philipp Lettner, who had entered the church in the meanwhile. He held his hand to his hip, and his face was contorted with pain; he'd apparently injured himself falling over the wall outside. "Load your crossbow. The dog may be cornered, but he's still dangerous."

Grumbling something incomprehensible, Friedrich began to crank the crossbow again.

As another wave of fever washed over him, Kuisl considered his options here behind the altar. He'd run straight into their trap! Once Friedrich's bow was readied — no more than a few moments from now — Philipp would flush him out from behind the altar like a rat. The hangman had no doubt the bolt would hit its mark this time. Friedrich made quite clear with his first shot that he hadn't forgotten how to wield a crossbow. Kuisl bit his lip; the fever had made him very agitated. He had little time before his fate would be sealed, by either the crossbow or the katzbalger.

Is this the end? he thought. *Here, where my new life began, will it also come to an end?*

Again he risked a glance from behind the altar. Philipp Lettner waited at the church door with sword raised. Friedrich, still cranking his crossbow, would be ready in a matter of moments. Kuisl studied Friedrich's face, ravaged by fire, a face he last saw on the trip to Regensburg. The skin had congealed into a hard mass like the burned, cracked bark of an oak, but the eyes behind it remained the same — cold, blue, evil. All around Friedrich wasps were buzzing, evidently disturbed by the commotion in the ruin. They were exceptionally large, black and yellow, and their wings shimmered in the midday sun.

Wasps?

Only now did Kuisl realize these weren't wasps at all but mean-looking hornets, each grown to nearly the length of a man's finger. They buzzed about Friedrich's scabby nose, and again and again the mercenary had to interrupt his cranking to swat them away. Where were they all coming from?

Kuisl's gaze wandered along the wall, over the ivy- and moss-covered stones, until he spotted the nest. It hung from the ceiling, hidden among charred beams and blackberry bushes.

Directly above Friedrich.

"Goddamn it, how long is that going to take?" Philipp Lettner said angrily. "Can't you see we've got him holed up behind the altar like a wounded boar? We've got to drive him out of there together."

"Just one second," Friedrich replied. "The bowstring is so taut the bolt could pass straight through three men like a knife through butter. I just have to—"

He didn't finish his sentence. Like an avenging angel, Kuisl rose up behind the altar and hurled a fist-size rock at the hornets' nest. The stone made a direct hit, and the nest swayed and finally fell to the ground at Friedrich's feet, where it burst open like a full wine pouch.

Hundreds of furious hornets swarmed out and enveloped Friedrich Lettner in a dark, tremulous lethal cloud. With a shout he dropped the crossbow and raised his hands to cover his face, but the hornets were already busily exploring his scars.

The seething black-and-yellow mass stung the man's face over and over.

Simon heard the fuse crackle as it burned inexorably toward the entrance to the mill. Through a crack in the door he thought he could see the gleam of gunpowder about to ignite. Having reached the door, the spark traveled now along the fuse toward the pile of flour, wood shavings, and small boards Silvio had positioned at the end of the cord.

In desperation the medicus thrashed about, but his bonds wouldn't give a fraction of an inch. He tried to slither to the door, only to find the Venetian had also tethered him to a beam. The rope jerked him back, and he collapsed, exhausted. Flour drifted like a white fog among the remaining barrels, sacks, and crates, one of which — Simon was painfully aware — contained several pounds of gunpowder just waiting to explode.

"Help! Doesn't anyone hear me?" he croaked hoarsely, though he knew it was pointless. The rumbling and pounding of the Wöhrd mill wheels would drown out even the loudest shout. Though the huge grain mill still ground away, in just a few moments it would burst with a single thunderous clap — likely the last sound the medicus would ever hear.

But maybe it won't explode at all, Simon thought. Maybe it will just catch fire and I'll burn to death, slowly. If I don't suffocate first, that is . . . Good Lord, at least let the mill blow up and spare me the longer agony.

By now sparks had eaten their way along the fuse into the mill proper. The dust was so thick Simon could hear the crackling flame better than he could see it.

Now . . . The time is at hand.

With a loud crash the door swung open. The air was too thick to see exactly who was there, but Simon could make out an oddly familiar figure through the haze.

"Dzoo have any idea what cheeth like that cosht?" the voice lisped. "I should really let you roasht right here, but then who'd fix my cheeth?"

"Nathan!" Simon shouted. "Good God, Nathan, here I am! The fuse! Everything's about to blow up!"

"Then we chuddn't waysht any chime!"

With a little knife, the beggar king severed the rope that

bound Simon to the beam. Then he grabbed the medicus, threw him over his shoulder, and made for the exit. Stooped and groaning, he cleared the door and staggered another dozen steps before tossing his heavy bundle roughly behind a pile of boards.

"Ouch," Simon shouted. "Watch what you're doing! You want to break all my —?"

At that very moment a loud explosion shook the entire island with such force the medicus was temporarily deafened. Entranced, he watched an enormous fireball rise into the sky. Splinters of wood and stone — even entire sections of walls — flew through the air above him. The blast was so strong that even behind the pile of boards where he crouched, Nathan was blown back like a frail sapling. Hot air smothered them like a dragon's deadly breath as beams and boards rained down on them.

"Quick, letch's get out of here," Nathan cried into the deadly storm. His voice was muffled, as if he were shouting through a heavy woolen blanket.

"How?" Simon shouted back. "I'm still tied up!"

Cursing loudly, the beggar king lifted him onto his shoulder again and carried him away from the fire. Hidden behind a hazelnut bush at a safe distance, they watched the conflagration. The mill was no more than a pile of rubble now, and flames rose high in the air like a bonfire on Saint John's Eve. Even here, more than a hundred paces away, the heat was palpable.

"How — how did you find me?" Simon finally gasped after what seemed an eternity.

"I knew . . . damn!" Nathan poked around in his mouth for a while until he seemed half satisfied. "My people were watching you as you left for the Wöhrd and alerted me right away," he said, more clearly now. "Actually I put a price on your head. No one who punches Nathan the Wise in the face goes unpunished!" He mockingly wagged his finger at Simon, but his eyes were cool, almost threatening. "And then I was rather curious about what you might be doing down here in secret all by yourself, so I

sent the boys home and followed you myself. Even a blind man
could read your tracks in the sawdust. And what do I find here?
This Venetian ambassador fleeing with a loaded wagon and my
trusted medicus nearly blown to pieces in Regensburg's largest
mill. An explanation is in order, at the very least."

"And if I don't feel like explaining?" Simon replied.

Nathan shrugged. "Then I'll toss you back into the fire,
trussed up as you are. You're not in a very good position to negotiate, are you?"

"Very well, then." Simon sighed. "I know now what's so special about this powder and why everyone's been trying to get
their hands on it. You probably already know the secret, too."

He then told the beggar king all he'd learned. Nathan listened attentively, but his face betrayed nothing. When Simon
finished, the leader of the Regensburg beggars just stood there
for a long time, picking his nose. "As God is my witness, that's
the most insane plan I ever heard," he muttered finally, counting
off on his fingers the puzzling series of events. "So, this madman
wants to poison the entire Reichstag—"

"Oh, don't pretend you're so surprised to hear all this!"
Simon interrupted angrily. "I'm sure you knew even before I did
what this powder was! I know you're in league with the various
factions at large in the city. Tell me, who ordered you to spy on
us?"

Nathan raised his eyebrows, amused. "Ah, so that's why you
left so hastily! I should have guessed." He raised his hand in a
solemn oath. "I swear by Saint Martin, patron saint of beggars, I
had no idea about any of this. Anyway, this is hardly the time for
sermons." He pointed at the burning remains of the mill. Guards
who had begun to arrive from the Stone Bridge were immobi-
lized at the sight of the catastrophe. It was far too late to save the
mill; all that could be done now was to prevent the fire from
spreading to the surrounding buildings.

"It's only a matter of time before that pack of morons over

there discovers us," the beggar king said. "As far as they're concerned, you've already set fire to half the city, and if they find you here now, you'll most certainly be eviscerated, drawn, quartered, and burned as the infamous Regensburg arsonist. At least this way you'd go down in the city's history, and in a few hundred years people will probably still be reading about you. That's something to consider."

Simon, lost in thought, mumbled something unintelligible.

"What are you muttering about?" Nathan asked. "Didn't you hear me? We've got to get away from here as fast as we can!"

"I'm wondering where Silvio may have taken Magdalena and the ergot," Simon said softly. "He was talking about some alternative plan, one that would claim far more victims. What the devil could that be?"

"Maybe he wants to make some other use of the ergot," Nathan replied with a shrug. "He could slip it into wine or beer, or God knows what else."

Simon shook his head. "With wine or beer, he'd have to find a willing brewer or vintner to play along, and that's much too risky. Things didn't work out too well with Master Baker Haberger, as you know. It has to be something much simpler. But what?"

He paused, trying to recall Silvio's last words as he left Simon to die in the mill. What was it again the Venetian had said exactly?

Man does not live by bread alone . . .

What do humans need to survive? Something to eat, a roof over their heads, a fire for warmth, water . . .

Water.

Simon slapped his forehead. "Of course!" he exclaimed. "Everyone in Regensburg needs water! For washing, drinking, brewing . . . Silvio intends to dump the ergot into the city wells—it's the only way he can really be sure everyone in the Reichstag will come into contact with it!"

Nathan shook his head, thinking. "How can he do that?" he wondered. "There are wells all over Regensburg. Will he go to each one individually and pour his poison in? Somebody would surely notice that."

"Of course not! He'll have to introduce the ergot into the water *before* it gets to the wells . . ." Simon stopped for a moment, then asked excitedly, "Is there a spring somewhere around here that could be the city water supply? A reservoir? An aquifer perhaps?"

"I don't know about an aquifer," Nathan replied. "But—"

"What is it? Speak up!"

The beggar king's mouth stretched into a broad grin, and his one remaining crooked gold tooth sparkled in the midday sun. "Of course, it's a real possibility. This Venetian is a sly old fox indeed."

"What do you mean?" Simon asked. "Magdalena's life is at stake! Speak up before I throttle you!"

Nathan gave the medicus a look of pity. "How will you do that, seeing as you're tied up?"

He bent down to Simon. "I'll make a deal with you. I'll untie you and tell you where Silvio took your sweetheart. But in return, when this is all over, you'll have a look at my teeth and make them look exactly as before. Promise?"

"I'll personally make you a brand-new set of teeth, if necessary," Simon promised. "Now cut these damned ropes!"

Magdalena heard the explosion as the wagon was rumbling over the Stone Bridge. Bound and gagged, she lay among sacks in the middle of the wagon and winced when she heard the first ear-splitting sound. Something in her snapped.

God! Simon! she thought. *It can't be! Not Simon, not after everything we've been through together!*

To the last second she'd been hoping for a miracle; she'd prayed to each of the Fourteen Holy Helpers to intercede, to keep the mill from exploding, but her miracle hadn't happened. The building had erupted around her beloved Simon, with whom she had fled to Regensburg to live and grow old.

Why in God's name did we ever leave home?

Tears streamed down her cheeks, mixing with sweat, flour, and soil, while all around her shouts went up. Even under the sacks she could hear the muffled babble of many voices and the pounding of men's feet as they ran to the bridge railing to gape at the crackling, fiery drama.

"It's the big grain mill on the Wöhrd!" Magdalena could hear someone shout. "I bet the flour exploded. My grandfather once told me about something like that happening . . ."

"No doubt the miller was drunk again . . ."

"He was smoking! That new, hellish tobacco they're importing! Lit his pipe and blew himself straight up to heaven, along with home and grain."

"Step aside, folks! A shipment for city hall, make way!"

The last voice belonged to Silvio, who shouted and cracked his whip as he tried to get through the gathering crowd. Magdalena had heard him bribe the watchman at the ramp with a handful of clinking coins. The people up here were so busy watching and gossiping about the catastrophe that the large wagon barely attracted any attention.

They weren't stopped at the gate leading from the bridge into the city, either. As the wagon rumbled on through the streets and alleys, Magdalena heard the occasional sound of marching feet—presumably guards rushing to the Wöhrd from all parts of the city—and bells ringing somewhere. No one seemed interested in the overloaded wagon carrying Silvio and the five raftsmen. Once in a while a hand pressed to Magdalena's mouth—apparently to check that she was still breathing—then took the opportunity to grope her breasts or her legs or tighten her bonds.

Finally the wagon came to a halt. Magdalena tried to guess

where they were, based on the sounds around them, but except for distant voices and bells she heard nothing. Her whole body itched; bugs crawled through her hair. She couldn't move a muscle. She lay there like a living sack of grain, breathing in dust, flour, and ground ergot.

"Haaaalt! In the name of the city, come down from the wagon!"

It was the commanding voice of a gate guard, clearly used to giving orders and having them heeded, too. Magdalena held her breath. Could he be her salvation? Perhaps one of the raftsmen had told them, and now the entire city was looking for the poison!

"What is this all about?" Silvio asked indignantly. "Don't you see we're in a hurry? Open the gate!"

"I'm sorry, but we have to search every wagon leaving the city," the watchman replied. "The Regensburg monster has escaped, the one responsible for the double murder in the Weißgerbergraben. We've got to be sure he doesn't flee the city."

Magdalena clenched her fists. At least they hadn't caught her father yet! But why was Silvio trying to leave the city with the wagon? She'd assumed they were on their way to city hall or perhaps the Heuport House. What could the Venetian do with the poisoned flour outside of town?

"A worthy task, constable," Silvio replied, now distinctly more polite. "But with me that's really not necessary. My men loaded the sacks themselves. Do you think the Venetian ambassador would provide cover for a murderer?" He laughed softly, and again Magdalena heard coins clinking.

"I—I—didn't recognize you," the guard gasped. "Excuse me, Your Eminence. But this is just a modest little wagon, and I would have expected you—"

"A little unannounced trip to the country; I do like to see what my servants are up to. Now would you please let us pass?"

"Well . . . naturally, Your Excellency. And a good day to you!"

The wagon rolled on again while Magdalena cursed through her gag. That was her last chance! Silvio would soon be force-feeding her the ergot, and what awaited her then? She thought of Resl, the maid of Schongau baker Berchtholdt, imprisoned in her own nightmares, her limbs turning black, crying and howling until the dear Lord released her from her pain at last.

Would that be her fate as well?

After about another quarter-hour the wagon stopped and the raftsmen climbed down, whispering softly to one another. Evidently they'd reached their destination. Bags were hastily offloaded and carried away. Squinting at the blinding sunlight, Magdalena took a while to recognize Silvio standing over her, smiling.

"If you could promise me you'd be quiet, I just might be persuaded to remove your gag," he said, pushing a lock of sweaty, matted hair from her face. He plucked a bug from her hair and crushed it between his fingers. "Do you think that's possible?"

Magdalena nodded silently. When the Venetian untied the knot behind her head and pulled the gag out of her mouth, she spat in his face.

"Murderer, damn you! You've killed Simon! For that you'll roast a thousand years in hell. I'll rip your puny balls right off, I'll—mmmmhhhh!"

Silvio forced the gag back into her mouth. "That wasn't our agreement," he whispered. "So once again, will you keep silent?"

Tears of anger welled up in Magdalena's eyes, but she nodded a second time. When Silvio removed the dirty rag again, she kept quiet.

"Take this stubborn woman down below!" Silvio ordered. One of the raftsmen tossed Magdalena over his shoulder like just another sack of flour and climbed down from the wagon, panting.

Though she was upside down now, the hangman's daughter could see that the wagon had come to rest on a wide road that wound through fields and meadows. The city wall lay less than a half-mile behind them. Nearby, on a hill that rose over rolling meadows, stood a strange, three-legged structure. Lifeless bodies hung from it, swaying in the gentle summer breeze. Despite the midsummer heat, Magdalena shivered.

My God, the Regensburg gallows hill! What do these insane men intend to do with me?

But the raftsman headed off in another direction entirely, along a little path where bushes, red poppies, and yellow broom grew wild, toward a stone staircase that led underground. Silvio, who was already waiting at the bottom of the stairs, opened a heavy iron door and bowed slightly as Magdalena entered a dark room on the raftsman's back.

"After you, *bella donna*," he purred. "Welcome to your new home. You'll be spending the next several days and weeks here. It may be a bit damp, but we all must make some sacrifices in the name of science, mustn't we?"

They were standing in a subterranean room built of huge stone blocks and filled with the sound of splashing water. The broad-shouldered raftsman set Magdalena down roughly on a stone bench and lit a torch. Only now could she see that the splashing came from a small waterfall that cascaded down the wall and emptied into a shallow basin at the back of the room. Stone tablets were mounted on the walls, but it was too dark to read the inscriptions. Behind the basin an arched passageway led to another vaulted area from which a loud rushing sound emanated.

Working silently, the five raftsmen carried the bags of flour past her and Silvio, through the knee-deep basin and into the rear vault. When they finished, the Venetian signaled to them.

"Stand guard up above. Only Jeremias will stay with us." He pointed at a hefty raftsman to their left, who nodded politely and planted himself next to Magdalena with arms crossed. "Just in case you should refuse to take your water cure," he reassured the hangman's daughter. "As you know, patients can be a bit uncooperative at times."

With a creak, the iron door swung closed.

"Don't worry." The Venetian fetched a tin cup from his pocket. "You won't have to eat any flour. You'll drink the ergot diluted with water. Sadly, I can't offer you wine, as that would distort the effect." Silvio took out a silver teaspoon, scooped some flour from an open sack, and stirred the pale blue powder into the cup.

"We still don't know exactly how strong the poison is in humans," he declared, "and above all, how fast it acts. If we dilute the ergot with well water rather than baking it into bread, it will presumably take effect later." He sniffed the cup and shrugged. "We expect the Reichstag to last a few weeks, and that should give us enough time. For you that means, unfortunately, the experiment may be a bit prolonged, but your hallucinations promise to be quite interesting in such an environment. May I?" Silvio set the cup down, pulled out a dagger, and with a flourish cut the ropes binding Magdalena's feet. "Since you'll be here a few weeks, you ought to be allowed to move about freely at least. You simply must have a look around your new home. It's really . . . well, come see for yourself."

Silvio climbed over the edge of the basin and waded toward the dark vault in the back.

He really intends to lock me in this place for the next few weeks and force me to drink cup after cup of this damned ergot! Magdalena thought. She closed her eyes, hoping to suppress her growing panic. The noise of rushing water was already getting on her nerves, and the echo in the underground vault intensified the volume until it sounded like a single towering waterfall.

How long will it take the nightmares to overwhelm me? And what will they be like down here, in this pit?

Magdalena decided to keep quiet and followed the Venetian and his stocky companion into the vault in back. She ducked under the low archway, then took an involuntary step backward.

The room was gigantic.

Torches illuminated a narrow corridor at regular intervals until, past where the eye could see, the light was swallowed in darkness. The vault had to be over a half-mile long. Water shimmered across the floor, but she couldn't tell how deep it might be. Even more water streamed into the basin from holes and pipes in the wall—some small, some large—and the sound of splashing filled the room, echoing from the walls and ceiling. To either side, more than two dozen flour sacks were lined neatly along narrow elevated ledges.

"Welcome to your new home," Silvio shouted over the roar. "The entire world drinks from this spring!"

He ordered Jeremias to hand him the tin cup, then pointed at the sacks. "We'll store the ergot here until the Reichstag begins, and then we'll slowly start dissolving the thirty one-hundred-pound bags in the water. You needn't be afraid that anyone will find you down here, since I'm the only one with a key. And now . . ." With a solemn gesture Silvio held the cup under a small stream. Carefully he swirled the water to dissolve the ergot, then put the cup to Magdalena's lips. "It's time for our experiment. One cup a day. Be good now, and drink up."

With her hands still bound, Magdalena turned her head from side to side. Nevertheless, Jeremias held her in his viselike grip while Silvio maneuvered the cup.

"Oh, by the way . . ." Silvio was speaking almost directly into her ear now. "I do hope very much that your visions are not all gloomy and gruesome. I've heard ergot can stimulate physical desire. If that's the case, do let me know. I'd be glad to share a few dreams with you."

The cup had reached Magdalena's lips.

• • •

Screaming, Friedrich Lettner writhed on the floor of the ruined church as hornets swarmed over his face and upper body. He thrashed about as if possessed, crushing dozens of the insects in his swollen hands, even as new ones kept coming.

Meanwhile Kuisl sought shelter behind the altar, out of sight of the angry hornets. Leaning against the huge stone slab, he peered out to observe an utterly bewildered Philipp Lettner. Only after a few moments did the raftmaster run toward Friedrich and attempt to swat the hornets away from his brother's shirt collar. But in doing so he was stung several times himself.

"Damn you, Kuisl!" Philipp Lettner shouted, waving his katzbalger through the air as if warding off invisible ghosts. "Damn you and your whole clan! Damn you forever!"

Kuisl had no time to waste now. Sword raised, he ran toward his opponent, who was still preoccupied with the hornets circling around him while trying to help his brother. The raftmaster cast an irritated sidelong glance at Kuisl, then, with a growl, left Friedrich to his own devices as he prepared himself for battle. A cloud of hornets circled his head and clouded his vision.

"You damned son of a whore!" Lettner shouted, brushing away a few angry buzzing insects with his left hand. "For this, Jakob, I'll slit your belly open and hang your entrails from the church steeple."

"Spare the talk and fight, will you?"

Without another word, Kuisl lunged at his enemy. He felt the hornets sting his arms, face, and back, but the pain was eclipsed by his fever and the excitement of battle. The hangman was horrified to realize that the clanging swords aroused something like lust in him.

Just as before . . . the smell of blood, the screams of dying men. It's like a fog that suddenly engulfs a man — only much clearer . . .

He could see Philipp Lettner clearly in front of him now, but the former mercenary's movements seemed strangely slow. Kuisl lunged with his sword, flailing away at his opponent, who con-

tinued to retreat, for the first time with fear in his eyes. Finally
Lettner's back was to the wall, and the two warriors stood face-
to-face, less than an inch apart, with crossed swords.

"The letter in the bishop's palace," Kuisl gasped. "What was
that sentence supposed to mean? Did you really think I would
believe such utter nonsense?"

Philipp Lettner's eyes lit up as he flashed his wolfish grin
again.

"It's the truth, just as sure as I'm standing here before you!"
With great effort the raftmaster forced Kuisl's sword a hand's
width to the side. "I had to make only a few quick calculations. I
learned from the Venetian how old your daughter is — twenty-
four! Barely a year before that, late in the fall, we were here in
Weidenfeld. Your Anna had screamed at the time, but believe
me, Jakob, they were screams of desire."

"You dirty lying bastard!" Anger blinded Kuisl like a corro-
sive poison. Over and over a line flashed through his mind, a line
from the letter slipped into his pocket just the night before in the
bishop's palace . . . That one line hurt more than all the torture
he'd experienced in the Regensburg dungeon.

*Kiss my daughter Magdalena for me . . . her mother tasted like a
sweet ripe plum . . .*

"Bastard!"

Kuisl shoved Lettner so hard he cried out in surprise as he
staggered back to the wall. This put the raftmaster just beyond
Kuisl's reach, so Lettner took a deep breath, planted his feet
firmly, and braced himself for the next attack. Scornfully he spat
on the ground and swung the katzbalger through the air while
his brother still rolled around on the ground, howling.

"I may be a dirty bastard," Philipp Lettner whispered, "but
I'm not a liar. I took Anna-Maria like a steer takes a cow. And
what do I learn all these years later? That shortly after our rendezvous pretty little Anna was pregnant. What a coincidence!"
He licked his lips and giggled. "Take another look at your daugh-

ter, Jakob! How could she not be mine? Her soft eyes; her matted, always-snarled hair; her full lips. She doesn't take after you at all, does she?"

"She takes after her mother," Kuisl said between clenched teeth as doubts started to grow in his mind. Anna-Maria never told him the name of the village she came from, and that was likely why he'd forgotten the name Weidenfeld completely. He knew she'd experienced horrible things there, but just what and *how* horrible these things were she'd never said.

She tasted like a sweet ripe plum . . .

Blood-red spots appeared before Kuisl's eyes and his head began to spin.

I can't let him get to me, he thought. *He wants me to lose control . . . But why else would Anna have never spoken about it? Her sad face, when I took my baby girl in my arms and sang her to sleep . . . I can't let him get to me . . .*

"She's my daughter," the hangman replied flatly. "My daughter, my—"

"Maybe you're right," Lettner interrupted. "Perhaps she isn't mine after all. Or maybe she is." He chuckled. "You know something funny? A while ago, in the bathhouse, I very nearly burned her alive, along with that little quack. I was there just to cover my own tracks. When someone came in, I hid up in the attic but later ran down to smoke the intruders out of the cellar. By God, I didn't know it was Magdalena at the time, but when the Venetian told me about it the next morning, I really did feel bad." The raftmaster laughed loudly. "Whether you believe me or not, I like the girl; I feel close to her. I could have killed her a dozen times, but I didn't. And do you know why? Because I know I'm her father."

"Never!" the hangman yelled. "You—you damned liar!"

Philipp Lettner sighed theatrically. "Oh, Jakob, why must you be so pigheaded? Let's agree that Magdalena has two fathers.

That's more than fair, isn't it?" He snickered when he saw Kuisl clutching his sword so hard the blood drained from his fingers.

"I've sown doubt in your mind, haven't I?" the raftmaster said. "I've given you a wound that will never hea . From now on, whenever you look at your daughter, you'll see my face, too. That's my revenge. Now, *fight!*" Philipp Lettner rushed the hangman like a man possessed, his teeth bared, holding the katz-balger out in front of him.

Kuisl lowered his sword feebly to the ground and, with a vacant look in his eyes, awaited the final blow.

"How long will it take us to get to this damned wellspring?" Simon asked Nathan, gasping as they hurried along the low corridor. "That madman may already be forcing ergot down Magdalena's throat!"

Just as they had the last time they visited the Wöhrd together, the beggar and the medicus made their way through the underwater tunnel connecting the city with the island. Foul water stood knee-deep in places in the muddy passageway, and falling bits of stone kept reminding Simon that only a thin wall of rock, clay, and dirt separated them from the Danube. And the decrepit bricks and beams of the ceiling weren't reassuring.

Stooping, the beggar king ran ahead, carrying a lantern that bobbed like a will-o'-the-wisp lighting the way. Nevertheless, Simon managed to stumble several times. At one point his boot stuck on a half-submerged stone, toppling him over into cold brown muck. Grinning, Nathan held the lantern up to the medicus's mud-splattered face.

"If you keep doing that, we're never going to get there," he squawked, his voice still hoarse from all the smoke at the mill. "The wellspring and the new chamber they've built around it lie to the south of the city, in the fields near the gallows hill. We still have quite a ways to go."

"Near the gallows hill?" Simon asked as he stood up again and wiped off his jacket as best he could. "Not exactly the ideal place for a freshwater spring, is it? Are you really certain we'll find them there?"

Nodding, Nathan marched ahead with the lantern. "Quite sure. The well chamber at Prüller Heights was built only a few years ago. It feeds into the fountain on Haid Square, as well as the bishop's palace, but most importantly, it feeds into city hall. If someone wishes to poison the Reichstag, that's where he'll be. Ouch!" He bumped his head on a jagged rock on the low ceiling. "Moreover, our dear Venetian friend will be absolutely undisturbed there. Except for a fountain guard, no one has access to the chamber. As far as I know, it's under lock and key. And because it lies deep underground, Silvio can store the stuff there for months and simply pour his poison slowly into the spring."

"A perfect place to imprison and poison someone with ergot over the coming days and weeks," Simon mused. "Come, we must hurry!"

"Don't worry. And if you didn't have to lie down and take your mud baths all the time, we'd be there faster," Nathan replied.

Finally they reached the end of the tunnel. As before, they climbed a matted fishnet like a rope ladder to a hole in the ceiling. They emerged at last into the roomy trunk that smelled as badly of fish now as it had a few days ago.

When Nathan opened the lid, fresh air rushed in. Simon eagerly took several deep breaths before he ventured a look outside. Barrels, bales, and crates towered all around them, and in the distance they could hear shouting. Every now and again it sounded as though someone passed close by.

Nathan whistled between his fingers, and shortly thereafter they heard a whistled reply. The beggar king nodded contentedly.

"Good fellows," he said. "Told them to wait here for me. The men will be glad to see you again—most of them, in any case."

Simon swallowed hard. Soon Hans Reiser, Brother Paulus, and two other beggars emerged from behind the barrels, waving and grinning when they caught sight of Simon. Hans Reiser, whose eyes were apparently fully healed now, spread his arms wide to welcome the medicus.

"Simon!" he cried out. "You just up and left us and knocked out the king's teeth to boot! That's no way to behave! And where have you left Magdalena?"

"This isn't the time for long explanations," Nathan said. "I've forgiven Simon and his girl. Everything else I'll tell you along the way." He looked around. "Where are Trembling Johann and Lame Hanres?"

"Down at the tavern by the Stone Bridge," Hans replied. "A great day for thieves. The mill on the Wöhrd is burning, and everyone's standing there gawking at it and—"

"I know," the beggar king snapped. "Quit blathering and get the others. We'll all meet outside Peter's Gate. Now, get moving."

Hans headed off with a shrug, while Simon hurried through the city with the other four. As word spread around town that the Wöhrd was on fire, people came running from every direction to congregate on the raft landing, making it difficult for the ragged band of beggars to navigate the narrow streets. But no one stopped them, and not a single person wasted so much as a glance on Simon.

How comforting! I look just like one of them, he thought as he glanced down at his wet, mud-stained jacket and sighed. *When this is all over, I'll be lucky if the beggars let me sleep at Neupfarr Church Square and maybe bring me a piece of stale bread now and then.*

Soon they arrived on the other side of the city at Peter's Gate, where guards were still searching farmers' wagons. By now Nathan had told the other beggars all that had happened at the mill. Whistling cheerfully, he turned left toward a tumbledown shed that leaned against the city wall, looking as if it might collapse at any moment.

Carefully the beggar king opened its rotten wooden door and motioned to the others to follow. Inside, Simon was astonished to find a narrow door in the city wall just wide enough for one man to pass through. Nathan tapped on the door — two long knocks and three short — and soon a bearded, boozy-eyed guard appeared.

"So many of you?" the man asked, assessing the group with bloodshot eyes. "This will cost you extra." Suspiciously he eyed Simon, who just stood there, soaking wet and trembling. "You look somehow familiar to me. Where — "

"This is Quivering August," Nathan interjected, pressing a few dirty coins into the hand of the confused guard. "He just joined us, the poor old dog. He has the English sweating sickness and probably won't last long."

The guard stepped back a pace in horror. "Good Lord, Nathan! Couldn't you have told me that sooner? Get out of town, and take your infected friends with you!"

The man crossed himself and spat. Giggling, the beggars stepped out into the turnip and wheat fields that bordered the city wall. The door slammed shut behind them.

"These one-man doors are a wonderful invention!" Nathan gushed, as they turned southward onto a broad highway. When they spotted Hans and two other beggars waiting for them in a radiant field of wheat, Simon assumed they'd made it out of the city through a similar door.

"Anyone can leave the city, any time of day or night, if he pays enough," the beggar king told Simon as they continued on. "That is, if he's not wanted for murders or intending to poison the Reichstag. But even then, if the price is right — I love this city!"

He spread his arms to heaven and, still whistling, set out at the head of the strange retinue — a dirty, ragged band of men, some hobbling, some babbling, but all determined to save the great city of Regensburg from destruction.

It seemed as if Philipp Lettner had pronounced a curse on Jakob Kuisl that made his arms and legs as heavy as lead.

The pain returned to the hangman's left shoulder, compounded by the hornet stings on his back and face. He staggered backward, raising his right hand mechanically to ward off his opponent's blows, but it was only a matter of time before Lettner would find an opening and deal him a *coup de grâce*.

Friedrich Lettner still lay on the floor in the middle of the church, gasping for air. The hornet stings seemed to affect the broad-shouldered giant much more than his slender brother. Friedrich's hands had swollen to twice their normal size, and he was vomiting saliva and bile, his breath constricted, as if someone had clamped iron buckles across his chest and was pulling them tighter and tighter. The worst, however was his bloated, scarred face, which glistened bright red from the stings, like the head of a freshly slaughtered pig. Out of the corner of his eye Kuisl noticed the man had started to twitch and seemed to be growing weaker. Once more Friedrich arched his back as if he'd been struck, then collapsed like a monstrous doll.

"For Friedrich, you scoundrel!"

With a shout, Philipp Lettner lunged, his *katzbalger* cutting through the air toward Kuisl's head. The hangman ducked this blow only to be faced with yet another.

"For Karl!"

Again Kuisl stepped aside just in time, but his movements were slower now and he was tiring. The fever came and went in waves—the ground beneath his feet as soft as butter—and he sensed he might not be able to fend off the next blow. Then his legs gave out beneath him, and he fell to his knees. Raising his head with great effort, he found Lettner standing over him, gloating, his sword held high in both hands. Lettner drew his hands back and to the right to get a good angle on Jakob's neck. Spellbound, the hangman stared back at his enemy; Lettner was about to do to Kuisl what Kuisl had been perfecting his whole life.

A clean decapitation.

"You don't really deserve such a merciful death, Kuisl," Philipp Lettner growled. "I'm doing this only for old times' sake. Well, that and—" He bared his fanglike teeth. "How many people can say they've beheaded an honest-to-God executioner? I'm sure the devil himself would have a laugh at this. So off to hell with you!"

Kuisl lowered his head, closed his eyes, and waited for the blow that would end it all.

It didn't come.

Instead, an almost ethereal silence prevailed, one interrupted only by a loud metallic whir. When Kuisl looked up, he was astonished to find Philipp Lettner standing before him, wide-eyed and dazed. The katzbalger lay on the church floor. Lettner clutched desperately at a charred, splintered beam that protruded from his stomach, staring down in disbelief, as if he just couldn't comprehend he might really be dying—as if, up until this moment, he'd never imagined his own death could be part of some divine plan.

He slowly toppled over and didn't stir again. Once the light left his eyes, they stared blankly at the collapsed roof of the church, where two swallows chirped furiously at each other, then flew off.

Behind Lettner stood Philipp Teuber. Although the Regensburg executioner swayed, he was still standing. He wiped his hands on his bloodstained jacket with care, hands that had wielded the charred wooden cross only moments ago.

"Let's hope that old thing was consecrated," he said, tapping his foot against the raftmaster, who lay impaled on the floor in front of him. Teuber had gored Lettner using the tip of the crucifix like a spear. "Perhaps that will drive the evil out of him," he said.

"For a bastard like that, you'd have to douse him in holy water, then dunk him in the baptismal font—and even that might not do any good," Kuisl answered hoarsely.

Still swaying, the Regensburg executioner smiled. With a stony gaze he regarded the bolt in his chest.

"I . . . don't . . . feel . . . very well," he spluttered. "The bolt . . ."

Kuisl pointed at Friedrich Lettner's corpse where a few hornets still circled about. "At least there won't be another bolt," he said. "Every villain has his weakness, and for this one it wasn't the big arrow but countless little stings. I hope the poison doesn't—"

He broke off as Teuber crashed to the ground like a tower collapsing. He didn't move again.

"My God, Teuber!" Kuisl shouted as he ran over to kneel down alongside his friend. Kuisl tried to concentrate despite his fever. "Don't do this to me! Not now, not after it's all over! What will I tell your wife?" He shook the executioner, but there was no response. "She's going to kill me if I carry you back home like this!"

Teuber opened his eyes once more, and a faint smile crossed his lips. "Not like you . . . deserve . . . anything better . . . you old dog . . ." he managed. Then his head sank, and his breath became a shallow rattle.

"Hey! Wake up, you slacker! Don't go to sleep now, damn you!"

Kuisl leaped up and grabbed Teuber's shirt. At once blood

flowed in dark rivulets over his hands. The bolt was as firmly embedded in Teuber's chest as a carpenter's nail. For a moment Kuisl was almost paralyzed; then it seemed he'd decided what to do.

"Hold off a bit on the dying. I'm coming right back!"

Without another thought about his own wounds or the hornet stings, the hangman ran into the blazing midday heat. A gentle wind moaned through a window opening and echoed through the forest like the cry of a little child. But Kuisl paid no heed to anyone or anything. Frantically he searched the bushes, birches, and willows surrounding the ruined village.

Lady's mantle, yarrow, bloodroot, shepherd's purse . . . I need shepherd's purse!

Teuber's blood wasn't foamy and bright, so the lungs had likely been spared. If Kuisl could find the right herbs, there might still be hope. The most important thing was to stanch the bleeding and prevent infection.

It took the hangman a while to find what he needed in the shadow of an oak, an unremarkable little plant, which he carefully plucked. Shepherd's purse was held to be a true miracle worker, integral to every executioner's pharmacy as far back as anyone knew. With little purse-shaped pods, the plant relieved fever and gout, helped induce labor, and was especially useful in treating open bleeding wounds. When Kuisl had collected enough, he began to tear moss and bark from surrounding trees. He shoved them all, along with a handful of other plants, into his open shirt and ran back to the church where Teuber still lay motionless. When he bent down, Kuisl was relieved to find Teuber still breathing.

"I'm going to pull the bolt out now," he whispered into Teuber's ear. "So clench your teeth and try not to yelp like a washerwoman. Are you ready?"

Teuber nodded almost imperceptibly. "Just my luck that I wind up in the hands of a quack like you . . ."

Kuisl grinned. "This is my revenge for you rancid ointment." Then his face turned serious again. "I can't top the bleeding completely. For the rest we'll have to go back to Regensburg."

"But . . . they'll lock you up again . . . the torture chamber . . ." Teuber stammered, apparently suffering fever dreams
already.

"Don't worry about me. The most important thing now is
that you get better."

As Kuisl tore out the bolt and pressed moss and yarrow to
the open wound, his lips formed a silent prayer.

"There are four of them," Simon whispered, pointing to the
raftsmen crouched lazily among waist-high stalks of rye, list-
lessly carving willow branches. "Do you think we can take them
on?"

Nathan cast a disparaging glance at the thickset, already intoxicated men. "Those fellows? As you know, we fight dirty and
mean. They'll think the sky is falling down around them."

"Very well." Simon nodded. "Magdalena is probably down
below with Silvio and the fifth raftsman. When I give the command, I suggest you attack the men up here while Hans, Brother
Paulus, and I storm the well chamber and take care of the rest. Is
that all right?"

Nathan grinned, showing off his crooked gold tooth. "A
brilliant plan — one I might have thought up myself. No tricks,
no finesse, just bust right in shouting and start thrashing away."

"You idiot!" Simon snapped. "Then tell me what you can
come up with offhand."

"Calm down. Everything will work out." The beggar king
tapped the medicus reassuringly on the shoulder, then whispered
to his men to spread out over the area.

In the course of their long march down the broad highway
and then along the small path across the field, the beggars had
armed themselves with sticks and branches. To their arsenal they

now added pebbles and heavy rocks from the surrounding fields. Then, concealed behind stalks of wheat, broom, and poppies, they approached the raftsmen who were passing the time drinking, chatting, and whittling.

Upon a signal from Nathan, Lame Hannes reached under his tattered shirt for a leather strap with a broad, spoonlike depression in its middle. He laid a flat stone in it, swung the strap in circles overhead, and finally sent the stone soaring toward the raftsmen.

The stone flew through the air like an arrow, striking the forehead of one of the men, who collapsed without a sound. Moments later more stones rained down on the raftsmen. The beggars shouted and ran out from hiding, slashing away at their astonished opponents as Lame Hannes fired more stones with his leather slingshot.

"Now!" Simon ran toward the stairs, followed closely by Hans and Brother Paulus. The medicus stumbled down the steps, coming at last to a heavy arched iron door. Struggling for air, he threw himself against it, only to realize it was already ajar. As the door swung open, he tumbled into a dark torch-lit room that ended in a large basin filled with rushing water. Behind it he saw dim light emerge from a small archway and heard panting and the muffled, high-pitched cries of a woman who sounded as if she'd already gone mad.

It was Magdalena's voice.

As the cup of dissolved ergot approached her lips, the hangman's daughter was at first transfixed with, and paralyzed by, fear. But her will to live reasserted itself: she would *not* resign herself to this fate without a fight. She was still standing with Silvio in the long, flooded passageway, the raftsman Jeremias gripping her head tightly. Magdalena went limp, as if she'd given up.

"Well, then," said Silvio. "Now, it seems like—"

All of a sudden she brought the full force of her right knee to

Silvio's groin. With a gasp, the Venetian collapsed like a pocket-knife, and the tin cup fell to the floor, where it sank in the turbulent water. The burly raftsman saw his leader collapse, was distracted for a moment, and loosened his grip. Magdalena took advantage of the moment to slip eel-like from his grasp. Without a glance backward, she ran for the exit, but the nearly knee-deep water slowed her so that she lost her balance and fell headlong into the basin.

"Stop her, you fool!" Silvio shouted at the confused Jeremias. "The damned bitch! I'm going to stuff her mouth so full of ergot that it comes gushing out of every last pore in her body."

The Venetian sat doubled over on the ledge along the wall, his legs dangling in the water. Magdalena's blow still seemed to cause him a lot of pain. His makeup ran in black and milky-white rivulets down his otherwise well-groomed face, and his sopping wig looked like rotten seaweed in the dim torchlight. Magdalena couldn't help but be reminded of the statue at Heu-port House of the handsome young man from whose back rats, snakes, and toads came crawling out.

It's all a mask, and behind it there's nothing but filth, she thought. *And dumb little slut that I am, I almost fell for it*

She'd just stood up again and was about to slip through the narrow corridor into the anteroom when Jeremias's hand seized her from behind, dragging her inexorably back into the dark vaulted chamber. Silvio had gotten up from the ledge now, and after wiping his nose with his wet shirtsleeve, he reached into a sack of flour.

"No one can say I didn't treat you courteously," he gasped. "But you leave me no other choice, you stubborn wench. Can't you see you're serving a great cause? Your insignificant little life will change the history of this empire forever! No more backward little nation-states governed by their tariffs and narrow minds! At the end of our journey lies a vision of a single state extending from the Black Sea to the Rhine! Once the Grand Vizier has seized Vienna, there will be no stopping him. Those who prepare the path for his victory will receive princely rewards. Don't be so damned stubborn. Submit yourself to a glorious vision!"

"If it's so important to you, why don't you eat this poison yourself!" Magdalena screamed as Jeremias gripped her shoulder tightly and pushed her toward the sacks of flour. Her hands were still tied, but she felt the rope loosening a bit in the water.

Silvio smiled. With smudged makeup and wet, stringy hair, he looked like some kind of evil, bewitched toad. "A nice thought," he said. "Unfortunately the Grand Vizier has plans for me that require I keep a very clear head. And who knows? Perhaps on the far side of madness lies eternal happiness. Just wait and see; you'll thank me for allowing you to sample this divine substance. *And now, open your mouth, damn it!*"

Silvio shouted these final words like a madman, every syllable echoing off the walls many times over. The ambassador had run out of patience. Dripping with sweat, he beckoned Jeremias to throw Magdalena onto the narrow ledge. As Jeremias held her down tightly with both hands, Silvio bent over her to force the flour into her throat like a goose being fattened for slaughter.

Magdalena clenched her teeth, but the Venetian held her nose until she had to open her mouth and gasp desperately for air. At once she gagged on the bitter, damp powder and could feel stomach acid rising in her throat, but she struggled not to swallow. Flour spilled out of her mouth, and she spat and screamed for help.

"Magdalena!"

At first the hangman's daughter thought she was hearing a ghost. It was quite clearly the voice of her dear deceased Simon calling down from heaven. How was this possible? Could the ergot be affecting her already?

Is this what crazy is?

Then in the doorway she spotted a short figure in a soiled

shirt, wearing an unkempt Vandyke and disheveled shoulder-length black hair. Clever black eyes sparkled back at her. If the man before her was an illusion, this ergot was some damn good stuff.

Simon! Is it really you?

Magdalena felt her heart leap. This was no hallucination! Simon was alive and had come to free her! Just a few more steps and . . .

Suddenly she realized Silvio had released her and was sprinting along the slippery ledge toward the entryway. As Simon entered the vault, Silvio picked up a rock and heaved it, striking the medicus hard on the forehead, then charged his surprised opponent with a shout. Both men collapsed in a foaming whirlpool, arms and legs flailing wildly. Magdalena could only watch helplessly as the Venetian held Simon underwater with both hands. The medicus spluttered and thrashed about, but Silvio didn't let go.

"You fool!" the Venetian shouted, his words echoing again through the vault. "You were supposed to have gone up in smoke with the mill. That would have been less painful. Now I'm going to have to drown you like a rat."

Simon surfaced briefly, but Silvio grabbed him and pushed him underwater again. The Venetian's wig had come off completely, revealing thinning hair and a receding hairline. His eyes flashed like those of an evil hobgoblin.

"Pigheaded lowlife!" Silvio yelled. "You just won't accept it's all over. Die now, you stubborn old dog!"

Desperately the hangman's daughter tried to escape Jeremias's clutches, but this time he held her as tightly as if she were bound to the rack. He grinned and bent his pockmarked face close enough that she could smell the wine on his breath.

"If it's true what they say about ergot," he growled, "then over the next few weeks we'll have a lot of fun, you and —"

Disgusted, Magdalena spat the rest of the ergot still stuck be-

tween her teeth and to the roof of her mouth right into the raft-
man's face. Mid-sentence, Jeremias's lips were wide open, and
the sticky little lumps flew straight into his mouth. He coughed,
gagged, and flailed about, apparently fearing he'd been poisoned.

"You whore! You'll pay for that!"

Magdalena rolled off the ledge, disappearing into the dark
ice-cold water and out of Jeremias's reach. When she ran out of
breath, she resurfaced to see that two more figures had arrived in
the meantime. With relief she recognized Hans Reiser and
Brother Paulus, who were beating the raftsman with sticks and
forcing him, step by step, against the wall.

When she turned around again, Simon and Silvio had disappeared.

It took her a while to locate them in the darkness further
back in the vault. In near silence they were fighting in waist-deep
water as torches on the walls cast them in long, distorted shadows. Magdalena couldn't tell which shadow belonged to which
man—they merged into one monstrous silhouette that had
sprung to life and, freed of its earthly form, now stalked ghost-
like up and down the dark corridor. The slender shadow of a
sword rose up, then lunged, yet the other part of the shadow retreated. The second part shoved the first part, and the shadow
split in two again, one half stumbling and falling underwater
and, a moment later, rising to the surface and attacking. For a
brief moment the shadows merged again into a single dense tangle, only to fly back apart and then merge once more.

"Simon! Don't give up! I'm coming to help!"

Magdalena waded through waist-high icy water, which felt
like a deep morass, an endless swamp separating her and her beloved. Through the powerful sound of many rushing streams she
could hear the muted shouts of the beggars and raftsmen behind
her. Frantically she fumbled with the rope around her wrists. It
was loosening, and after a while she was able to slip her hands
free at last.

Meanwhile one of the two combatants seemed to have gained the upper hand. He held the other underwater until the latter's movements grew erratic and devolved into wild convulsions. Now Magdalena was close enough to make out the face of the victor.

It was Silvio, grinning scornfully, his pale face framed by wet, stringy hair. He wore the concentrated, impassive expression of a professional killer. In a few seconds the Venetian would strangle Simon to death.

"Nooooo!" Magdalena shrieked, her voice echoing off the walls. "Simon! My God, Simon!"

"In the name of the city, I order you to stop!"

The hangman's daughter flinched. Turning around, she saw only the raftsman Jeremias, who lay face-down in the water, blood forming a halo on the surface around him and a finger-length bolt protruding from his back. The two beggars alongside him lowered their clubs and stared down the long corridor. There, in the dim torchlight, stood a high official in a fur-trimmed cloak, his thinning hair hidden beneath a red hat.

Paulus Mämminger.

The Regensburg treasurer gave a sign to two guards at his side to lower their crossbows. Then he gazed reproachfully at the violent disarray in the well chamber. His voice resounded through the vaulted room like a clap of thunder.

"The game is up, Silvio Contarini! We know about your scheme. Come out now and surrender!"

"Never!" The Venetian, who like everyone else was bewildered by the new arrival, turned from Simon and retreated a few paces. He was immediately swallowed up in darkness. "A Contarini doesn't surrender so easily! We'll meet again, Mämminger, on the floor of the Reichstag, if not before!"

Silvio's laughter mingled with the noise of the rushing water, which, as the many individual streams merged into one, generated an infernal uproar. For a moment they heard splashing in the distance; then the insane laughter that echoed back to them suddenly broke off.

In the meantime Simon had hoisted himself up onto the ledge, where, panting and gasping, he coughed up water and bile. Magdalena waded over and wrapped her arms around him.

"Simon, my God, Simon!" she whispered. "I thought you were dead."

"And I thought this madman had actually poisoned you," Simon gasped.

Magdalena wiped the last bits of ergot from the corners of her mouth. "I really made an effort not to swallow that stuff," she said. "I guess we'll find out in the next few hours whether I was successful. But for now let's get out of this frigid water before you catch a chill and die on me."

Supporting Simon, she waded through the pool toward Paulus Mämminger. The old treasurer blinked. It took him a while to recognize who stood before him — but then his face lit up.

"Ah, the mysterious beautiful woman from Heuport House!" he cried. "Tell me, how are you liking Regensburg?"

Magdalena wrung out her hair. "Too many lunatics in one place, if you ask me. And it's too wet here."

Paulus Mämminger laughed and handed her his cloak. "I'm certain you have some stories for me." Then he turned to leave. "But I suggest we save that for the open air. It smells too much of death and madness down here." A slight smile twitched on his lips. "Besides, I have to express my thanks to a loyal servant up there. I hope he's satisfied with his reward."

It was late afternoon when Jakob Kuisl returned to the raft landing in the little rowboat, knowing he wouldn't be able to escape his fate this time.

A carnival-like atmosphere prevailed on the landing. A huge crowd had gathered, and guards were running about, trying in vain to shoo people back into the city. From the Wöhrd a huge column of smoke rose into the sky, and piles of charred beams, some still smoldering, littered the ground. The sheds and mill wheels looked like bonfires among towering piles of collapsing boards, and the large grain mill seemed to have been swallowed up by the earth. Now the fire had spread to surrounding buildings, and the entire island was one raging inferno.

Spectators on the raft landing gawked at the scene as they would at a public execution. They cheered whenever a building collapsed and pointed excitedly at embers blowing their way. The watchmen, having already given up on saving the island, were now busy trying to keep the fire from spreading to the bridge, the other islands, and the city wharf.

When the guards finally noticed the small rowboat with its two passengers, they hesitated, whispered to one another, and pointed anxiously at the Schongau hangman tying the boat to a post on the wharf. Kuisl seemed as disinterested in the spectacle as any old fisherman from out of town. Finally the guards approached cautiously with pikes raised.

"The . . . monster!" one stammered. "Now we've got him! We must stay together! Or he'll rip our throats right open."

"He probably blew up the mill," the second man whispered. "Ever since he's been here, misfortune has come over this city like the Plague."

Kuisl raised his hands to ward off the guards, but he was much too tired to resist them. He'd been racing so long now — first lugging the deathly pale Teuber almost two miles from Weidenfeld to the rowboat, then rowing back from Donaustauf against the current. The Regensburg executioner hadn't regained consciousness after speaking his last words in the ruined village. Throughout the boat trip Kuisl watched blood seeping slowly through the moss, herbs, and bandages. Teuber's face was waxy like a corpse's, so Kuisl repeatedly checked to make sure his friend was still breathing.

"He needs help," the Schongau hangman pleaded in a hoarse

voice as he climbed out of the rowboat. Almost unconscious himself, he offered no resistance as the guards seized him and bound his hands and feet. "Bring Teuber to a surgeon," he muttered, "a real one, or I'll wring your necks. Do you understand?"

"Hold your tongue, monster!" one guard shouted, punching him so hard his upper lip split open and he fell to the ground. "Your game is over; you won't get away from us again. That was you who did that to the mill, wasn't it?"

As other Regensburgers began to recognize the man being led away, a murmur went up that gave way to cheers and shouting.

"The werewolf!" an old woman shouted. "The werewolf's back! And look, he's in league with our executioner! Throw them both on the mill—into the fire with them!"

"By Saint Florian, they should burn!"

"No, hang them instead! Right here!"

"Hold on, people!" one of the guards interjected. "We can't say whether the Regensburg hangman—"

But his voice was drowned out by the crowd. People were already down by the great crane on the raft landing, tossing boat ropes over the crossbeams. They tied the rope into a noose and began to fashion a makeshift gallows. The first sticks and stones flew through the air now, and the guards, silent and pale, formed a circle around Kuisl and the Regensburg executioner, who was lying unconscious on the pier. They couldn't hold off the crowd for long.

"Go get a city official!" a high-ranking officer shouted at the other guards as he braced himself against two farm workers who'd already drawn their knives. "If you can, bring Mämminger! Right away! Before they kill Teuber. Run! Get going, damn it!"

As one of the guards broke from the circle and ran toward town, the crowd amassed into one enormous, furious, screaming creature that charged the desperate bailiffs behind him. Kuisl looked out on the riotous mob, registering a cold, bestial look in their eyes.

Predators, he thought. *This is what they always look like at an execution.*

This time the execution was his own.

"Nathan!" Simon cried as he stumbled out of the dark well chamber and into the bright daylight. "I should have known!"

The beggar king was counting out and distributing shiny coins to the beggars standing around him. Only reluctantly did he look up.

"Beg your pardon?" he mumbled.

"You told the treasurer we were here!" the medicus cried, kicking the beggar in the shins. "Who else do you work for? The kaiser? The pope? The Virgin Mary?"

Grimacing in pain, Nathan rubbed his shins. "If the price is right." Finally, he grinned. "Be happy. Without the esteemed treasurer, you'd be fish food now. And your little sweetheart would no doubt be trapped in a fit of hysterical laughter, trying to claw her own eyes out, having gone stark mad. So don't make such a fuss."

"Great," Simon muttered. "So we've been rescued from the well chamber only to be burned at the stake for arson and God knows what else. Thank you very much."

Suddenly he felt the treasurer's hand on his shoulder.

"We've been working with Nathan a long time," said Mämminger, who'd emerged from the well chamber right after Simon. "He's been keeping us up to date on what's happened since you first sought refuge with the guild."

"So it's true," Simon whispered.

But the treasurer seemed not to have heard him. "I just didn't know what role you were playing in all this," Mämminger continued. Removing his official red hat, he passed a hand over his sweaty forehead. "So I had Nathan keep an eye on you. When it

became clear you had nothing to do with the powder, it was unfortunately too late. You had sought amnesty in the bishop's palace, and as long as you were there, there was nothing I could do
to help you."

"You knew about the powder?" asked Magdalena, her
clothes and hair dripping in the bright light. She eyed the treasurer suspiciously. "Then why didn't you just put a stop to Silvio
Contarini and his game?"

Paulus Mämminger shook his head slowly, deep in thought.
"We only suspected the freemen were planning something for
the coming Reichstag, but we had no real evidence. When we
heard that Hofmann was experimenting somehow with alchemy, I asked Heinrich von Bütten to find out more."

"The kaiser's agent," Simon added softly. "We thought for a
long time he was trying to kill us."

Mämminger shook his head. "His job was only to learn more
about you two. Later, he wanted to warn you about Contarini,
but the Venetian somehow always managed to distract you."
Mämminger removed his sweaty pince-nez to clean them.
"Heinrich von Bütten was the kaiser's best agent," he continued.
"A brilliant swordsman — inconspicuous, intelligent, and incor-
ruptible. Leopold I wanted him to serve as a spy at the Regensburg Reichstag. His Excellency won't be happy to hear he's
dead." Mämminger sighed. "Von Bütten had long suspected that
Contarini was working for the Grand Vizier. When he saw the
Venetian in the company of a beautiful woman, a stranger, we
started to snoop around. And lo and behold . . . !" He smiled at
Magdalena. "It just so happened that beautiful stranger was the
niece of the bathhouse owner under suspicion of plotting against
the kaiser. Naturally, this gave us more than a moment's pause,
especially when it turned out her father was said to have killed
the very same bathhouse owner."

"Did you really think my father killed his sister and brother-in-law?" asked Magdalena, tying her wet hair into a bun. "Even a blind man could have figured out he walked right into a trap!"

The treasurer frowned. "Don't judge too quickly, young lady. Your father was the brother-in-law of a leading free-man—an *insurgent*. For that reason alone he came under suspi-cion. We had to subject him to some pretty severe interrogation just to find out whether he knew anything about this powder." He shrugged. "Your father is a tough nut to crack. We aldermen therefore reached the decision, after long discussions in my house, to suspend the torture for the time being. The following night I left a note in the cathedral for Heinrich von Bütten, tell-ing him to see whether he could find some connection between Contarini and the freemen—and exonerate your father." Mäm-minger put his pince-nez back in place. "Unfortunately Kuisl fled the very same night, thus renewing suspicions. It's too bad; we very much wanted him to identify the true leader of the free-men for us."

"I think we can help you in that regard," Simon said. "It's the raftmaster, Karl Gessner. He also set the trap for Jakob Kuisl."

The treasurer's eyes widened in disbelief. "Gessner? But why . . . ?"

"Revenge," Magdalena chimed in. "Gessner and my father knew each other from the war. But that the raftmaster was the leader of the freemen you could have also learned from *this* gen-tleman."

She pointed at Nathan, who only smiled back innocently and continued counting coins into a pouch. Mämminger raised his eyebrows and scowled at the beggar king, who had turned to pick his nose.

"I really don't know what the two of you are talking about," Nathan replied. "I would never—"

"What's going to happen with Contarini now?" Simon asked. "Has he escaped?"

The treasurer squinted, irritated, and turned back to the medicus. "To date no one has ever explored all the caves the water carved through the rock down there," he explained earnestly. "It's a wet, dark labyrinth, and no one can really say how far down it goes. Maybe the Venetian will find the entrance to hell down there, but he might also get lost or eventually return to the well chamber. Just in case, we sealed the exit. No one can get out. And now—"

Just then they heard the sound of someone approaching through the field. A watchman, drenched with sweat, came running up to Mämminger. He whispered something in Mämminger's ear, and the treasurer frowned, placing his official red hat back on his head, hurrying down the path, and beckoning to the others to follow.

"We hope your father will soon be able to answer all the outstanding questions in person," he said as he hastened toward the city with the watchmen and the beggars. "They caught him down at the raft landing, and if we don't hurry, there won't be much of him left."

Jakob Kuisl barely felt the cabbage stalks, stones, and rotten fish that hailed down on his body and face. The shouts of the crowd, too, echoed strangely, as if they came from the end of a long tunnel. Straining to turn his head, he saw Philipp Teuber next to him, his consciousness quickly fading again and, like himself, with a noose around his neck. The Regensburgers had finished erecting a gallows on the harbor crane high above the raft landing now, and both hangmen stood on crates piled high to form a makeshift scaffold. Leering and smirking at the hangmen, a few carpenters waited beside a crank that would eventually hoist the ropes and, with them, the men high in the air. Kuisl let his gaze wander along the rotten wooden structure that rose at least twenty feet above them.

Must at least be a great view of Regensburg from up there, he thought.

Kuisl's fever had returned now in full force, and despite the midsummer temperatures, Kuisl was freezing. Even if he weren't in pain and dizzy, though, there was no possibility of escape now. He was shackled, and when he looked out over the crowd, he saw several hundred pairs of angry eyes, all eager for a summary execution. A few guards were scattered among them, but they'd abandoned their official duty now to join the onlookers. After a brief and futile resistance, most bailiffs had withdrawn and given the two prisoners over to the screaming mob. Kuisl counted himself lucky that the Regensburgers hadn't stoned him to death yet.

Another clod of dirt hit Kuisl on the head so hard his gaze went black. Still, he was able to remain upright. Next to him, however, Philipp Teuber was close to losing consciousness again, and, because he was no longer able to support himself, his body weight tightened the noose around his neck like a garrote cutting off his air supply. Teuber's eyes were closed, his face chalky except where blood vessels had burst, and his mouth open like a carp gasping for air.

"Monster! Monster!"

All around him Kuisl heard the roar of the crowd as if through a wall, a seething mass of high-pitched screams and shrill laughter rising and falling. Blood dripping from his forehead, he blinked, blinded by the sun; still, he had the impression he could clearly see each individual in the crowd below — bull-necked raftsmen and carpenters, snotty-nosed children and journeymen bare to the waist, but also fishwives. Even a few fine ladies looked on from the rear with their finely powdered male companions, whispering and pointing at the two figures on the makeshift gallows. For all these people the two hangmen were a marvelous spectacle, an experience they could share with their children and grandchildren. Unleashed, the people's anger demanded a blood sacrifice.

"Hey, Teuber," a skinny, pockmarked youth shouted from the first row. "How does that noose feel around your neck? You hanged my brother. I hope you dance just as long as he did."

"They say the other one's a hangman, too. Perhaps they can hang each other," a young maid joked.

As laughter broke out, the crowd surged toward the teetering stack of crates that threatened to collapse at any moment. Atop the hastily built scaffold and beside the two shackled executioners stood four grim raftsmen, the apparent ringleaders. With grave self-importance, they held the crowd back, preventing them from storming the gallows. Kuisl had to assume the four men had designs on the ropes and victims' clothes and bodies. Bloody talismans were thought to have magical powers, especially those from a pair of hangmen.

"String 'em up! String 'em up!" At first just a few voices chanted, but then others joined in and the shouts rose to a mighty chorus that resounded over the pier.

"String 'em up and let 'em dance!"

Now Kuisl could feel the carpenters beginning to turn the crank on the winch. The cords tightened, pulling the hangmen slowly upward. At first Kuisl could still touch the ground with his toes, but soon he was swinging freely in the air.

The rope squeezed Kuisl's throat and Adam's apple tight, crushing his windpipe as his legs began to thrash involuntarily. The hangman knew from experience that death didn't come immediately to hanged men, and for this reason he often tugged on victims' feet to break their necks and put an end to the torment. But it was obvious that no one here had any interest in mercy. Kuisl jerked and strained; he could hear blood pounding in his head and, in the background, the crowd's cries and laughter.

"Look at them flounder! The scaffold is like a dance floor!"

When the hangman opened his eyes again, it was as if a red

veil hung in front of his face. The crowd's voices merged in a senseless, meaningless melee. Images rose within and flashed all around him. He saw himself in the Great War, sword in hand, and in the background a city in flames. Then there was blackness. He saw his father die beneath a hail of stones; he saw soldiers seeking recruits as they passed through Schongau, waving to little Jakob at the side of the road; and finally, he saw himself in his mother's lap with a soiled headless little wooden doll.

Mama, why does Daddy kill people?

The bloody veil before his eyes moved on like a storm cloud, and behind it a soft, warm blackness appeared, with a tiny light shining at its center. The light grew closer and closer, opening onto a tunnel. At its end stood a form wreathed in light.

Mother, I'm coming home to you . . . I'm coming . . .

"Stop! In the name of the city, stop at once!"

Suddenly Kuisl felt himself falling. When he landed with a thud on the hard crates below, his body, which had been drifting off into another realm, suddenly reasserted itself with intense earthly pain. The light and the tunnel disappeared, and at that moment, blissfully, air came streaming back into his lungs, somehow cold and hot at once. His throat burning, he rolled on his side, spitting up bitter bile. When he felt the unpleasant taste on his tongue, he knew he was still alive.

"Everyone stand back! Back to your houses, or I'll have you all thrown in the stocks and whipped! Do you hear me? That's an official city order!"

Kuisl opened his blood-encrusted right eye to see a man in front of him dressed in a fur-trimmed cloak and official crimson cap. A half-dozen city guards stood defiantly at his side on the crates, crossbows trained on the crowd below. Snarling like fierce toy dogs, if less playful, the crowd backed away, bit by bit. Only a handful of spectators seemed to object, but in no time the bailiffs gained the upper hand and drove them all into the narrow streets along the Danube. Within a few minutes the uproar had subsided and the docks were as deserted as on a Sunday morning during mass.

Panting, Kuisl stood up and staggered toward the edge of the scaffold, where Teuber was doubled up in a pool of his own vomit, the bandage on his chest soaked in blood. The Regensburg executioner coughed and spat but for the time being seemed to have at least regained consciousness. Kuisl knelt down beside his friend and passed his hand through Teuber's sweaty hair.

"You think I'll let you die on me here?" the exhausted Schongau hangman gasped. His throat felt like it was on fire, and he could speak only in fits and starts. "Better forget that idea . . . I didn't drag you here all the way from Weidenfeld so that you could give up now. We hangmen are tough dogs. Don't forget that!"

Teuber seemed to nod; then he turned away like a sick animal and didn't stir. His breath whistled and rattled, though, as if he wanted to let everyone know he wasn't dead yet.

"We'll take him home," an official's voice spoke up from Kuisl's right. "His wife will take care of him. The rest is in God's hands."

Kuisl turned around and looked straight into the eye of the man with the crimson hat. He had an old wrinkled face and wore a pince-nez on his nose, but his gaze was as sharp and clear as that of a man in his thirties.

"So you're this Jakob Kuisl fellow," Mämminger said, looking him up and down with a severe but curious gaze. "You haven't made it very easy on us. You can't be locked up, and torture won't make you confess—and evidently you can't be hanged either. Who are you? The devil? A ghost?"

The hangman shook his head. "Just a Kuisl," he murmured. "We're a tough breed."

Mämminger laughed. "I'll believe you there! Indestructible, the whole lot of you—your daughter and future son-in-law included." He turned to a guard alongside him. "Cut this man's bonds; he's suffered enough. Then bring the other two over here. Now that the mob has cleared out, they have nothing to fear."

The bailiff cut the ropes from Kuisl's wrists and jumped down from the scaffold. Shortly thereafter he returned with Simon and Magdalena.

"Thanks to the Virgin Mary and all the saints in heaven! You're alive!" When the hangman's daughter caught sight of her father again, she was unrestrainable. With outstretched arms she rushed to the scaffold, clambered swiftly up the pile of crates, and wrapped her arms around her father, squeezing him so hard he thought he was being strangled a second time.

"I don't want you ever to leave me again, do you hear?" she whispered, placing her hands on his face as if she still couldn't believe he was alive. "Promise?"

"And don't you ever leave me, either, shameless wench," Kuisl replied. "Just think what you've done to your mother, vanishing from Schongau like that. She must be crying her eyes out day and night."

He let out a chest-rattling cough as Magdalena ran her hand through his hair. "We're on our way home now," she said, "but first you've got to get better. You've got a fever — that much is clear — and there's something wrong with your shoulder as well."

The hangman blinked warily at Simon, who'd climbed onto the scaffold in the meantime. "Don't you think for a moment I'm going to let myself be treated by this dubious little quack," he growled. "I'd rather smear Teuber's stinking ointment all over my body again."

Simon grinned and bowed slightly. His clothing was still ripped and wet from his fight with Silvio, but some color had returned to his face. "Please do. You're more than welcome to saw your own arms off, if you like. Less work for me."

"Impertinent little shit. If you lay so much as a finger on my daughter again, I'll smack you in the face."

"In your condition?"

Kuisl was about to let loose a tirade, but Magdalena cut him off. "If you're well enough to quarrel, your fever can't be too serious," she snapped. "And now let's clear out of here before the Regensburgers change their minds and decide to hang the hangman again."

"Just who are all those people back there?" Kuisl inquired, pointing to the band of beggars gathered around an elderly man in a tattered coat and wide-brimmed hat. When the old man noticed Kuisl looking at him, he grinned, revealing a sparkling gold tooth.

"They look just like the people I have to beat up and run out of town back home. Are they with you?" the hangman asked.

Magdalena smiled. "You might say that, or we with them."

She jumped down from the scaffold and skipped off between the crates while Simon, Kuisl, and the old treasurer stared after her.

"A headstrong girl, that daughter of yours," Mämminger said. "Takes after you."

Suddenly the hangman's face darkened, and he stared off into space. The two nooses swayed back and forth in the wind like two enormous pendulums.

"Whether she takes after me or not, she certainly is one hell of a woman," Kuisl replied. "A hangman's daughter is always in league with the devil."

He climbed down from the scaffold with Simon and walked toward the pier. For a while they stood silently on the shore, watching waves splash and foam between the grimy pillars under the dock. The hangman took a crumpled piece of paper from his shirt pocket, tore it into small pieces, and scattered them over the water. Like tiny white leaves, they drifted away until finally the waves swallowed them up.

"What was that?" asked Simon, surprised. "The letter you received last night?"

Kuisl stared a few moments longer at the water, then turned abruptly toward the Stone Bridge, where Magdalena was already waiting.

"Nothing important—just a little piece of the past. Who cares what happened so long ago?" he answered.

Magdalena let her legs dangle over the side of the pier and watched them approach, her eyes black and sparkling like two embers on a cold night, a broad smile on her lips.

The hangman felt he'd never loved his daughter so much in his life as he did at this moment.

EPILOGUE

BY THE END OF OCTOBER BARONS, DUKES, FREE-
men, and counts had started streaming into Regensburg. With
their colorful costumes, boisterous servants, and countless
coaches, wagons, and carts—all pulled by handsome steeds—
they gave just a taste of what Regensburg was in for when the
Reichstag would officially begin in January. The strangers, an
exotic crowd from the farthest reaches of the German Empire,
filled the narrow streets and houses with noise and life. Speaking
in exotic tongues, servants brawled in the taverns with the locals
while noble gentlemen shopped the markets until the shelves
were bare. The locals whined and complained, and many already longed for the day the kaiser would leave again.

Jakob Kuisl didn't see much of this, though. For the first few
days his fever was so high he woke only from time to time for a
sip of thin barley soup. As was customary among hangmen, he
stayed at Teuber's house, where for the next two months Simon,
Magdalena, and Teuber's wife nursed the two executioners back
to health. Caroline Teuber said she'd never seen such good
friends curse each other so much. When their fevers finally broke

after almost ten days and their strength began to return, the two hangmen lay in the Teubers' wide marital bed quarreling like sick, bored children, complaining constantly about the medicine, the lukewarm mulled wine, and the mushy food.

"I can only hope they get better soon," Caroline sighed as she stood alongside Magdalena, stirring a pot of fragrant green oil. "I have my hands full with my five youngsters and don't need to hear any more arguing."

During those first few days Philipp Teuber had been on the brink of death. He woke up screaming with recurrent fever dreams of being hanged by a furious mob. His chest wound healed surprisingly quickly, however. The bolt, which had missed his lung by less than an inch, pierced straight through the muscles in his shoulder. When Teuber first regained consciousness, he credited the successful cure to his own ointment. Jakob Kuisl, on the other hand, was convinced that bad weeds don't die. Even Kuisl's shoulder and the severe burns on his arms and legs were healing well. His blisters left little pockmarks, however, that would remind the hangman forever of his time in the Regensburg torture chamber.

Soon after Kuisl was spared execution at the raft landing, Mämminger proposed to the city council that the Schongau executioner be declared innocent. The treasurer was able to convince the patricians that Kuisl was a victim of the scheming freemen, who after the death of their leader had vanished as suddenly as they'd appeared—almost as if they'd never even existed.

City guards burned the thirty bags of ergot in a field near Regensburg. In the end only Mämminger and a few patricians in the inner circle knew about the monstrous plan to poison the Reichstag. The treasurer considered it advisable to let as few people as possible in on the incident—in part, not to upset people unnecessarily, but also to avoid giving any visiting nobles the wrong idea. Even Nathan fell silent, and Simon had to imagine the beggar king had received a tidy sum of money from Mämminger for that.

On a cold, wet October morning, the medicus installed Nathan's new set of gold teeth as promised. It was on this occasion that Simon learned something interesting about his adversary, the Venetian.

"Yesterday I was out at the wellspring," the beggar king said casually as the medicus packed his instruments. "And just imagine—they've found Silvio!"

"After all this time?" Simon was so astonished he almost dropped his stiletto. "Is he alive?"

Nathan grinned. "Only if there's life after death." Then he told the excited medicus what he learned after bribing one of the guards.

The bailiffs ordered the well house opened when farmers began complaining about a disgusting odor coming from the door. Just inside the guards found Silvio's half-decomposed corpse. Evidently the Venetian had wandered for days through the labyrinth of corridors and subterranean springs but, finding no exit, had slowly starved to death inside the well house.

"Do you know what's so funny about the whole thing?" Nathan said as he admired his gold teeth in a polished copper mirror. "All his pockets were full of that bluish stuff. He must have hidden a little sack somewhere the guards hadn't seen. As his hunger grew, it seems he ate the flour. His whole jacket was white with it; he must have really stuffed himself full. And now listen to this . . ." Nathan paused for dramatic effect and winked at Simon. "They swore they'd never seen a corpse with such a horrified expression—his eyes wide with fear, his mouth open in a fixed scream, his cheeks sunken in. And they say his hair was white as snow, as if he'd caught sight of Satan and all the demons of the underworld at once! What a gruesome death!" Nathan shuddered before turning to examine his teeth again, extracting a filament of meat lodged there.

"Alone in the dark for days, a prisoner of his own madness!" Simon mused. "I wonder what sort of nightmares he suffered. Well, in the end, at least he found out exactly how that damn ergot works."

By early November they were finally ready to leave. Simon and Magdalena paid a final visit to the beggars down under Neupfarr Church Square where they celebrated all night. Hans Reiser cried a bit, but when Simon promised him one of his books about herbs, the old man quickly calmed down again. The medicus knew he'd found a worthy successor in this man who was so thirsty for knowledge, that soon the beggars in Regensburg would be able to seek help from one of their own. After all, healing herbs grew in every garden in town and needed only to be gathered secretly, under the light of the moon.

Long after the little group cast off from the Regensburg raft landing, Nathan and his men stood on the pier waving farewell. Cold November rain lashed the faces of the passengers, and the horses made slow progress along the muddy towpath as they pulled the raft against the current. And in the days that followed, the weather didn't improve. Wrapped tightly in their cloaks, hoods pulled far down over their faces, Simon and Magdalena stood in the bow, staring into a fog that hung low over the forests and fallow fields. Smoke rose from fires in the fields and wafted westward, homeward. Magdalena had written her mother a letter weeks back announcing they'd be returning, and now home-sickness was consuming her with a yearning stronger than anything she'd ever felt.

After two endless weeks of travel, they came to the broad Lech River, and here at last, through the fog, the familiar church towers and gabled roofs appeared atop a hill.

"Schongau," Magdalena said in a muted voice. "I thought we'd never get back."

"Are you sure you really want to go back?" asked Simon, pulling her close.

As the cold rain whipped her face, Magdalena grew silent. Finally, through clenched teeth, she whispered an answer. "Do we have a choice?"

As soon as they left the Schongau raft landing and started up toward the Tanners' Quarter, they noticed something was wrong. It was almost noon, but there was no one in the streets. Many doors had been bolted shut and the windows nailed closed with thick boards. A few stray dogs and cats scurried through the muddy streets, but it was otherwise as quiet as a cemetery.

"Somehow I pictured our homecoming differently," the hangman said. "Where is everyone? At mass? Or have the Swedes attacked again?"

Simon shook his head. "It looks to me like people are afraid of something." Little bouquets of St. John's Wort hung from doors, and some windows were marked with pentagrams and crosses drawn in chalk. "For heaven's sake," he muttered. "What happened here?"

Walking faster, they finally arrived at the hangman's house at the far end of the Tanners' Quarter. Unlike the other buildings, the door here stood open, and as they arrived, a figure that Magdalena didn't recognize at first emerged from the house into the gloomy daylight.

My God, Mother . . .

With a pail of garbage in her hand, Anna-Maria Kuisl shuffled into the yard. Stooped, she looked smaller and more fragile than Magdalena remembered. The hangman's daughter also thought she noticed a few new white strands in her mother's black hair.

She's gotten old, Magdalena thought, *old and sad.*

When Anna-Maria lifted her head and saw her daughter

and the others before her, she dropped the bucket and uttered a loud cry. "Thanks be to all the saints! You're back! You're really back!"

She ran toward her husband and daughter and, embracing them, began to sob. For a long time they stood there in the rain, a little bundle of humanity lost in their love for one another. Off to one side Simon could only shift uncomfortably from one foot to the other.

Finally Kuisl straightened up, wiped his eyes, and began to speak.

"What's happened here?" he asked, gesturing at the surrounding houses. "Speak up, wife; what pestilence did the Lord God send this time to test us?"

"The Plague," his wife whispered, making the sign of the cross. "The Plague. It's already claimed more than two hundred people, and every day there are more, and . . ."

In a flash all the color drained from Kuisl's face. He took his wife firmly in his arms. "The children! What's happened to the children?" he gasped.

Anna-Maria smiled weakly. "They're well, but for how long I don't know. I made them a potion of toads and vinegar according to a recipe from the hangman Seitz in Kaufbeuren, but Georg won't drink it."

"Nonsense!" Kuisl snapped. "Toads and vinegar! Woman, who talked you into this nonsense? It's high time I put things in order around here. Let's go inside. I'll make the children a cup of angelica powder and—"

The sound of footsteps cut him short. Turning, he saw Johann Lechner in the yard behind him. The Schongau secretary wore a long brown fur coat over his nondescript official garb. He looked as if he'd stepped out for a short walk and just happened to drop by the Tanners' Quarter. To his left and right stood two nervous guards with cloths tied over their mouths, looking for all the world as if they wanted nothing more than to get out of here at once.

"How nice you're back," Lechner began softly, a sardonic smile on his lips. "You can see we've removed the garbage from town ourselves while you were away. Actually, that's the hangman's job, but when he's nowhere to be found . . ." He paused briefly, menacingly. "Believe me, Kuisl, there will be consequences."

"I had my reasons," the executioner said tersely.

"Of course, of course." Lechner nodded almost sympathetically. "We all have our reasons. But more than a few people believe the terrible odors and fumes from the trash brought the Plague to Schongau. And that the hangman is therefore to blame for all our misfortune. What do you have to say to this theory, huh?"

Kuisl remained defiantly silent.

Finally the secretary continued, drawing patterns in the mud with his walking stick as he spoke. "I'll admit that when I heard you were coming back, my first thought was to have you dragged out of town in an animal hide and pushed into the nearest manure pit," he said casually. "But then it occurred to me what an outrageous waste that would be." Lechner looked the hangman in the eye. "I'm going to take pity on you one more time, Kuisl. The city needs you — and not just to haul the garbage away. People are talking about the wonder of your healing practices, and it just so happens that we could stand a few miracles right now, especially since we don't have a medicus at the moment . . ." Lechner's words hovered in the air like the Sword of Damocles. He turned his gaze to Simon, waiting for a reaction.

"What . . . what do you mean by that?" Simon felt as if the ground were slipping from under him, and his throat was suddenly parched. "My father . . . is he . . . ?"

Lechner nodded. "He's dead, Simon. Your father didn't hide

from this terrible sickness; he visited the sick in their homes. You can be proud."

"My God," Simon whispered. "Why him?"

"Only the dear Lord can say. It's often the bravest doctors who leave us first."

Simon was overwhelmed now by countless images and thoughts. He'd left his father angry, and now he'd never see him again. Simon remembered when, as a little boy, he accompanied his father and the camp followers in the war. He remembered the years he'd looked up to his father. Bonifaz Fronwieser had been a respected army surgeon at the time, a good doctor and healer, not the drunken, hot-tempered quack he later became in Schongau. Simon hoped he could remember his father as he used to be. Indeed, it seemed he'd regained some of his earlier dignity just before the end.

For a long time no one spoke. Finally Lechner cleared his throat. "We'll need a new doctor in town," he said. "I know, Simon, you never completed your university studies, but no one has to know that."

Simon gave a start. In spite of his grief, hope sparked within him. Had he heard correctly? Had Lechner just proposed he take over as town doctor? He felt Magdalena squeeze his hand, and right then he knew what to do.

He embraced the hangman's daughter and held her close. "Thank you for your offer, Your Excellency," he whispered. "But I'll accept only on the condition that you also welcome the new doctor's future wife. Magdalena knows more about herbs than anyone. She'll be an invaluable help to me."

Lechner frowned. "A hangman's daughter, the town doctor's wife? How do you figure that?"

"You don't have to *call* him a medicus," Magdalena replied defiantly. "If it's only a question of the title, then Simon will . . ." She thought for a while, then her face brightened. "Then he'll become a bathhouse owner."

There was a brief silence broken only by the crows cawing from rooftops.

"Bathhouse owner?" Simon stared at her in disbelief. "Cleaning dirty wooden tubs, bleeding people, and shaving their beards? I don't think I'd care for that. It's a dishonorable vocation that—"

"Exactly; then *you* will fit in with *me*," the hangman's daughter interrupted. "And I'll be glad to take care of the shaving, if you really find that so disagreeable."

Lechner shook his head thoughtfully. "Bathhouse operator? Why not? Actually, that's not a bad idea at all. We do have one in town already, but he's a drunken scoundrel, and the only thing he knows how to do is bleed people of their money. For all intents and purposes you'll be working as a medicus, I guarantee that. After all, there's no doctor in town, so you won't have any competition." Satisfied, he nodded. "Bathhouse operator. That could be a solution."

"And the people?" Anna-Maria interjected. "What will people say? When I think of Berchtholdt and the way they taunted my poor Magdalena . . ." She shook her head. "I never want to live through a night like that again."

"You don't have to worry about Berchtholdt anymore," Johann Lechner replied. "The Plague claimed him two days ago. Not even his wife shed a tear." The secretary shrugged. "All the St. John's Wort, rosaries, and Ave Marias in the world couldn't save him in the end. Last night they took him down to Saint Sebastian's Cemetery and buried him as fast as they could. May his soul rest in peace." The secretary quickly crossed himself. "So are we agreed, Fronwieser? Bathhouse owner for life, and I'll do what I can to get the council to approve marriage with the hangman's daughter."

Simon hesitated for just a moment, then they shook on it. "Agreed."

"Just a moment," Kuisl grumbled. "You can't go ahead and

arrange a wedding here without first asking *my* permission. I always said the Steingaden executioner would make a good match
for Magdalena—"

"Oh, stop with that foolishness!" Anna-Maria interrupted.
"You can't keep hiding the fact that you actually like Simon, and
after everything he's done for you, it would be an outrage if you
were to refuse him now. So give him your blessing, then leave the
two of them be. You've played the surly old bear long enough."

Kuisl stared back at his wife, his mouth hanging open in astonishment. But words apparently failed him, and he said nothing more.

"Then I'll leave the young couple to themselves." A hint of a
smile played across the secretary's lips as he turned and hurried
abruptly off with the guards in the direction of the Lech Gate.
"I'll expect to see you in two hours at your father's house," he
called back to Simon. "And bring your woman along; there's a
lot to be done."

The freshly crowned bathhouse owner grinned. As so often,
Simon had the feeling Lechner had achieved exactly what he
wanted. Simon took Magdalena by the arm and strolled back
into the town with her, toward his father's house.

As the couple disappeared through the Lech Gate, Kuisl and
his wife entered the house and went up the stairs to the room
where the twins were napping. They stood for a long time in
front of the little beds, holding hands and watching their children's calm and even breathing.

"Aren't they beautiful?" Anna-Maria whispered.

Kuisl nodded. "So innocent. And to think their papa has so
much blood on his hands."

"You numbskull! The children don't need a hangman but a
father," she replied. "Remember, you're the only one they have."

A shadow passed over Kuisl's face. He let go of his wife's
hand and stomped down the stairs without a word where he sat

on the bench beneath the family altar for a long time, staring off into space and cracking his knuckles now and then.

When his wife saw him brooding there, she couldn't help but smile. Anna-Maria had grown accustomed to her husband's moods; she knew he'd take his time before speaking again. Sometimes it took days. Without a word, she began pounding angelica root in a stone mortar. For a long time the rhythmic scrape of the pestle and the crackle of the flames were the only sounds in the room.

Finally, when she had had enough, she put down the pestle and ran her hand through her husband's black hair, which was beginning to show the first signs of gray.

"What's the trouble, Jakob?" she asked softly. "Don't you want to tell me what happened in Regensburg?"

The hangman shook his head slowly. "Not today. I need some time."

When Kuisl finally cleared his throat, he looked his wife directly in the eye.

"I'd just like to know one thing . . ." he began haltingly. "Back then, in Weidenfeld, when I saw you for the first time . . ."

Anna-Maria bit her lip and drew back. "We weren't ever going to talk about that again," she whispered. "You promised me that."

Kuisl nodded. "I know. But I have to know, or it'll tear me apart worse than the rack."

"Then what is it you want to know?"

"Did any of those men touch you? You know what I mean—did they attack you? Philipp Lettner perhaps, that filthy bastard?" Kuisl put his hand on his wife's shoulder. "Please tell me the truth! Was it Lettner? I swear it won't change anything between us."

For a long time the only sound in the room was the crackling birchwood on the hearth.

"Why do you want to know that?" Anna finally asked. "Why can't things stay the way they were? Why must you hurt me?"

"Yes or no, for God's sake!"

Standing, Anna-Maria walked over to the family altar and turned the crucifix around so the wooden Jesus faced the wall.

"The Savior doesn't need to hear this," she whispered. "No one does, except us." Then, haltingly, she began to speak. She left nothing out. Her voice was hard and even, like the pendulum of a clock.

"Do you know how I washed myself after that?" she said finally. She stared off into space. "I washed for hours in the icy brooks along the way, in the rivers, ponds, whatever pool of water there was. But it didn't help. The filth remained, like a mark of Cain that only I could see."

"You kept silent a long time," the hangman said softly. "You've never said a word about this until today."

Anna-Maria closed her eyes for a moment before she continued. "When we got to Ingolstadt, I slipped away from you for a while. I went to visit an old midwife down by the river. She gave me a powder to get rid of it. The blood flushed it out—it was nothing but a little red clot." Tears welled up in her eyes. "A week later, we made love for the first time. I held on to you, and I thought of nothing else."

Kuisl nodded, his gaze transfixed by the past. "You clawed at my back. I couldn't figure out whether out of pleasure or pain."

Anna-Maria smiled. "The pleasure helped me forget the pain. The pleasure, and the love."

"The powder from the midwife," he asked. "What was it?"

His wife bent over him and ran her finger across the creases in his face. They were deep, like furrows in a field, and she knew each one intimately.

"Ergot," she whispered. "A gift from God, or from the

devil—take your pick. Just don't take too much or you'll fly off to heaven and never return."

"Or to hell," the hangman replied.

Then he took his wife in his arms and held her tight until all that remained of the birch on the hearth were glowing embers.

TRAVELER'S GUIDE TO
REGENSBURG

The book you have just read is actually a love letter. If a person can be said to love a city, then I love Regensburg, and I hope you will feel the same after reading this book. If you're planning a visit, let me reassure you that today Regensburg doesn't stink, all the roads are paved, and you won't be locked up in the House of Fools if you're out and about after eight o'clock in the evening.

While Regensburg is part of Bavaria, it feels very Italian — with its narrow lanes, café tables in the open air, any number of churches, a real cathedral, and a history that dates back to the Roman Empire. A wonderful city, it was just recently named a UNESCO World Heritage site.

If you want to learn more about Regensburg, I recommend a tour, either with one of the city guides or with STADT-MAUS — an organization whose novel tours bring old Regensburg back to life with actors and dramatizations. But perhaps you'll want to set out in the footsteps of the hangman's daughter and visit the places that play a role in my book.

If you're the type of person who insists on reading the last pages first, consider yourself warned: if you continue reading, you'll learn who the villain is. Is that what you want? No? Then go back to the Prologue and start from the beginning. I hope you enjoy it!

On the other hand, if you've already finished, and enjoyed, the book, then take a trip to Regensburg, perhaps for a weekend. Pack comfortable shoes and a copy of this book and go! For the following city tour, you'll need at least a day or, better yet, two. After all, you're on vacation, not running a city marathon.

Just like Magdalena and Simon, we'll start our tour through Regensburg down by the pier next to the **Stone Bridge.** The oldest stone bridge in Germany, it marked the border between the Free Imperial City of Regensburg and the Duchy and Electorate of Bavaria, right up until the nineteenth century. With its fifteen arches, it was — for people of the Middle Ages — one of the wonders of the world, if not one of the devil's masterpieces.

In the seventeenth century, at the time of our story, Regensburg was still an important trade junction, thanks to the Danube, which was navigable by ship and connected the city with Vienna and, farther downstream, the Black Sea. The Danube landings teemed with rafts and raftsmen — and no doubt with any number of shady characters. You would search in vain here for raftmaster Karl Gessner's house — it's just an invention of mine — though brandy and tobacco smuggling were certainly common. That said, you'll have a fine view here of the two **Wöhrd Islands.** On the Upper Wöhrd, the larger island, there were actually mills at the time — hammer mills and sawmills powered by the waters of the Danube. And local rumors claim there was once a smuggler's tunnel under the Danube, just as in my story.

Fortify yourself with some Regensburg bratwurst, preferably at the famous **Wurstkuchl,** probably the oldest bratwurst restaurant in the world. The quaint little tavern stands right next to the bridge and was a popular meeting place, even in Jakob Kuisl's time. The first written record of it dates back to 1616. Look for markings on the wall here that denote historic high-water river levels. The beautiful blue Danube may not seem so harmless anymore.

Walk west along the Danube and turn left into Weißgerbergraben. Three hundred years ago a bathhouse stood on this corner. Of course, there was no secret alchemist's laboratory here and, as far as I know, never a devastating fire, either. The old house was torn down in the eighteenth century to make way for an imposing structure that housed a doctor's office—a building still in the hands of the same family today.

Heading south along Weißgerbergraben, cross Arnulfsplatz and turn right onto Jakobsstraße. Farther still from the center of town stands **Jakobstor (Jakob's Gate),** the gate by which the Schongau hangman entered the city and the place where he was first imprisoned overnight. The execution site was located only a few steps away at the time but has long since been torn down and built over.

Far more exciting is **Jakobskirche (Jakob's Church)** with its famous "Scotch" portal. Itinerant Irish monks, called "Scoti" at the time, laid the cornerstone of this building at the end of the eleventh century. To this day, experts are still trying to decipher the meaning of the innumerable figures depicted in reliefs on the portal. Some represent society's outcasts, like those who appear in my novel: prostitutes, street performers, beggars, witches. Try to find them all—it took me quite a long time, but in my search I realized society's outcasts would be a central motif of the novel.

After crossing the **Bismarckplatz (Bismarck Square),** stroll back into town by way of Gesandtenstraße. Once called **Scherergasse** or **Lange Gasse,** this is where patricians and, later, the representatives to the Reichstag lived. Today it's a shopping district, but the buildings still retain a certain touch of the distinction that characterized Regensburg at the time of the Perpetual Reichstag of the Holy Roman Empire (Der Immerwährende Reichstag, 1663–1806). The building at 2 Gesandtenstraße, by the way, was my model for the home of city treasurer Paulus Mämminger — a figure who, like the Regensburg executioner, Philipp Teuber, really existed.

Moving along, we come to **Neupfarrplatz (Neupfarr Church Square),** where the remains of the **Jewish Quarter** can be found. In 1519 Jews were driven out of Regensburg, their homes razed. A church was built in this place, and the cellars of the old houses, which were often interconnected, were not rediscovered until 1995, during construction work on the church.

The entrance to the **Document Neupfarrplatz,** the subterranean museum, is rather inconspicuous. Because a tour there is possible only with a guide, you'll need to inquire at the tourist office. But it's worth seeing! The catacombs offer a vertical cross section of almost two thousand years of Regensburg history. Over Roman ruins the basements of Jewish homes were built, and above them a Catholic pilgrimage site and then a Protestant church. In the Second World War bunkers were built there, and after that, a public restroom. At the end of the twentieth century, when the cellars were partially excavated, a hoard of old gold coins was found there. The catacombs serve as the beggars' hideout in my novel. I had been seeking such a historically documented setting for a while, and the first time I found myself down below amid the rubble, I knew I'd found it. I also liked the idea that the beggar king, Nathan, was living in catacombs built by his ancestors. Incidentally, Nathan is my favorite character in the novel, and that's why I featured him in the title.

From Neupfarrplatz we turn into Residenzstraße and then right onto the **Domplatz (the cathedral square).** Here stands Regensburg's landmark cathedral. Much has changed inside since Jakob Kuisl's time. If you want to see the statuette of Saint Sebastian where Paulus Mämminger inserted his message for the kaiser's agent, you'll have to visit the cathedral museum next door. The statuette's long arrow is in fact a tube from which the faith-

ful used to sip consecrated wine during the festival of Saint Sebastian. History is indeed often stranger than fiction.

Nowadays you can doze in the sun or take a short nap on the
steps of the cathedral without being assailed by a mob like Magdalena. Take a little break here, but if you'd like to see something
really grandiose after lunch, walk over to the **Haus Heuport
(Heuport House)**.

The former patrician's house stands directly across from the
cathedral. In my novel it's the home of the Venetian ambassador,
Silvio Contarini, but today it's a restaurant. Even if you're not
hungry, go and have a look around! Nowhere else can you get a
better sense of how a patrician or an ambassador must have
lived — with a secluded interior courtyard, magnificent halls,
and large windows overlooking the Domplatz. On the stairway
you'll see the statue of the handsome young man with rats, toads,
and snakes lodged in his back: an early clue to Silvio's true character.

To the left of the cathedral stands the **Bischofshof (bishop's
palace),** where the hangman sought asylum. At that time an in-
dependent jurisdiction began just behind the west side of the
great portal. The bishop's brewery has since moved to another
location, but the beer is nonetheless still highly recommended.
I myself took refuge in the restaurant there during a long rain
shower, and my appreciation for the brew grew with each
glassful.

If you walk around the bishop's courtyard, you'll come to the
adjoining **Porta Praetoria,** Regensburg's oldest cultural monument. The Roman gateway, dating back to 179 AD, is one of the
last remains of the castle Castra Regina, which gave Regensburg
its name. In 1649 the gateway was part of the bishop's brewery
and wasn't rediscovered until about two hundred years later.
The walled-up passageway from the bishop's residence into the
street **Unter den Schwibbögen (Under the Arches)** is my inven-

tion, although the arches really existed as covered passageways. They led across the street from the bishop's courtyard to some houses that belonged to the bishop's residence.

A bit farther from the center of the city but on the same street was the tavern **Zum Walfisch (the Whale),** where Magdalena and Simon stayed. All that is left of this disreputable establishment is the sign in front showing Jonah and the whale. (The current establishment has nothing at all in common with the legendary Whale.) One of the most enigmatic figures in Regensburg history frequented this place in the late seventeenth century: the English ambassador Sir George Etherege, a dandy par excellence. The quirky nobleman and author of comedies surrounded himself with whores, gamblers, and magicians; held wild parties; and longed for his former profligate life in his native London. To escape boredom in Regensburg, he patronized the most infamous dives and danced half naked with prostitutes in the street. Do you recognize him now? I've tried to breathe new life into this strange figure in the character of the Venetian ambassador, Silvio Contarini. But surely Sir George was a lot more likable than the sleazy Venetian scoundrel.

Another character in my novel is based on a historical figure: the madam Dorothea. In the eighteenth century a certain Dorothea Maria Bächlein ran a house of prostitution at **Peterstor (St. Peter's Gate)** on the south side of the city. Unfortunately nothing remains of the gate or the bordello, and the **Henkershaus (Hangman's House)** at the present-day 2 Königsstraße is no longer standing, either.

My search for the **Regensburger Brunnenstube (Regensburg well chamber),** where my final showdown takes place, turned out to be a difficult one. Once located near the **Galgenberg (gallows hill)** south of the city, it lies under the busy Universitätsstraße today. When I expressed my wish to visit the well chamber, the city informed me regretfully that such a visit would require setting up a detour for all local traffic. I had to rely on a few photos, and you'll have to rely on the description in the book.

The **Rathausplatz (city hall square),** the end of our present tour, is easy to reach by heading west along Unter den Schwib-bögen. The little House of Fools, where Simon meets the drunken Father Hubertus and spends a few unpleasant hours, was once attached to the magnificent city hall. Right next to it was the entrance to the dungeon where Magdalena sneaks past the guards to visit her father.

The tourist information center is located in city hall itself. By all means book a tour through the **Reichstagsmuseum** and the **Fragstatt (Reichstag Museum** and the **torture chamber).** The Reichstag is an absolute must-see in Regensburg! Nowhere else in Germany can you get such a good feel for the politics of the period as in the assembly hall where representatives from all parts of the German Empire met and debated for 150 years (though they debated more than they actually made any real decisions). Anyone trying to understand the European Union or the German parliamentary system need only come to Regensburg, where it all began. If you're a German speaker, you'll learn the origins of some German phrases, such as *auf die lange Bank schieben* (to procrastinate, or literally, "to push onto the long bench") and *am grünen Tisch* (to negotiate, literally "at the green table").

Just as interesting is the gloomy torture chamber next door, in whose dungeons major portions of this novel take place. I hope you get a sense of what Jakob Kuisl might have felt when he saw the rack, the Schlimme Liesl (Bad Lizzie), and the Spanische Reiter (Spanish Rider). The Regensburg torture chamber is the only one in all of Germany still preserved in its original condition. All the instruments of torture actually come from here. And the niche for the inquisitors behind the lattice-work, as well as the little bench with half a backrest, is historical.

After so many grisly scenes, treat yourself to a mocha in the **Café Prinzess (Princess Café)** on the city hall square, the oldest coffeehouse in Germany, according to its owners. Admittedly the café didn't open for business until 1686, but I simply opened it a few years early for Simon and Magdalena. I beg your pardon for this; perhaps I can humor you a bit with the exquisite pralines the café offers.

If you plan to stay a second day, that would be a good time to board a boat and take a trip down the Danube. Just like our two executioners, you'll float along at a leisurely pace until you reach the town of **Donaustauf** and the **Walhalla,** a reproduction of the Parthenon commissioned by Ludwig I. While this national monument didn't exist at the time, a visit is nevertheless worthwhile. From here, a path leads up to the ruins of the nearby Donaustauf Castle, which was destroyed by the Swedes in the Thirty Years' War. But please don't go looking for the ruins of Weidenfeld there! You'll just get lost in the woods and starve to death — though not without first cursing my overactive imagination.

With this tour you've seen only a fraction of Regensburg, of course. You'll have to find a reason to come back — perhaps with a new book of mine? There are countless stories yet to be told about this grandiose city.

Wishing you much pleasure in reading, strolling about, and poking around,

—OLIVER PÖTZSCH

ACKNOWLEDGMENTS

Many people have helped me in the writing of this book. My special thanks to the late local historian Karl Bauer. His book, *Regensburg,* is a treasure trove of true stories, upon which many of the ideas for this novel are based. Without such tireless and energetic historians, books like mine wouldn't be possible.

Special thanks also to Matthias Freitag of Regensburg, the team of STADTMAUS, and Dr. Heinrich Wanderwitz, curator of the city archives, whom I pestered with endless questions. Any errors that may have slipped in are, of course, my responsibility.

Thanks also to Rainer Wieshammer, who taught me how to make green oil; the Wagner family, who guided me through the Weltenburg Enge (Weltenburg Narrows); the incomparable colleague and writer Günther Thömmes, who, over ten mugs of wheat beer, introduced me to the secrets of brewing beer; Dr. Peter Büttner of the Bavarian Agricultural Department for his information about ergot; Till and Christian for the Italian translations; Ingo for the idea of the hanged hangmen; my agent, Gerd Rumler, for wine and truffle ravioli; my editor, Uta Rupprecht, who's taught me what a confoundedly difficult language German is; and above all, to my brother, Marian, and my wife, Katrin: first readers who once again did a first-rate job.

TURN THE PAGE FOR A PREVIEW OF

THE WARLOCK:
A HANGMAN'S DAUGHTER TALE

𝕷IGHTNING FLASHED FROM THE SKY LIKE THE finger of an angry god.

Simon Fronwieser saw it directly over Lake Ammer: for a fraction of a second, it lit up the foaming waves in a sickly green. It was followed by a peal of thunder and a steady downpour — a black, soaking wall of rain that drenched the two dozen or so pilgrims from Schongau in seconds. Though it was only seven in the evening, night had fallen suddenly. The medicus gripped the hand of his wife, Magdalena, tighter and, along with the others, prepared to climb the steep hill to the Andechs monastery.

"We were lucky!" shouted Magdalena over the thundering downpour. "An hour earlier and the storm would have caught us out on the lake!"

Simon nodded silently. It wouldn't be the first time a ship of pilgrims had gone down with all hands in Lake Ammer. Now, barely twenty years after the end of the Great War, the crowds of pilgrims streaming to the famous Bavarian monastery were larger than anyone could remember. In a time of hunger, storms, ravenous wolves, and marauders, people were eager to find protection in the arms of the church more than ever. This longing was fed by reports of miracles, and the Andechs monastery in particular, a full thirty miles southwest of Munich, was renowned for its ancient relics that possessed magic powers—as well as for its beer, which helped people to forget their worries.

When the medicus turned around again, he could just make out through the rain clouds the wind-whipped lake that they had just managed to escape. Two days before, he had left Schongau with Magdalena and a group from their hometown. The pilgrimage led them over the Hohenpeißenberg to Dießen on Lake Ammer, where a rickety rowboat took them to the other shore. Now they were proceeding through the forest along a steep, muddy path toward the monastery, which towered far above them in the dark clouds.

Burgomaster Karl Semer led the procession on horseback, followed on foot by his grown son and the Schongau priest, who struggled to keep a huge painted wooden cross upright in the wind. Behind him came carpenters, masons, and cabinetmakers and, finally, the young patrician Jakob Schreevogl, the only city councilman along with Semer to heed the call for the pilgrimage.

Simon assumed that both Schreevogl and the burgomaster had come less in search of spiritual salvation than for business reasons. A place like Andechs, with its thousands of hungry and thirsty pilgrims, was a gold mine. The medicus wondered what the dear Lord would have to say about this. Hadn't Jesus chased all the merchants and moneylenders from the temple? Well, at least Simon's conscience was clear. He and Magdalena had come to Andechs not to make money but only to thank God for saving their two children.

Simon couldn't help smiling when he thought of three-year-old Peter at home and his brother, Paul, who had just turned two. He wondered if the children were giving their grandfather, the Schongau hangman, a hard time.

When another bolt of lightning hit a nearby beech, the pilgrims screamed and threw themselves to the ground. There was a snapping and crackling as sparks jumped to other trees. In no time, the entire forest seemed to be on fire.

"Holy Mary, Mother of God!"

In the twilight Simon could see Karl Semer fall to his knees a few paces away and cross himself several times. Alongside him, his petrified son stared open-mouthed at the burning beeches while, all around him, the other Schongauers fled into a nearby ravine. Simon's ears were ringing from the bone-jarring thunderclap that accompanied the flash of lightning, so he heard his wife's voice as if through a wall of water.

"Let's get out of here! We'll be safer down there by the brook."

Simon hesitated, but his wife seized him and pulled him away just as flames shot up from two beeches and a number of small firs at the edge of the narrow path. Simon stumbled over a rotten branch, then slid down the smooth slope covered with dead leaves. Arriving at the bottom of the ravine, he stood up, groaning, and wiped a few twigs from his hair while scanning the apocalyptic scene all around.

The lightning had split the huge beech straight down the middle. Burning boughs and branches were strewn down the slope. The flames cast a flickering light on the Schongauers, who moaned, prayed, and rubbed their bruised arms and legs. Fortunately, none of them appeared injured; even the burgomaster and his son seemed to have survived the disaster unscathed. In the gathering dusk, old Semer was busy searching for his horse, which had galloped away with his baggage.

Simon felt a slight satisfaction as he watched the animal run through the forest, bellowing loudly.

I hope the mare took off with his big moneybags, he thought. *If that fat old goat shouts one more* hallelujah *from up there on his horse, I'm going to commit a mortal sin.*

Simon quickly dismissed this thought as unworthy of a pilgrim and quietly cursed himself for not having brought along a warmer coat. The new green woolen cape he'd bought at the Augsburg cloth market was dapper, but after the rain it hung on him like a limp rag.

"One might think God had some objection to our visiting the monastery today."

Simon turned to Magdalena, who had directed her eyes at the sky as rain ran down her mud-spattered cheeks.

"Thundershowers are rather common this time of year," Simon replied, trying to sound matter-of-fact and somewhat composed again. "I don't think that—"

"It's a sign!" cried a trembling voice off to one side. Sebastian Semer, son of the burgomaster, held out the fingers of his right hand in a gesture meant to ward off evil spirits. "I told you right away we should leave the woman at home." He pointed at Magdalena and Simon. "Anyone who takes a hangman's daughter and a filthy bathhouse owner along on a pilgrimage to the Holy Mountain might as well invite Beelzebub, too. The lightning is a sign from God warning us to do penance and—"

"Shut your fresh mouth, Semer boy," Magdalena scolded, narrowing her eyes. "What do you know about penance, hmm? Wipe your britches off before everyone notices you're so scared you've peed in your pants again."

Ashamed, Sebastian Semer stared at the dark spot on the front of his wide-cut reddish purple petticoat breeches. Then he turned away silently, but not without casting one last angry look at Magdalena.

"Don't mind him. The little rascal is the spoiled offspring of his father."

Jakob Schreevogl now emerged from the darkness of the forest, wearing a tight-fitting jerkin, high leather boots, and a white lace collar framing an unusual face with a Vandyke beard and a hooked nose. A fine rain trickled down his ornamented sword.

"In general I agree with you, Fronwieser." Schreevogl turned to Simon and pointed at the sky. "Such violent storms aren't unusual in June, but when the lightning strikes right beside you, it's like you're feeling God's anger."

"Or the anger of your fellow citizens," Simon added gloomily.

Almost four summers had passed since his marriage to Magdalena, and since then a number of Schongau citizens had let Simon know just how they felt about this marriage. As the daughter of the hangman Jakob Kuisl, Magdalena was an outcast, someone to be avoided if possible.

Simon reached for his belt to check that a little bag of healing herbs and medical instruments was still attached there. It was quite possible he'd need some of his medicines during this pilgrimage. The Schongauers had often sought his help in recent years. Memories of the Great War still haunted some of the older people, and plagues and other diseases had swept over Schongau again and again. Last winter, Simon and Magdalena's sons had also fallen ill, but God had been merciful and spared them. In the following days, Magdalena prayed many rosaries and finally convinced Simon to make a pilgrimage to the Holy Mountain with her after Pentecost, along with nearly two dozen other citizens of Schongau and Altenstadt — citizens who wanted to show their gratitude to the Lord at the famous Festival of the Three Hosts. Simon and Magdalena had left the two children in the care of their grandparents — a wise decision, in view of the last hour's events, the medicus again admitted to himself.

"It looks as if the rain will finally quench the fire." Jakob Schreevogl pointed at the storm-ravaged beech, where only a few flames still flickered. "We should move along. Andechs can't be far off now — perhaps one or two miles. What do you think?"

Simon shrugged and looked around. The other trees were smoldering, but the rain had now become so heavy that the pilgrims could hardly see their hands in front of their faces in the growing dusk. The Schongauers had taken refuge beneath a nearby fir to wait out the heaviest rain. Only Karl Semer, still looking for his horse, was wandering around somewhere in the nearby forest, shouting loudly. His son had decided in the meantime to sit down and pout on an overturned tree trunk, trying to drive the cold from his bones with help of a flask he'd brought along. His Excellency Konrad Weber frowned at the young dandy but didn't interfere. The old Schongau priest was not about to pick a fight with the son of the presiding burgomaster.

Just as the pilgrims were beginning to calm down, another bolt of lightning struck not far away and once again the Schongauers ran like spooked chickens down the muddy slopes, farther into the valley below. The priest's wooden cross came to rest, filthy and splintered, between rocks.

"Just stay together!" Simon shouted into the thunder and rain. "Lie down on the ground! On the ground you'll be safe!"

"Forget it." Magdalena shook her head and turned to leave. "They don't hear you, and even if they did, they'd hardly obey a dishonorable bathhouse owner."

Simon sighed and hurried with Magdalena after the others. Beside them the carpenter Balthasar Hemerle carried an almost thirty-pound pilgrimage candle. Though its flame had gone out, the powerful, nearly six-foot-tall man held it up as straight as a battle flag. In comparison, Simon looked even smaller and more slender.

"Stupid peasants!" Hemerle grumbled, stepping around a muddy puddle with great strides. "It's just a thunderstorm! We have to get out of this goddamned forest—fast! But if those cowards keep running around like that, we'll get completely lost!"

Simon nodded silently and rushed ahead.

In the meantime darkness had descended completely under the dark canopy of trees. The medicus could see only vague shadows of some of the Schongauers, though he heard anxious cries farther off. Someone was praying loudly to the Fourteen Holy Helpers.

And in the distance now howling wolves could be heard.

Simon shuddered. The beasts had multiplied considerably in the years since the Great War and now plagued the land just like wild pigs. The hungry animals were no threat to a group of twenty hardy men, but for Schongauers wandering alone through the forests they presented a real danger.

Branches lashing his face, Simon struggled not to lose sight of at least Magdalena and the sturdy Balthasar Hemerle's pilgrimage candle. Fortunately, the carpenter was so tall that Simon could see him over the tops of bushes and even some low trees.

When the huge man stopped as if rooted to the spot, Simon stumbled and almost bumped into him and Magdalena. The medicus was about to utter a curse when he froze and felt the hair on the back of his neck stand on end.

In a small clearing directly before them stood two wolves with drooping jaws, growling at the three pilgrims. Their small eyes were red dots in the night, and their hind legs were tensed, ready to pounce. Their bodies were thin and scrawny, as if they hadn't found prey for a long time.

"Don't move!" Hemerle whispered. "If you run, they'll attack you from behind. And we don't know if there are any more nearby."

Slowly Simon reached for his linen pouch, where along with his medical instruments and herbs he kept a stiletto as sharp as a razor. He wasn't sure the little knife would help against the two famished beasts. Beside him, Magdalena stared at the wolves, unmoving. A few steps away Hemerle raised the heavy candle above him like a sword, as if he were about to smash the skull of one of the beasts.

A pilgrimage candle sullied with wolf's blood! Simon thought. *What would the abbot in the monastery have to say about that?*

"Stay calm, Balthasar," Magdalena whispered to the carpenter after a few moments of silence. "Look at their tails between their legs. The animals are more afraid of us than we are of them. Let's just slowly step back—"

At that moment, the larger of the two wolves lunged for Simon and Magdalena. The medicus dodged to one side and, out of the corner of his eye, saw the animal rush past. Scarcely had the wolf landed on his feet than he turned around to attack again. The animal snarled and opened his mouth wide, revealing huge white fangs dripping with saliva. Simon imagined he could see every drop individually, magnified as if through a microscope. The wolf prepared to jump again.

From somewhere a shot rang out.

For an instant, Simon thought lightning had struck again nearby, but then he saw the wolf writhing. He yelped and whined before falling to the ground, where he twitched one more time and died. Red blood flowed from a wound in his neck onto leaves on the ground. The second wolf growled once more before running off and, a second later, disappeared into the darkness.

"The Lord giveth and the Lord taketh away. Amen."

Now a broad-shouldered figure appeared between the trees holding a smoking musket in one hand and a burning lantern in the other. He wore a black habit and a hood drawn over his face. In the pouring rain, he looked like an angry forest spirit in search of poachers.

Finally, the stranger pushed back his hood. Simon found himself looking into the friendly face of a bald man with protruding ears, crooked teeth, and a bulbous nose furrowed with veins. He was probably the ugliest man Simon had ever seen.

"Allow me to introduce myself. I'm Brother Johannes from the Andechs monastery," said the fat monk, squinting at the three lost pilgrims. "Have you by chance seen any bloodroot growing nearby?"

Rain and cold sweat pouring down his face, the medicus was

too exhausted to answer. He slid to the ground alongside the trunk of a beech, mumbling a little prayer of thanks.

Indeed, he'd have to dedicate another candle up on the Holy Mountain.

Half an hour later, the Schongau pilgrims, led by Brother Johannes, climbed the narrow path up to the monastery.

Everyone was filthy, their clothes ripped or tattered; some had suffered a few scratches and bruises. But otherwise they all appeared unharmed. Even the burgomaster's horse showed up again. Right behind the fat monk, old Semer rode at the head of the procession, trying to make a dignified impression, an attempt that was not entirely successful, however, in view of his battered hat and muddy coat. In the meantime, the rain had turned to a steady drizzle as the storm moved east toward Lake Würm. The sound of thunder was faint and distant.

"We have you to thank, brother," declared Karl Semer in a stately voice. "Had you not appeared, some of us would have gotten lost in the forest."

"What a stupid plan to leave the road with a storm coming on and take the old path to the monastery," grumbled Brother Johannes as he shifted a sack bulging with iron tools to his other shoulder. "You can count yourself lucky that I was out foraging for herbs, or the wolves and the lightning would have finished you off."

"Considering the approaching darkness, I thought it was advisable to—uh—take the shorter route," the burgomaster retorted. "I'll admit that—"

"It certainly was a stupid idea." Brother Johannes turned to the pilgrims and examined the large white pilgrimage candle that the carpenter was still holding in his callused hands.

"Damned heavy candle you have there," he said, obviously impressed. "How far have you carried it?"

"We come from Schongau," interjected Simon, who was just

behind the monk with Magdalena. The medicus's vest was filthy, the red rooster feathers on his new hat were bent, and his leather boots from Augsburg looked like they needed new soles. "We've been traveling for two days," he continued wearily. "Yesterday, near Wessobrunn, we heard a pack of wolves howling, but they didn't dare to attack us."

Brother Johannes panted as he continued up the steep forest path, his lantern swinging back and forth like a will-o'-the-wisp. "You were very lucky," he mumbled. "The beasts are getting fresher. In this area they've already killed two children and a woman. And to make matters worse, we are plagued by vagrants and murderous gangs." He hastily crossed himself. "*Deus nos protegat!* May the Lord protect us in these uncertain times."

In the meantime, the forest had thinned. Before them the Schongauers saw the warm and inviting lights of the small hamlet of Erling, located on a plateau at the foot of the Holy Mountain. Simon breathed a sigh of relief and squeezed Magdalena's hand. They had reached their goal unharmed—a blessing not shared by all in these hard times. He fervently hoped their two children were well in Schongau. But he had no doubt they were, in view of the overflowing love of their grandparents.

"I hope you all have a place to stay," Brother Johannes said. "Sleeping outside in the field on such damp June nights is unpleasant."

"We Schongau council members are staying in the monastery guesthouse," replied Burgomaster Semer coolly, pointing to his son and the patrician Jakob Schreevogl. "We've arranged for the others to be boarded with farmers in the area. After all, our journey is for the benefit of the community, isn't it?"

Brother Johannes chuckled. His face, already lopsided, contorted into a grimace. Once again Simon couldn't help noticing how ugly he was.

"If you mean the repair of the steeple, I must disappoint you," the monk replied. "The farmers don't give a damn about the condition of the monastery, but the abbot promised bread and meat to any resident of Erling who provides shelter to a needy mason or carpenter. So it shouldn't cost you anything."

Semer nodded contentedly and stroked his horse's mane. "Thanks be to God," he exclaimed. "I promise that if the Savior sends us good weather, the work on the church will be finished soon."

The Festival of the Three Hosts, one of the largest pilgrimages in Bavaria, was still a week off, but Abbot Maurus Rambeck had sent messengers to pilgrims in the surrounding villages asking them to come early to the Holy Mountain. More than a month ago lightning had damaged the steeple of the monastery church. The roof truss had been destroyed, as well as a large part of the south nave. Many strong hands were needed to assure the festival could take place as planned. For this reason, the abbot had given the local craftsmen an indulgence for a year and good pay—an offer that a number of hungry men in the area were all too happy to accept. Along with the usual pilgrims, four masons and a carpenter had come from Schongau, and in Wessobrunn three plasterers joined their group.

"I myself am here—uh—on an urgent business matter," Karl Semer declared. "But I'm sure this pious group will be quite happy to help you with the construction work," he said, pointing to the bedraggled crowd from Schongau that had just begun singing an old church hymn.

In Erling, a number of windows and doors opened to reveal village residents who eyed the pilgrims suspiciously. A few dogs barked. These strangers could hardly expect a warm reception in town—too often strangers had brought death and destruction in recent decades. This time, at least, the villagers would be well compensated for the annoyance.

"What's that light up there?" Magdalena asked, pointing to the monastery that towered above the village like the castle of a robber knight.

"A light?" Irritated, Brother Johannes stared back at her.

"The light up there in the steeple. Didn't you just say the tower had been destroyed in the fire? There's a light burning there, though."

Now Simon, too, looked up to the steeple. Indeed, a tiny light flickered above the nave just where the lightning had struck the belfry four weeks ago—more than just a weak glimmer. When the medicus looked more closely, however, the light had vanished.

Johannes shielded his eyes and squinted. "I can't see anything," he said finally. "Probably sheet lightning. In any case, no one is up there; it would be much too dangerous in the dark. Much of the tower has already been rebuilt, but the roof truss and the stairs are still in bad shape." He shrugged. "Anyway, why would anyone be up there at this time of night? To enjoy the view?" Although he laughed briefly, Simon sensed the laugh was fake. The monk's eyes seemed to flicker before turning to the other pilgrims.

"I suggest you all spend tonight in the big barn on the Groner farm. Tomorrow we'll send you out to individual towns and houses. And now, good night." Brother Johannes rubbed his eyes tiredly. "I hope very much my young assistant has prepared the carp with watercress that I'm so fond of. Saving lost pilgrims makes one terribly hungry."

With the three aldermen, he stomped off toward the monastery and disappeared in the darkness.

"And now?" Simon asked Magdalena after a while. The other Schongauers had marched off praying and singing to the newly built barn next to the tavern.

Again the hangman's daughter stared up at the dark belfry; then she rubbed her hand over her face as if she were trying to shake a bad dream.

"What else? We'll go where we belong." Sullenly she walked ahead of Simon toward the village outskirts where a single little house stood at the edge of the forest. The roof was holey and covered with moss and ivy, and a rickety cart by the door gave off a smell of decay. "Unlike the other pilgrims, at least we know someone here."

"But who?" Simon muttered. "A mangy knacker and distant relative of your father. Isn't that just great?" He held his breath as Magdalena walked determinedly to the crooked door of the Erling knacker's house and knocked. Once again Simon thanked God they'd left the two little ones with their grandfather in Schongau.

A light flared up again in the belfry. Like a huge evil eye, it shined out again into the night, searching for something in the forests of the Kien River valley.